Strings Attached

To order additional copies, please contact us:

littleedenpress.com

Little Eden Press
11862 Balboa Blvd. #205
Granada Hills, CA 91344

NICK NOLAN

STRINGS ATTACHED

LITTLE EDEN PRESS
2006

Strings Attached

For Jaime,

And For Margaret

PROLOGUE

He was late, but there wasn't a damn thing he could do.
And just like this freeway he was stuck on, his life had become one big gridlock.

Take Tiffany, for example: he'd pretty much given up hope of ever moving forward again with her, but then she'd called saying she wanted to see him and needed to talk. She'd even sounded cheerful and he'd started getting his hopes up...until she slipped into her baby-talk voice; that old Shirley Temple routine usually meant trouble was waiting for him up the road.

For the last half-hour all eastbound traffic had been stopped, and only in the past few minutes had the vehicles around him begun to squeeze into the bottleneck ahead made by the fire trucks parked higgledy-piggledy across the lanes.

He eased out the clutch and nosed in.

When he saw the twisted motorcycle and yellow tarp under the semi he averted his eyes and scanned, instead, the roadside crowd: some chatting firemen, three highway patrolmen, and what was probably the semi driver—a skinny old hick wearing a grease-splattered t-shirt, camouflage pants and a black cowboy hat. But instead of looking dazed or shocked or remorseful, as Jonathan thought anyone would under similar circumstances, the man seemed to stare down each of the rubberneckers from beneath his Stetson, while his jaw worked a big wad of something, like a cow chewing too much cud.

Jonathan had nearly passed when their eyes locked. Instantly the cowboy's scowl cracked and he smiled, then winked at him and tugged down the brim of his hat in an old fashioned, black-and-white-movie-type salutation. That this man would *howdy* him with a corpse beneath his load of gaily-packaged dairy products was unsettling. Disturbing even. But then he figured it wasn't often one saw such a young, good-looking guy driving a brand new 1988 Porsche, much less a top-of-the-line *Carrera*.

i

Probably thinks I'm a movie star, or something.

He returned the greeting with a vacant smile, then dropped the clutch and shot forward into the deserted freeway, like a fighter jet off a carrier.

Sometime later he reached the cracked heels of the San Bernardino foothills, where the sloping lanes and black-as-velvet curves ascended lazily. He hit the gas and snapped on his headlights; night was coming fast. His tires squealed around a curve as the car fishtailed. He thought about little Jeremy and slowed down. His headlights hit a sign and it lit up like white neon:

Lake Estrella 3 mi.

He continued along the road lined with looming pines and dark-windowed cabins, then downshifted, making the engine wail as he approached, at last, the brightly-lit intersection leading into the Estrella Village shopping center. He made a right at the stop, then continued past the fire station in the loop that dropped towards the water's edge. A left led him down Shoreline Drive, past the familiar lakefront mansions behind their long stone walls and curlicued gates. He accelerated up the final rise in the road, then veered around the last bend to where his family's monolithic, Modernist structure sat at the end of a long gravel driveway. He crossed through the open gates then coasted to a stop.

Filling the open doorway was Tiffany's curvaceous silhouette—arms crossed, chin up, shoulder to the jam. Her pose was languid, reflexively seductive still, in spite of everything.

"Hi Johnny," she offered in baby voice, upon his approach.

"Don't start," he replied, stomping past her.

She turned and followed him in after squeezing shut the heavy wooden doors. Once inside his nostrils twitched; since the chalet had only been completed a couple months before the scent of milled cedar still hung in the air like a freshly decimated forest.

"I'm kind of hungry," he said, finally turning to her. "Anything to eat?"

"Rosie left some stuff in the fridge," she answered. "I'd fix you something but I gotta run upstairs."

"For some coke?" he smiled.

"To check on our son," she replied icily. "And...to pee."

"Where is she? I need to give her a check."

"Rosie?" she asked, raising her penciled eyebrows.

"Yes, Rosie." He glared stupidly at her.

"I sent her out for some things. You can give it to me."

"That's OK I'll wait. How's my son?"

"Our son's OK," she answered, ignoring the jab. "He's bigger now, and he's getting into everything. Rosie's been trying to toilet train him; I get real sick of that shit." She rolled her eyes and his rolled back at her.

Mother of the Year.

"I didn't tell him you were coming 'cause he would of been too hyper to sleep." She crossed her arms. "Besides, you were late."

"I'll see him tomorrow. Go ahead and...do whatever."

After she left he made his way to the breakfast bar, dragged out a stool and lifted himself into it. Then he yawned. His stomach rumbled. He was both starving and nauseous. He hopped down, crossed the floor to the refrigerator then opened it, startling a cluster of beer bottles. After grabbing a Pepsi and a half-empty cellophane tube of Oreos he went back to the barstool and sat, then shoved two cookies in his mouth.

"Whatcha thinkin'?" She'd slipped on a pink ski parka, as if headed outside.

Strange.

"I'm *thinkin'* you called me here because you want something."

"Well." She slipped her hands in her pockets. "As a matter a fact, I do."

"Too bad," he mumbled through crumbs. "Because I'm not giving you anything until you tell me what you meant about Bill..." he chewed, then swallowed "...being able to 'make it snow in Hollywood'. What exactly did you mean by that?"

"I said something I shouldn't of. To piss you off."

"You're lying."

"Anyhow, I didn't tell you to come here to talk about that old prick. Besides, if you've got a problem with him you should deal with it yourself. He's part of your stuck-up family, not mine."

"That's OK Tiff, don't tell me; it'll all come out anyway. And when it does you'll be prosecuted as an accessory." He smiled brightly. "Then again, maybe you'll tell me when I remind you that one court-ordered drug test will make sure you never see Jeremy again. Or any of my money."

"I don't need your money anymore."

"Really?" He laughed. "For Christ's sake, Tiff, who's gonna keep him from falling down the stairs…or drowning in the lake when you're out whoring for cash?"

"I'm off coke," she stated imperiously. "And you know I'm not gonna let anything happen to him and Rosie won't either. What kind of mother do you think I am?"

"You don't want to know."

"And you don't want to know what kind of father, or husband, I think you are."

"At least I didn't get knocked up for someone else's money."

"I didn't get that way by myself, in case you forgot. And from what I heard-" she glared at him "-you had your own little reason for screwing me."

"You listen to too much gossip," he laughed. "I just wonder if he's really mine. I've heard things, you know."

"We're not going through all that again, Johnny. He's all yours, like it or not."

"I wish I could believe you." But he did believe her, at least about this one thing: his son was the image of himself at the same age, right down to the emerging cleft in his chin.

"I've got something to tell you," she said finally.

"Yeah, so I figured," he said, then shoved his tongue between the crevices of his teeth to extract cookie mush.

"I'm dating someone. It's serious."

"Really?" His eyebrows arched. "You actually found someone stupider than me? That wasn't part of the terms; we both agreed not to see anybody else until we work this out."

"There's nothing left to work out, and you know it. Besides, C.J.'s helped me get clean, which is more than you ever did; I haven't done any coke in almost a month now. And I'm really in love now—with a real man—so we're getting married."

"That's hilarious considering I never agreed to divorce you," he laughed. "But you go ahead and do whatever the hell you want to until I do…you can screw Bill for all I care." He jumped off the stool then crossed the room to the open doors that faced the lake, turning his back on her. "Just don't do anything that'll put my boy in danger."

He glanced down at the reflection of the crescent moon swimming to the left of the boat dock in the water, then up at the stars that sparkled over the ridge of darkened mountains. Then something caught his eye. Was there something down there by the boathouse? He squinted, but couldn't see anything.

Might've been a deer.

"Well, you might give a shit when I tell you I'm going to sue you for divorce and permanent custody of Jeremy, as well as for child support and alimony and all of the community property I'm entitled to by California law." She recited this as if reading a cue card. "And there's nothing you can do to stop me."

"Oh, come on now, Tiffany, this isn't *Dynasty*, this is our lives! And apparently you've forgotten who you're dealing with...my aunt has more attorneys at her fingertips than you've got rotten teeth. They'll snatch Jeremy away from you, then kick your ass off this mountain. You'll never see my son again, and you'll never get another Tyler penny!"

"We'll just see what the judges have to say about it."

"And since when do judges award anything to a coke whore with no way to support herself, and...oh yeah...no attorney?"

"F-Y-I, I get three or four phone calls every day from lawyers who're begging for my business because I'm divorcing a Tyler. And everyone knows that judges always give the kids to the mother."

"Unless they're unfit, which I can prove with a few entertaining stories that half of Ballena Beach will witness to!" He turned to squint again into the darkness beyond the opened window. *What's down there?* "How the hell could I have fallen for a slut like you?"

"You're talking to the mother of your son," she said, reaching into her pocket. She then withdrew a pack of cigarettes, shook one out, put it between her glossed-pink lips and flicked her lighter.

"I told you never to smoke around the baby!" He snatched the cigarette from her mouth and crumbled it, then backhanded the pack out of her hand. It flew across the room and landed with a splash in the sink piled high with dishes.

She rubbed her hand. "The courts also take the kids away from abusive husbands, which you are, besides being an asshole." She sauntered by him to the sink and retrieved the dripping cigarette pack.

"You ain't seen nothin' yet."

"Is that a threat, Mr. Tyler?" she asked, inching dangerously toward him.

"Take it however you want."

"Tell me, Johnny, are you threatening me?" She jabbed him hard in the chest with her finger.

"Don't you fuckin' touch me!" He grabbed her hard.

He shook her and she threw her arms in the air and screamed.

The room exploded with twin lightning-bright flashes from outside the opened doors. He was blinded momentarily by floating emerald-green spots. He blinked crazily until the silhouette of a standing man began to emerge in the darkness outside the house. The spots faded. He could see now that the man held a camera up to his face.

He threw down his hands and clutched his belt hoops.

"You'll live to regret this, you filthy bitch. I swear it on my life."

She giggled. "Keep threatening, Johnny, 'cause I got all that on tape too." She dug a small cassette recorder out of her ski jacket and waved it in the air. "Now I don't have to wait for you to give me a divorce, I can sue because you're a wife beater. And now I've got proof."

He reached up to snatch the contraption and another flash exploded. His shoulders dropped as he turned away and walked toward the foyer.

"I'm going," he announced quietly.

"Good idea." She popped a soggy cigarette into her mouth and tried to light it with her cheap disposable. *Flick...Flick...Flick.* "Goddamn lighter..."

He turned and leapt up the stairs two at a time to the room where Jeremy was asleep.

Tiffany's shrill laugh rose banshee-like from the stone-floored entry.

The nursery was empty.

"Where is he?" His eyes suggested murder.

"Don't worry," she said, then her cigarette sizzled as she sucked on it. "Jeremy's with Rosie, on their way down to visit her family in Colton. I thought you'd try something, so I sent him with her and gave her a couple days off." She took another hit and exhaled as she spoke, the words blown-out in vaporous puffs. "She was happy to leave; I told her C.J. was staying the next couple days, I guess she doesn't like him, as if I care."

He shoved past her through the doors to his car, the metal underside ticking as it cooled from the race up the hill not twenty minutes earlier. He opened the door then turned to her.

"You won't get away with this." He shook his head. "There's no way in hell my aunt or I will let you. I'll kill you before I'll let you steal my son!"

"Ooh! Now I've gotten two threats from you in five minutes, and each worth at least a million!" She held the recorder up in her hand. "Now you better get out of my house before C.J. shows up," she warned. "He'll whip your ass."

She waved goodbye parade-style.

"You goddamn bitch, Tiffany. If you only knew how much I hate you."

"Tell someone who gives a shit." She smiled, and then slammed the door.

The Porsche sprayed gravel at the house as he sped up the long pine tree-lined driveway toward the dim street. Within minutes he was back on the highway headed down the mountain, his chest heaving and his molars grinding.

What could he do now?

He glanced at the dashboard clock and figured he could get home to Ballena Beach to consult with Aunt Katharine before she settled into bed.

She'd know what to do.

Her voice echoed in his head: *One should never marry outside one's social class; the ensuing resentment on both sides is insurmountable.*

He was driving even more furiously now than during his ride up, grateful that it was a weeknight and there were practically no other cars around to slow him. And the roads were dry.

He cranked down his window and sucked in the crisp night air, heavy with the scents of pine and dust and sage, and just cold enough to numb the side of his face and make his eyes water.

At the Twin Peaks junction just outside Lake Estrella he hit his brakes hard when a black Suburban with a tangle of CB antennas pulled stupidly out in front of him. The vehicle then lumbered along at an excruciating crawl. After a few minutes of tailing the car he flashed his headlights to urge the driver into one of the scarce turnouts, but the idiot refused to yield, and even seemed to speed up whenever he tried to pass.

He was losing valuable time.

He honked his horn and flashed his high beams again.

The driver's hand emerged from his window and flipped him off.

His heart thudded in his ears.

There was a long straightaway about two miles further down where he was certain he could pass the big truck. He would hang back a bit before that section of road, then build up speed and fly past the Suburban like it was standing still.

He eased off the accelerator and let his car coast casually around the series of hairpins, noting with satisfaction that his plan seemed to be working; he was beginning to build some distance now between the Suburban and himself.

A sign drew into view: *Passing Lane 1/4 mile.*

He downshifted and stomped the gas, and the speedometer needle swung clockwise. As the final turn emptied into the straightaway he jammed the gas pedal to the floor and his adrenaline surged with the scream of the engine and the moonlit mountainside along the road blurred to fuzzy gray.

"Fucker! Fucker! Fucker!" he yelled as the Suburban's engine roared like a dragster's.

The two cars strained neck-and-neck for a moment until the superior horsepower-to-weight ratio of the Porsche allowed him to shoot in front and cut back out of the oncoming lane. He eased off the gas and pulled his knotted shoulders from his seatback. His review mirror told him that the big Chevy's headlights were shrinking. He was free.

He glanced at the speedometer and saw that he was doing better than 70, while the flashing yellow 35 mph sign ahead with the squiggle on it announced that another series of hairpins were approaching, fast. He hit the brakes hard then downshifted, slowing the car as much as he could without locking up the wheels.

He cranked the wheel and leaned into the approaching blind curve.

Then he saw it: a snowplow-wielding dump truck...in his lane...its mammoth iron blade headed straight for his windshield.

But there's no snow!

He twisted the wheel hard to the left and felt his back tires break free. His thoughts scrambled nonsense as he spun, Frisbee-like, over the dirt embankment, then become airborne as the motor wailed traction-less through space. And as he plummeted tail-first toward the inevitable boulders his headlights cut a swath towards heaven through the up-rushing clouds.

CHAPTER 1

The mid-October sun broiled the town of Fresno as it had every day since early July, blasting through mini blinds, baking walls so cold tap water ran hot, and painting mirrors on distant asphalt. Cars stalled. Pretty young mothers screamed at their kids. And throughout the blocks of slum where the lavish hum of an air conditioner was as rare as a green lawn, poor folks fanned themselves on their junked-up porches with the same thought: the relief of Winter seemed a century away.

It was almost four in the afternoon, and a haze hovered over a row of peeling apartment buildings identified by laughable names like *The Capri* and *The Riviera* and *The Monte Carlo*. The scene could have been some gritty gallery photograph if not for the teenager zigzagging his way between the curbside trains of beaten cars, and a mongrel that paused, panting, to appraise him.

Eventually the boy turned down the walkway of a pink apartment building clad with bars. He pushed his key into the security gate, twisted the knob then shoved open the door with his shoulder.

He trudged up to the second floor, continued down the concrete walkway then stopped in front of the unit he shared with his mother.

What would he find inside? This morning she had cracked a beer at sunrise.

He fished his key from his pocket, unlocked the door then stepped in. As usual the drapes had been tightly drawn. The stench of cigarettes pinched his nostrils.

"Mom? You home?"

He stepped over a pile of magazines that tilted next to the coffee table then tiptoed his way toward the kitchenette. Sticking out of the trashcan he saw an empty vodka bottle, poorly camouflaged by junk mail.

He turned and padded to her bedroom, not hesitating to knock before throwing open her door; as it swung wide a ghost of boozy air rushed past him.

He approached her and bent down, then reached through her sweat-matted hair and pressed his fingers on her neck, the way he'd seen people do on TV.

It took him a couple tries to find her pulse.

It was faint as a kitten's.

Here we go again!

He trotted through the apartment to the outside, then loped down the stairs to Mrs. Jackson's unit on the bottom floor near the laundry room at the back. She had a phone; his mother's had been shut off months ago. Or was it last year?

"Mrs. Jackson? Mrs. Jackson!"

Their eyes met through the screen door as she fanned herself with a newspaper. "Lord, don't tell me..."

"Could you call 911 again? She's almost dead, I think."

She nodded. "I'll call. You go up and see to her."

He turned, then took the stairs two at a time.

Halfway through their living room a waft of pukesmell put its hands around his throat. He moved through the bedroom door in time to see her vomit again, softly, a gurgle really, her body looking as though she were dozing peacefully instead of inching toward eternal rest. He grabbed a corner of the bed-sheet and wiped her mouth, then dragged her to the side of the bed so her head dangled over the edge. His hand snatched the wastebasket that sat next to her night table and he threw the contents onto the floor, then stuck the receptacle under her mouth. Her back heaved like an alley cat's and her stomach contents roared out, mostly missing its target.

"Mom! Mom!" He shook her shoulders. She hadn't been this bad since going into rehab the last time, nearly two years ago.

Mrs. Jackson's footsteps shook the floor. "Child, I'll see to her. You stay outside and show the men where to go."

He pulled himself upright and ran out of the apartment, then flailed down the stairs to the curbside. "Don't let her die too," he muttered reflexively to balance out the part of himself that wished she would, and not expecting anyone to hear his plea, or even allowing himself to think for a moment that his life might improve even if she pulled through. He knew better. He shifted his weight from right foot to left and back again then stood on his tiptoes, hands in pockets, eyes and ears straining for any sign of an ambulance or fire truck.

And he imagined what was to come. The last time this happened he'd stayed at Mrs. Jackson's, where he devoured hearty breakfasts, neatly packed school lunches, and hot meatloaf and mashed potatoes dinners with ice cream for dessert served on a flimsy TV tray in front of her big old RCA console. But after a week he began feeling like an intruder, even though he cleaned up after himself and minded his manners and listened attentively to her recount the same stories he'd heard many, many times before. The only thing that helped his guilt was his dead father's rich relatives in Ballena Beach had sent Mrs. Jackson a thousand dollars to help with the food and utilities, and had paid a couple of months rent on his mother's place besides.

Both women, in the long run, had been delighted.

Would the same thing happen this time?

Something told him *no*.

Finally the wail of a siren kissed his ears. He turned and watched with relief as the spinning scarlet of the ambulance's emergency lights sliced the rising afternoon shadows.

CHAPTER 2

Jeremy stepped into the street and began hopping up and down, waving his hands back and forth in a panicked jumping jack. He heard the acceleration of the vehicle as it passed the last stopped cars before veering to the curb in front of him. Both driver and passenger doors were thrown open and two strongly built men stepped out, heavy red cases in-hand.

"She's upstairs in number 'F'."

The boy followed the paramedics inside then up the stairs, accidentally clipping one of their boots with his toe.

"In the bedroom, she's in there." He pointed at the prone figure on the bed through the doorway, and saw that Mrs. Jackson kneeled in prayer at her side.

Oh, now that's gonna help.

"How long she been like this?" the shorter one asked. He wiped his dripping brow before popping a stethoscope into his ears.

Should he answer now or wait until he was done listening to her heart? He decided to wait, then changed his mind. "I don't know. She was OK when I left for school. I just got home and found her like this... it's not the first time."

"You got a father?" the other asked.

"He's dead."

"You stay outside now, we'll do everything we can." He threw open the big red case, then dug out a syringe and a teeny glass bottle.

Mrs. Jackson sidled around the paramedics and their equipment and came out of the bedroom next to where Jeremy was standing. She reached out and grasped his hands, smiling bravely.

"Is she gonna be OK?" he asked.

"Let's wait outside and let those men do their job. She's in good hands."

She wrapped her arms around him, and he put his head in the crook of her neck and breathed the familiar scent of her moist, spicy skin. He thought about crying, that he should somehow be more upset under the circumstances but strangely wasn't. Truth be told, he was more pissed-off at her than anything.

So he made a sniffling sound and hid his face.

"It's OK now baby. Jesus will heal her," she whispered in his ear. "He brought you home just in time to save her today. Lord be praised." She rocked him slowly back and forth in her arms. "Lord be praised."

Good—she bought it.

They were waiting together outside on the walkway when the tall paramedic emerged from the living room. He looked from Jeremy and back to Mrs. Jackson. "We're trying to stabilize her so we can take her to the hospital. Her vital signs are improving, but it looks like she aspirated her vomit, we can hear a rattle in her lungs. We should be ready to go in about ten minutes." He nodded, and then descended the stairs.

"Sure." Jeremy knew the drill.

She might get stabilized but he suspected now that she was in the worst shape of her life, in the last couple months he thought she'd aged another ten years. He could hardly believe she had ever been that teenage girl with the perfect smile and supermodel body who once matched the physical perfection of his dear, doomed father.

What happened?

The *clung* of the paramedic ascending the metal stairs startled him.

"How old are you?"

"Seventeen...and a half."

"You got any relatives to stay with while she's in the hospital?" he asked, popping the gurney upright.

"He's staying with me," Mrs. Jackson announced. "His mother and me arranged it, long time ago."

"You got that in writing?"

"Not exactly," she said. "But I practically raised this boy. He's like my own my baby, though he don't look like one no more. I'll see he gets what he needs."

"Sure. I'll just need to get your name and telephone before we go. And I'll tell Social Services they can find him here tomorrow. Can you find him a ride to County?"

"I'll drive him," said Mrs. Jackson. "And his name's Jeremy."

"Jeremy Tyler," added the boy.

Mrs. Jackson dropped him off at the entrance to County General then sped off to her sister's who lived nearby, with instructions to be out front in exactly an hour. He sidled past the bums panhandling on the front steps and made his way up to the security station, where a walking skeleton of a man argued with a security guard about smoking inside the building. He emptied his pockets and stepped through the metal detector, afraid sirens would go off even though he was smuggling nothing, the same way he was always reluctant to pass through those shoplifter detectors in stores. He was given the obligatory little pink wristband with his mother's room number on it from the information lady, who, he couldn't help noticing, had one eye swollen shut. *This place is a human junkyard*, he thought, shoving his hands deep into his pockets while shuffling down the corridor past the banks of doors, each one a gateway to someone's Brush With Death, toward the sign at the end with the room numbers on it.

He followed the arrows until he found it.

Room 260

He paused, sucking in the first half of a sigh before crossing the doorway. The doctor, a petite and efficient-looking woman was standing at the foot of his mother's bed jotting notes in a large blue binder. She took a few moments to finish, snapped the folder shut and turned to peer at him through rimless glasses which revealed soft brown eyes—intense but friendly. Safe.

"Are you Jeremy?" She appraised him with her head cocked to the side, looking through him really, and then smiled as if to say *you poor kid, I'll bet nobody knows what hell you've been through all these years.*

"Yes ma'am. Doctor."

"Call me Dr. Kathy," she said. "Your mom's still asleep, but I think she'll be waking up soon."

"Then she's gonna be O.K.?"

"Let's talk outside." She put a birdlike hand on his elbow and escorted him into the hallway.

Their eyes held. "Jeremy, your mom's really...sick. She'll be somewhat recovered from this episode in a few days, but there are some long-term effects of her disease that need to be treated. *Aggressively.*"

"Yeah?"

"Her blood-alcohol was very high. She's lucky she didn't die. She's very dehydrated, and her chest X-rays tell us she aspirated, which means she's at risk for pneumonia."

He'd heard all this before. "So what else?" he asked, spying a piece of the floor's molding that was peeling away from the wall.

"She'll be here for about two weeks, between the detoxification process and the pneumonia. After that, if she's willing to go I'm recommending she check into a rehab program that treats people like her."

"Yeah, that's what I figured. But you know it probably won't work."

"This one might. It's different."

"How?" He blinked.

"It's six months long...six months of therapy and hard work. It's kind of like one of those boot camps for teens, only this one's for substance abusers."

"Six months. Six months." he nodded dumbly, wondering if he could stand hearing Mrs. Jackson's stories for that long. "But I don't know if my neighbor can take care of me for six months." He shook his head. "And please, I don't want to go to a foster home again or one of those group homes."

"I thought there might be a problem so I referred you to one of the social workers here. She'll be talking to your mother here tomorrow, then will meet with you at your neighbor's house, if that's where you'll be, after school. She'll be able to outline your options better than I can."

"But maybe after she gets better this time she can just come home. I could take care of her, I've done it before," he said. "Anyway, maybe she won't *want* to go into the six month program."

"That's where she's going to need your help. No one can make her go, so it'll be up to you to encourage her. She has to be the one to want to change...for her sake as well as yours."

"So what'll happen if I can't convince her, if she won't go?"

"We both know what'll happen, Jeremy. And I'm going to be honest with you because you're old enough and you should know: your mother's tests show she's been diabetic for some time. And her liver has what's called *Portal Hypertension*, which means it's failing due to the alcohol abuse; and her kidneys have nearly shut down from dehydration, as well as the high blood pressure she's developed from diabetes and smoking.

The bad news is these diseases are usually progressive." She raised her eyebrows. "But with long-term treatment the prognosis isn't all bad. How much time she has left *depends* on her never drinking again. She almost didn't make it this time—I understand that you got home just in time to save her life." She smiled, then glanced at her watch. "I've got to go see another patient. You can stay here as long as you like. Think about what I've said; I know you'll help her make the right decision."

He was at her side when she regained consciousness.

"Where the hell am I?" She slurred, while drifting her bloodshot eyes toward him.

"The hospital. Again."

"What..." She looked away from him toward the windows with their twinkling brown streetlights beyond. Would she remember anything? He pictured the wheels in her head wobbling like clown car's tires as she tried to remember the day's remarkable events.

"Oh, shit," said she.

Bingo!

She turned to face him. "Baby, I'm sorry."

Jeremy looked down. "Yeah, sure you are." He slumped over in his hospital chair, his limbs wooden, his breaths shallow. He wanted to run over and slap her across the face, then jump up and down on her bed, chimpanzee-style, howling at her crazily.

"What the hell is that supposed to mean?"

"Nothing."

"For your information, I have a disease."

"Yeah. I know."

"You're lucky. You weren't old enough to realize how hard it was when your father died...not that I'm going over all that again because I know you don't care...I've just been through too much today...I'm just sorry you don't understand." She turned from him and faced the window and tried to cross her arms across her chest, but the tug of the IV tube stopped her. She winced. "Can't you see I've been through enough?" she sniffled.

"Yeah, Mom. I understand. Sorry."

She faced him again and affected a brave a smile. "Honey, get me some water, will you? And turn on the TV. And go ask where I can smoke. I'm dying for a smoke, did you bring my smokes?" She delivered these demands in baby talk, a device she used, he figured, because her voice sounded like sandpaper on a chalkboard from the decades of chain-smoking and booze-chugging. It was actually funny to hear her go between the two voices; he figured anyone standing outside the door would think he was watching an old movie starring Shirley Temple and the old fat guy neighbor from *I Love Lucy*.

But the situation wasn't funny to him. Not at all. His mother hadn't been awake for two minutes and she was already issuing orders like a sergeant. She had, of course, no concept of what the last few hours had been like for him. She hadn't witnessed the group of neighbors who huddled in front of their apartment, smirking as the paramedics hauled her blathering self into their rig. And over the coming days while she lounged in her hospital bed ordering the nurses around, he would have the revolting task of cleaning and dismantling their apartment before being shipped off to Foster Care Hell. And finally, as her dutiful son, he would do whatever he must with the knowledge that she was an alcoholic time bomb with an unpredictable hair-trigger. Who knew but God what would set her off? And when would it be—next month, next year, tomorrow? He should have come home later...he vowed never to cut swim practice again.

What could he say to get even?

"No, mom, I didn't bring your cigarettes."

"Oh. Well you've got some money don't you? They've probably still got a machine in the cafeteria; you know most of the doctors smoke here, it's really not as bad for you as-"

He held up his hand to cut her off. "They're taking me away again Mom, for a long time I think. I don't know where I'm going, but they're coming tomorrow."

"What?" Her jaundiced cheeks flushed orange. She searched his face for any sign that he was lying. She expected him to be angry, she could count on that. And it wasn't unlike him to make up a story; after all, he was her son. "What do you mean they're taking you away? They can't do that, you're nearly grown! You can stay with Mrs. Jackson for a couple days 'til I get out of here."

Her smug expression said *and that's that.*

He pushed down a grin. "The doctor said a social worker will be at

Mrs. Jackson's tomorrow to tell me what's gonna happen. They say I can stay with her for a couple days, maybe even a week or two."

"Then what's the problem?"

"You've got to face the fact that you're an alcoholic, Mom, *big time.*"

"I'm aware of my disease, thank you."

"Just listen to me. *Please.*"

"Fine." She rolled her eyes.

"The problem, Mom, is that the doctor says you have diabetes now, and liver and kidney failure too. Besides, you choked on your puke and you'll probably get pneumonia. Dr. Kathy says you almost died."

"What else did that woman tell you?"

"She says another binge like this'll kill you…and she thinks this six month program she knows about is your only chance now."

"That's bullshit. I've survived a lot worse than this."

"But that was before the diabetes. The doctor said your life depends on your never drinking again, forever."

"Well doctor's make me sick," she said. But she assumed that what her son had relayed from the doctor was correct; she had, in fact, felt her body deteriorating. She had no energy, her pee was now a brownish-yellow, she wobbled from a loss of balance and had bloat that never drained. She had even thought about moving downstairs because the climb to the second floor was becoming too difficult. In fact her latest binge was fueled partly by the desire to know if she could still pull one off, or if the party was indeed over. She had been sleeping more and more lately, forcing herself to rise and brush her scant remaining teeth barely ten minutes before her son was expected home each day.

If she were as ill as her situation indicated, and if she didn't want to die a miserable death filled with dialysis, blindness and hacked-off limbs, she really had no choice but to try another program. And this would also mean sending him away to some god-awful foster family, or worse yet, a group home filled with teenage thugs.

There has to be some other way.

This time maybe there was some angle she hadn't thought of—some bridge she hadn't yet burned that could take them both to where they needed to go.

Had enough time gone by that she could send him to Katharine?

There was no one else, so Katharine it had to be.

But what about Bill?

She could deal with Bill, even if it meant...

She smiled sweetly and reached out for her son's hand, which he accepted limply.

"You know I love you," she said, Shirley Temple-style.

He nodded.

"So don't worry, I'll talk to the doctor tomorrow. And I think I've got a way to take care of us, to give us both what we need."

"Like how?" he asked suspiciously.

"I can't say yet, 'cause I don't want you to get your hopes up. Leave it to me, everything's gonna be OK." She nodded with conviction. "Trust me."

"So you're gonna go into that Program?" he mumbled.

She inhaled dramatically, then blew a vodka-scented sigh at him. "Yes, honey, I'll go. I'll tell the doctor tomorrow. Now I think there's still this big dikey nurse out there, looks like an old man with boobs, she works nights. She smokes. Go find her and tell her I gotta have one, bad. Then you go on home. We'll talk more tomorrow after I fix everything."

CHAPTER 3

At a quarter to eleven Jeremy plodded up the stairs to their unit. His mother's bodily fluids had combined with the day's oven-like heat to make the apartment smell like a dumpster, so he pushed rolled-up towels along the underside of her bedroom door and shoved his sofa-bed up to one of the louvered windows that faced the street. He then slept coma-like, fully clothed, and impervious to the hizzing glare of the amber streetlights, or the cars that sped by throughout the night.

By sunrise the stench had dissipated enough that he was able to enter her bedroom. He spent the earliest part of the day cleaning and going through their belongings, and around lunchtime was coming down the stairs with the last two bags of trash when he heard a car pull up to the curb in front of the apartment house. He watched the white Honda creep to a stop, its engine fan blowing like a hairdryer under the hood, the young woman behind the wheel craning her neck to make out the numbers on the front of the building. She switched off the motor then ratcheted the parking brake.

He continued more slowly down the stairs, his stomach tight, watching as she scooted out of the car hefting an expensive-looking briefcase, then sashayed toward him. She stopped next to the bus bench, flipped her hair back and smiled.

"Hi," she announced perkily with eyes purposefully widened. She was pretty and he figured she knew it. "Can you tell me where I can find Jeremy Tyler?"

He looked across the street and saw a filthy man eyeing his bulging trash bags. "That's me," he said.

"Thought so. I'm Ms. Klugburm, from DCFS." She walked closer but extended no hand. "You can call me Kelli. The hospital sent me. Is there somewhere we can talk?"

"Um, not at our place, it's kinda gross right now. But we can go to Mrs. Jackson's, she's right back there." He turned around to point just as the woman herself emerged from the shadow of her screen door, arms folded like a sumo wrestler.

Jeremy led the way to her cozy apartment as his neighbor grunted a welcome to the young woman, and then directed them to sit on her long, autumn-leaf patterned sofa. Mrs. Jackson then took a seat in her own sagging recliner, which had been placed in the room opposite the front door, affording her a commanding view of the comings and goings of everyone in the building. *Troll under the Bridge*, she called herself.

"I'm Louise Jackson." Her voice filled the room. "This boy's mama directed me to care for him when she's away, and I'm prepared to do so. I've done it in the past and when I do, I look after him like he's my own. Now what's your business?"

Ms. Klugburm shot what was supposed to be a disarming smile first at Mrs. Jackson, then at Jeremy. Then she snapped open her briefcase and withdrew a series of stapled forms. "Mrs. Jackson, Jeremy, I've just come from interviewing Mrs. Tyler about your placement. And please keep in mind this is only temporary." She handed them each a set of papers. "I understand in the past his staying with you has worked out really well. However this time, because of Mrs. Tyler's lengthy hospital stay, some other arrangements had to be made."

"What other arrangements?" Jeremy demanded. "Where'm I gonna live?"

"I'll speed this up, Jeremy, as I can see that you've been through a *lot*," she looked sad for a second, turning to face him. "And *please* keep in mind that this decision was made in your best interest."

"We'll see about that," said Mrs. Jackson.

"The Court has arranged for you live with an aunt of your late father's in Southern California, in Ballena Beach. Her name is," she looked at the paper in her hand, "Mrs. Katharine Tyler."

"Oh God, not Aunt Katharine!" Jeremy shouted, jumping up. "My mother hates her! Why would she send me there?"

"His mother speaks wickedly of that woman," Mrs. Jackson added.

"I understand that there were some disagreements in the past." The girl scratched her nose. "But the Court believes that her and her husband will be the best-equipped of all your relatives to care for you. They've got no children of their own. And although your mother hasn't wanted you to stay with them in the past she said she'd rather see you with them than in foster care. And when I confirmed the arrangements with Mrs. Tyler she seemed very friendly, and really excited about your staying with them. The paperwork's still being processed, but you should be ready to go by tomorrow morning."

"Tomorrow!" exclaimed Jeremy. "Why so soon?"

"The Court doesn't like children missing school, especially when placement has already been determined and the new school year has started. The County has purchased a bus ticket for you. I'll be by tomorrow, I think the bus leaves at one in the afternoon," she looked at her notes. "Yes, so I'll be by at noon to pick you up. Do you think you can be ready by then?"

"Do I have a choice?"

She smiled. "No, honey, you really don't." Then turning to Mrs. Jackson she asked, "Can he stay with you one more night?"

"He could stay with me forever," she said. "But I'll do as you say and see he's ready tomorrow by noon, sharp."

"Great," she replied, snatching her briefcase and then pushing herself up from the sofa. She held out her hand. "Thank you for your time, Mrs. Jackson. I can see that Jeremy would be very well taken care of here."

Mrs. Jackson took her hand. "Promise me that if it don't work out with that woman you'll come talk to me before you put him somewhere else. This boy's been through enough already. He needs a good home and lots of love, I'll give him that."

"I promise I'll do that, Mrs. Jackson."

"Call me Louise."

"I promise, Louise. See you both tomorrow."

By eleven the next morning Jeremy had two pieces of luggage packed, for himself an old green canvas army duffel stuffed with balled-up clothes, his journal and his pillow, and for his mother a trash bag. In it he placed her freshly washed and folded pink bathrobe, her only pair of decent jeans, her scuffy slippers, two worn T-shirts and the shoebox covered with layers of masking tape that she had carried dutifully from apartment to apartment over the years. He had long ago given up asking her what was inside; when asked she would only reply, "Some old crap."

He hoisted the duffel in his right hand and her bag in his left, but then noticed that one of the corners of the box was already sticking through a hole in the black plastic. He set both bags down, pulled the box from the trash bag then pushed it past his pillow deep within the duffel—just to be safe, just for now. After all, everyone knew that things got lost in hospitals. And maybe he would open it up himself, just to spite her.

At a quarter to twelve he went downstairs. Jeremy and Mrs. Jackson said their good-byes and, judging by her glistening eyes when the Honda pulled up in front, his leaving appeared to be difficult for her. But not so for him. During the early years they had moved a lot, so he never become attached to people or places. It was easier that way. He hadn't even bothered to call the hospital to say good-bye to his mother—he knew he'd be hearing from her as soon as she needed something.

When they got to the bus terminal, Jeremy thanked Ms. Klugburm for the ride, slung the duffel over his shoulder then waved at her, ticket in hand. She responded with a happy smile, and then drove off to the hospital to deliver the trash bag and, he assumed, to cart off more children to some moldy orphanage.

As he stepped up into the long, silver bus he scanned the remaining empty seats and saw that the back row was unoccupied. He made his way to it, tossed his bag on the netted shelf above the scratched and tinted windows, and then slid himself onto the vinyl bench seat.

After a few moments the bus driver, a frighteningly gaunt black man dressed in a flawlessly creased gray uniform, slammed the folding door shut, then gunned the engine while simultaneously farting the air-brakes. The immense vehicle shuddered, and then began rolling down Mission toward Highway 99.

The bus made two stops on its journey south; the first to pick up more passengers in the farming community of Tulare, the second at a depot on the outskirts of Bakersfield. Here they had a twenty-minute rest stop, so Jeremy got off the bus to spend some of the five dollars Ms. Klugburm had insistently pushed into his hand for food. He needed to pee, besides.

He surveyed the outrageous prices of the snacks in the half-empty vending machines lining the back wall of the station, and then came to the conclusion that he had just enough money for some M&M's, a bag of Doritos and a Coke.

He had only just retrieved his snacks, torn open the package of candy and unscrewed the soda cap when a friendly voice startled him from behind.

CHAPTER 4

Where ya' headed?"

Jeremy turned, and then jerked away from the pear-shaped man standing too closely behind him. He wore jeans and a black satin shirt that was unbuttoned but shouldn't have been, considering his flabby torso. His eyes were hidden by glasses tinted so dark they looked like space.

"L.A.," the boy replied as icily as he could, and then made his way over to the row of orange, hooked-together fiberglass and chrome chairs. There he sat.

"That so," the man said, and sat next to him. "You gonna be in the movies?" The man grinned, revealing front teeth like piano keys and an absence of molars.

"No," he laughed.

"Looks like yours, you could be."

"Thanks." He looked away, trying not to encourage him. He checked the clock over the ticket counter: fifteen more minutes before his bus left.

"I got a buddy who makes movies in Hollywood. And I know he's always lookin' for boys like you to make into stars. I could hook you and him up—you'd be rich. What's your name, son?"

I'm not your son. "Josh."

"Well Josh, glad to know you. I'm Bud Stygian...rhymes with pigeon." He held out his hand to Jeremy, who automatically shook it because that's the only thing he'd ever been taught about what men are supposed to do. But after his hand made contact with the skin he recoiled—it felt dry and cold and hot and wet at the same time, like the man was sick in a hundred different ways.

"Josh, like I said, I could do you a favor and hook you up with him—give you his number for when you get into town. So I do you a favor," he murmured, "and you do me one, know what I mean?" The man looked around nervously as his hand secreted down to trace a finger along the boy's thigh. "By my count, we still got about twelve minutes before your limo leaves for Beverly Hills," he whispered, leaning in. "Truck's out back. Whatcha say?"

Was this happening?

"No way." Jeremy rose from the chair as the loudspeaker announced they would be boarding in five minutes. His bladder was about to rupture, so he trotted towards the men's room while keeping Mr. Stygian in his peripheral vision in case he followed, which he did not.

Jeremy was zipping up himself at the urinal when he heard footsteps behind him and turned to see the man entering the restroom, his piano-key mouth snarling.

"Look you shitty punk, you think you're better'n me? I can tell trash when I see it, 'specially faggot trash. Could see it all over you like neon lights when you climbed off that bus."

"Get away!"

Stygian spat on the floor. "You're just another worthless queer boy on his way to LA. One a day just like you comes in this station. The smart ones sees I can give 'em something they couldn't get from where they come from, but not you...so not only are you faggot trash, you're *stupid* faggot trash."

"Fuck off!" Jeremy pushed past him as he trotted from the stinking restroom toward the lobby. He glanced out of the windows and saw, with relief, that a group of passengers was already pulling themselves up the steps of the bus.

Some time after the adrenaline had worn off and he was rocking again with the motion of the highway he ran the incident over in his head, from start to finish and back again. The episode bothered him more, he figured, than it should have; he'd heard stories of guys at school getting hit on by dirty old queers. So why did it bug him so much?

For starters, he hadn't fought back, he'd just run. Any other kid his age would have flattened the old creep and been justified in doing so. So he'd cheated himself out of the opportunity to stretch his manly wings and fly; after all, bashing a fag was supposed to score you even more Dude Points than losing your virginity to the hottest cheerleader at school. But he hadn't slugged the man, hadn't pushed him down or shoved his head into one of the un-flushed toilets.

He'd just run away.

Secondly, he was not naive enough to think that he looked like anything other than white trash; he had long ago resigned himself to the social status he'd inherited. He usually never even gave it a second thought that his clothes were torn, his hair hadn't seen scissors in years, and his old running shoes had holes in the soles. But all-in-all he figured he looked about the same as the other guys who slouch their way through their teens, alarming convenience store owners and pissing off their parents. So what was it that had drawn the man to him?

He knew he looked pathetic, but it hadn't occurred to him until now that he also looked gay. How else could some stranger in a bus station know the part of him that was hidden in the masking-taped shoebox buried inside his head?

But what shook Jeremy to the foundation of his being, as the bus lumbered toward the crimson sun, was the kinship that the old pervert had assumed: Bud Stygian and Jeremy Tyler were the same kind of folks.

But I'll kill myself if I ever end up like that.

He needed a change. It was now or never.

Ballena Beach. He'd seen it on TV, and it looked like the kind of place where the rest of the planet dreams of living. Stretches of sunny beach, million-dollar houses, shining sports cars, beautiful girls everywhere. Guys his age hanging out together on the beach, surfing and skating and even kite boarding; weekends spent at parties and weekdays spent getting ready for adulthood.

But how could he ever fit in there, of all places? After all, they had laughed at him in Fresno. *Geraldine Trailer*, the tough boys had named him in 6th grade.

And a quiet, very mean voice in his head had secretly called himself that ever since.

But maybe this Aunt Katharine would buy him some new shoes, for starters. He decided he would ask her, probably not tonight, but for sure tomorrow. And eventually he could get some new clothes then make some friends, and then he could have someone to talk to besides a stinky old drunk lady.

He might even be able to have his own room.

If nothing else, at least now I won't have to take care of my mom.

Could all of this actually work out?

His eyes drifted out the windows as the fading light gilded the rows of bean fields as they rolled by, and the first stars of the evening glimmered up high in the East.

He sat back in his seat and hummed quietly.

CHAPTER 5

The bus hit a snag of traffic outside Bakersfield at the base of the Grapevine, so from his window all he saw were brake-lights blinking in the darkness. His anxiety had mounted with each minute that crept past their scheduled arrival time of 8:05 PM, culminating in a state of full-fledged terror as he glanced at the black plastic watch on the wrist of the sleeping army guy in the row in front of him. It read 9:17.

Would his aunt and uncle have waited for him? What would he do if he were stranded? Who would he call? Where would he stay?

He felt like throwing up.

Try to think positive thoughts the school counselor had once suggested after following up on a referral issued by one of his teachers upon noting how anxious the boy looked. Then he added *picture good things happening to you,* and sent him back to American Lit. Such was his over-the-counter remedy for Jeremy's jumpy demeanor.

Well OK then.

He couldn't, for the life of him, place himself in any sort of lavish scenario, and neither could he imagine what his aunt and uncle looked like, so he gave up trying. But he'd seen plenty of movies about rich people. Did they have a stuffy English butler who carried things on big metal trays? How many Rolls Royces did they own? And what about racehorses? Did they have any, and if so were they named *Luck's Wicked Girly* or *Favorite Blue Ladybug*?

How big was their private jet?

He'd seen fancy Las Vegas hotels on TV with Roman statues and Gilligan's Island-type swimming pools. Is that what their house looked like? He hoped they had a pool, he'd been on the swim team for the last few years and discovered that he loved it. All rich people had pools, he told himself.

Finally something to look forward to!

At the top of the Grapevine the traffic cleared and his anxiety diminished as the road descended. At a quarter-to-ten they exited the freeway and a few minutes later pulled into the driveway of the bus depot in Van Nuys.

After the vehicle stopped, he lifted his duffel from the overhead and took his place behind the line of passengers shuffling toward the door. Once outside, he watched the people greeting their families or being swallowed by taxis, and within minutes the parking-lot was deserted except for a few cars, including a dirty gold Camry, a beat-up BMW and an old Ford van.

No Rolls Royces.

Maybe his aunt and uncle had come and gone already. Or maybe she'd forgotten, or this was the wrong stop.

He wasn't used to relying on adults.

What should he do?

He entered the depot and looked around. No rich ladies here, but no creepy old men either. He'd better find out if any message had been left for him, so he made his way across the gum-pocked linoleum floor toward the ticket booth against the far wall. Inside, as if on display, sat an ancient woman sporting a jet-black wig. She was still as a corpse.

As he approached, she looked up from her magazine but said nothing.

"Yeah, someone was supposed to pick me up and they're not here," Jeremy told her. "I was wondering if anyone came by already and left before the bus pulled in. A nice-looking lady and her husband?"

"Couldn't tell 'ya. Just came on at nine myself," she replied. "But we're open 'till two AM, so you can wait around 'til then." Her attention returned to an article about Mariah Carey. "Phone's over there, next to them chairs." She pointed without looking up.

"Thanks."

He was making his way toward the row of chairs when he noticed a snow-white Jaguar glide into the driveway of the station and then pull underneath the portico next to the lobby. As it got closer he saw that the driver was a well-dressed middle-aged woman, and the passenger an older, grandfatherly man. The sight filled him with both intense relief and anxiety.

He hoisted his duffel from the floor, and then pushed the glass door open.

The driver's door swung wide and she got out. "Jeremy?" The woman held out her arms. "Is it really you?"

Her voice was pleasant, with an elegant accent.

He had no recollection whatsoever of this woman. "Aunt Katharine?"

He went to her and they embraced briefly.

"Oh, it is *wonderful* to see you again!" She beamed, studying him from head to foot, her face unreadable—until she grimaced at the sight of his shoes. "You are..." her throat caught and she cleared it "...the very image of your father when he was your age. Isn't he, dear?" she glanced at her husband.

"He is." The older man nodded from the passenger seat.

"Jeremy, please put your things in the trunk. Bill, do help him."

The man got out of the car, and then made his way toward Jeremy. "Bill Mortson." He held out his hand and made a smile, in spite of his nonexistent lips. "Call me Uncle Bill, just like your father used to."

Jeremy shook his hand. "Hi Uncle Bill."

The trunk popped open.

He examined the attractive, delicate woman in front of him, and guessed that she was in her late fifties or early sixties. She wore a beige suit and tortoise-shell glasses, and her reddish-blonde hair was cut in a simple fashion that stopped just above the shoulders. She wore very little make-up and had a curious lack of lines on her face, and she looked even younger than his own mother. But then so did anyone under ninety.

"I'm...I'm sorry I don't remember either of you," the boy stammered.

"Of course not, dear. You've been kept so far from us since your father's accident. But here you are again; I must tell you that I'm so excited to have you staying with us!"

"Yeah, thanks for taking me in." He looked from one to the other. "I hope it's not too much trouble."

"Oh, nonsense! There's just Bill and I rambling around that big house together. We're both so glad to have one of those extra bedrooms put to good use. Have you eaten?"

"Not since Bakersfield," Jeremy replied, trying not to think of Mr. Stygian.

"Then get in and let's get you some dinner."

He threw his bag into the trunk, and then slid himself into the Jaguar's sumptuous backseat. The smell reminded him of an expensive shoe store he used to pass in the Fresno mall.

"My, it's late," Katharine stated after starting the motor and glancing at the clock on the dash. The interior lights dimmed like the house lights in a theater, extinguishing the sight of the saddle-colored leather and gleaming wood. "There are fast food places open, but I'd prefer that you eat something more nourishing...we're still about an hour from the house. Could you wait until then?"

"Sure." He was used to going days without decent meals. What was another hour?

"Wonderful! Bill, will you please call ahead and have Arthur order something for him?"

"Of course," the man replied. He snatched a cell phone from the console and made the call.

Who was Arthur?

"What would you like to eat, Jeremy dear?" She notched the gearshift into Reverse.

He pictured his favorite meal: a steaming bowl of macaroni and cheese, the cheap kind that comes in a box. But that seemed completely pathetic so he said the next thing that came to mind: "I don't know. Pizza?"

"Tell Arthur pizza, but without pepperoni, plenty of vegetables." She threw the transmission into Drive and hit the gas.

"Pizza, but no pepperoni, plenty of vegetables," Bill echoed into the phone, and then snapped it shut.

For the rest of the trip Bill was silent, while Katharine generated a stream of questions about Jeremy's life in Fresno: his likes and dislikes, his friends, his academic strengths and weaknesses, his mother's condition prior to being hospitalized and so on. Which sports did he like? She expressed delight at his enthusiasm for swimming. What did he wish to study in college? Most of his responses were monosyllabic, due to the fact that she made him nervous and he was starting to feel carsick.

Really carsick. His head was throbbing and his stomach had begun to flip-flop. Jeremy imagined his M&M speckled vomit splattering the immaculate leather in front of him.

After switching freeways and directions a few times they headed west over a treacherous mountain pass, with Aunt Katharine chattering constantly as the heavy car glided and heaved in the dark atop the curving asphalt, seemingly oblivious to the jutting mountain boulders to the right and the speeding oncoming headlights and abyss to their left. His aunt's manner of driving on this road indicated to Jeremy that either she knew this strip of road really well or she was nuts. Or maybe bad driving just ran in the family.

She threaded the car through a tunnel bored straight through the mountainside, and finally the road began to dip and straighten toward the base of the hills. He made out a dim strip of twinkling lights winding along an edge of glassy blackness that he figured to be the ocean.

"This is so much prettier during the day, Jeremy. I'll take you around tomorrow and show you around town. We'll go shopping, have lunch at *Jeffrey's*. How does that sound?" she asked.

"Terrific. Great." He was seeing spots.

They came to the stoplight at Pacific Coast Highway, turned right, then headed north past the miles of rolling lawn at Pepperdine University. Eventually the car made a left, and then crawled along a narrow street that descended as it approached the ocean, past an assortment of gargantuan homes in varying architectural styles with artfully lit gardens and glowing windows. Katharine motored open the sunroof, filling the car's interior with the ripe tang of sea air. At the end of the cul-de-sac the Jaguar's headlights flashed upon a looming, cursively intricate black wrought-iron fence supported by hefty adobe walls that ran interminably in each direction, over which cascades of scarlet and tangerine bougainvillea billowed in the night sea breeze. She tapped a button on the dash and the gates swung open majestically, revealing a cobble-stone drive encircling a carved stone fountain, and beyond that an immense tile-roofed villa surrounded by orange trees and rose gardens and carved topiaries.

The effect was more like pictures Jeremy had seen of a grand European hotel than someone's house. He nearly expected to hear trumpets blasting a short, regal tune at their arrival.

"Home at last," she announced, wheeling the car past the fountain and down the side driveway lined on both sides with up-lit palm trees.

"Jesus, this is one beautiful house," Jeremy said as they pulled into the garage, estimating that the parking garage and its adjoining guest-house was nearly as large as the apartment complex that had been his home in Fresno just this morning. With delight, he spied the gleaming black Range Rover 4.6 HSE and the platinum Bentley Continental parked in wide adjoining stalls.

"Thank you for saying so," she said. "It's exciting for us to see it through someone else's eyes from time to time; I'm afraid one becomes numb to its beauty after awhile."

Living with my mother in Fresno for a week would slap you out of your numbness...

As the three exited the car and Jeremy went to the trunk to retrieve his bag, he saw a door open, and the light from inside made known the silhouette of a strongly-built man.

Arthur?

The man grinned at him as he made his way up the steps of the house with his duffel over his shoulder. "Here, let me take that," he said, as he took the burden from Jeremy.

CHAPTER 6

I'm Arthur Blauefee," he said. "Welcome home."

"Hi," was all the boy could think to say. Relieved of his bag, yet still heavy with fatigue, Jeremy lurched through the doorway then froze. There was no way he belonged here; no way would he ever feel comfortable enough in this palace to have it feel like home. *Home* meant chaos, and a dumpster ten feet from the front door.

"Come in, dear." She waved him in from the back entry into the kitchen as Bill brushed past them. "Mr. Blauefee takes excellent care of us, so if there's anything you should need, please see him."

"Call me Arthur." He smiled and nodded and the boy nodded back. "The pizza place was closed so I had to whip up something strange and exotic," he said, with a wink. "Mac and cheese, a salad and some garlic bread, choice of beverage. Have a seat and the waiter will be with you shortly." He motioned to a barstool.

Jeremy hesitated, complied, and cocked his head.

How had Arthur known?

He looked around and saw that over his head hung an iron rack the size of a king-size bed, from which dozens of gray metal pans and copper pots dangled between ropes of garlic and dried plants he didn't know the names of. To his right, a vault-like refrigerator stood beside twin restaurant-sized ovens, and at the far end of the room was a fireplace so immense he figured he could walk inside it and stand up. The opening was topped with a thick wooden mantel, above which hung a gloomy painting of a whale harpooned by a sailing ship that seemed about to smash upon the rocks. And to his left, a series of plate-glass windows so large that the moonlit ocean beyond loomed as if projected on a drive-in theater screen.

And as he scanned the room he caught a glimpse of his reflected self in the glass and realized he looked like a runaway getting a charity meal in some fancy restaurant. He looked down, checking to see if he'd tracked in dirt.

"We're going to the salon tomorrow, dear boy. First thing," his aunt announced. Their eyes locked and he nodded. Had she read his mind?

"I think a Crew-Cut would work," Arthur suggested, sliding a plate of steaming food under his nose. "Very *Bruce Weber*."

"Very who?" Jeremy snatched his fork and dug in, the first bite scalding the roof of his mouth.

"Never-mind," Arthur chuckled, leaning against the bar. "Careful, it's hot."

In spite of his nervousness it took him only a few minutes to shovel through his meal, which he barely tasted due to the screaming in his head to take smaller bites and chew with his mouth closed and use his napkin. In the meantime Arthur attended to his kitchen duties, while Katharine scrutinized her great-nephew's table manners from across the room with narrowed eyes, Jane Goodall-style.

"Are you finished?" she asked.

Jeremy blinked up at her. Wasn't it obvious? His plate was scraped clean.

"Would you like some more?" she offered.

"No thanks," he replied, wanting more.

"Then come. I'll show you the grounds, it's a lovely evening." She held out her hand and he jumped from the barstool, and together they stepped out of the kitchen onto an immense patio.

It does look like a hotel, Jeremy thought again, noting the white-cushioned chaises arranged around the huge rectangular pool that bathed the area in flickering turquoise light, as well as the clusters of tables and chairs with their white canvas umbrellas flapping in the breeze.

"The house was modeled after the *Villa de Flores* in *S'Agaro* on the *Costa Brava* in Spain, where Bill and I spent our honeymoon," she said, hooking her arm through his while gesticulating grandly with her free hand. "The original dates back to the late Renaissance, but ours was finished in 1963, which now makes it one of the older structures in Ballena Beach."

They made their way to the edge of the patio to peer over the stone balustrade, where Jeremy saw that the house sat on a peninsula surrounded by a sheer drop on three sides to a shadowy beach below. On the western end of the compound a jetty protruded away from the main property, upon which, high above the sea, a small round wooden structure perched, appearing then vanishing between puffs of fog.

"What's that?"

"That's the gazebo. Your parents were married there."

Parents. For so long it had just been himself and his mother, so it was strange to have himself referred to as part of a trio instead of the usual miserable pair. But he liked the reference. It sounded homey.

She continued with the tour, telling him how the waves could be illuminated at night by powerful beacons installed on the cliff's edge, then walked them through the immense cross-shaped rose garden, which had been established with cuttings brought in from Tuscany, while the drizzling fountain at its center was copied after one carved for Catherine de Medici.

"I've never seen anything like this," was all he could say.

"It is remarkable, yes," she replied. "Your father dearly loved this place." She paused for a moment, her face frozen. Then her eyes met his. "My hope is that you grow to love it as much as Jonathan did. And that you never take it for granted, or become 'numb' as I'd mentioned earlier." She turned to him and the careful smile vanished. "No matter what happens in the future to any of us, I don't want you to forget that we are a very special and fortunate family." She reached her hand to his face and pushed the hair from his eyes. Then she smiled. "You're like him you know. I can feel it in you, all that Tyler blood. I see it, too, in your eyes. Your father is inside you."

Jeremy looked away.

"Oh, I've made you uncomfortable. Will you forgive me?" She broke out her smile again then threaded her arm through his. "Now where was I? Yes, well there had been an old termite-ridden Cape Cod on the site originally, it'd been built by my grandfather in the Twenties, but fire took it while your uncle and I were on our honeymoon. And when the old house perished we couldn't imagine being happy anywhere else, so we built this on the same spot. As I recall we were notified of the fire during brunch at the Villa, and by dinnertime we'd gone nearly crazy sketching measurements and taking photos all day. We've had some close calls through the years, with those dreadful *El Nino* storms and the fires in '96. But somehow we've been spared."

They turned around, and then climbed the steps back to the kitchen. Once inside she touched him lightly on the wrist. "I should think you'd like to wash-up and unpack your things—it's been a very long day for you, I'm sure. After all, we have tomorrow to catch up and talk about your future." She turned and leaned over to a small panel of numbers and blinking lights on the wall, then pressed a button. "Mr. Blauefee, please come back to the kitchen for a moment," she said, and then, "Arthur will see you to your room. I'm certain he's set out everything you might need for the night. I'll see you bright and early for breakfast, and then we can go into town for that haircut and some shopping." She smiled brightly, smoothing his hair again from his eyes. "It's so good to have you here, my dear. You've no idea how long I've waited for this day. "

"Thanks. I'm glad I'm here too." He tried a smile.

"Wonderful then. Goodnight." She made an about-face and left.

After she had gone he, beckoned by the film of mac and cheese coating his mouth, stood before the refrigerator, tempted to yank the door open but afraid some shoplifting-type sirens would go off.

"I expect you'll need a map for the first few days. To find your room, I mean."

He spun around and found himself staring into Arthur's broad grin.

"Oh, I was just…"

"Sit down, I'll fix you a plate you can take to your room."

"Thanks Mr. Blauefee. Arthur." While the man prepared the snack Jeremy saw that initially, he'd misjudged the man to be in his thirties, but the silver specks in his army-style haircut and the friendly wrinkles fanning the corners of his eyes placed him comfortably into his next decade. But he was still quite handsome for an older man, with an angular jaw and the body of an athlete. And there was something nice about him, something that Jeremy couldn't name, except that it made him feel somehow…teeny. And safe. Like instead of being a servant, he was the kind of guy you'd see in the park playing catch with his son.

A few minutes later, with a cellophane-covered plate in one hand and a sports-bottle of milk in the other, Jeremy followed the man down a hallway to a narrow back staircase that wound upward in a tight spiral. Once at the top he followed him down another hall to an open door.

"This one's yours." Arthur nodded, and they went in. "There are fresh towels in the bathroom there, along with every grooming product known to man." He then crossed the room to a bank of shuttered doors, pulled open the nearest and flooded the room with fresh air. "Your own patio is out here—you look pretty worn-out, so I'll show you how to work the alarm system and the intercom tomorrow. Just don't open any of the exterior doors or go downstairs after midnight, which's when the motion sensors come on. If it gets too hot or cold you can adjust the thermostat on the wall, or you can ring for me...just press one, then three on the keypad." He smiled. "Is there anything else I can get you?"

"No thanks." Jeremy shook his head. "Oh...just one thing, if it's not too much trouble could you make sure I don't sleep too late? I'm going out with my aunt kind of early."

"I'll wake you at seven, and in the meantime ring me if you need anything. Remember, lucky thirteen."

"Great. Thanks." How could he make this man go away? He couldn't wait to be alone.

"No problem. Anything you need out of that duffel bag before I take it to the laundry?"

"That's OK. I can do it myself. I've been doing the wash since I was little."

"Hey, it's what I'm here for, but suit yourself. I'll show you where the machines are tomorrow. Call me if you need anything."

"Lucky thirteen. I know."

Arthur smiled, turned, and then pulled the door shut behind him.

Jeremy looked around.

His quarters were about the same size as the old apartment back in Fresno, with a main area furnished with a fancy queen-size bed, a prissy-looking sofa and two matching club chairs, a fussy desk and chair that looked like it would break under his weight, and an old carved wardrobe encrusted with beveled mirrors. Every fabric in the room was the same guacamole-green, the walls were painted butter yellow, and the trim and woodwork gleamed white. A bouquet of fresh sunflowers drooped their heads from a crystal vase on a marble stand between the two pairs of French doors leading to his own terrace and a pair of luxuriously padded chaises. And beyond that stretched the Pacific, as well as the faraway sparkle of other rich folk's homes hugging the coastline.

After finishing his leftovers Jeremy kicked off his shoes and flopped down on the bed, his nose aimed at the chandelier. He lay that way for some time wondering why, in this fantastic place, he felt so sad and even scared, like he'd just been shipped off to battle.

And then it hit him.

From now on every aspect of his life would need to pass a very rigorous inspection based on a code he knew little of: his grades, his manners, his clothes, his grooming, how he spoke, even his friends if he ever made any. And every choice would now be made for him months, even years in advance. But what terrified him most was the realization that he was now expected to be, by Tyler standards, *successful.* Valedictorian, Class President, Dude-Most-Likely-To-Succeed.

So he *had* been shipped off to war, only this was the battlefield of manhood and he was armed with a squirt gun.

What would he do when, inevitably, he failed?

He closed his eyes and made a wish.

I guess I should write that down.

He found a pen in the nightstand drawer, dug his journal out of the duffel and then cracked it open.

A few minutes later he closed the cover, having found the courage to scrawl, with pessimistic fingers, his most secret wish on the blank page. He got up and stuffed the book far in-between the mattress and box spring, went over and locked the patio doors, turned off the lights then laid on top of the comforter face down.

An hour or so later he reached the conclusion that he couldn't sleep.

He got up and went to the duffel bag and pulled out his pillow and threw it on the bed. He buried his nose in it. It stunk like home.

He slept.

CHAPTER 7

He was rubbing the sleep from his eyes as he rounded the corner of the kitchen and nearly bumped his aunt off her barstool, causing the teacup in her hand to splatter the skirt of her beige suit.

"Oh!" said she.

"*Shit!* Oh God I'm sorry." He blinked stupidly, waiting for her to scream at him, while at the same time amazed by how put-together she looked for so early in the morning. Like the First Lady in a commercial for children's literacy, only classier.

"*Shit,* indeed." She examined first her skirt, then peered at him over the rims of her horn-rimmed glasses, her momentary irritation melting into amazement at how much, by the light of day, he resembled his father—in spite of that awful hair. Could it be the boy was salvageable, in spite of that whore's DNA?

"I trust you slept well?" She switched her attention back to the Stocks page; the very sight of him reminded her of those awful dreams she used to have where Jonathan was suddenly here again, grinning and laughing and sublimely ignorant of the fact that he was dead.

"Uh-huh. Thanks." He shifted from one foot to the other.

"You need to eat breakfast. Sit." She pointed a perfectly manicured finger toward the stool opposite her, and then arose. "Arthur prepared a meal for you, which I will have to reheat, because apparently you are a late riser. But I don't mind." Her lips made a thin smile. "You're welcome to anything we have here. This is your home now—that is, so long as you leave the '*yeahs*' and '*uh-huhs*' and '*oh shits*' back in Fresno with your mother where they belong." She made her way to the microwave and tapped some buttons, making the dish inside light up and spin. "Here we use perfect manners, Jeremy, especially when addressing each other. Is that clear?"

"Yes Ma'am."

"Then help yourself."

"Thank you."

"By the way, you'll be starting school tomorrow at Ballena Beach High, so we've no time to lose for making you look like a Tyler. We'll be leaving for the salon as soon as I finish my paper and...change my skirt. Have you bathed?"

"No, ma'am."

"Finish your breakfast then run upstairs and ready yourself—and from now on, please do not come downstairs until you've made yourself presentable. Mr. Blauefee pulled together an outfit for today, you'll find it there." She motioned to a *Barney's New York* bag on the floor, and then read from a list on the counter. "29x33 flat-front Khakis, Large navy-blue Oxford button-down shirt, size ten and one-half *Kenneth Cole* shoes with belt to match. Dark brown socks. Oh, and some *Calvin Klein* items. Will these fit?"

"Yes, ma'am. Exactly."

"Good. Don't ask me how he does it."

"I won't."

"And Jeremy, dear?"

"Yes ma'am?"

"Please do not call me 'ma'am', I am not your department store customer. You will call me 'Aunt Katharine'."

"Yes, Aunt Katharine."

"Now hurry and eat, we don't want to keep Walter waiting."

"Yes, Aunt Katharine."

Salon Polendina was part of a modern commercial complex built along a bluff leaning over Pacific Coast Highway, all steel beams and tinted glass and white walls like some government laboratory. Katharine was the one with the appointment with Walter, which was good because the overly-tanned owner of the salon made Jeremy jumpy, as the man made no effort to mask his hungry smile and crotch-checking eyes upon their introduction. Instead his stylist turned out to be a stunning young woman with sparkling eyes and a jet-black flat-top haircut.

"I'm Carmen." She held out her hand and Jeremy shook it.

"Hi."

"Young lady," Katharine announced from the neighboring chair, "I'm picturing for him something that a young Kennedy...a *respectable* young Kennedy might wear. Ivy-league and not bowling league, if you will."

"Uh-huh." She confirmed her understanding with a bite of her lower lip and a scrunching of eyebrows. "It *would* be a shame to cut all this off." She shook her head. "But—" her voice dropped to a murmur "—it would be even worse to hide all this." She studied him with one eye shut, scrunching his hair in a ponytail with one hand while standing to the side and scrutinizing his face. "Yep. I know *exactly* what I want to do to you." Their eyes caught at reflected angles in the mirror.

He looked down.

Gay she concluded. *And just Carlo's type.* "How about real short in back, buzzed even, but long enough in front to bed-head it for school or gel it back for going to church with your grandma."

"I'm his great aunt, and that sounds fine," Katharine muttered into her *New Yorker.*

"Well how about you? It's your hair."

"Like she said, it sounds fine. Anything's better than this." He laughed, pushing the mop out of his eyes. "Anyhow, my aunt's trying to make me look respectable."

"I think I can make you look better than *respectable.*" She smiled, revealing two rows of perfect teeth between rosy-brown lips. "So let's see what we can do. But first tell me about yourself, I've never seen you around before." She grabbed his hand. "Let's go over and wash your hair, my assistant's out sick today so I'll do it."

"Your *assistant* didn't look sick the other night dancing his little butt off on the go-go box at the *Frat House*," Walter corrected, brushing red goop onto Katharine's head.

"Are you suggesting Carlo is neglecting his duties here, Walter?"

"That boy's *duties* are his business, sweetie. All I know is what I and most of West Hollywood saw; your baby brother's healthy as a horse. How else could he have put on such a memorable show?"

"Don't pay any attention to him," Carmen whispered into Jeremy's ear as she guided his head back into the sink. "So where've you been hiding all this time?"

"I'm from Fresno. I just got here last night."

"You visiting or here to stay?" She sprayed some warm water through his scalp then massaged in some bubble-gum scented shampoo.

"Kind of both, I guess. My mom's sick and Aunt Katharine, actually she's my dad's aunt, told me I could stay with her until my mom gets better. But that's gonna be awhile."

"You go to school?"

"I'm starting at Ballena Beach High tomorrow."

"You're kidding! That's where I graduated from last year, and my brother Carlo is a Senior there now too. His real name's Carlos, but he thinks dropping the 's' is more European or exotic or something. You'd like each other I think...I'll tell him to keep an eye out for you."

"Thanks." He shifted in his seat.

She rinsed the lather out of his head. "So where's your dad, if you don't mind me asking."

"He died when I was two. Car accident."

"That sucks. Lots of accidents up here. Mostly drunk tourists pulling out of the restaurants on PCH. Do you drive?"

"Not yet."

"Well then if you need someone to show you around, call me. I was born here, in fact, my brother and I were raised on one of the oldest *ranchos* in the area, way up in Topanga; it's been in my family since the 1800's, so there's not an inch of this town I don't know. Now let's get to work."

She toweled him dry, then began combing and snipping his hair with quick precision while he watched his covered lap and the floor around his chair become littered with long moist strands, the only remaining evidence of his former life.

After she finished she ran some gel through his hair, then stood back and grinned while blocking his view of the mirror.

"What's so funny?" he asked.

"See for yourself," she replied, stepping aside.

He caught his reflection, but then looked away.

"Too sexy?" she asked.

"It's fine, I guess." He smiled at her.

She unpinned the huge plastic bib. "Now go show your aunt."

He got up and shuffled over to where Walter worked and Katharine sat reading, her glasses threatening to drop from the tip of her nose, her hair now wig-perfect.

"Aunt Katharine?"

She looked up and narrowed her eyes. "Turn around."

He complied.

"I'd pictured something shorter on top, like your father used to wear...more collegiate...more conservative. Young lady?"

"Yes Ma'am?" answered Carmen.

"I must say this is not what I was picturing—but I suppose it will do for now; we've shopping to do and reservations to keep. Next time shorter, if you will."

"Absolutely." Carmen nodded. "Shorter." And then, "Here," Carmen said, pressing a *Polendina* business card into his hand. He saw that a phone number was scribbled on it. "Give me a call, OK? I mean what I said about showing you around, and I'll tell my brother to look for you at school. Like I said, you two are gonna hit it off."

CHAPTER 8

As they sped down Pacific Coast Highway toward Santa Monica, Katharine phoned, upon Arthur's suggestion, the *Banana Republic* store in the Third Street Promenade. "I need an autumn wardrobe for a seventeen-year-old boy. Listen carefully and have these items bagged and ready to go in, say, fifteen minutes? Do you have a pen? Good. Just a moment, please."

She handed the phone to Jeremy as she rolled through a reddening yellow light at the corner of Temescal Canyon and PCH. "Tell the young man your measurements. Mr. Blauefee wrote them on that little yellow paper in my handbag."

"Hi, hold on a sec," the boy said into the tiny silver phone, feeling very uncomfortable at rummaging through his aunt's purse. Finally he came upon the paper, and began reciting the specifications. "I have a 29 waist, a 34 inseam, wear a large shirt, and..." he was amazed that Arthur had been so precise in his recommendations "...look best in olives, tans, rusts, beiges and black. Absolutely no orange or light green or turquoise. A nice mix of dress and casual. And flat front pants, no pleats."

"Anything else?" asked the voice.

"Uh, nope."

"OK. Let me talk to your mom."

"She's not my mom."

Jeremy handed the phone back as they made a sharp left on Chataqua, and then continued up the steep hill to the stoplight at the top across from Palisades Park.

"We'll need five pairs of slacks, five jeans, five sweaters, five sweatshirts, Three jackets, three belts, two pairs of athletic shoes and two pairs of dress shoes..." the light turned green and she gunned the engine, nearly hitting a man crossing the street sipping from a *Starbucks* cup, "...some colored socks. Oh, and a nice leather book bag of some sort. We are now ten minutes away. Please meet us in the alley with the bags. My American Express number is five-nine-one-seven..." she recited her fifteen digit card number from memory while navigating between a merging transit bus and two bicyclists "…yes, yes. You're most welcome."

She snapped the phone off as they roared down West Channel, made a right on 7th, then another right onto Wilshire. Just past 5th Street they turned left into an alley lined with yawning dumpsters and sagging cardboard boxes. At the end of the roadway two well-dressed young men, laden with a dozen or so shopping bags, emerged from behind a heavy metal door.

"For the record, I believe that shopping this way is crass," she said, slamming the car to a halt while popping open the trunk in front of the silent salesmen, who dutifully filled the trunk with her purchases and then presented her with, through the driver's window, a lengthy receipt to be signed. "But the *paparazzi* is so brazen now that anyone noteworthy can't take the chance of trying on clothes in a fitting room." She scribbled on the receipt, handed it back, and then nodded to the young men. "But alleys are tricky business, my darling. Those with anything to lose should *never* be caught in one alone."

Thirty minutes later the pair was headed again along the Coast Highway, traveling further north past The Colony. Jeremy squinted through the windshield as the noonday October sun danced on crayon-blue waters. Tilting his head back, the rush of the clouds and tree branches through the sunroof made him dizzy, like he was flying upside-down.

She glanced at her watch. "Good. We've made better time than I'd expected."

"Why the big hurry?" he asked.

"We have twelve-thirty reservations."

"Wouldn't they wait for you?"

"Of course they would hold our table, but that isn't the point. There are two kinds of people in Ballena Beach: those with manners and everyone else. And Tylers have manners, of which you are one…officially, as of yesterday. Our first lesson takes place this afternoon, when we review the dying art of dining in public."

"Oh."

"We have so much to discuss, young man. Ah, and here we are."

She waited for the traffic to clear and then made a left into a driveway that plummeted sharply down and to the left, where she nearly plowed into two handsome valets in navy blazers.

"Good afternoon, Mrs. Tyler," the first said while opening her door and offering his hand, which she took. The second opened and held the door wide for Jeremy.

"Thank you, and good afternoon to you, Miguel. This is my nephew, Jeremy Tyler."

"A pleasure to meet you," the man said. "And this is Ernesto. He's my cousin from *Durango*."

"*Mucho gusto, Don Ernesto*," stated Katharine, with a coy smile. And with that Ernesto bowed to her.

"Hi." Jeremy waved first at one and then the other.

"And how are the children, Miguel?" she asked while gathering her purse and sweater from the back seat.

The man smiled broadly. "Oh, they're growing up so fast, Mrs. Tyler."

"Miguelito—is he ten now? And Carolina, she must be in third grade this year."

"Yes, Mrs. Tyler. Thank you for asking."

"I would love to see pictures of them—I'll bet they're both simply beautiful." She waved Jeremy along. "Miguel, I would so appreciate your parking my car in the shade, if it's not too much trouble."

"Of course, Mrs. Tyler."

And with that they climbed the steps toward the maitre-d, who greeted Katharine as if she were his very best friend, and then guided them past the other diners toward her favorite table at the far end of the flagstone terrace, tight against the railing overlooking the ocean. On the way, two sharply dressed men lunching together waved a cheerful hello to his aunt, and she returned their gesture with equal enthusiasm. Jeremy noticed, as soon as she looked away from them, that the men tracked his own progress across the patio.

"Who are they?" he asked when they reached their table.

"They are two of my best clients from the gallery."

"What gallery?"

"Oh, it's nothing much..." The maitre d' pulled out her chair and she folded herself down into it as gracefully as the Queen. Jeremy followed suit. They were handed menus. "A few years back I bought a little shopping center near the center of town, and then found that I couldn't rent out the last two spaces. Primitive art has always fascinated me, so I decided to combine the spaces and build a gallery to showcase some of the Chumash Indian art from this region. With its success I've branched out of course, and now feature antiquities as well as work done by some of the local artisans; I have a special passion for woodcarvings, as you'll see. I'll swing you by the space sometime, it's called *Galleri Collodi*."

"Sounds interesting," he noted blandly. He looked over and caught the men stealing glances at him. One threw him a bold smile. Jeremy grabbed his menu and studied it. "What's the name mean?"

"It's an obscure reference to the author of *Pinocchio*; there's something about that story that I've always loved. And there are those woodcarvings that I mentioned."

Presently their waitress, a pretty young blonde dressed in a spotless white shirt and slacks, took their drink order. Aunt Katharine decided on a glass of Chardonnay for herself and an iced tea for Jeremy, then ordered a grilled salmon for him and a *Salad Nicoise* for herself. The waitress nodded courteously, and then disappeared.

"I suppose you'd prefer a soda, which is fine at home," she said, "but not in a place like this."

"It's OK, there's sugar here."

"Yes, of course." She smiled thinly, then knitted her hands together. "If you don't mind, I'll suggest your food order the first few times we dine together. To help refine your tastes."

"Sure, Aunt Katharine. Whatever."

"Good."

"Can I ask you something?"

"You *may*."

"What was with those guys in the parking lot? Back in Fresno, my mom said you shouldn't talk to Mexicans."

"That doesn't surprise me, Jeremy; Tiffany had the breeding of a rodeo clown. So your first lesson for the day is this: a true gentleman treats everyone with the same respect, from a Senator down to the lowliest beggar on the street. Unfortunately our society confuses class with money, both of which are often mutually exclusive. Your second lesson is that it is always good form to show interest in other people's lives, even if you have none. And while we are discussing good form, we need to discuss your poor posture…hasn't anyone told you to walk and stand tall, imagining that a string is holding up your head?"

"A string?"

"Yes, a string, such as that which holds-up a marionette. If you accustom yourself to visualizing this you shall, with practice, never slouch."

"OK. I'll try it."

"Very well. But these are trivial matters." She removed her glasses, squinted at him, then slipped on a pair of sunglasses drawn from her purse. "Jeremy, please tell me, are there any serious character flaws which you possess? I'd much prefer you tell me now so that I might get you the help you need."

"I'm not sure what you're talking about." His eyes shifted.

Their conversation halted as the waitress deposited their drinks on the table, then fled. "What I mean, if I may speak frankly, is that you are your mother's son."

Jeremy stiffened. "Why's that so bad?"

"It's worse than you might think." She stopped, took a sip of her wine, grimaced, and then continued in a softer voice. "How much do you know about her past?" She touched him on the wrist.

"Not much, only what I can remember. She wouldn't tell me much about my father or herself, she always said there was no point in digging up buried garbage."

"What, if you don't mind me asking, did she ever tell you about me?"

He looked down at his iced tea, snatched some packs of sugar, tore them open and then dumped them into the glass. The substance floated atop the ice cubes like a miniature snowy island. "I only knew that she talked like…she hated you."

"She hates me?" she snapped. "That is lunacy! If not for that woman my Jonathan would still be alive! If anyone should hate it should be I!"

"What do you mean by that?" he asked, nervously stirring his now cloudy tea.

She sighed. "Well, I'd better start at the beginning if I'm to make any sense of this for you." She glanced over her shoulder. "Where is that waitress? I'm going to need a better Chardonnay to get us through this."

CHAPTER 9

"I assumed guardianship of your father in 1973, when he was just six years old, under much the same circumstances as yours. But let me go back even further, so you might know the entire story.

"Jonathan's parents, my brother John and his wife Donna, had divorced rather suddenly. Their separation came as a shock to the family, as we all knew how much he loved his wife, and how happy he seemed after having begun his own little family with her. After the divorce little Jonathan went to live with his mother in Lakewood or Bellflower or some other dreary little suburb, while John remained here with us.

"As I mentioned it was the early '70's, and my brother was called, as were so many young men, to fight in Vietnam. Naturally we were sick with anxiety, and our father schemed and pulled strings and plotted for him to stay here, or at the very least to be shielded from combat if he had to serve. But none of us predicted that he would himself decide to go to that God-forsaken country and fight that hideous war, which at that time was winding down into a humiliating defeat for our soldiers.

"You see, my brother had just lost his family and was understandably discouraged, and being a headstrong and honorable Tyler male he believed it was his duty to go there and battle the Communists, and to our dismay there was no reasoning with him otherwise. He was killed in a helicopter crash only two weeks after his arrival in Saigon. But as heavily as we grieved, at least we had the comfort knowing he hadn't become one of those unfortunate POWs or MIAs, rotting forgotten in those jails, while our politicians made deals with their lying diplomats.

"The last time I saw Jonathan's mother was at my brother's memorial service. You could tell she blamed herself for his death; she knew, as did we all, that if she hadn't divorced him he'd never have volunteered to fight overseas. Donna looked physically ill that day, as if every fiber of her being was woven with regret. And poor little Jonathan, just old enough to comprehend that his beloved daddy was never coming back. It was enough to break your heart just seeing him standing bravely in his little navy suit, saluting his father's flag-draped casket."

"So why do you think she blamed herself?" asked Jeremy.

"There had been rumors, of course. Still no one was certain what had destroyed their marriage so suddenly. If she'd been unfaithful to him, which I believe she had, he was too much the gentleman to make that information known, even to his immediate family. Whatever had been the cause of their divorce died with him, and then a short time later with her."

"She died too?"

"The coroner ruled it an accidental death, but I believe it was suicide. She ingested more than a few Valium and, if memory serves, a fifth of *Southern Comfort*. She was only twenty-seven at the time, as had been my brother. Your father was only four. A four year-old orphan from a broken home.

"Of course I volunteered to be Jonathan's guardian. And I'll tell you right now that there was no more heart-wrenching sight than your father as a boy, wandering around this house by himself, never playing or laughing or running, at least not for the first few years or so that he was with me.

"It wasn't until he reached twelve or thirteen that he began to heal and come out of his shell, at that time in life when most boys are retreating into one. Eventually he pursued sports and other extracurricular activities. In fact, he won a few State ribbons for Swimming and later Debate.

"And your father grew into one of the most handsome young men in the area. We Tylers are Irish, but Donna had been Italian, and the mixture of the two bloodlines was quite spectacular. Jonathan was clearly what is referred to as 'the best and the brightest'. Bill and I were certain that he was headed on the straight and narrow road to a brilliant, fulfilling life." She turned her head, looked out to sea and then sighed heavily. Then she turned back to him and removed her sunglasses and Jeremy saw that her eyes were actually copper-colored. "In 1987 your father was a Senior at Ballena Beach High, and with his athletic ability as well as having earned excellent marks all through school, we were expecting he would have his choice of the finest colleges and universities in the country, if not the world. He'd been approached by Harvard, Yale, Stanford, even Oxford."

"This must be the part where my mom comes in," said Jeremy.

"A clever assumption, dear boy," she replied with a sad laugh. "You'll please forgive me for saying so, but your mother was what I will euphemistically refer to as *common*. And please know that I do not refer to her family's unfortunate socioeconomic status. To be blunt, she scratched her way into Jonathan's social circle by using her floozy looks, and by being a colossal manipulator. From what I recall, the more respectable girls would have nothing to do with her because they knew if they looked cross-eyed at her she would steal their boyfriends or worse, just for sport. Eventually she clawed her way to the position of head cheerleader or drill-team captain or some other such nonsense, which unfortunately put her in close proximity to your father at all the school functions, including his illustrious swim meets."

"She was a drill-team captain?" Jeremy asked, wide eyed.

"Yes, and to be honest, she was quite a knockout. I remember overhearing some boys describing her as a *stone fox*, whatever the devil that meant, although I quickly came to understand the *stone* part. With her bleached blonde hair she looked just like that girl from, what was that insipid television show? Yes, *Dynasty*. Heather something-or-other. Only more impressive. In the early Eighties every young woman in Ballena Beach looked as though she were impersonating that actress; only with your mother it looked as though *Heather Whatever* were impersonating her.

"I'll never forget seeing her for the first time at the High School Swimming Championships, after Jonathan had placed First in the Butterfly competition. We had unwittingly sat next to her in the front row of the bleachers, down by the pool's edge. I didn't know at the time who she was, but I took one look at her and thought, *that girl is trouble*. Imagine my horror when Jonathan rose from the water in his black swimsuit, all glistening muscles and white teeth, and this squealing bimbo ran to him and pressed her breasts against his half naked body.

"The rest is history. Of course she 'accidentally' became pregnant by him, and even though every girl in the country was routinely running off for abortions Tiffany remembered suddenly that she was Catholic and had no choice other than to have the baby. And predictably, Jonathan offered to marry her.

"Of course I knew the only reason she wanted the baby was because it would be her ticket out of the trailer park, which it was, literally; her family actually lived in a mobile home if you can believe the cliché. Jonathan and she married shortly after the end of the school year, and then took up residence in the guesthouse at the rear of our property. Naturally, they were miserable.

"You were born in March following their graduation. But if I had been opposed to her having decided to keep you, after you were born I was equally relieved she'd made the decision she had. You were the most agreeable and beautiful baby, so calm and quiet, never a trouble to anyone. Everyone loved you; even I began thinking myself a grandmother."

His aunt paused for a moment, deep in thought, staring intently out to sea, the faint breeze tousling her hair. Suddenly the waitress appeared, and with flourish placed the wrong dish before them.

"Enjoy!" the girl piped.

"The other way, dear," she corrected. "And a better Chardonnay this time." She tapped the crystal rim. "Or better yet, a glass of that lovely *Viognier* that Maurice keeps in back."

Jeremy watched with interest as his aunt's tongue loosened with each sip of wine, and he began to feel afraid of what he might hear next. He stabbed at his salmon steak, she ignored her salad. A fly landed on the rim of her plate, she waved it away absently.

"As I'm certain you know, your parents were ill-suited as a couple, and they grew visibly more unhappy with each passing week. Your mother left one night, taking you with her, claiming that Jonathan had hit her during a disagreement which, of course, he had not. She even called the police and tried to press charges.

"We assumed that divorce was imminent, and I consulted with the family lawyers and a private investigator about deeming her unfit to care for you. After all, you are Jonathan's son, and would eventually inherit a substantial share of the Tyler holdings.

"Of course your mother's family got involved in the dispute, they all had a nose for other people's money. In any case both parties began building cases for when the time came for custody to be determined."

"But why would my mother's family want to keep me?"

"Jeremy dear, has no one told you that on your eighteenth birthday your Trust becomes available to you?"

"What Trust?"

"*What Trust?* Good Lord, that woman! She's kept you in the dark about everything, hasn't she?"

"I guess..."

"I'll explain the Tyler Trust to you with the assistance of the family attorneys at a later time. Suffice to say that this coming March you will be a wealthy young man. But please allow me to finish my story."

The waitress returned to deliver Katharine's wine and to refill his tea. Jeremy watched his aunt skewer a plump pink shrimp with her fork, swirl it in some dressing and pop it in her mouth without a sound, chewing noiselessly while dabbing at the corners of her mouth with the end of the napkin that she kept anchored on her lap with her other hand. And suddenly he felt faraway, as if he were watching this event on television. *A wealthy young man*, she had just said. *A wealthy young man.* Her throat worked as she swallowed. "Overcooked," she remarked, then threw back a swig of her freshened wine. Her cheeks were fast becoming the same color as the curled headless creatures lying still atop the lettuce.

"As I was saying, the divorce proceedings began and the custody battle ensued. Because your father had gallantly opposed a pre-nuptial, your mother was entitled to half his assets. Fortunately, your father's financial advisors had invested his share of the Trust well before the marriage, and the dissolution of these numerous investments would have taken considerable time. Our attorneys astutely suggested your mother might be happier with a cash settlement, which could be dispensed immediately.

"Of course she opted for the payoff, which at the time was in the neighborhood of two-hundred thousand dollars. Little had she known that if she'd waited three months for even a partial dissolution she would have been set for the rest of her life—although with the way she ran through money she would've eventually become destitute. It was like she was determined to make a shambles out of her life.

"And with the property having been settled the only battle left was over the custody of you, my dear. Our private investigator had dredged up some interesting facts about your mother, about her indiscretions and such that I won't embarrass you with. There even seemed to be some question as to whether or not you were Jonathan's son, but one look at you told your lineage better than a blood test. You had just turned two, and were the spitting image of your father at the same age, just as you are now at seventeen.

"Our attorneys felt that they had the case against your mother sewn up tight, and the final court date to grant custody was set.

"What happened next was terrible; it took me years to stop blaming myself. I should have demanded that he not go see her that night, and I've asked myself a thousand times why I did not."

"The accident?" asked Jeremy.

"Yes, *the accident*, only it wasn't. On the Friday night before the court date your father went up to our chalet in Lake Estrella to try to work things out one last time with Tiffany. And don't ask me why, because his life finally seemed to be in order; he'd been accepted to Harvard and was dating this beautiful girl from a good family that lived down the road in *Castellamare*, Kimberly Van-Something. And it looked as if the Courts would agree that I should raise you as I had Jonathan, at least until he could finish college and set himself up professionally. For the first time since throwing his life away on a girl who was so beneath him, the vision we'd had for Jonathan's life appeared to be materializing.

"There were no witnesses to the crash. It was late, and he'd just left Tiffany after visiting with her. The police concluded that his mishap was unfortunate, but rather routine for that infamous stretch of road. He had, the report stated, lost control around a curve and had gone over the edge of the mountainside, having narrowly missed the stretch of guardrail that might have saved his life. Your father was killed instantly, of course. Only..." her voice caught suddenly, her composure shattered by a burst of emotion. "...only I used to lay awake at night imagining what thoughts must have gone through his head as the car went over the side. Poor Jonathan, orphaned as a boy and then sailing over the edge into blackness to his own death. Dying all alone on that mountainside. It just devastates me even now to think of it!"

Jeremy looked away as she used the ends of her napkin to dab at the corners of her eyes then blow her nose. He fidgeted in his chair, gathering the courage to ask the question he dreaded hearing the answer to.

"So what makes you think his death...was my mother's fault?"

Moments passed before she answered. "Your father kept that car, that black Porsche, in *perfect* order, and he was an exceptional driver. In fact I sent him to driving school, it was the only way I'd let him drive something so powerful. And the weather was clear—no rain, no fog, no snow."

"So then what happened?"

"Of course a deer might've jumped in front of him, and it would've been in keeping with his nature to avoid hitting a defenseless animal. The police offered that as a probable cause, because there were no tire tracks of another vehicle or any other evidence that pointed to his having contact with another car. It's just my intuition, and the timing of it all, which tells me that he was murdered. That and the look on your mother's face at Jonathan's memorial."

"What do you mean?"

"Tiffany had the same look on her face that Donna had at my brother's funeral. The very picture of guilt, of regret, of deep grief for a man whose life she'd single-handedly ruined, all because of lust. It was evident to me that Tiffany had experienced all too clearly the consequences of her filthy greed: that beautiful young man who'd once loved her, or more correctly had once *made love* to her was dead. *And it wrecked her*; you've seen the proof of it yourself all these years. Only, and you'll forgive me for saying this, she hadn't the strength of character to redeem herself the way Donna did, at least not as *quickly or efficiently*."

She paused, sighed, then pushed the virtually unmolested salad away from her and replaced it with her nearly empty glass of wine which she stared at for a moment then drained unceremoniously.

"You see, without Jonathan around, the courts had no choice other than to award sole custody to her. So she took you and her settlement money to Fresno, claiming she wanted to bring you up in a more *wholesome* environment. I learned later that she'd followed some man there whom she had designs on, the son of some Armenian dairy owner, if memory serves. But Jeremy dear, what I think...*what I know* is this: your mother is in some way responsible for your father's death, for his murder. Don't you see? It was she who murdered my son and stole my grandson, then made off with two hundred thousand dollars of my money. Now you tell me who should hate whom!"

No. His mother was a lot of things, and nobody knew this better than he did, but this was too much. How could it be true what Katharine was alleging? If she had been responsible, wouldn't she have been found out? It made no sense to think that his mother, all by herself, could have pulled-off the perfect murder.

Jeremy saw his inebriated aunt sitting in the blazing afternoon sun, her tipsy mind reliving the details of devastating events nearly two decades past. And in spite of her weakened state he saw a powerful woman righteously angry about having someone stolen from her whom she still dearly loved, a man she had just referred to as her son even though he was not, just as he himself was not her grandson. And he felt, deep within himself, the first great connection he'd ever felt with anyone: his aunt and he had both suffered deeply for the loss of his father. And now they could grieve together.

"Aunt Katharine, let's go home."

She nodded sluggishly, fished her phone from her purse, and then handed it over. "Press number two to call Arthur. Tell him we are at *Jeffrey's* and that I am in no condition to drive. He'll know what to do."

CHAPTER 10

A gang of belligerent seagulls on the balcony startled Jeremy from his afternoon nap; for a moment he didn't know where he was, and it took a concerted effort to reorient himself and calm his pounding heart. And after his panic melted and it all started making sense again he swung his feet to the floor and pushed himself up from the bed to stand before the windows, looking west. He saw that the October sun's reflection on the western sea made twin fiery pumpkins: one hovering above, the other shimmering on the water. He turned and glanced at the clock.

Good, he hadn't missed dinner.

He then left his room, having been drawn toward the faraway drone of a vacuum cleaner. He followed the sound down a labyrinth of halls until he found Arthur propping one corner of a delicate-looking antique sofa up with this left shoulder as he shoved the complaining machine under it with his right hand.

"Hey!" Jeremy shouted.

"Hey," Arthur replied, his concentration focused on a stubborn piece of lint.

"When's dinner?"

"Hold on a minute." He switched off the appliance and stared, doing his best to mask his amazement, at Jeremy from head to toe and back.

Jonathan, back from the grave.

"Well, I guess it's true what they say about diamonds," was what he said.

"That they're a girl's best friend?" Jeremy asked.

"No. That the rough ones polish up...and rather nicely I might add." He reached down and unplugged the machine then recoiled the cord. "Really Jeremy, you look great. You'll do more than just fit right in with the young Ballena Beach elite, and I imagine you'll turn more than a few heads."

"I'm used to that, only usually for the wrong reasons."

"You sell yourself short, young man. Certain things are always visible to the discerning eye—like intelligence, poise...and a swimmer's build. But there's no substitute for a decent haircut and tasteful clothes. Speaking of, how did that stuff fit that I picked out for you?"

"Like, perfectly so far, but I haven't tried on everything. How'd you know my sizes?"

"I am a keen observer of the male form. Plus, I apprenticed as a tailor in one of my stabs at an earlier career."

"Before you were a butler?"

"Yes, before I became a butler."

"What made you change?"

"I fell in love, but that's another opera. You're too young."

"Yeah, like I'll be eighteen in five months," he declared. "Anyway when's dinner? I'm already starving. Aunt Katharine only ordered me some fish for lunch. It was stinky so I didn't eat it all."

"She *ordered* for you? Please tell me you were in the restroom when the waiter came."

"No, she said she wants to make sure I eat the right stuff. And she even wanted to have my hair cut a certain way, and ordered a bunch of stuff for me from the *Banana*, and she corrects the way I walk and the way I talk. It's kind of driving me crazy."

"Figures." Arthur nodded. "You have to understand that she wants to carve you into her vision of the man she thinks you should become, which means she probably wants you to be as much like your father as possible. And I can't say I blame her. Your dad was quite a guy."

"You knew him?"

"Not the way I wanted to, believe me," he said, then smiled. "Just from afar. He was one of those amazing people with everything going for him, and I mean *everything*. He was smart, rich, gorgeous, athletic, popular, and the nicest guy you ever met. Everyone wanted to be his girlfriend or his...buddy. The swim meets were standing room only when he competed, and when he got his black Porsche for graduation, five other kids from Ballena Beach High traded in their cars for black Porsches. I graduated a couple years ahead of him, but I heard about when the whole scandal took place with Tiffany, with your mom getting pregnant I mean. By the way, I'm sorry she's in the hospital again."

"I'm not, but thanks anyway. So can I get myself something to eat?"

"Sure, but one more thing. Your aunt needs to remember that one of the best things about your dad was that he was nobody's puppet—he made up his own mind about everything he did. Unfortunately that became his downfall, too. No pun intended."

"Huh?"

"Bad joke. Just learn what you need to from her, and when the time's right to stand on your own two feet you'll do it. So what're you hungry for?"

"Can you make me a peanut butter and *Fritos* sandwich?"

"No, but I can make one for you. Just go change your clothes before you spill on them; I'll have your disgusting sandwich ready downstairs in five minutes—your wish is my command."

Arthur was arranging a corn chip happy face on one slice of the peanut butter-smeared bread when Jeremy entered the kitchen wearing stiff new jeans and a T-shirt with the packaging creases visible in a large grid across his torso.

"I'm back, Arthur."

"I can see that."

"After I eat could you show me around the house? I don't want to get lost or walk in somewhere I shouldn't. Maybe you could even show me the guesthouse where my parents lived." He remembered what his aunt had alleged about his mom; maybe Arthur had an opinion on the matter. "And I have a lot of questions for you, when you have time."

"Sure, I don't think your aunt would object to my showing you around, and it'll be a while before she's up, probably not until dinnertime. But only after you sit down and eat." He slid the plate in front of the boy.

Jeremy devoured the sandwich. "There. Should we start on the first floor?"

"Drink your milk first."

They ambled from room to room, while Arthur explained to Jeremy the proper names for everything. They visited the *Grand Foyer* with its flying staircase, *Carrera* marble floor and Louis XVI chandelier; the drawing room with its green velvet drapes, gloomy portraits and elegantly carved baroque settees, and the formal dining room with the Inquisition-sized table flanked by rows of Italian Renaissance chairs. Eventually they made their way to the conservatory, a kind of room that Jeremy had never seen before.

The structure was attached to the western end of the house in order, Arthur explained, to catch the fog-dimmed rays from the afternoon sun. The walls and even the ceiling were constructed almost entirely of glass panes, which rose up two stories to a point in the middle that formed a glass pyramid, through which the drifting clouds were visible beyond the crystal chandelier hanging at its apex. The glass room had been crammed with exotic plants and trees sprouting chartreuse and emerald-green leaves, and some even drooped the most delicate and intricate flowers Jeremy had ever seen, with petals of pink, orange, purple and yellow. The furniture in the room consisted of a battered Victorian chaise and a few crumbling arm chairs gathered in a circle around an ottoman; the other pieces included some mismatched English bamboo side-tables, and finally a moldy wall fountain that drooled water from the mouth of an angry stone chimpanzee.

Arthur explained that Katharine had shipped the items over from England one summer after nodding hello to an old friend at an auction and inadvertently outbidding a famous designer known for her chic and 'shabby' interiors. Upon arrival from her trip she'd had the Conservatory built to house the pieces which, she explained, were too expensive to be put out by the curb, yet too ratty to be seen by polite company in the rest of her home. Ironically, Arthur had discovered since that if he could not find his employer in her office working, she was usually reading or asleep on the chaise in the conservatory, a cold cup of tea on the table by her side.

Jeremy stood in the doorway of the room, quite taken with the magic of the place. The air even smelled differently than the rest of the house—it was velvety and sweet, like a warm bubble bath.

"Come sit down with me and watch the sunset." Arthur pointed to an armchair.

They sat and watched the sky before them as if from the first row of a movie theater, heads tilted back.

For Jeremy this felt like the first sunset of his life. He watched as the cobalt sky dimmed to lavender, and the silhouetted clouds before him rose up like ragged mountains, while the amber sun kissed the watery horizon and gilded the whitecaps.

"People say they move to Ballena Beach to be near the water, but the real reason is the sunsets," stated Arthur, breaking their silence at last. "I always like to watch a good one with someone who's not from around here, it's like seeing it through their eyes again for the first time. Makes it fresh."

"I can see what you mean. We didn't have sunsets in Fresno," Jeremy said, then paused in thought. "At least not that I remember—it just gets dark all of a sudden."

"Oh, I'm sure Fresno, like all places, has sunsets…it just sounds like you didn't have the time to enjoy them."

"You're right about that, I guess," the boy replied. "Anyway, how do you know so much about me?"

"I'm sorry, maybe I shouldn't have said anything. It's just that I've overheard conversations between your aunt and uncle. This house may be big, but it doesn't keep secrets well. Not even its own."

"I guess not." Jeremy paused, noticing that the moon had slid up into easy view now, illuminating the jungle of plants enveloping them, as well as their two figures with silver light. "So how much do you know… about my situation?"

"I guess I know about everything your aunt and uncle know, at least about your 'circumstances'. But I can't say that any of us here knows the real Jeremy Tyler."

"Except me."

"Of course, except for you," the man said, then smiled.

Jeremy sighed. "Well, maybe that's not even true."

"How is that so?" asked Arthur cautiously.

"Do you remember what it's like to be seventeen?"

"Of course I do, although parts of the memory grow dimmer with each year. But some parts seem like they happened yesterday."

"Really? Like what?"

"Like graduating from high school, starting my first job, my first kiss, all the really important events. The first time I knew I had fallen in love."

"So how do you know when you're in love?"

"Just like you know when you're hungry and then you know when you're full."

"It's that easy?"

"Sometimes. Unless you try to make yourself fall in love with the wrong person. Just remember, you can't make yourself hungry when you've stuffed yourself, or convince yourself you're not hungry when you're starving. Unless of course you have an eating disorder."

"If you know so much then how come you're not married?"

"How do you know I'm not?"

"Well, you live here, don't you? And I haven't seen any maids besides you."

"You're correct. I'm a single man, as I've been, unfortunately, for some time now."

"Then you were married?"

"In every sense of the word, except legally. My spouse passed away."

"How?"

"I'd rather not say. It's hard for me to talk about it."

At first Jeremy didn't know what to say; he'd never known anyone beside himself who owned a tragedy. "It's OK, I know what you mean," the boy said finally. "It seems like everyone here in Ballena Beach dies young, like my dad and both my grandparents. None of them even got to thirty."

"Well fortunately that doesn't always have to be the case, as is evidenced by my presence here this evening." Arthur laughed, rising from his chair to switch on the chandelier overhead. Jeremy also pushed himself up, as he sensed that their conversation had grown too intimate for them to remain in this room together.

"Can I see the rest of the house now, Arthur?"

"I'm afraid I am neglecting my 'maid' duties, Jeremy. And besides, this talk of love and death has left me a bit melancholy. Maybe tomorrow morning."

"But tomorrow I start school," Jeremy reminded. Not that he really cared about seeing the rest of the house, but he did have more questions to ask. And he liked the man's company.

"Tomorrow afternoon, then, so I can hear all about your first day of school. In the meantime I expect you'll want those shopping bags emptied and the heaping contents laundered?"

"You don't have to wash them," Jeremy laughed. "Nobody's worn them."

"Yes, of course. I'd forgotten." He grinned.

"Arthur?"

"Yes, young man?"

"Do you know anything about my father's accident?"

His smile vanished. "Jeremy, at one time just about everyone in Ballena Beach had their own theory of what happened that night. All I can say is you've got enough to deal with without listening to rumors or imagining things about a tragedy that happened so long ago. Just believe in the fact that the truth always comes out. And the important thing is that you're here now, and you're safe. I'll make sure of that. Now what do you want for dinner?"

CHAPTER 11

The pounding on the door rescued him from his recurring dream of having to pull his complaining mother around the beach in a little red wagon, the tiny wheels sticking in the sand like ice skates in wet cement.

"Jeremy, wake up."

"Yeah," he answered, muffled and sleepy. He half-cracked open an eye. It was still dark.

"It's Arthur. May I come in?"

"OK." He turned over and propped himself up against the headboard as the door swung open and Arthur entered backwards, his biceps straining under the weight of the heaping bed-tray piled high and chinkling with silver and crystal.

"Wow, where's the princess?" Jeremy asked, rubbing his eyes.

"That would be you. Your aunt wants you to get an early start for school. She'll drive you there herself, but says you've got to eat a good breakfast first."

"I don't eat breakfast," Jeremy stated, bunching the covers around his lap to camouflage his morning erection.

"Your aunt expected you'd say that, so she told me to tell you that from now on you'll be eating a full breakfast every morning. Now straighten out your covers so I can put this down. It's heavy."

Carefully, he pulled the bedclothes evenly around him, and Arthur, bending from the waist, settled the large tray on the bed, trapping the boy's legs underneath.

"I'll kill you if you spill anything on that comforter. It fills up the whole back of the Rover when I take it to the cleaners," he said.

"I'll try not to."

"And don't get used to this breakfast-in-bed business. This is strictly a back-to-school present."

"Don't worry. So what's in here that's so important to eat?"

"Per Mrs. Tyler's orders: a fresh basil and sun-dried tomato omelet with mozzarella and turkey sausage, home-made biscuits with butter and marmalade, fresh grapefruit juice and freshly-ground *Starbuck's* coffee."

"I don't drink coffee."

"You should know that your aunt is of the opinion that people who don't drink coffee shouldn't be trusted. I suggest you use the sugar in that bowl." He pointed.

The boy rolled his eyes.

"You'd better get used to this."

"Yeah, I know, I know. I guess there are worse things." He surveyed the foods before him and decided to try the biscuits. He knifed some butter and pushed it on the steaming bread, then popped it in his mouth. "Are there any other orders from her?" he mumbled through crumbs.

"As a matter-of-fact there are. She says you are to wear khakis and a white long-sleeve oxford, brown leather shoes and a matching belt."

"What are khakis?" Jeremy asked.

"Beige twill pants."

"What's twill?"

"Not denim, or jeans."

"And when do I have to be ready by?"

"Seven-fifteen, sharp. Class today starts at eight, but tomorrow you'll need to be up and ready by six for swim team tryouts."

"*Six?*"

"Six."

"I'll be ready. And thanks for the breakfast."

"You're welcome. Just leave the tray on the table over there and I'll pick it up later. And good luck today."

She was already outside warming-up the Jaguar in the circular drive when Jeremy, in designated uniform, bounded down the flagstone steps toward the rear of the car with its twin plumes billowing from the tailpipes. He could see she was yammering into the little silver phone in her hand, and as he approached the car she clipped the device shut and hit the switch for the passenger window to descend. She then snatched the sunglasses off her nose and glared at him.

"Stop," she ordered.

He stopped.

"Open the door, but don't get in. Let me see you."

He obeyed, his right hand frozen on top of the car's window frame. She examined him from hair to shoes. "Let me see your socks."

He raised up one foot and then the other for her to see from her position in the driver's seat, not thinking that one would have satisfied.

"Turn around, slowly please."

He revolved in response, and when he'd completed the circle he saw, with relief, that she was smiling.

"Excellent! You look respectable and eager—the perfect prep school attendee. Now please get in, we mustn't be late—Principal Riley does not tolerate tardiness."

As he buckled his seatbelt the car zigzagged down the cypress-lined driveway to the two iron gates that swung wide, releasing them onto the street. She cranked the wheel to the right, swinging them onto Zumirez Drive, then up to Pacific Coast Highway where she nearly killed them both while making a left turn into the northbound lanes. Within moments they were passing the other cars at double the speed limit.

"Damned tourists. I still haven't figured out where to buy a good used stoplight I can install back there."

"You really have to buy your own stoplights in Ballena Beach?"

She threw him a frown. "Of course not, dear. Are you nervous, or don't you have a sense of humor?"

"I guess I'm a little nervous."

"Thank God. And your being apprehensive is completely understandable, considering where you were a week ago and all the change that has taken place since. I must say you're doing remarkably well, Jeremy. You're holding up like a true Tyler. I'm proud of you."

"Thank you."

"You're welcome. Just remember who you are and where you've come from—consider it it a type of boot camp if that helps. You're much stronger than you know."

"It's just that I'm afraid I'll be a little behind in the classes here, even though I was doing pretty good back in Fresno." He was lying, he was lucky to maintain a 'C' average, and here she was already talking about his being the perfect prep school attendee.

"Well how could anyone be expected to make the Dean's List under such circumstances, half-starved and wearing rags, and having to spend your precious homework time looking after the one who should be looking after you, or searching the cabinets and toilet tanks for booze?" The car roared suddenly as she floored the accelerator to make the yellow light at Corral Canyon.

"We only had one toilet."

"Of course…" She paused, apparently deep in thought. "As I recall, Arthur has a Master's Degree in something. I'll ask if he'd be willing to oversee your studies. Would that help you?"

"Sure, I like Arthur, and I get along with him."

"Good. Just don't get along with him too well."

What was she implying?

"I don't understand…"

"I mean that…that one should never lose sight of the true nature of the relationship between employer and employee, especially as it concerns domestics. One needs certain tasks accomplished, the other a paycheck. Do you understand?"

"Yes, Aunt Katharine."

But be extra nice to the guys that park your car…

"Good. And if things go the way they should, I might even have Arthur teach you to drive. You'd like that wouldn't you?"

"Are you kidding?"

"I'll take that as a 'yes', my dear, and in the meantime you see to it that you satisfy the requirements for your learner's permit. Arthur can teach you on that old black Range Rover Bill refuses to sell. It's big and safe and slow as a school bus. It'll be the perfect first car for you."

"Do you mean that, Aunt Katharine? I could have my own car?"

"I don't see why not. Just don't get any ideas about sports cars. There will be no more sports cars in this family." She smiled sadly at him, and then slowed to take their place in a line of expensive cars turning right up a tree-lined street. "And here we are," she announced as the driveway crested and a sign came into view.

Ballena Beach Senior High School
Home of the Orcas

His stomach twisted at the sight. Everywhere were doorways and sidewalks and balconies and cars and lawns teeming with teenagers of every race, size and shape gabbing with each other in pairs or groups, ambling and shuffling toward their familiar morning destinations, all knowing where to go, what to do and whom to do it with, except for him.

His legs began twitching. His face flushed and his armpits moistened, and he felt an embarrassing bubble of gas floating its way down to the end of his digestive tract.

She wheeled the car over to the curb. "Jeremy dear, this is where the mother bird shoves her fledgling from the nest. I'm going to let you off here with your class schedule and a map of the school. And here's a Twenty for lunch. Arthur will be by to pick you up in front at three."

"Yeah, Aunt Katharine?" he asked. "I don't think I'm ready yet, if you don't mind. I just think I need another day or two to get used to everything. Could you just stay here for awhile so I can look around the campus?"

"Jeremy, look at me," she began, taking one hand off the steering wheel to grasp his. "Clearly you have less faith in yourself than I have in you." She peered over the top of her sunglasses at him, and he saw the kindness in her eyes. "I understand your fear. Your father's death and your mother's lack of control over her own life have taught you that this world is an unsafe place. But I intend to change this perception of yours."

"How?"

"By giving you the same things I gave your father: love, guidance, discipline, structure, education, and privilege. Only this time I won't make the same fatal mistake."

"Which was?"

"I gave your father freedom. You can't mix freedom with such powerful ingredients—it makes for a lethal recipe when one is young. I knew better, yet I still allowed it. Having done so, regrettably, I believe his death was my fault as much as his own."

"Do you really blame yourself for what happened to him?" He began to feel calmer the more she spoke about something other than himself. Maybe if he could get her to keep talking he might miss his first class.

Her face hardened. "Only in the abstract, dear one. Sooner or later the true culprit will be made to pay." She nodded thoughtfully. "But enough about that, you need to be on your way. And Jeremy darling, as you walk through this school today I want you to stop at every mirror, every plate glass window, every puddle on the ground and take a good look at yourself and ask, 'What does Aunt Katharine see in me? How will I achieve my destiny? And how ever will I suffer through the adoration when the world falls in love with me?'" She squeezed his hand. "Now off you go. I have to be at the gallery by eight to meet with a client."

"Really?"

"Really. Go."

He blew out a sigh, grabbed his bookbag and pushed himself up and out of the car. He made a tiny good-bye wave as she threw the car into Drive.

"Three o'clock out front!" she yelled as the car lurched away from the curb and nudged its way into the snarled line of cars heading their way back down toward PCH.

He was nearly paralyzed with dread. He could always cut class, as he had on occasion in Fresno, but then he had only his drunken mother to lie to.

His aunt was a different story, entirely.

There was just too much at stake; he had a real chance now and wouldn't screw it up.

So where should he begin? He held up the class schedule and groaned out loud. Each successive entry was worse than the previous: US Government, English Literature, Geometry, Biology and Spanish. At least his PE class at Zero Period tomorrow should be fun: Men's Swimming. He loved to swim.

An electronic chime blasted, and groups of students at once disintegrated into ambling lines, like ants drawn by the scent of a dead bird. He re-checked his schedule and glanced at the crinkled map in his hand, then made his way toward the throng, hoping to disappear into it.

CHAPTER 12

Jeremy turned the map upside-down and sideways in an attempt to figure which of the rectangles corresponded with the rows of buildings in front of him that held the classroom in which he was supposed to be, at that very moment, introducing himself to his first teacher. Unfortunately, the creator of the map had neglected to include any fixed landmarks, such as a hillside or even the ocean to help decipher the drawing. *Building A* could just as easily have been *Building F* or *Men's Gym* or *Administration Building*.

"Fuckity fuck!" he exclaimed, wholly exasperated.

"You look lost, can we help?"

He looked up to see two pretty girls smiling identical smiles, their books held across their chests in exactly the same pose. There was something so similar about the pair that they appeared sisterly, except that one was fair with nearly platinum hair, while the other was dark and exotic, like she had African or middle-eastern blood.

"Yeah, I sure could use some help. I need to get to room A-32, for US Government."

"With Miss Irwin?"

"That's the name on my schedule."

"We're going there now, come on." The blonde girl grabbed him by the arm. "She's a total bitch if you're late. Makes you recite the *Preamble* in front of the class."

"Actually she's just a total bitch," said the other. "By the way I'm Reed, she's Ellie."

"I'm Jeremy." The threesome dodged oncoming students as they headed toward the farthest building.

"Where are you from, Jeremy?"

"Fresno, up north. I just moved here a few days ago."

"*Fresno?*" they chorused.

"How'd you move from Fresno to Ballena Beach? Sue somebody?" asked Ellie, flipping her hair.

"Actually I came here to live with my aunt and uncle," he mumbled.

"Don't pay any attention to what she says. Ellie's got a chip on her shoulder the size of the dumpster she was born in."

"That's all good and fine coming from a girl who's so poor she recycles her tampons," snapped Ellie.

"Ooooh! Ellie girl, you kiss your granny with that mouth? No wonder Coby dumped your classless self!" Reed swung her pink backpack, barely missing the side of her head, and Ellie swung back with her own purse and they both squealed with laughter. Jeremy grinned apprehensively.

The door to room 311 had been propped open with an overflowing wastebasket, and as Jeremy and the girls approached he caught the nasal drone of the teacher, a homely silver-haired woman with buck-teeth and glasses thick as English Muffins. The girls scooted directly to their seats as the teacher scrawled *The Intolerable Acts of King George III* on the chalkboard. And he stood just inside the doorway with backpack in hand, not wishing to interrupt and waiting for some sort of acknowledgement from her, while at the same time doing his best to ignore the thirty pairs of eyes on him like branding irons, ready to mark him according to the high school caste system.

"Raise your hand if you can think of three repercussions of the British having closed the Port of Boston after..." the woman stopped, shot Jeremy a glance, pointed to an empty chair-desk in the back, then continued, "...the Boston Tea Party."

Silent eyes followed him as he sidled down the narrow aisle to the vacant seat. He removed his backpack and slid into the cramped desk, ran a hand through his hair, leaned back in the flimsy plastic seat and aimed his eyes straight at the teacher while affecting the bored expression and slumped shoulders that suggested he'd been sitting there for weeks.

Ellie raised her hand. Miss Irwin nodded.

"The colonists used the Port of Boston to generate money for themselves as fishermen, merchants, and shipbuilders." She raised and lowered the pitch of her voice exaggeratedly as she spoke, in classic know-it-all fashion. "In addition, the ships traveling in and out were the colonists' only way to communicate with the outside world, including the other New England colonies and their families back in England."

"That's correct, Miss O'Neal. And thank you *so much* for joining us this morning."

"My *pleasure*," she answered, with forced enthusiasm. Students tittered.

Reed's hand shot up. "Yes, Miss Banks?"

"That girl over there forgot that closing the Port also limited the varieties and quantities of food that came into Boston, not to mention medical supplies."

Ellie scratched the side of her head facing Reed with her middle finger.

"Good point. I can see that at least some of the ladies in the class are ready for the essay test tomorrow. Now let's hear from the gentlemen."

No raised hands.

"Young man?" She glared at Jeremy. "What is your name?"

"Jeremy Tyler."

"Mr. Tyler, can you think of any other repercussions of the British having closed the Port of Boston in addition to those previously stated?"

The room was a mausoleum. Nearly every student in the class had turned to watch, strained halfway around in their seats. In Fresno he'd never offered any information in school unless absolutely necessary as the good students were always ridiculed, unless they were jocks. But he was counting on everything here being different. Luckily he hadn't hated History as much as his other subjects, and had been preparing for a test on a similar chapter the day his mother went on her most recent bender. But he'd not anticipated having to perform so soon.

He licked his lips.

"Weapons and gunpowder were smuggled, by land, into the Port of Boston even though it was closed, and every day that the Patriots' stash of weapons grew, so did the threat of war against the British."

All heads swiveled forward to Miss Irwin, whose teeth protruded through her orange lipstick in the weakest of smiles.

"That's sufficiently correct, Mr. Tyler. And where did you drop in from?"

"Hoover High School in—" *don't say Fresno* "—Northern California."

"Welcome, Mr. Tyler."

He fought a grin with every muscle in his head.

Having proved himself to the teacher and to the class, at least for the time being, he halfway listened to the teacher while scanning the room and taking mental notes on those surrounding him. And after a few moments he reached the conclusion that they were pretty much like the kids from his last school, only better dressed. But then so was he. In fact no one besides the two girls, Ellie and Reed, really even stood out, with the exception of a tall, good-looking boy sitting in the row to his right and up one seat. He examined the young man's high-bridged nose and scraggly blonde hair, the rosy smear on his tan cheeks, the athlete's frame flopped over the yellow plastic chair. And Jeremy thought *if I could look like anyone it would be him.*

Just as the teacher finished her review of *The Articles of Confederation*, the chime rang. The room erupted into shuffling feet and zipping backpacks.

"Essay test Monday on the causes of the American Revolutionary War!" the teacher yelled over the chaos. Jeremy trailed his classmates out the door, and saw that Reed and Ellie were waiting outside.

"We figured you for Cute n' Stupid, guess we were wrong," said Ellie.

"I never said anything about him being stupid," corrected Reed.

"Thanks." He smiled. "Well maybe I am, because I could use some help getting to my next class."

"We'll show you the way," Reed offered. "So you just moved here? Tell us more." They began walking.

"Yeah, a few days ago. I moved in with my aunt and uncle down on Morning View. Overlooking the beach."

"We know where Morning View is," declared Ellie. "Streisand and what's-his-name live there too. So where's your next class?"

"It's..." he fished in his pocket "...English Lit in S-14."

"That's the building there, next to the tennis courts." Reed pointed.

"So then just meet us right over there after each bell." Ellie gestured towards a wall of vending machines. "We'll aim you in the right direction. And if you're nice to us we might even eat our lunches with you."

"Then after you can watch Smelly Ellie throw hers up."

"Speaking of that, look Reed!" She pointed to a heavy-set girl. "There's Mandy Adams, back from the clinic. And it looks like she's put on fifty pounds!'"

"Ooh, I know what she did last summer..."

"Yuck. And she's eating one of those jumbo chocolate cookies. In public!"

"Can you believe it?" Reed wrinkled her nose. "Watching a fat girl eat dessert is like seeing an alcoholic get drunk."

"Oh my God, you are so right!" exclaimed Ellie.

And Jeremy nodded his head, although he disagreed. Strongly.

"So what about it, Jeremy?" Ellie asked. "Do you still want to eat lunch with us, or are we just too much?"

"Sure." He was about to ask where the bathrooms were when he saw Reed's expression switch from smile to snarl.

"Hey Ellie, trouble at two o'clock."

It was the blonde boy from Government, headed their way. "And just what the hell do you want?" Ellie shouted as soon as he was within earshot.

"I was curious about the new history whiz."

"Coby Carson Jeremy Tyler Jeremy Tyler Coby Carson," Ellie babbled.

Jeremy's arm shot out to shake hands while the other kept his shoved deep in his jeans. "Hey," Coby offered instead, jerking his head backward as if there were a fly on his forehead.

"What, Coby, are you too *bitchen* to shake hands," asked Ellie, "or were you doing him a favor because you forget to wash your hands again after visiting the toilet?"

Coby turned to Jeremy. "Dude." He held out his hand and Jeremy took it. Their eyes held for a fraction of a second longer than custom dictated. Coby turned back to Ellie. "I was wondering if I could call you for some of the notes I missed for the test."

Ellie rolled her eyes and huffed. "Oh, I guess. But I'll be over at Reed's tonight studying. Do you remember her number, or for that matter how to use the telephone?"

"How could I forget anything about Reed, especially her number?" He pursed his lips at her and kissed. She wrinkled her nose and turned away.

"Because you forget how to count to twenty-one unless you're naked," said Ellie, turning her back to Coby and flipping her mane of platinum. "Jeremy, we'd *love* to walk you to your next class, it's really no trouble."

Bells chimed.

"I gotta go." Coby announced. "See you, ladies."

The three watched him walk away with his hands back in his jeans, his flannel shirt flapping, pants falling off narrow hips.

"Don't mind him," Reed said. "Ellie and he broke up again, and he considers every guy to be a threat," she lowered her eyes, then looked up with a smile, "especially *cute* guys." They began walking in the direction of the classroom buildings. A minute later they pointed out his class and waved good-bye.

At lunchtime Jeremy did not see either of the girls waiting for him at the vending machines, so he took a place at the end of a long line that led up to the concession windows. Disappointment and insecurity built steadily as each passing minute was reported by the clock over the menus, and he resolved to eat the first of what would surely be many solitary lunches here.

Oh well.

He checked the Twenty in his pocket and considered his day.

He'd just left Geometry, taught by a guy that was so uninteresting he might have been in black-and-white. One person in the class did catch his attention, however: a cute guy with coffee-colored skin and hair like mink. Jeremy thought he'd seen him out of the corner of his eye glancing his direction twice during the class. And Jeremy pretended not to have seen him looking.

The lunch line inched along. He was close enough now to scan the menu board and smell the French fries. His stomach growled.

As the girl in front of Jeremy grabbed her order Ellie and Reed ran up to him, all smiles and flying hair.

"Jeremy, thanks so much for keeping our places in line!" panted Ellie.

"Yeah thanks," Reed added. "I can't *believe* the Vice Principal kept us so long. Did you order for us?"

Jeremy looked over his shoulder, noting the angry glares being hurled their way. "Not yet," he replied. "I couldn't remember...what kind of dressings you wanted on your salads."

"Silly, you know we *always* have fat-free Ranch!" Ellie giggled, nudging him with her shoulder.

"Just hurry up and order, you stuck-up bitches!" A girl hollered from the back of the line.

"Anyway," Reed said and rolled her eyes, "two chef-salads, no ham, both with fat-free Ranch, two diet Cokes and-"

She pointed to Jeremy, who jumped in "...a chicken burrito and a Coke."

"Let's eat up at the football field; you can see the ocean from there," Ellie suggested as she took her salad. "Besides, I want to see the men practice their football drills."

After getting their lunches the three walked abreast up the wide steps that led from the quad to the gymnasium and athletic field, chatting about nothing and everything. The sun knifed through the brisk October air, while a mild Santa Ana wind rustled the fronds from the swaying palm trees that tilted like giant shaggy lollipops over the campus. Jeremy gulped the air, held it for as long as he could, then exhaled slowly through his nose. He felt the tension draining from him, his shoulders un-hunching.

"Is Brynn coming to the party with Coby?" Reed asked Ellie as they trudged up the ramp and turned past the gymnasium toward the bleachers.

"Not if I can help it. I've hated that little social-climbing slut since Girl Scouts. I'll throw her to the sharks if she dares set foot in my house."

"Who's Brynn?" asked Jeremy.

"Oh, she's Coby's new plaything..." Ellie threw a kiss to a dozen jocks who whistled and whooped and waved at her "...Head Cheerleader, Homecoming Queen, Coke Whore *Deluxe*."

"Coby, your ex-boyfriend?" Jeremy asked.

"Yeah, that charming Neanderthal you met this morning."

"So how long ago did you guys break up?"

"Last August," Reed interrupted. "She keeps changing her mind about being with him, and him about her. They're the stars in their own little soap opera that no one cares to watch anymore. The whole situation is *Snoresville*."

"Reed, Sweetie, at least I've had at least one steady boyfriend since puberty, which is more than you can say." Then turning to Jeremy, "In case you didn't read all the graffiti in the bathrooms, Reed prefers brief relationships with men. Anyway, we want to know more about you. Tell, tell." She flung her hair to the side while fishing in her purse, then withdrew her cell-phone. "Voice mail," she announced.

"There's not much to say," he began. "You already know where I live and where I came from."

Ellie turned to Reed. "Missy, we have a mystery boy on our hands!"

"Oh, I just *love* a mystery!" Reed sighed. "Pass me a fork, you cow."

Ellie complied, throwing three napkins at her. "Have some of these, they're sanitary *and* recyclable."

The girls cackled. Reed sucked at her soda straw, then continued, "Don't even try to pretend there's not some great story about your being some long, lost relative coming here out of the blue to live with the richest family in Ballena Beach."

"I'm hardly rich," Jeremy confessed.

"Oh, right," Ellie laughed, her eyes drifting to a shirtless figure jogging around the football field, while Reed dug silently into her salad with her plastic fork.

Jeremy took the last bite of his burrito then scrunched the wrapper in a ball. "So what's there to know about you two?"

"Well," Reed drawled, "Miss Ellie and I are just two, simple-minded gals who wish to meet the men of our dreams and have *oodles* of children."

"Yay-yes," Ellie responded, holding her soda cup with her pinkie straight out while making burbling sounds with her straw.

"Hey girl, isn't that the former man of your dreams out there on the track?" Reed asked.

The figure bounded closer. "Yep, it's him, I'd know those chiseled pecs a mile away."

"Kind of makes ya' sick to know that Brynn gets to gnaw on them now instead of you," said Reed.

"Why Reed, such language is really not appropriate in front of our luncheon guest. In any case, Brynn doesn't look like the gnawing type."

"Yeah, she's more the type to be gnawed on," Reed added, "by coyotes."

Coby had apparently recognized the figures in the stands and decided to pay them a visit. He slowed his pace as he approached, then took the stairs two at a time to their picnic spot.

"Don't come any closer with your sweaty self," Ellie screeched. "My bulimia has a hair trigger."

Coby grinned in spite of the jab, his glistening chest heaving. "What's goin' on?" He looked from Ellie to Reed, ignoring Jeremy.

"We were just planning our costumes for Ellie's Halloween party this weekend, weren't we?" stated Reed.

"Why yes," confirmed her friend. "And we were wondering if you were coming with that pretty girl friend of yours, Brie. To the party, that is."

"Brynn is her name," he corrected. "Brie, for your information, is cheese."

"Cheese that smells like urine, to be exact," said Ellie.

Coby sneered. "Anyway I'm not sure if we'll make it there, we've got so many other parties to go to Saturday night."

"I know that all our friends will be at my party, so you must be referring to Brie's friends' parties. Reed, were you aware that Brie had any friends?"

"You mean that are out of jail?" She cocked an eyebrow.

The girls hooted.

"Don't be such a bitch, Ellie, It ain't pretty," Coby said, wiping a drip of sweat off the tip of his nose.

"Ain't? *Ain't?* I see that Brie has been teaching you some of her hillbilly slang, Coby. Your Junior League mother must *love* her influence on you." She snapped her half-eaten salad closed and placed it next to her on the bench.

"Why is it that the two of you broke up months ago but are still acting like an old married couple. Huh, Jeremy?" Reed asked.

He'd been staring into the distance during their hostile exchange, made all the more uncomfortable by Coby's naked torso only inches from his face.

"I better stay out of this," he mumbled.

"Good man," Coby bellowed, coach-style.

The girls rolled their eyes.

"Jeremy's coming to the party," said Reed.

Jeremy turned to Ellie, who smiled and bulged her eyes.

He understood. "Can't wait."

"I can," said Coby. "Anyways, I gotta finish my laps."

"Then run along," Ellie ordered. "We're just leaving anyway."

The four slowly descended the bleachers, Ellie and Reed yammering about their costumes, the mute boys trailing.

"What's your next class, Jeremy?" asked Reed as they reached the bottom of the stairs.

"Biology, with Ms. Lessner in Room A-22."

"Our friend Carlo is in that class," said Ellie. "He's nice, you guys might get along."

"That is, if you're a fag," laughed Coby.

"Since when did you graduate to full-fledged redneck?" asked Ellie.

"I think he's channeling Brie," observed Reed.

"Brynn," he corrected.

"Whatever. The bell's gonna ring. We're off to CAD, which reminds me, Jeremy, what's your e-mail so I can send you the directions to the party?"

"Mine isn't set up yet."

"Well Reed and I are coming down with colds tomorrow so we can get stuff ready, but you can get the directions from Carlo. He's been over to my house a zillion times."

"Maybe you two can be each other's dates," said Coby. "You could go as Ballena Beach Ken and Barbie."

"And I lay awake at night and wonder why we ever broke up, having so much in common. It must be comforting to finally date someone of your own social class."

"If you had any class maybe you could do the same."

Coby jogged away as the threesome descended the ramp by the gymnasium.

"So what does this Carlo look like?" Jeremy asked, trying to sound indifferent.

"Very cute with black hair, dark skin. A little on the short side, with a big smile and very pretty eyes," said Reed.

"You didn't mention his bubble-butt," added Ellie. "For once."

"You'll know Carlo when you see him, Jeremy. He'll make sure of that."

"Does he have a sister named Carmen?" he asked.

"Yeah, he does," answered Reed. "How did you know?"

"She cut my hair yesterday."

"Oh." They nodded.

"So is he really gay?" he asked, sounding politely disgusted.

"Why don't you ask him when you see him," said Ellie. "He's very *out.* Now you'd better be there Saturday night, and bring someone if you want. But no costume, no admittance."

An attractive, petite woman who looked more like a Beverly Hills trophy wife than a school teacher met him at the door to his next class. She was beautifully dressed in white and navy, and not one blonde hair was out of place.

Did everyone in Ballena Beach just step off a yacht?

"Happy to have you Jeremy, I'm Ms. Lessner." She smiled cordially, holding out her hand. Jeremy shook it. "Please find a seat, anywhere you like."

The class had not yet filled up, so Jeremy walked to the back and stood awkwardly as all but two of the desks were claimed by noisy students returning from lunch. He looked around and noticed that the boy in the front left corner was the same one who'd peeked at him in Geometry.

He fit the picture the girls had painted.

Ms. Lessner stood from behind her desk and the room hushed. "We'll be having the test on Biomes tomorrow afternoon. I'll be assigning one to each of you randomly. You'll be required to state the regions, including latitude in which yours may be found, an extensive list of the flora and fauna, the temperature range and average rainfall for each season, and any other distinguishing features. The test will be a combination of fill-in and essay. Today will be review, so I suggest you use your notes and quiz each other. Are there any questions?"

The class erupted into a sea of raised hands and note-scribbling while Jeremy leaned back in his chair; after all, no teacher would make a brand-new student take a test on his second day. And he began planning what he might dress as for the party. A baseball player? A hippie? A vampire? *Pinocchio?*

"Mr. Tyler, I don't see you writing anything down. Is there something wrong?" She had crept up behind him.

"You mean I have to take the test?"

"Of course."

"But I…"

She cut him off. "Is there anyone in the class that might be willing to share their notes with our new student?"

No hand went up.

"Then I'll pick someone." She gave the room a quick scan. "Carlo, would you be willing?"

"I hear he's always willing," someone stage-whispered. Those around him giggled.

Carlo ignored the comment and nodded at Ms. Lessner.

"Thank you, Mr. Martinez. Your cooperation is noted."

The boy turned and grinned at him. Jeremy nodded back.

The class continued reviewing until the bell rang. Jeremy stood up, giddy that he'd made it through his first day. He pulled his book bag over his shoulder and then looked around for Carlo, who was already outside waiting. Jeremy went to him.

"Hey, I'm Carlo."

"Thanks for lending me your notes." They shook hands. He tried not to smile or look too friendly; he didn't want to give the wrong impression.

"Well, here's the thing," Carlo began. "I can't really lend them to you because I need to study them tonight, and I could Xerox them, but the machine in the library's been down for a week."

"Oh, man. What can I do?"

"I could scan them and e-mail them to you when I get home."

"I'm not on-line yet; I just moved here a couple days ago."

"Then I guess you could study over at my place."

"I don't have my license. Jesus, I'm sorry to be such a pain."

"Then I'll come by your place….if it's OK."

Jeremy couldn't think of why it wouldn't be OK. "Sure."

"Here. Write your address and phone on this…" he handed Jeremy a paper from his pocket "…and take mine." His information was already scribbled on the paper. "I'll come by about seven. We can either stay at your house or go out for coffee. There's a great little place down near Trancas."

A first date? No thanks.

"We've got lots of room at my house. And thanks for your help."

"Hey, it helps me to study with someone too. So I'll see you at seven?"

"Yeah, see ya."

Jeremy smiled down at his new shoes thinking Carlo seemed friendly and honest, like someone he could talk to and be himself around. So what if some of the others made jokes about him? After all, if Ellie and Reed were friends with him he couldn't be a total geek.

He turned and jogged towards his Spanish class, which would start any second. And he thought *I've got so much to tell Arthur.*

CHAPTER 13

"I hear you're going to be taking over my beloved Rover," Arthur grumbled as they sped down the highway toward home.

"Mine, all mine," the boy gloated, running his hands over the walnut dashboard and ebony leather seats. He reached over and turned the radio up, then shoved his hands up and out of the open sunroof. "Wheeeee!"

"I'm glad to see you enjoying yourself at my expense," the man shouted, snapping off the radio. "Now I'm going to have to run errands for your family in my dreadful Taurus."

"I'm happy you're glad."

"Don't get sassy with me, young man. Someone still needs to teach you how to drive this behemoth, and I don't really see your aunt or uncle doing it any time soon. Or your mother, for that matter."

"Ouch. Okay I'll stop. It's just that this has been the best day, Arthur. I mean, I was dreading everything and everything turned out OK."

"That's great. I'm happy for you. Later on I want you to tell me all about it." He hesitated. "But in the mean time I need to talk to you about something before we get home."

"Oh God, what?"

"Your mother called today. I overheard your aunt on the phone with her."

Fear stabbed his belly. "So what were they talking about?"

"I can't say...obviously she wanted to keep the conversation private. But I did hear the words 'attorneys' and 'restraining order' mentioned."

"Shit! Just when I start to get something good happening she comes along and fucks it up! I should've known better than to think things would change."

"Jeremy, don't get ahead of yourself," said Arthur. "You've got no idea what's going on, so you should ask your aunt. Tell her I told you she called, and you want to know what's happening. You've got a right to know. Things are going on right now that'll affect the rest of your life."

"No way, Arthur." He shook his head. "I don't want to know. What's gonna happen will happen anyway, I'm only seventeen so I don't have any control over my life. I'm just going to enjoy this for as long as I can—even if it's only until next week."

"Are you sure you don't want to know?" he asked, glancing his way. "Maybe it's not what you think."

"Yeah, I'm sure," he replied, folding his arms across his chest. He figured she'd checked herself out of rehab and wanted him back home; it was likely that she'd forgotten that they didn't have a place to live anymore. Or she was threatening to live here in Ballena Beach, which would explain the talk of 'restraining orders'. Either way, she was back in the picture, and the thought made him want to open the door and hurl himself out of the moving car. He turned to the window so Arthur wouldn't see the tear burn down his cheek. "Nothing's ever going to change for me."

"Well…it's your decision. Just know that I'm here to help in any way that I can." He smiled, placed a hand on his shoulder and squeezed. "You've got to have faith that everything will turn out for the best. And believe me, you can trust your aunt to do what's right for you."

"I don't trust *anyone*."

"I can't say that I blame you," he said as they crept to the stoplight at the *Porto Marina* bridge and stopped. Arthur looked at him squarely. "But there are a couple of trustworthy people around here who really do care about what happens to you. Not everyone is as unreliable as your mother has been, at least in the past."

He ignored the encouragement. "What'm I gonna do if she makes me go with her?"

"For one thing you're assuming things about their conversation. But even if you had to leave you would just make the best of it until you turn eighteen, then you'll come back to Ballena Beach if it's what you still want."

The light turned green and they lurched forward.

"But I can't do that."

"Why not?"

"I know it sounds crazy, Arthur, but if she's out of rehab then she's going to need my help, especially if…I mean *when* she has another relapse. I can't just leave her all alone. She's my mother, she'll die without me."

Arthur nodded. "Then you need to do all the living and growing and laughing you can in the meantime. Speaking of which, why don't you tell me about your day? Did you make any new friends?"

"Well, kind of. This one girl's named Ellie and the other's named Reed. They're nice. I like them. In fact they're having a Halloween party this weekend and invited me."

"Good! You need to get out. Did you meet anyone else?"

"Yeah, this asshole guy named Coby and this nice guy named Carlo. I'm going to study tonight with him."

"You're going to study with the 'asshole'?"

"No, with Carlo."

"Of course. And what's he like, this Carlo?"

"He's nice, I guess."

"How descriptive. And how were your teachers?"

"Fine I guess. Arthur, can I tell you about all this later? I just don't feel like talking right now, if it's OK."

"I understand."

"Oh! I almost forgot." He pulled his wrinkled schedule out of his pants pocket. "I have swim team tryouts first thing in the morning and I have to be there by seven. Could you take me?"

"I guess. With your swimming I suppose it'll be a good thing for you to have your own car after all. Plan on going with me to the DMV tomorrow after school to get your Learner's Permit."

"You mean you'll start teaching me to drive?" he asked, beaming.

"Yes, Jeremy. I'll teach you." He considered what a tragedy it was that this boy's father wasn't here to guide him along the road to manhood, a road Jeremy had apparently grown accustomed to maneuvering with his mother's hands over his eyes. "I'll help you with everything I possibly can."

CHAPTER 14

He emerged from the shower dripping wet footprints on the carpet in his bedroom as an insistent buzzer sounded, followed by his aunt's teeny electronic voice. "Jeremy dear, there's a young gentleman waiting for you downstairs in the foyer."

He clutched a towel in front of his nakedness as he leapt to answer. "I'll be there in a second," he yelled while stabbing the button with his finger. He checked the clock on the nightstand. Carlo was early.

He pulled on a T-shirt, some shorts and socks, grabbed his backpack, then bounded down the flying staircase to where his classmate sat looking around nervously on a gilded settee, his tattered book bag on the marble floor beside his well-worn tennis shoes. At Jeremy's descent Carlo's face blossomed into a grin.

"Hey, Carlo. Thanks for coming over," he announced, his wet hair falling into his eyes as he jumped onto the floor from the third step up. He reckoned that he might be starting to look the part of the carefree rich kid and the thought made him woozy.

"Hi, Jeremy, what a great house you have. It's really beautiful." His voice was softer and more feminine than he'd remembered at school, and he had dragged-out the words *really beautiful*. So Coby had been right after all. He hoped no one else in the house, especially his aunt, had overheard his new friend's telling delivery.

"Thanks. I'm still pretty much getting used to it myself; half the time I'm not sure which room is which."

"Yeah, well I don't really have that problem at my house," he laughed, grabbing his bookbag and standing. "By the way, my sister Carmen says 'hi'. She wanted a report on how your hair looks and I told her it's *fab*. So, where can we study?"

"Uh, anywhere, I guess." He paused, not wanting to suggest his bedroom. "We can use the conservatory."

The boys made their way through the labyrinth of sumptuous rooms while Carlo gave his run-down on Jeremy's stable of teachers, as well as the various groups and cliques on campus and their rank within the school's pecking order.

At last they came to their destination. Jeremy threw open the twin glass doors and motioned toward one of the wicker armchairs. Carlo fell into the chaise instead. "What a wild room this is!" the boy exclaimed, his head swiveling as he surveyed the exotic vegetation, the baronial chandelier and the mossy, trickling fountain. "It's right out of a horror movie. God, if I had a place like this to go to I'd never leave it." His eyes twinkled. "When can I move in?"

"Maybe when I move out, which might be sooner than I thought," he replied sourly, surprised at his own disclosure.

"What do you mean?" Carlo's dark eyebrows knitted fiercely together. "You just moved here."

"It's nothing for sure yet, I'll let you in on the details some other time." He shook his head. "So...I guess we should start at the beginning of the test material."

"Oh. Just a sec, let me find my notes. By the way, I can't believe Ms. Lessner is making you take this test on your second day." He unzipped his bag and pulled out a bulging green notebook, then pawed rapidly through the stack of pages. "Here it is: Biomes."

Jeremy fished for a pencil. "Biomes."

For the next couple of hours Carlo read and Jeremy listened intently while scribbling facts and terminology, until his hand was nearly cramped into a claw.

"That's it?" Jeremy asked, eyebrows raised.

"Yep, but now you've gotta memorize everything." He yawned, flexing his swollen biceps back over his head, his shirt riding up to expose a strip of lean brown abdomen. "If you wanted, I could stay for awhile more and test you."

"Let's take a break first," he suggested, avoiding Carlo's stare. "So... what can you tell me about Ellie and Reed?"

"Oh, they're crazy and gorgeous, and they're my best girlfriends. I'll tell you anything you want to know...but first let's talk about you." He kicked off his shoes and tucked his legs up under himself.

"There's not much to know."

"That's not what my sister said." He grinned salaciously, cocking an eyebrow. "But why don't you tell me why you're here? I'd rather it come from your mouth than hers."

"My mom had to go into the hospital for awhile, so I came here to finish high school. That's it."

"Jesus, I'm sorry." His manner softened, the bravado extinguished. "I guess she must be pretty sick. She doesn't have cancer, does she?"

"No, no. Nothing like that." He shook his head thinking that would probably be easier to deal with.

"That's good to hear," he said. "My mom died of cancer last year, right about this same time. It was horrible—the surgeries, the chemo, the tests. She'd be in the hospital for awhile then get out and things would get back to normal, then a month or so later she'd be in so much pain she couldn't get out of bed again." He turned away, almost talking to himself. "I still jump every time the phone rings. But I guess I'm doing OK now and so is Carmen, but my dad'll never be the same."

"Oh, man. I'm sorry," was what he said, when actually he was relieved at learning of another's tragedy. That another boy his age had tasted a slice of the same miserable pie he'd eaten all his life gave him hope that his isolation might be ending. He felt like dancing. "Yeah, let's take a walk down by the cliff," he suggested brightly. "I don't know about you, but I could use some air."

They left the conservatory and strolled shoulder-to-shoulder along the pathway that connected the west wing to the gazebo. A gentle breeze swirled around them, and the thunder of waves filled the air. Neither spoke.

"I've always loved being by the ocean," Carlo said finally. "I don't care if it's sunny or foggy, Summer or Winter."

"Yeah, me too. It would be nice even to just walk around here sometime by myself and get things straight in my head. But I haven't had time yet."

"Maybe you should take that walk with someone who could listen; I think it really helps when something's bugging you."

"My problems are so boring. I'd have to force someone to listen to me."

"You wouldn't have to force me," Carlo offered. "As long as we could take turns boring each other."

"Thanks, but I'm kind of used to going through everything by myself."

"I know how you feel. It's like...when you figure out you're gay and you think you're the only one in the world. It took me nearly two years before I could tell anyone. Of course Carmen knew before I even said anything, she's got the best *gaydar* in the world. Maybe because she works in a salon," he laughed. "She could even tell about you right off."

"About me what?" Jeremy asked defensively.

"About you being gay?"

"But I'm not."

"Oh." He cleared his throat and shifted his stance, stuffing down his disappointment. "Jesus, Jeremy, I'm sorry. I just thought..."

"It's OK. You and your sister aren't the first to think so."

"That's good, I *guess.*"

"Let me ask you something, but I want you to tell me the truth."

"I'll try."

"So what is it about me...that makes people think I'm gay?"

Carlo sighed. How could he restate the obvious? "It's probably a combination of things." He nodded. "But don't take that to say that you lisp and swish and say 'fabulous' all the time."

"But neither do you."

"I can, believe me, but only when I want to *girl* it up." He giggled, and then crossed his arms across his chest. "For one thing you're a really... cute guy, but in a quiet way. Most straight boys as good-looking as you are totally gross, strutting around talking about 'pussy' and 'titties'. You also dress well. I mean, what straight guy wears those shoes you had on today with khakis to high school? And from what I can tell you have a nice bod; your lats show through that Mormon-looking shirt you had on earlier," he laughed. "And of course you have the most excellent haircut."

"Is that all?" Jeremy was relieved that most of the exterior items on the list were either Arthur's or his aunt's doing, and most were exchangeable. And he figured he didn't mind the observations about his body.

"That's just about everything. The rest is too hard to explain."

There was more? He gathered his courage. "Could you try?"

The boys leaned against the stone balustrade overlooking the shadowy beach below; their nearly-touching elbows like flipping magnets, attracting then repelling.

"OK, but don't hate me," Carlo warned. "But you know how you can tell where someone is looking when they talk to you?"

Jeremy nodded.

"It's like when a straight guy talks to you he might make eye contact, then he looks away totally like he's trying to find something he wants to stare at and you're not it. But a gay guy locks eyes with you then looks away only to check out your nose, or your neck or ears or mouth or hair. And that's how I know...when I think a guy is gay like me. It's like both of us have eyes that are hungry, and the other dude is an all-you-can-eat buffet."

"And you're saying I do that?"

"Well I thought you did."

"So then a girl like Carmen probably gets the same thing from most guys."

"And she didn't get it from you."

"Maybe she just wasn't my type," he suggested.

"You're right, Jeremy. I guess she wasn't." He smiled. "But anyway, I've gotta go. It's late."

They began the long walk back to the conservatory. "Thanks for coming over and helping me out. And...thanks for being honest."

"No prob."

"Oh, and one more thing before I forget. I need directions to the Halloween party on Saturday at Ellie's." He dropped her name as if they were old friends.

"I thought you didn't have a license."

"I don't yet."

"Then why don't I pick you up at eight on Saturday? That is if you don't mind people seeing you come with me. Everyone knows I like boys and people might talk."

Jeremy hesitated. "So I figured by that comment in class about you always being *willing*."

"So you caught that. You're quick."

"Thanks. Anyway, I'd like to go with you to Ellie's," he lied, figuring he could back out if he needed to. "Why should I care what people think because I show up with someone who's gay?" he laughed. "I know who I really am, and that's all that matters."

"Yep," Carlo replied, buttoning his book bag. "That's what matters. By the way, will you be honest with me if I ask you something?"

They stopped walking and Jeremy nodded.

"If you *were* gay would you be interested in someone like me?"

Their eyes locked in spite of the darkness, and Jeremy took a step backwards, as if pulling against an invisible bungee-cord. "I really can't say," he stated, his mind racing. "It'd be like you asking if I...liked cheesecake even though you knew I hated desserts."

"Oh, well thanks." He threw his book bag over his shoulder. "I get the picture, in spite of the shitty analogy." He turned and marched back toward the villa with Jeremy in tow. "But you forget one thing Jeremy Tyler—" he called over his shoulder as they neared the door. "—Nobody doesn't like *Sara Lee.*"

Arthur smiled benignly while scrutinizing Jeremy's face for some hint of what had happened. He could tell the boy was upset, but beyond that he was as unreadable as a Chinese newspaper.

"So where do you want to eat your dinner?"

"Upstairs. I've got to study some more." He clutched his backpack to his chest like a shield and marched out of the kitchen without looking back.

"Jeremy?"

"What?" His voice cracked.

"I forgot to tell you earlier. Your Uncle wants to see you in his office right away."

He paused. "What about?" *Am I moving back to Fresno?*

"I've no idea. But he asked where you were over an hour ago, and I told him I'd send you along right after your session was over. Just take that hallway on the left to the end," he pointed, "then the long stairwell all the way down until you come to a door with his name on it. Knock, then wait."

He followed Arthur's directions down the staircase, then padded along the carpeted hallway toward the cluster of rooms from which his uncle commanded the family's various corporations. His arms blossomed into goosebumps as a stream of frigid air blew past him. There was no echo of waves inside these tomb-like corridors, no sounds but his breath.

The door at the end of the hall held a gold plaque with *BILL MORTSON* engraved in a stately font. He knocked softly.

"It's open, Jeremy," came the pleasant voice from somewhere.

He placed his hand on the icy doorknob and twisted. The door glided open.

The light in the chamber was eerie, emanating from the blinking computers as well as a fire that had nearly burned itself out in the elegant fireplace on the far wall. The rest of the office was fenced with dark, floor-to-ceiling bookshelves crowded with crumbling books and paperback manuals, bronze statuary and framed credentials, degrees and awards. And on the floor was something Jeremy had seen only in movies: a flattened polar bear's body with the roaring head attached, as if the creature had been run over by a steam roller that stopped just in time to be too late.

Bill hunched in a red, high-backed chair behind a castle-sized desk, his glasses reflecting like mirrors the green light from the triple monitors in front of him, while his fingers tapped between a trio of keyboards and mice. "Just a moment, my boy." His hands slid to each mouse, clicked twice, and the glowing screens extinguished one-by-one. "Have a seat over there, son." He motioned to the pair of leather armchairs on either side of the fireplace.

The boy nodded, then seated himself in the chair furthest away. His uncle rose finally, grasping the edge of the desk to steady himself.

"Would you care for anything to drink, a soda, or a beer, perhaps?" he offered, teetering over to a refrigerator disguised to look like another bookshelf.

"No thank you. I don't drink," he replied, trying not to sound ungracious.

"Probably better that way." His uncle smiled then stepped carefully, as if his shoes were a size too small, to the empty wing chair opposite Jeremy. Then with a grunt he fell into the chair. "I know that we haven't had much time to get to know each other yet, as I've been busy with a new software we're developing."

"Oh yeah?" He tapped his foot.

"Our family's consumer software division is always running to stay ahead of the competition, of which there is aplenty."

"I'll bet," he responded, wondering how long it was going to take for him to break the news that he'd be going back to Fresno.

"In any case, when things calm down a bit I hope we can do something together as a family. Your aunt and I were never fortunate enough to have children of our own; the closest we came was having the privilege of raising your father, of whom I was extremely fond." He paused here, and Jeremy figured his uncle might be expecting him to say something.

"I don't remember him," Jeremy said.

"Of course not, you were far too young." He shook his head. "After your father's tragic accident my wife and I tried desperately to bring you back home, but to no avail. But you know this already." He stood again. "What I am trying to say in my awkward fashion is that we, your aunt and I, are so very pleased to have you back with us again, at long last."

"I hope I never have to leave," Jeremy replied sourly.

"You've no idea how that makes me feel to hear you say that." He smiled. "In any case, I won't take up any more of your time, as I'm certain you've had a long, arduous day. But before you go, I want to give you something."

He tottered over to a pair of closet doors, then pulled them open to reveal a storage room piled high with large boxes. "Come and get this, son. The one on the floor here."

Jeremy sprang from the chair to where his uncle bent over, feebly dragging backwards a large carton from inside the doorway into the office itself.

"A computer!" Jeremy exclaimed. The box had been opened already and he saw that a printer was inside, as well. "Thanks so much, Uncle Bill!"

"I expect you'll need this for your studies. It's a rather good starter machine, and when you're ready I'll get you something faster. It's heavy, why don't you let me ring for Arthur to help you take it to your room?" He reached for the intercom button on the wall.

"It's OK, I got it." He began sliding the box toward the door, knowing that he wasn't yet up to fielding Arthur's questions about his study session with Carlo. "I've never had my own computer before. I really appreciate this, Uncle Bill."

"It's my pleasure, young man," he replied. "Incidentally, I've ordered the best man in my company to come by and configure your high-speed line while you're at school. By this time tomorrow, you'll be on-line with your own e-mail address."

"I hope I can make this up to you somehow," Jeremy offered

enthusiastically, pushing the box along the carpet ahead of him toward the hallway. The door swung magically open for him.

"You can start by testing our new email software that I've installed on that machine. It may have some glitches, so I want you to let me know just as soon as you have any problems. Will you do that?"

"Sure I will," he replied over his shoulder. "I'm glad I can help out."

"Good! You're already speaking like a Tyler. You're aunt will be so proud."

Jeremy stopped and stood facing him, holding out his hand. "And Uncle Bill? I really want to thank you for taking me in. I don't know what I would've done otherwise."

The man reached out and took the boy's hand, grasped it then pumped slowly. "Son, you have to understand something," he began, "For the past seventeen years it's been my wish to do for you exactly what I did for your father." Jeremy saw that although the man's eyes were looking at him he got the feeling they were seeing something from long ago, instead. "We just had to wait for the right opportunity to come along, and God bless us all, here it is."

He'd nearly lugged the computer to the very top of the stairs when the phone in his room rang. It was nearly ten; who could be calling him at this hour? Had Carlo forgotten something, or was it Ellie or Reed about the party? With a final push he hefted the box over the top few risers then leapt through the doorway, snatching the handset as he belly-flopped onto his bed.

"Hello?" he puffed.

"Jeremy Tyler?" He did not recognize the voice.

"Yeah?"

"Jeremy, it's Mom. I need to talk to you about something important." She didn't sound drunk. Instead her enunciated words were as careful and deliberate as a newscaster's. And no baby voice, for once.

His body snapped upright as he whirled around and sat up on the edge of the bed. "What's goin' on?" he asked innocently, disguising his dread.

"How's everything going there? And be honest with me."

Why did she sound suspicious?

"It's going great so far, I mean it's only been a few days. So how're you doing in the hospital?"

And be honest with me.

"Same old bullshit rehab, it never changes. You'd think someone would be able to come up with something new by now. But that's besides the point." She began speaking so fast now her words rear-ended each other. "Listen, I can only make local calls here, and I can't talk long because I'm on one of the nurse's cell-phones and she doesn't know I'm using it. So I need for you to listen carefully to what I'm going to say."

"Sure. I'm listening," he sighed.

"Watch out for Bill. Don't trust him for a second."

"And what the fuck do you mean by that?"

"Don't cuss at me, Jeremy. I mean he might try to do something bad to you," she whispered. "Have they told you about the Tyler Trust yet?"

"Yes Mom, Aunt Katharine just did," he said. "Why didn't you tell me about it before? Our family has more money than God, and up 'til now I've been wearing the same shoes for three years..."

"It's a long story, and I'll explain—" she paused to take a drag on her cigarette "—the whole thing later. You've got to believe me when I say that Bill might try to get you out of the way, like he did your father."

"You better slow down and explain exactly what you mean..." he was appalled that she would bring up his father's death as part of whatever scheme she was working "...because Uncle Bill's been *really, really* nice to me." No wonder Arthur had overheard Katharine talking about restraining orders and attorneys!

"Of course he is. That's how he works." A deep rattling cough sent her into spasms. "Like Satan."

"So now you're trying to tell me he had something to do with dad's accident? That Uncle Bill murdered my father and suddenly, oh by the way, I'm next?"

"I'm pretty sure he did, but I can't prove anything yet."

"And being the world's best mom you sent me away to a place where you felt there was a chance I could get murdered too?" he laughed bitterly. "Why are you doing this to me?"

"Because I'm worried about you."

She almost sounded convincing.

"Bullshit! You've never been worried about me!" he yelled,

remembering the old joke: *How do you know if an alcoholic is lying? Her lips are moving.* "You're trying to scare me into running to your side because someone at the hospital pissed you off and now you've had enough of this *bullshit rehab*, or you just saw a beer commercial and boy did it look good." He stomped across the room toward the balcony. "Well you can stay there or leave or do whatever the hell you want because I'm not going anywhere." His voice rose to a pitch he'd never heard come from himself. "You're on your own, *Mother*!"

"Jeremy!" she hissed. *"Listen to me!"*

"I'm never leaving this place, do you understand? This is my new home and Aunt Katharine and Uncle Bill are my family, *they're my new parents.* Something good has finally happened to me and you're not going to steal it from me again!" He felt his eyes brim with tears. "She told me how she fought you in court to keep me here and all you wanted was the money. You fucked my father to get pregnant and then you only had me because of the money!" He began crying, his words now nearly incoherent. "Then he died! Isn't his death and seventeen years of fucking up your son's life enough for you?"

"I understand you're angry, Jeremy," she pleaded. He could hear the tears in her own voice—were they real? "It wasn't like that! I'll explain it all to you later if you'll give me the chance. Just promise me you'll watch out for yourself. Promise me Jeremy!"

He heard a second voice yell through the earpiece. "Bitch, gimme back my phone!"

Sounds of scuffling, then dead air.

With a shaking hand Jeremy hung up, his mother's words spinning in his head. He fell face forward onto the bed, his body jerking with sobs as he buried his face in his pillow. What was happening to him? He'd never dared talk to her like that before! And only this afternoon he'd told Arthur that if she relapsed he would be the good son and tend to her. What if after the way he acted she never called him again, or it caused her to go on another bender and she died? And then, what would happen when he screwed up or failed his classes or *his serious character flaw* was discovered and Katharine and Bill wanted nothing to do with him?

Where would he go then?

CHAPTER 15

With a heave he pulled the leaden door open, and then froze. The thunder of male voices, spraying water and slamming metal blasting him from beyond the doorway made him want to flee; if he went further he'd be subjecting himself to the sharpened beak of the school's pecking order. But he had to do this, it was his only chance. So he pictured the string going through the top of his head and lifted himself higher, then entered.

"Where's the Coach?" Jeremy asked a tall Asian boy who'd just slipped his shirt off.

"The cage." He pointed absently then unbuckled his belt. Jeremy made his way to the end of the locker room where a sunburned, crinkle-faced man with a whistle around his neck leaned against the doorway to a chain-link room. Jeremy saw him scrutinizing his clipboard, shaking his head.

"Coach?"

"Coach Tunny," the man replied, not lifting his eyes.

"Coach Tunny, here's my admission slip." He offered the dog-eared paper to the man.

"What's your game?" He punctuated his question with a gum snap.

"Two hundred meter Backstroke, but I'm a little out of practice."

"Best time?"

"Just under 3."

"Gotta suit?"

"Not yet."

"Get one from the box over there, then meet the team poolside for drills." He pointed with the clipboard at a box on the floor, then reached into a cubby and retrieved a strip of paper. "And here's your locker combo."

"Thanks, Coach Tunny."

He raised his eyes finally. "Just 'Coach'," he mumbled.

Jeremy bent and fished through the assortment of spandex *Speedos* until he found a black one that appeared to be his size, and then stretched it to the slim width of his hips.

Perfect.

After changing, Jeremy hugged his shoulders against the cold and tip-toed along the slippery cement toward the sounds of splashing water and the coach's shrieking whistle.

The air outsider was thick with chlorine, it scorched the lining of his nose and singed his eyes. The huge rectangular pool was furious with thrashing and kicking as the swimmers windmilled along the lanes with frantic arms. Watching them called up a memory of himself as a child, hooking his fingers through the chain-link at the swim park while watching the young men practice. Their grace had mesmerized him; he imagined them to be flying boys, skimming the water like geese before lift-off. So he'd been delighted when, at the age of eight, his mother had enrolled him in lessons so she wouldn't have to look after him during the endless summer days while school was out. And he learned to love swimming. It was the one physical activity he excelled at naturally.

His stomach clenched. He probably had no business trying out for this team, as he hadn't practiced at all since last season ended, nearly four months ago.

"You!" The coach pointed at Jeremy. "Lane four!"

Although he executed the best start he knew how, he still hit the surface with too big a splash; he'd always had trouble with his start and so instead relied on his long, strong stroke to make up time and distance. The shock of the frigid water tensed his body, but he knew the sensation would pass quickly. He flipped onto his back, then reached behind himself first with his left arm then his right, and the top of his head pushed a wake like a breaching submarine headed toward the target mark at the opposite wall of the pool. He swam lazily at first, letting his muscles stretch and pull as they pumped themselves with rich, warm blood. After a lap and a half his limbs resumed the rhythm and cadence of a swimmer at one with the water.

On his third lap he spotted a boy, two lanes over, whose Butterfly pace was only slightly quicker than his own Backstroke. Jeremy deepened his breaths and began pulling his arms through the water with more force, the way he knew how to make them ache. His legs kicked mechanically as if driven by a motor; he knew his speed came from concentrating on his arm strokes and breathing. Soon he was abreast of the other, and whoever it was had apparently taken notice of his competitor and was pulling ahead. Jeremy judged the other swimmer's reach to be longer, but no more able than his own.

But this past summer, while Jeremy had lolled around watching talk shows in his mother's smoke-filled apartment, the athlete in lane six had been training. *Hard.* His lead stretched to almost half a length by the start of the seventh lap, and by the time the coach's whistle signaled the end of the practice Jeremy was barely able to make it to the side of the pool and lift himself out. His arms and legs shook as he toweled himself vigorously from hair to ankles.

"Not bad, except for your start," the coach growled. But the crooked grin on the man's face told him what he'd hoped for.

"I'm just...out of...practice."

"Well, even out of practice I could see you were giving Carson a run for his money. What was your name again, bud?" He took the pencil from behind his ear and poised it over the clipboard.

"Jeremy Tyler."

"Knew another 'Tyler' once, about twenty years ago." The coach scribbled. "Johnny Tyler, fastest Freestyler in the State; think his record still stands. You're not a relation, are you?"

"He was my father," Jeremy beamed.

The man's eyes snapped up to meet his. "You're jokin'!" He squinted at Jeremy, scanning him up and down. Then the hard creases around his eyes and scowling mouth softened and he looked suddenly gentle, like someone's grandfather. "Good God, you are his boy!" He clapped a hand on Jeremy's shoulder, nearly knocking him into the pool. "Where the hell you been hiding? We could use you!"

"I just moved here to my aunt and uncle's." He wrapped his sopping towel around his hunched shoulders and shivered, in spite of the sun cresting the ridge of hills to the east.

The coach turned to the troop of boys heading to the locker room. "Men! We've got the son of another celebrity on our team!"

They stopped and turned and Jeremy saw Coby in the center of the group, his easy smile melting.

"Men, this is Jeremy Tyler, the son of Ballena Beach High's '86 State

Champion Jonathan Tyler, AKA *Tyler the Freestyler*, who was twice the swimmer you girls will ever be!"

The boys jeered and laughed, and a few lolled over to introduce themselves. The last to pass was Coby.

"Jeremy, this is Coby Carson, our star Butterfly."

"Yeah, we met already," he responded coldly, ignoring Jeremy's outstretched hand for the second time in two days.

"Hey, don't be such a *prima donna*, Carson. He don't know it yet, but if he's anything like his father his game's gonna' be the Crawl for the 800 Relay, so you don't have to worry about him snatching your crown. Now shake hands, you're gonna' work together. He's part of the team."

Coby obeyed. "Good to have you, dude."

Their hands pumped each other.

"Thanks." A grateful smile split Jeremy's face.

"Go hit the showers. Tyler, see me in the cage before you go."

Steam filled the air like fog. Whoops and howls echoed, and the water streaming against tile sounded like a tropical downpour. As Jeremy made his way to his locker he glanced sideways at the assemblage of young naked men, trying to ignore how each that he passed seemed more exquisitely muscled than the last.

Coby was peeling his suit down his thighs as Jeremy approached his own locker two over. He avoided looking at him by verifying the numbers on the slip of paper with those on the lock, even though he'd already memorized them.

"Hey," Coby said.

"Hey."

"So what's your best time on the Backstroke? he asked, balling up his *Speedo* and throwing it in his locker.

"Just under three in the Two Hundred."

"Cool. So your dad was really a State Champ?"

"Yep. But I don't remember his time off hand."

"So where's he now, some three hundred pound attorney?"

"He died in a car accident right after I was born." Saying the words had no effect on him anymore, like telling someone what time it was. He slid his own suit off.

"Bummer."

They walked to the shower area, Coby in the lead. Jeremy slyly appraised the other's sculpted ass as he strutted in front of him with a towel in one hand and soap in the other. They took side-by-side places at an empty pair of spigots in the middle of a bunch of sudsy guys.

"We train fuckin' hard, hope you can take it." He stepped under a spray of water and threw back his head, the ricocheting droplets splattering Jeremy's face. Jeremy in the meantime peered sideways from under his own steaming spigot, secretly studying the other's physique.

Coby's torso twisted and flexed, the bar of soap sudsing first his bulging shoulders, then the armored muscles of his chest, and next sliding in descending circles to lather his buckled stomach, then finally lingering over the crisp ridge where his abdomen tapered to join his tan-lined hips. His thighs glistened like wet marble in the streaming water, and wagging between them hung his hefty cock, swinging in opposition to the salacious movements of its master. He was statuesque and powerful, with limbs rigidly defined but not yet overbuilt, and skin so evenly bronzed and free from blemish it looked like miraculous plastic. Jeremy quickly concluded that in all his life he had never seen a more perfect human being—like an anatomically correct G.I. JOE come to life, but without the empty joints.

"Got soap?" Coby held the bar out to a squinting Jeremy.

"Thanks." He took it and began rubbing himself quickly from neck to feet.

"Hey, did you say you were going to Ellie's party tomorrow?" Coby rinsed himself, then stepped away from the showerhead and shook his head like a dog just out of the rain. He snatched his towel off the wall hook and rubbed it over himself, then tossed it on the floor. He turned and leered splendidly, throwing his naked beauty at the other.

"Yeah, I guess so," he said, feeling exposed even under the protective cover of the spray.

"Then I'll see ya' there." Coby strutted away between the banks of lockers and then disappeared.

Jeremy twisted off the water then dried himself, cinched the towel around his waist, and then walked to the cage. He found Coach Tunny thumbing through a peeling three-ringed notebook, his feet tapping the air atop a junkyard-looking desk.

"Coach?" he asked from the chain-link doorway.

He looked up. "I need to weigh and measure you. Over there." He motioned with his clipboard to an ancient scale in the corner. Jeremy dropped his towel and stepped up onto the cold metal platform while the coach adjusted the sliding weights.

He raised a bar and brought it down on Jeremy's head. "Five-eleven and a half, one sixty-nine." He frowned. "You could slim down a bit, but I can see you've got some strong meat on your bones. If you shed about eight pounds it'll help you get further under two-minutes, so long as you keep your muscle mass. So how long you been swimming competitively?"

"Since I was eleven."

"Good. Here's the deal: No smoking, no drinking, and absolutely no drugs. If I find out about you doing any of the above you're off the team. But if you train hard, quicken up that start a' yours and become one of my champs I'll see you go to any college you want. Deal?"

"Yes Coach, sir."

"Good man. Go dress." he paused in mid head toss. "Wait a second, I think I got something you might like."

Jeremy retrieved his towel and tucked it around his waist.

"Somewhere here…" he threw open, then slammed shut each of the desk drawers "…here it is, 1986 California State Champs. Your pop is the one in the middle wearing the medal. He won the Relay for us." He handed over a long, dog-eared photograph.

Jeremy looked. Even through the layer of dust, Jonathan's dazzling grin jumped out from the rest, dead center in the back row of a dozen bare-chested swimmers squinting in the sunlight of twenty years past. He held the picture up closer and came to the conclusion that Katharine was right, his father had been stunningly handsome. He handed the photo back to the coach, afraid of somehow having his thoughts read.

"That there's an extra you know. We keep the others framed in the Main Hall of the Administration Office. You can have it if you like."

Jeremy looked up. "Thanks a lot, Coach."

"And Tyler? I just wanted you to know how much I liked your old man." A sad smile creased the skin around his eyes. "He was quite a guy, one in a million, and like a son to me. I can remember hearing about his accident like it was yesterday, just like I'll never forget that funeral. One of the biggest, saddest funerals I ever went to. They had to cut down the eulogies, there were so many broken-up folks. This whole town mourned for him, everybody was crazy for him. Specially your mom. By the way, how is she?"

"She's not doing so good."

"I'm sorry to hear that. She was one beautiful girl." He gave a low whistle.

"So I've heard." Jeremy shifted from foot to foot, wanting to get back to his locker. He didn't want to be late again to Miss Irwin's.

"I'll bet if he were alive today he'd be proud to call you his own." His gray eyes held Jeremy's and the boy's said *I don't think so.*

"You bet he would, son." He rose from his chair and rested a leathery hand on his shoulder. "I can tell just by lookin' at you you've got natural ability and intelligence. The only thing we got to work on is your start and your stamina, you already got the moves." He smiled and nodded reassuringly. "You're built almost as strong as him, and if you lean up and train hard and get your start down you'll be the team's anchor for the Relay, just like him. But remember, the start is where the magic is. You got to picture yourself like a rock out of a slingshot. Pull baaaack..." he pantomimed with his hands "...then release. Instead you're pushin' off; there's a difference. Now how you gonna practice it?"

"Pull baaaack, then release. Like a rock from a slingshot."

"Good boy! And one more thing." He snatched the photograph out of Jeremy's hands. "I changed my mind. You let me take this and I'll frame it and hang it here in honor of your pop." He held it up against the chain-link, under a rusting sign stating *No Girls Allowed.* "I'll give it back at the end of the season, and in the meantime it'll be a reminder for you to push yourself hard as you can, every day. Now go get dressed, bell's gonna ring. Be here Monday, Six-thirty sharp. And remember our deal."

CHAPTER 16

He'd been lying awake for some time waiting for the blanket of sleep to shroud him. He lay naked on his back under the sheets clasping his fingers behind his head, already feeling the delicious ache in his flexed biceps from this morning's workout. He yawned closed-mouthed, pulling the pungent sea air through his nostrils, then popped his eardrums as he expelled it. Turning his head toward the French doors he squinted at the white glare of the full moon as it hovered big as a searchlight over the twisted iron of the balcony railing and threw flat, cartoon-like shadows on the carpet and along the walls of his bedroom.

The house was silent but for the crash and fizz of the waves on rocks and sand. Further away, a siren mimicked itself as the plaintive wail echoed off the palisades walls and skimmed out across the bay to open sea.

He sighed. Nights had always felt lonesome, apparently it didn't matter that he was in Ballena Beach now instead of Fresno.

He thought about school. Neither Ellie nor Reed had shown up today, which he'd expected; he was lost in Geometry, which he'd also expected; Carlo hadn't shown up for their class, so he missed the test they'd both studied for. He hadn't expected that. Had their conversation at the end of the evening killed their fledgling friendship? He'd need to call him in the morning to see if they were still going to the party together. Otherwise maybe Arthur could drop him off.

He blinked up at the ceiling, then checked the clock on his nightstand. It was already Saturday and he had nothing really planned for the coming day but a driving lesson with Arthur, and in the evening Ellie's party. Nothing terrible was pressing, so why couldn't he sleep?

He'd awakened hard and sweating after midnight just like, he figured, every other seventeen-year-old male did on occasion. And even now, some two hours later, his aching erection still tented the sheet covering him. Of course he knew how to relieve himself in a matter of minutes, he'd done it hundreds, perhaps thousands of times since discovering how at the age of thirteen. But he hadn't yet allowed himself to do so since his arrival here, in fact he was terrified to do so. He told himself he wouldn't think about it, wouldn't picture it, wouldn't even touch it until he knew he could do it the *right* way. And he made a deal with himself: when he couldn't stand it any longer he'd indulge himself only in the dark; he didn't want any visual reminders of his fascination with male anatomy. Otherwise, if he violated his code, he'd spend tomorrow and the next few days in a state of self-hatred, dreading his 'date' with Carlo for the Halloween party as well as every future moment in that torture-filled locker room.

He'd known for years that he was attracted to guys but figured it was something like his mother's addiction; if she'd only nipped it in the bud soon enough nothing catastrophic would ever have happened. So that's what he was determined to do: *nip it in the bud*. And find the right girl—that magical combination of beauty, sexiness and intelligence that could make him forget any disturbing urges and help him become the man he dreamed of becoming, especially since being handed all but one of the pieces to the dream-life jigsaw puzzle.

But who? Ellie was gorgeous, there was no question about that. But she was also wickedly bitchy, and they had no chemistry between them. Reed, on the other hand, was beautiful and seemed to be giving off interested vibes. She'd even referred to him as 'cute'. And he couldn't remember anyone mentioning her boyfriend.

There was no question now that Reed fit the bill, at least for tonight. He could allow himself some pleasure by thinking about her; it might even start things rolling for the coming evening and maybe even beyond.

He reached down, grasped himself and began picturing her deeply creased cleavage, imagining those lovely soft breasts naked as he made circles with his fingers around her hardening brown nipples. He saw her mouth open and her tongue slither out to lick the insides of his cheeks, then draw his tongue deep within her mouth. He could almost hear her whimper as they kissed.

He saw himself kissing her nipples, then slide his tongue down the center of her belly toward the space between her legs. Her stomach muscles tightened and flexed and she drew in sharp breaths as his mouth crawled like a horny snail down the centerline of her body.

His hand moved faster under the covers and his breathing quickened. With relief he discovered he had no difficulty imagining her tight belly, her firm hips, the wetness between her legs waiting for him, craving his hardness. He was a man now, he could do manly things. He would mount her forcefully yet gently, but not before pleasuring her the way women loved.

His hand was jerking madly back and forth now, and he threw the bed sheet aside so as not to get it wet. The shock of the cold night air tensed his naked body and his skin erupted in goose flesh. His body and mind were consumed with the pleasure his hand was giving himself. He knew it wouldn't be long.

And as his cherished climax approached, so well-deserved and wholesome with images of heaving breasts and lipsticked lips, Reeds curvaceous waist morphed into Coby's rippling abdomen, his mushroomed manhood aimed obscenely at Jeremy's gaping mouth. He imagined with delicious panic the sensation of his tongue making contact with the exquisitely molded flesh as he took him down his throat while watching the marbled thighs flex with ecstasy, then scissor crazily with pleasure. He was ambushed by visions of Coby's crooked smile, Coby's heroic chest, Coby's sculpted ass, his own feet in the air as Coby grabbed his ankles and mounted him face to face with blonde stubble scratching madly against brown, Coby's drooling spit as their tongues twisted against each other's as *Coby slowly entered him…*

Jeremy's toes curled and his back arched off the bed as he gasped and locked his wrist and streaked his torso with sperm.

And it was over.

It took him a minute to catch his breath. His chest heaved as he peered down the length of himself and saw that in spite of the frigid nighttime air he was covered in perspiration that glistened silver in the moonlight. Then he watched numbly as the puddles on his chest turned clear, then trickled onto the sheets.

He hopped out of bed to clean himself in the bathroom. He snapped on the light and snatched some tissues from the box on the counter beside the sink, then carefully wiped the evidence from his cock and stomach and chest as he checked his face in the mirror.

Did he look as queer as he felt? He was approaching his eighteenth birthday and the problem wasn't going away.

"You are a *faggot*," he whispered contemptuously to his reflection in the mirror over the sink, wincing as *the word* caught his ears.

"You are a God-damned fucking faggot."

He threw the clumped tissues into the toilet and flushed it, switched off the light then tip-toed his way back into bed, shivering. He buried his head under the stack of pillows and tried to push out the roaring waves outside but it made no difference. He flipped over onto his back, then his side, then his belly, then back again. He sighed. He asked himself *why was being gay so bad? After all Carlo was, and he seemed OK.*

But he knew why it would never be OK for him. Every movie or TV show or commercial that depicted a cheerful dad, a fashionable mom and their normal, self-assured kids bit him like a snake, sending bitter poison from his heart up through his spinal cord to his brain and down through his body to his arms, hands and feet. *I'll never have any of that* was what that snake was made of. And when it bit, its teeth took days to let go.

He'd learned long ago to avoid the greeting card aisle of the supermarket, the categories held little relevance to his life and their captions made him furious. Once, while in a particularly black mood he'd stopped to read through the categories he'd never buy: *For Dad, For Grandfather, For Grandmother, For Sister, For Brother.* And he wondered *do people really feel this way about their family members?* But the ones that really pissed him off said things like *God Bless You Mother on your Birthday*, and *A Mother's Kiss is Sent from Heaven.* He sure as hell would never buy those. And neither, apparently, would he now have any use for the final three categories: *For Wife, For Son* or *For Daughter.*

He switched on his nightstand lamp and tumbled naked out of bed, then made his way to the nearly empty closet where he kept his shoebox of mementos, up on the top shelf next to the sealed one belonging to his mother. He slid his from the shelf and lifted the top, then found what he was looking for: the only picture he'd ever seen of his father and him, taken at the beach just after he'd been born. He hadn't looked at it in years.

He held it under the lamp on his desk while studying his father's image and decided he'd been stunningly good-looking, even by today's standards. And with him Jeremy, just a typical fat baby, eyes bugged and mouth slack. His shirtless father beamed at the camera, holding him by the armpits so his legs dangled in the air, diaper threatening to drop onto the sand. Had his mother held the camera, or had it been Aunt Katharine?

He shuffled over to the gilt mirror hanging on the wall, then examined the man in the photograph while scrutinizing his own features. Their faces shared the same heavily-lidded eyes that narrowed into squints when laughing, the high cheekbones set off by hollow shadows underneath, twin ruler-straight noses, and square jaws with identical clefts. They even had similar mouths, which relieved him, as he was self-conscious about his full lips, as well as the slight gap between his two front teeth. Their similarity was striking; now that Jeremy had matured—and cut his hair—he figured they could have passed for brothers.

He held the picture in his left hand and began petting it slowly with his right. Over and over again he drew his palm slowly over the photograph of his father holding him. He reminded himself that touching the glossy paper might ruin it but he didn't care. The simple gesture inexplicably calmed him, momentarily assuaged the lifetime of feeling like an orphan.

"If you were here we could spend time with each other," he whispered to the image as he stroked it. "We could talk about everything that's going on, and you could handle Mom and give me advice on what I'm going through." A great sadness swelled up from the deepest part of him and his throat knotted. "You could teach me how to drive and help me with my swimming and tell me you're proud of me and that you'd be there for me and love me no matter what I did or who I was." Tears streamed down his cheeks as he continued pawing the picture, simultaneously feeling both unexpected relief and embarrassment from what he was doing.

Then he collapsed onto his bed. His body heaved with sobs as he held the photograph to his bare chest, biting his pillow while wails of grief for all that might have been gushed forth. But almost immediately he began to feel ashamed and stupid so he quieted himself, afraid someone would hear him and think he'd set himself on fire or cut off a toe. He lay hiccupping and sniffling for a while, then drifted finally into an exhausted sleep.

Two figures ambled along the moonlit beach, bare feet sinking into the wet velvet sand squishing in-between toes, relaxed strides leaving twin trails of skidded footprints; one man-sized, the other tiny. Waves slapped the shore while rustling palm trees swayed and tossed their shaggy heads. A waterfall thrummed in the distance.

"I've been looking all over for you," the young man said to the little boy, his voice deep and sonorous, like he was inside a cave. "I was worried, I was afraid something bad had happened."

Jeremy looked up at the smiling face of his father, and marveled at how beautiful and crystalline his skin was in the moonlight. He glowed actually, as if he were lit inside by a million tiny white Christmas lights.

"You're here, I can't believe you're really here," he replied excitedly. "All this time I thought you were dead."

"I know. But what's important is that we've come together finally. That's what counts."

Jonathan held his son's hand, a miniature copy of his own. He grasped it gently and the boy squeezed back.

"But where were you?" The small face blinked up at his father, the hair blowing atop his head reflecting silver moonlight.

"I've been here all along."

"Where?"

He laughed as he bent down, lifted Jeremy by his armpits, laid him gently over his right shoulder then maneuvered his crooked arm under the boy's behind so they could have their faces at the same level. He turned so both looked across the black nighttime sea.

"I'll tell you someday. But now, I want you to see something." He raised his arm to point skyward. "Up there."

Jeremy searched the inky sky. "What is it, Daddy?"

"There, Jeremy. There is the *Father's Star*." His pointing hand stretched away from his body until it hovered far over the water, like a kite riding a brisk summer wind. "Make a wish, my son."

Jeremy then spotted it—a glistening speck high above the horizon that dimmed all but one of the lesser stars around it, pulsing pink one moment then silver the next. It was simply dazzling, and somehow magical. Seeing it called up pleasantly mysterious feelings, like a scent from his childhood that he couldn't place. He stared at it and let the sensations inside him swell.

"It's *beautiful*. What's it mean?"

"If there's something you need, you wish on it and it'll come true."

"Is that all I have to do?"

"I'll tell you the rest in a moment, but something's wrong. Tell me."

Jonathan bent over and dropped his son onto the sand, then caressed the hair on his head. As he did so Jeremy was transformed into a young man. "I want to be…a real man. Like you," he said, now eye-to-eye with his father. "I'm afraid I'll never be one. I don't know how. And you're not here to show me."

Jonathan chuckled deep within his chest, stretched himself a hundred feet tall as he did so, then pulled himself down to meet his son's eyes. "You *do* know how," he said.

"But I'm *gay*."

"Whom you fall in love with has little to do with it; to be a man you must be three things: courageous, honest, and selfish."

Jeremy cocked his head. "The first two I can see," he agreed, nodding. "But to be selfish? How'll that help me?"

"The three are inseparable," he began, placing his hands on his son's shoulders. "Courage is needed to be honest with yourself, and once you know your true nature you must be courageous enough to be selfish about your needs. The happy man pursues that which he *needs*, but at the same time uses great caution while pursuing that which he *wants*. You'll see that by doing this, you'll be able to give unselfishly to others, and to illuminate your life—as well as another's—with love. Otherwise you will only exist, chasing someone else's dreams instead of your own. It is a paradox that some people never figure out. Do you understand?"

"I think so. But how does wishing on a star come into this?

"I don't know, son, but it does. Maybe it has to do with God, or whatever made all of this, as well as the force that keeps you breathing when you're asleep, or makes your heart speed up when you're angry or excited or when you're in love. It's the spell that makes the trees turn their leaves orange, and birds fly in a perfect 'V'. It's the force that created you when your mother and I made love eighteen years ago—we shared a moment in time, and now here you are. It's the miracle of true friendship and laughter and empathy and the drive to improve yourself." He curled his arm around his shoulder. "There are many forms of magic out there, Jeremy," he whispered. "You don't have to understand how it works so much as you need to honor it. Magic, like love, is a phenomenal tool. And it's always there."

At once the Star began pulsating brighter and brighter until it washed the landscape around them into a world devoid of shadow or dimension. A ringing like a thousand wineglasses rubbed by wet fingertips grew from a hum to a deafening symphony as the star exploded with blinding radiance.

"Magic, my son, magic. Close your eyes and make a wish. *Now!*"

His mind spun behind his eyelids. Which wishes should he pick? Was it more important that Tiffany stop drinking forever and his parents be together again, or for him to find true love, or that he embrace himself and dive into the passions that stirred him so deeply, or that he become a real man? He decided finally that they were all important so he wished for them all—after all, Jonathan said he needed to be selfish. Then he opened his eyes and found his father, as well as the entire beach and even the Star itself, fading away.

"What do I do now?" he shouted as Jonathan's image dimmed, retreating genie-like to the magic bottle that was his childhood memory.

"Believe in magic," whispered the reply.

"Where will you be?"

"I'll be watching."

"But who'll show me the way?"

"Mr. Blauefee. Arthur knows all about the magic."

He lay blinking at the ceiling as it brightened with the sunrise. His father had a moment ago seemed so real to him, so real that his voice still echoed in his ears. Quickly, he tried remembering his father's messages, but as he ran the dream through his conscious mind the details began disintegrating like wet toilet paper.

He extricated himself from his twisted comforter and tottered toward the bathroom to pee. "Have courage, be honest and selfish, believe in magic." He flipped on the light and lifted the toilet seat. "The Father's Star," he muttered, watching the stream of amber urine as it foamed the water inside the white bowl.

CHAPTER 17

Jeremy, on his balcony, cocked a hip against the railing and looked out at the estate's ancient oaks, their twisted silhouettes like clipped black construction paper against the tangerine sky and sea. He was worried: he only had an hour before Carlo was to pick him up and he hadn't pulled together a costume yet. And he'd looked for Arthur to help him since early this afternoon, but discovered that the man was out running errands and wouldn't be back until dinnertime, which was usually about a half hour ago.

With relief, he heard a car roll down the driveway.

Jeremy found him hefting bags of groceries into the kitchen.

"Arthur? I need your help with something. Please please please?"

The man appraised him. "I thought you were leaving at any minute for some sort of Halloween extravaganza."

"I'm supposed to, but I need a costume and I don't have anything to make one out of." He grimaced. "Do you have anything I could borrow? Just for tonight?"

Arthur sighed and placed the bags on the counter. "You help me put these away and we can talk about it."

With their task completed, they hastened to Arthur's quarters, where the man threw open his closet doors. "Hmmm...Halloween costumes." He scratched his chin. "I haven't gone to any parties in quite a while, so they must be...way back...here." He dug his hand deep into the end of the racks and pushed hard. "Shoot. Nothing's here anymore." He shook his head. "I'd forgotten I gave just about everything away. Sorry, old buddy."

He saw the boy droop.

"Oh! Hold on there." He reached all the way to the left side and lifted a bulky object forward into the light, something carefully preserved in black plastic. "I knew I'd kept this for a reason. It'll be close to your size." He laid it on his bed and pulled the heavy zipper open.

Jeremy looked: it was a military officer's uniform in blackish-blue wool with red piping, brass buttons and gold stripes. He saw that a double bar, inlaid with multi-colored squares, was pinned above the left breast pocket, and a spotless white belt had been buckled across the midsection, as if the soldier wearing it had simply evaporated.

"Wow. Where'd you get that?" He pictured the expression on Reed's face as he entered wearing it.

"I was in the Marines. First Lieutenant," he declared.

"You?" Jeremy blinked.

"Is that so hard to believe?" he asked sharply.

"No, of course not. I mean, you totally look like a Marine. It's just that I thought..."

"You thought they didn't let faggots in," Arthur said flatly.

Arthur too? "No, actually I didn't even know you were...gay. No one told me."

"I figured your aunt warned you right off," he explained, "seeing as she instructed me, in some very well chosen words of course, to keep a healthy distance from you. 'Our nephew Jeremy is terribly vulnerable, you see.'" He mimicked the clip of her patrician speech perfectly. "'We trust you implicitly, but we also believe it wouldn't be wise to inadvertently influence his developing personality', or something along those lines."

"That sounds like her," Jeremy giggled. "But when I sounded surprised you were a lieutenant what I meant was, what are you doing working for them here? You're not old enough to be retired, are you?"

"Technically I am, but that's not the point, and thank you." He sighed. "Jeremy, do you remember when I said I was married in every sense of the word, except legally? And that my spouse passed away?"

"Yeah. On my first day here." He connected some dots in his head. "He didn't die of AIDS, did he?"

"No, thank God. We were both...are both, I mean...I'm fine." He paced to the opposite side of the room and sat on his desk, his hands grasping the edge. "I was stationed in Germany when my partner, his name was Danny, was killed in the attacks on the World Trade Center. He was a civil rights attorney who worked in Tower One. After the attacks, when I didn't hear from him, I requested an emergency furlough to New York, but they were only allowing personnel to leave who had immediate family that'd been affected. I was out of my head, hoping for a miracle that he was unconscious in some hospital somewhere, so I finally broke down and told my commanding officer that he was my lover and I had to find him." Arthur looked down. "He'd been missing for nearly two weeks before they found his body, or what was left of him. And I thought the Military would respect my grief, that they would honor the Tragedy." He shook his head. "Instead, just as the country went to war I was discharged, so I came back here to Ballena Beach where I grew up."

"Jesus, Arthur. I can't even picture what that must of been like."

"Thankfully, Jeremy, few people can. But similarly, I can't imagine what you've gone through all these years, either." He gave him a smile. "At least I have some really happy memories, and that keeps the bitterness away. I've just learned to be thankful for the time Danny and I had together." He nodded. "And you know, old buddy, we both have something pretty special in common."

"What's that?"

"We've both lost the man we loved most on this earth under tragic circumstances. And that makes us both very strong, very special people." He held out the uniform. "Go try it on. You probably have only a few minutes before your friend comes, so you might as well use my bathroom to change. I promise not to peek."

Jeremy closed the door and shucked his jeans and sweatshirt, then slipped on the funky, high-waisted pants and buttoned the complicated jacket over his T-shirt. When he finished he lifted his head and gazed into the medicine cabinet's mirror, startled by the dazzling young officer staring back at him. He turned from side to side. The coat was a bit loose through the chest and arms, but he figured he could manage for an evening.

"Does it fit?" said a muffled voice behind the door.

"I guess."

"Then get out here."

A bashful Jeremy opened the door.

Arthur grinned. "You do it justice. I should hope I ever looked that good."

"So don't I need some kind of hat?" He raised his eyebrows hopefully.

"I was saving the best for last." Arthur presented, from behind his back, a white lieutenant's cap with a black patent-leather brim. Gently, he placed it on the boy's head, as if this were his coronation. "The brim always goes two fingers over your nose, like this." He tugged the visor down so it covered Jeremy's eyebrows and shielded his eyes, making him look both mysterious and somewhat unrecognizable.

A distant horn honked.

"Your carriage awaits. Now run upstairs and put on those new black shoes I bought for you, mine'll be too big; and don't forget to wear dark socks."

"OK!" He sprinted for the stairs.

"Just don't spill anything on it that our dry cleaner can't get out," Arthur warned. "And I want to hear all the details tomorrow at breakfast."

Jeremy disappeared. The horn sounded again. He reappeared barefoot and grinning as he ran down the stairs, with shoes and socks dangling from his hands.

"And call me if you need a ride home. And don't get into a car with anyone who's been drinking!"

"Don't worry, Mom!" Jeremy yelled back, slamming the door behind him.

"I prefer *Fairy Godmother*," Arthur muttered, then turned his attention to the baskets of laundry on the floor of his room, waiting to be folded. He smiled, seeing much of it was the boy's.

Carlo sat in his sister's Tahoe drumming the fingers of one hand on the steering wheel while adjusting the draped white sheet that covered half his bare torso with the other. He checked his reflection in the rear-view mirror, then adjusted the tiara he'd constructed with a hot-glue gun and oak leaves, then spray-painted gold. The costume had been a risk, he knew, but he was determined to make a statement.

His gaze switched at once from the mirror to follow Jeremy as he trotted across the driveway toward him, opened the passenger door and heaved himself up into the seat, then slipped on a sock as he pulled on his seatbelt.

"Hello Sailor. Where'd you get that?" he asked.

"Don't ask because I can't tell you. It's a long story. And speaking of, what are you supposed to be?"

"Alexander the Great," he replied proudly. "He's sort of the patron saint of my people."

"I didn't realize the Mexicans of Ballena Beach prayed to him."

"Very funny. What I mean is that he was a proud gay man, and he's considered the greatest military figure of all time. His lover's name was Hephaestion, aka *philalexandros*, or 'best friend' of Alexander—which meant they were screwing each other." He slipped the transmission into Drive and rumbled down the long driveway. "That and they wore rainbow tunics."

They made a right out of the open gates and sped toward Pacific Coast Highway. "I hope we don't get there too early. Ellie's parties don't usually get started until after ten."

"Really," Jeremy replied, wondering how he'd look, walking into a room full of jocks with a gay guy dressed like Cupid.

They drove in silence.

"So what's with you? Aren't you looking forward to this?"

"Nothing's wrong. I just have lots on my mind."

"Well I'm sure you'll have a blast, especially with your new look." They stopped at the highway, and then Carlo gunned the engine and turned south toward Santa Monica. "You do look really good, Jeremy, I mean it. You'll be the hottest guy there."

"Thanks Carlo. You look really...good too."

"Gosh, do you mean it?" They both laughed.

They zigzagged south for another ten minutes, then the Tahoe turned right and slowed. "And here we are," Carlo announced, wheeling the vehicle into a line of waiting cars.

"Valet parking?" Jeremy asked.

"What else would you expect from Ellie?"

A man in a red vest jogged up to them and opened Carlo's door, then handed him a white ticket. "How's it goin'?" Jeremy said to the other valet, a guy barely older than himself.

"Just great," came the sarcastic answer.

"Come on, Major McHandsome." Carlo bounced from the car then headed toward the house while Jeremy followed, looking up at the unusual structure. The house looked like one big block of cement with its almost completely blank façade, except for a huge tongue of walkway suspended drawbridge-style that connected the luminous glass entry to the street, and two teeny windows that glowed red, like suspicious eyes watching their entrance. Dance music thumped louder as they approached.

They entered.

Eyes darted in their direction.

"Thank God! Finally some good-looking men!" Ellie exclaimed from across the room. Her platinum hair had been dyed black for the evening and was pulled tight into a bun at the back of her head. Her eyebrows were painted in high dark arches, her lips a luscious plum. She wore a tight black turtleneck and tighter black Capris, and on her feet perfect silk flats. Her hand held a martini glass, empty but for a bright red cherry.

"Oh my God, Maria Callas!" Carlo exclaimed, gently taking her hand and pressing it to his lips.

"An excellent deduction, Caesar, excellent. I had no idea you were an opera aficionado."

"Actually I'm Alexander the Great."

"Yes, of course," she waved her cigarette holder dismissively. "And what have we here, an officer or a gentleman?" Ellie batted her long false eyelashes.

"Thanks for inviting me."

"You're ever so welcome. Come and get yourselves stuffed and tipsy. We've got *everything*, and *everybody's* here. But don't stray too far; I'm expecting Coby to show up any time with that beast, and I'm gathering a small group to point and laugh at whatever she's wearing. In the meantime, Carlo, would you show the Commander around while I freshen my Manhattan?"

"As you wish, Miss Callas."

She sauntered away.

"I'm starved," Carlo announced. "Let's see what she's got."

The boys wove their way through the horde toward the buffet table, where Carlo filled his plate with sushi while Jeremy assembled a heap of nachos.

"Oh my God this is sooo good!" Carlo exclaimed, after shoving some smoked eel in his mouth.

"Yuck. How can you even put stuff like that in your mouth?" Jeremy scrunched up his nose.

"A tacky guy would make a nasty joke right now, but not Alexander the Great." He yanked Jeremy's hand. "Come on, *Nacho Man*, let's see who's here. I'll give you the dirt."

.He led Jeremy out to a deck that stretched out over the sand. From there they watched the party through the windows. "See that girl over there, the one dressed as Jewel?" Carlo pointed to a girl wearing ill-fitting bellbottoms and a sloppy gauze blouse. "She's the biggest slut at Ballena High. Been with the entire football team."

"Jealous?"

"You catch on fast. And see that dude over there with all that Abercrombie shit on? He's an escort—*a professional boyfriend*—and he goes both ways. But during normal business hours he folds sweaters at the Gap, and can you believe his clueless parents don't even question where he gets the money for his tacky yellow Corvette?"

"Juicy." Jeremy replied flatly, suspecting Carlo was trying to bring them back to their conversation of the other night. He changed the subject. "So what's the story about that one guy, Ellie's ex-boyfriend?"

"Oh, you mean Coby?" He cocked an eyebrow. "Why are you suddenly interested in him?"

"I made the swim team. I heard he's the best, my biggest competition."

"Oh. Well you should know right off that he's one screwed-up dude."

"Really? He seems OK to me; I thought he was pretty cool."

"Pretty, yes. Cool, no. Unless you like *game boys.*"

"Huh?"

"It's a loooong story. But if you want to know the dirt on Coby, *for competitive purposes*, no one knows as much as Ellie. Ask her. She'll set you straight. Pun intended."

"I *am* straight, thanks."

"Of course, I'd forgotten. Girl, I need a drink. You want something?"

"Yeah. Coke."

"You'll have to ask Avery for that; he's the one over there dressed like a rapper. How *tired.*"

"I meant to drink."

"No duh. I'll be back in a sec."

Jeremy watched as the expanding party spilled onto the sand below, while those inside yelled to each other over the thunder of the music. He saw how kids posed themselves like living sculpture, laughing while leaning or sitting on every surface within and outside the sleek house, drinks in-hand, eyes scanning back-and-forth for masquerading friends and potential evening hook-ups. Then a flash of black caught his eye. It was Ellie, the exquisite hostess, flitting like an elegant wasp to a variety of Halloween flowers, her manner even more grandiose than usual.

So where was Reed?

At once he spotted her, outfitted in a red one-piece bathing suit and a frazzled blonde wig. She giggled as she tried flipping a torpedo-shaped rescuer's float in the air, TV lifeguard-style. Only she bounced it off the ceiling and hit a pirate on the head, causing him to drop his sandwich.

Jeremy figured he should approach her before Carlo returned, so he threaded himself through the crowd and tapped her on the shoulder. "Hi Reed."

Startled, she turned to face him as her pink-lipsticked mouth split into a huge smile. "Oh! Mr. Sailorman!" Reed pointed her index finger at her chin. "Has your ship run aground out in that big old dangerous bay, the former pristine waters polluted by corporate greed?" she feigned a look of panicked concern, flipping her blond wig back from her face and blinking drunkenly.

"Yes Miss Lifeguard, and the boat's filled with Chinese orphans that'll drown if you don't save them."

"But I can't save your ship, Mister Sailorman, 'cause I've just broken up with my stunningly gorgeous boyfriend and my recurring eating disorder has made me too weak to swim. But please don't tell Mitch or I'll lose my job."

"I won't tell as long as you go out with me. By the way, what's your name?" Jeremy reached out and touched her shoulder, feeling her buttery skin for the first time, the delicious warmth of her body.

"Tarzana," she giggled hideously.

He laughed back, looking her up and down. "Honestly, Reed, you look great."

"Yeah? Thanks. You too, and I'm not just saying that. That uniform fits you great! Was it your father's?"

"Actually I got this from our butler." He loved saying *our butler.*

"As the saying goes, I love a man in uniform, so long as it's not a *McDonald's*. So where's Carlo? I thought you were coming together."

Jeremy blushed. "Yeah, he was my ride. Which reminds me, have you seen him? He's the one dressed as Alexander the Great in the toga; he was supposed to be bringing back drinks."

"Isn't that the greatest military figure in history over there talking to that tore-up drag queen?" Jeremy turned to where she pointed and saw that Carlo was indeed listening to a babbling, platinum-wigged transvestite who lasciviously traced the muscles of his bared shoulder with her hand. Carlo glanced across the room at them and rolled his eyes. He still held a fresh drink in each hand.

"I think I need to execute a rescue," declared Reed, grabbing her torpedo float and twirling it in the air, but once again missing the catch as it tumbled through her hands and bounced into the lap of a girl in a football uniform, splashing her drink. She apologized, then grabbed Jeremy's hand and pulled him toward their friend. "You coming, Mr. Great?" she shouted as they whizzed by, her free hand snatching Carlo's tunic as the drag queen's mouth hung open in mid-word.

They moved outside, where desert winds blew in circles like nosy ghosts, flapping costumes and blowing out candles in the jack-o-lanterns strewn about the deck and sand. And the three leaned over the deck's railing, watching a noisy game of strip volleyball on the sand below. They gabbed like old friends.

Jeremy learned that Reed's mother was Swedish and her father Jamaican, they'd met while dancing for a music video in the early eighties and lived now as a happy family of three at the northern end of Ballena Beach just south of County Line. Her parents had since made a small fortune selling real estate, and Reed's professional ambition was to have her own advertising agency some day. He also learned that Carlo came from an extremely traditional Mexican-American family, living on what was left of the *Rancho* that had been in his family since the 1840's. Up until recently they had operated one of the last working ranches in Southern California, where they raised and trained Andalusian horses. Then his mother had taken ill and his father had become a recluse, and they'd been forced to sell the last of the horses to settle their mother's staggering medical bills, as well as the property's gargantuan taxes. Sadly, their home was now in danger of being sold to one of the vulturous developers who'd been circling for years.

So Jeremy felt safe enough, finally, to disclose some details about his journey back to Ballena Beach, while leaving out the most sordid details of his mother's affliction, as well as the filth in which he'd been raised. They expressed polite approval about her finally being in rehab, and appropriate sorrow that his father had been dead for years. The pair nodded attentively and sympathetically as he spoke, making him feel, in his costume, like a war hero addressing reporters.

Then thoughts became romantic, so their conversation dwindled.

"What are you so deep in thought about?" Reed asked him, finally breaking the silence.

"I guess I was just wondering what time it is, or how much longer until I've got to get going."

"Don't worry Cinderella," Carlo giggled, grabbing his wrist. "It's only a quarter past eleven, so you don't have to worry about your carriage leaving for another hour."

"Carlo, you need to tone that faggot shit down," Jeremy snapped, yanking his hand away. "We all get that you're gay, and that's 'fabulous' and all, but *I'm not.*"

"Hmmm." Carlo's happy smile vanished. "I can tell it's time for me to freshen my drink. If you need me I'll be hunting for other sodomites; they're much more fun on Halloween than the Self-Righteously Insecure." He turned and disappeared into the crowd.

"What was that all about?" Reed asked.

"I guess it was just that, well, I think Carlo has the wrong idea about me. I think he thinks I'm like him. You know, gay."

"Well are you?" she asked.

"God, no."

"Have you told him that?"

"Yep. The night he came over to study."

"Then what's the problem? Or didn't you know that he kids around like that with everyone."

"I just didn't want you to get the wrong idea about me. That I don't like girls."

"I already figured that out," Reed murmured, touching his hand. "But I wouldn't mind being convinced."

"Convinced?" he raised an eyebrow.

"You know. Prove it to me, so I can testify at your court martial." She flicked the medals on his chest. Their eyes held.

"You mean like this?" He leaned in and pressed their lips together, then felt her mouth nudge his lips open and urge their tongues into a slippery game of tag. Jeremy was thrilled; he was finally having his first kiss, and he was enjoying it.

And the tingling between his legs told him he'd been right about her: she did, apparently, hold the puzzle's missing piece.

Their mouths separated finally and they hugged, but when their eyes met she could see he was faraway. "What are you thinking about?" she asked.

"Oh, just that we should probably go inside. I feel bad about Carlo."

Her expression clouded. *"That's* what you were thinking?"

"Sure, I mean...no. I'm just kind of embarrassed to say." He turned to survey the rolling waves. He couldn't possibly tell her what he'd been thinking.

"You don't have to tell me. It's OK."

"But I do, I mean, just a couple of weeks ago my life was so different, and now here I am with someone like you, and, what I mean is, I wouldn't have ever thought someone like you could go for someone like me, I guess."

"What, because I'm *black*?" Her voice dropped a notch.

"No! No." He shook his head. "I mean, someone who's...so beautiful and popular."

"So you think I'm beautiful *and* popular?" she giggled. She stretched up on her toes and whispered into his ear. "Do you think then that I'm out of your league?" He felt her breasts press against his chest.

"Well, yeah. Sure."

"Then come with me!" She grabbed his hand and led him from the balcony back into the house, where the party's population bulged now in the hundreds. They pushed and pulled their way through toward the industrial-looking stairway at the far end of the living room, then climbed the stairs quickly. Once at the top she led him down a hallway toward the bedrooms.

This was all going too fast. Ten minutes ago he was enjoying his first kiss, and now they were scouting out bedrooms? His stomach knotted as they stopped in front of a closed door. She knocked.

"What!" It was Ellie.

"It's me, bitch!"

"Go away, I'm busy." Her voice sounded far away.

Reed pressed the side of her head against the door. "If that's Coby in there with you I'm gonna knock your brains in, girl."

"It's not, so go the fuck away!" Ellie's giggling mixed with the muffled laughter of not one, but two male voices.

"Ugh, that filthy ho. Come on with me, Jeremy." Reed pushed open a bathroom door, "And *please* don't get the wrong idea; I'm not that kinda girl." She batted her eyelashes and shot him an innocent smile.

The pair entered and Reed switched on the light. Jeremy looked. They were standing in front of a generous mirror. It was the first time he'd seen himself as part of a couple with anyone other than his awful old mother.

"Do you see?" she asked.

"See what?"

"See us, you 'tard!" Reed grabbed him by the chin and pointed his face at the mirror. "Now do you still think I'm out of your league? Look at yourself. You're absolutely beautiful!"

"No, you're the beautiful one." He lowered his mouth again to hers, and this time their kiss was more passionate than before, more assured. As her arms slid around his back he reached up and ran his hand through her hair, for the moment forgetting it was a wig. Their mouths opened wider to each other, and their tongues danced wildly. At once Jeremy felt his genitalia tingle again, as if his naughty bits had been submerged suddenly in warmed-up soda pop.

A sharp knock on the door broke their moment.

"Ellie?" It was a deep male voice. Jeremy recognized it immediately. Reflexively, they released each other.

"What do you want, Coby? She's not in here," she said.

"I know she's in there with you. I heard you telling her she's beautiful…as if she doesn't think so already."

"Number one, you shouldn't go listening at bathroom doors and number two, it's none of your business who I'm in here with and number three, why do you care? Didn't you drag that girly-thing here with you?"

"Brynn's downstairs."

"Then what do you want with Ellie?" She stepped up closer to the door.

"It's some business that we gotta finish, so just open the door and let me talk to her."

Reed looked back at Jeremy, raising her eyebrows in a question. Jeremy nodded his head. She grasped the handle and swung the door open.

Coby was leaning his heavy shoulders casually against the wall opposite the bathroom doorway, his hands tucked casually into his back pockets and his hips thrust forward. He wore a baseball uniform so perfectly tailored to his body it could have been painted-on, so tightly was the white striped fabric stretched over the swells of his chest, crotch, and legs. The hallway's overhead lighting illuminated his golden curls and shadowed the hollows of his cheekbones, and defined the square jaw and aristocratic nose that gave his young face such robust, masculine beauty.

His overwhelming magnificence startled Jeremy.

"Satisfied?" Reed snarled.

"You know Reed, there's no need for such hostility." He nearly sang the words. "I was just looking for Ellie. Where is she?"

"Last time I saw her she had a football player on each arm and didn't want to be bothered, least of all by *you*."

"Really, well now you've gone and hurt my feelings," he replied innocently, then turned his gaze toward Jeremy, easing his mouth into a crooked smile. "Hey *Tyler*." He held out his hand.

"Hey." Jeremy took his hand and smiled back, thinking that since he'd been caught in the bathroom with a girl he should feel like one of the guys. But the suggestiveness in Coby's turquoise eyes shot down Jeremy's fledgling heterosexual confidence, and took him back to the memory of his shameful nighttime fantasy, which he'd successfully forgotten up until this very moment.

"That uniform looks really cool on you, Tyler. You must be a sailor, or something like that, huh?" Coby's eyes seemed to linger over every inch of him, from head to toe and back again, while ignoring the fuming Reed.

"Actually I'm dressed like a Marine. I got this from our butler."

"Wow, your *butler*..." his eyebrows arched. "It looks cool on him, doesn't it Reed?"

"Better than that tired baseball uniform, Coby. What is that from, like, eighth grade or something?" She rolled here eyes.

"He can't help it if he keeps growing more muscles," came a shrill voice from in back of the three. A big-chested, chestnut-haired girl ascended the last of the stairs wearing a scantily-cut French maid's uniform. "I think he's the best looking man here, by far." She turned and looked down her nose at Jeremy. "No offense, whoever you are."

"None taken," Jeremy replied.

"Hello Brynn, how *pretty* you look tonight." Reed sneered.

The bedroom door behind them flew open. Ellie emerged wide-eyed and disheveled. She gave Brynn's costume the once-over. "Thank God the clean-up crew's finally here," she announced breathlessly. "There's a pile of dishes in the sink and I think we ran out of clean glasses over an hour ago."

"Uh-oh," Reed whispered.

"And what are you supposed to be, Ellie?" Brynn asked cheerfully as two guilty-faced boys sidled from the bedroom past the group and down the stairs. "The village slut? Oh, I forgot, you wouldn't need a costume..."

"And when you're finished—" Ellie interrupted "—don't forget to take out the trash, I mean, let yourself out. Now off you go, time is money. Tick-tock, tick-tock."

Coby cut in. "Will you both just quit it?" He turned to Ellie. "I came up here to ask you to please be nice to her, just for tonight. Brynn already promised me she wouldn't start anything with you."

Ellie's eyes narrowed. "Coby, sweet simple Coby, are you forgetting whose house this is? You should've known better than to bring *her* here."

"You're the one who invited me."

"Exactly my point."

His face flushed. "If she's not welcome here than we're both leaving." He grabbed Brynn by the arm and headed for the stairs.

"Don't forget to tip the valet," Ellie sang.

As soon as they were gone she collapsed onto her bed, beating her fists on the rumpled sheets. "I hate her, I hate her, I hate her!"

Reed calmly turned to Jeremy. "You better find go find Carlo; it looks like I'm gonna be here awhile."

Jeremy nodded. "OK." He smiled shyly. "Can I call you?"

"Get my number from him." She stood on her toes and kissed him gently. "Call me tomorrow."

He tore down the stairs.

Carlo sat by himself on a long black leather sofa. He looked up as Jeremy approached, his eyebrows knitted together. "I suppose you still need a ride home," he said, folding his arms across his chest.

"Look, I'm sorry about what I said earlier. It came out different than I meant it."

"Yeah, whatever. I just want to get the fuck outta here. You're lucky I waited."

"Thanks Carlo. So do I. Let's go." He held out his hand and pulled Carlo up from his seat. "We need to talk."

CHAPTER 18

Carlo slowed the Tahoe in front of the Tyler Compound's fancy iron gates, and then stopped. The engine idled expectantly. Should he put the car in Park or leave it in Drive? Park meant they would be talking for awhile and he wasn't sure he wanted to. He only felt like sulking. And he was afraid that if they started talking he would wind up expressing the distress his heart was screaming, even if it meant Jeremy would shush him, or worse yet laugh. It was like they were both watching the same thrillingly romantic movie, only Jeremy was listening to dialogue radioed in from another theater.

Meanwhile, the boy in the passenger seat unbuckled his seatbelt, then puffed out his cheeks and blew an invisible tube of air at the windshield. The ride back from Ellie's party had taken only ten minutes but had felt like an hour; the tension between them flickered like distant lightning, too far away to hear, but hot as hell and headed this way. And now he just wanted to get inside the house; he wanted to think and needed to pee. Better get this over with. He looked over. "Hey, I said I was sorry. I just don't want Reed to get the wrong idea about me. I think you could understand."

His knuckles showed white on the steering wheel. "Jeremy, all I said was that we had an hour before we had to go."

"You grabbed my hand and called me 'Cinderella'. In front of Reed."

"Everybody knows I joke around like that."

"Well, it didn't feel like a joke then, or when you called me 'girl', or when you made your comment about Ellie 'setting me straight'." He spoke with the masculine self-assurance of a boy with the taste of girl on his lips. "I don't like you implying that I'm gay, especially in front of other people because I'm not. Or have you already forgotten our conversation, *Miss Sara Lee?*"

"If you were secure about your masculinity it wouldn't bother you." He shoved the gearshift into Park and switched off the motor.

"That's total bullshit, and you know it. Even if I was gay I wouldn't want you throwing it around. A person's sexuality is their business."

"Now *that's* total bullshit, Jeremy," he declared. "Everywhere I look I see breeders forcing their sexuality on me. Churches, billboards, at school, on TV, even in commercials where they drive their fat ugly kids around in their mini-vans. And if you don't see that then you're as homophobic as the rest of them." He sighed. "I'm just sick and tired of feeling like I'm from another planet."

Jeremy fiddled with his hat. "Then maybe you should stop acting like it."

"What's that supposed to mean?"

"What I mean is, why do you act so faggy sometimes?"

"I'm not in the closet, Jeremy," he snapped.

"That's great, Carlo, I respect that. But is being the queer poster boy really who you are? I mean, you didn't act as gay when you came over to study the other night—then it seemed like you were being yourself. But at the party, it was like you were someone else." He paused, searching for a way he could make himself understood. "Tonight you seemed kind of like a cartoon character. I mean, if a straight guy on TV acted the way you did tonight, you and all your little gay friends would get pissed off that he was acting like a stereotype."

Little gay friends? "When you've gone through as much shit as I have," he stated with furious dignity, "then I'll have the balls to listen to you talk down to me, then say I'm acting like a cartoon. But not before!"

"I've been through plenty of my own shit, Carlo."

"Of really?" He snickered. "Did Butler burn the toast again, Master Tyler?"

"That's not fair. Where I've lived for one week has nothing to do with it."

"I'll tell you what's not fair, Jeremy. It's not fair to listen to your mother crying as she dies, not from the cancer eating her alive, but because she says she'll never see you in heaven because you're going to hell." He was trembling suddenly, as if freezing. "And it wasn't fair when my father told me I killed her, *I killed my own mother*, because I'd broken her heart and she lost the will to live. He even told me—" his voice cracked "—that he hoped God would send me AIDS to punish me for what I'd done to her. He hoped, Jeremy, he *hoped!*"

"Oh dude," he shook his head. "That's totally fucked-up that he would say that. Of course it wasn't your fault…he probably just needed someone to blame."

"So blame her doctors, blame her fucking HMO, or better yet, blame *her* for not getting a Pap Smear for twenty years!" he exclaimed. "But not your son, not your grieving boy!" He sobbed now unabashedly, his face contorted as if his features had frozen in mid-sneeze. "Can you believe he wouldn't even speak to me at her funeral? And now he just he looks at me with hatred and disgust, like I'm some dog shit stuck to his boots." He pulled up a corner of his tunic and loudly blew his nose on it. "So now I make sure that I act like the very thing he hates the most in this world. I throw it in his face every day and every chance I get, so he can see that his son is a *joto*, that he was such a fucking horrible father he raised a *maricon* instead of a man." He wiped his eyes with the backs of his hands then heaved a leaden sigh. "And that's why I dropped the 's' from 'Carlos', because I was named after him, this 'father' that wishes a miserable death on his only son. And that's also why I won't *tone that faggot shit down*, Jeremy. I act the way I do because I've earned the right to."

Jeremy was speechless. He could only watch as Carlo's crying-hiccups diminished, then he laid a hand on his shoulder. "Hey, I know we haven't known each other very long, and you're right, I haven't been through anything like what you have. All I can say is…I know how it feels to lose someone, and to be thrown away by someone who's supposed to be there for you." He squeezed his shoulder, feeling the knotted warmth beneath his hand. "And if nothing else, I understand what it feels like to be hurt. More than you know."

Carlo looked back at him and saw the understanding in his eyes, and felt a rope being thrown his way. He nodded, and Jeremy smiled. He grabbed Jeremy's shoulder and squeezed back, and as he did so felt that rope become taut. "It's just so hard sometimes for people like us…being this age and all."

"I know it," Jeremy said softly. "It's like everything's turned up full blast when you're a teenager—you have all these choices but you also have people everywhere telling you who to be and what to do. But you're lucky in a way, Carlo, because your anger's helped you figure out what you really want, and I'm only now starting to think of what I want instead of what other people want for me. You're way ahead."

Carlo stared at him. "That sounds great and all, but if you really understood you'd never think of me as 'lucky'."

Jeremy nodded. "Okay, maybe I don't understand. It just seems to me that if you're mad at your parents, why take it out on everyone else?"

"What do you mean?"

"I mean…that if you act a certain way to piss off your dad, don't you think it might keep other people away too? Like people who want to be friends." His mouth made a shy smile. "Like me?"

"I never thought about it that way," he answered quietly.

"Well, maybe you should. It's your life and all, but if it's not really the true 'Carlo', then why do it? I mean, isn't that the whole reason for your being *out* in the first place, so you can be yourself?"

Carlo pressed his fingertips to his temples and made tiny circles. "My head hurts, Jeremy. I need to go home and think this whole night through…but I want you to know that I really appreciate your listening to me go off."

"Hey, that's what friends are for, right?" He grabbed the door handle and pulled.

"Right. But one more thing," Their eyes caught. "I need to confess something."

Jeremy waited.

"I made that Cinderella crack tonight because I felt a little left out because of how good Reed and you were getting along." He sighed. "So I think you were right after all…that in some way I was trying to piss you off. And I'm sorry."

"Thanks for the apology." He opened the door and climbed down. "So I guess I'll see you at school on Monday—oh, and Reed told me I could get her number from you. Is it OK if I call you tomorrow?"

"Sure. I'll be home." He started the engine then pulled the gearshift into Drive. "And if my dad answers the phone, tell him you're a gay porn producer that wants to hire me."

They waved as he drove away.

Jeremy punched his security code into the keypad and the gates swung open, and then he trudged up the remaining length of the driveway to the main house's side entrance. Once inside he meandered through the hallways to the kitchen in search of a tasty bedtime snack.

He found his uncle sitting at one of the barstools thumbing through a stack of complicated-looking papers, digging his fork into a triangle of oozy green pie.

"Hey, Uncle Bill."

"Jeremy!" the man blurted. "I didn't hear you come in." He flipped the stack of papers upside-down on the counter, then squeezed his eyes nearly shut as the reality of Jeremy's costume sunk in. "Where on God's green earth did you get *that*?"

"It's Arthur's," he told him. "He let me wear it to a Halloween party."

"Mr. Blauefee, of course. I keep forgetting about his 'colorful' past." He chuckled through his nose. "Well, it's good to see something like that put to use. Lord knows he won't be wearing it again." He patted the barstool next to him. "Sit down, young man, and cut yourself some of this Key-lime pie."

Jeremy hated Key-lime pie. "No thanks." He leaned against the counter, comfortable with discussing the subject since, apparently, it no longer applied to him. "That's too bad about his friend, isn't it? I mean, how he died and all on September Eleventh. And then for Arthur to be kicked out of the Marines on top of everything."

"Such a tragedy for him, losing his career." Bill shook his head. "Of course, if people didn't lie in the first place, they wouldn't have to worry about their awful truths being discovered, now would they?"

"Do you mean he shouldn't have ever gone into the military?"

"Of course! Those people have no business in the armed forces. It would be like my trying to be some Hollywood Hunk or Olympic athlete at my age. Some things just aren't meant to be."

"But aren't you talking about the way someone is physically?" he asked, then perched himself atop a nearby stool. "Arthur sure looks like a Marine, even still."

"What I am referring to is a weakness of the mind, my boy. It's a sickness..." he pointed to his head and tapped his finger over his ear "...up here. Would you want a mentally unstable person rescuing you from a burning building?"

"I guess I wouldn't care who rescued me...as long as they did," he replied.

"When you're older you'll understand. You will understand." His eyes narrowed. "Speaking of which, your eighteenth birthday is coming up in a few months, isn't it?"

"March fifteenth."

"And have you decided what it is you want?"

Jeremy's head dropped. "I've already gotten so much from you and Aunt Katharine. To be honest I haven't thought about it at all."

"Nonsense. You've just been deprived of so much your entire life, *by that woman*, that you've grown accustomed to having nothing. But all that's changed." He popped a piece of pie into his mouth, chewed noiselessly then swallowed. "So think, boy. What is it that would make your eighteenth birthday one you'll never forget?"

He'd already been promised a car, even though he couldn't drive yet; he had a computer, he had new clothes. So what didn't he have? A vision popped suddenly into his head of Coby and himself splashing and swimming through turquoise water, then sunning themselves side-by-side on an empty beach. "A trip to Hawaii this summer," he suggested happily, "with a friend."

Bill laughed, and a chunk of pie fell from his mouth onto his lap. "Jeremy, dear boy, you're still thinking like your mother's kind, like some cocktail waitress or the pizza man. You're a *Tyler*, and the sooner you start thinking like one the better." He picked up the renegade morsel and popped it into his mouth, leaving a stain the shape of Texas on his trousers. "So what will it be—an apartment building in East LA? Or maybe you'd prefer a well-diversified stock portfolio? Our shares of Wal-Mart have been doing magnificently."

Jeremy's smile vanished. *What fun were those?* "Uncle Bill, I guess I need to think about it. I mean, it's still a few months away."

"A very wise decision, young man. In the meantime you might find it interesting to know that I'm working on something very special for your eighteenth, an event of sorts."

"Really?"

"Yes. Something to make the momentous occasion unforgettable."

"Really." He was squirming with curiosity and hadn't a clue as to what the man could be thinking. "Could you give me a kind of a hint, please?"

"Mmm, well..." He looked at him like a shark eyeing an oblivious sea lion. "All I can tell you is that if what I'm considering takes place, it will involve your family and all of your closest friends, and will be an unforgettably elegant event."

"Really!" Jeremy exclaimed, almost gasping. He hadn't even thought of having a birthday party, he was so used to them passing by unacknowledged. Clearly his mother, with her ominous 'warnings' had been lying again; Bill had already done more good for him than she would in a thousand lifetimes.

"But it's a surprise, Jeremy. So *don't tell anyone anything*."

"I won't, Uncle." He yawned, then scooted off the barstool. "I've got to go to bed now. Thanks."

"My pleasure."

His heels on the stone floor made happy tap-dancing sounds as he trotted toward the stairs leading up to his room, then switched directions after realizing he needed to return the precious uniform to Arthur. But would he still be awake? He rapped gently on his door after spying the glowing bar of light coming from underneath. He heard shuffling feet, then the door swung open. Arthur wore a wife-beater T-shirt and boxer shorts with big Chihuahuas printed willy-nilly all over them.

"I'm sorry, I know it's late. I just wanted to give you back the uniform."

"Sure, come in. I was just wasting time online. And your sweats are over there," he hitched a thumb toward his crisply made-up bed. "I washed them for you." He sat back down at the desk and focused his attention on the computer.

Jeremy pushed the door halfway shut and unbuttoned the coat, then slipped off the pants, not bothering this time to sequester himself in the bathroom. "So what is it you're looking for?"

"Nothing that would interest you." His hand made figure-eights with the mouse. "It's a chat-room for ex-military personnel who've been discharged because of sexual orientation. We discuss legal issues and court decisions."

"Hmm. Listen, if it's not too much trouble do you think you could look something up for me? My computer's not set up."

"Sure," he replied absently. "What do you need?"

"I had this sort of crazy dream last night, Arthur." He began, pulling his sweats on. "I can't remember a whole lot about it, except that my dad and I were walking along a beach together and he was telling me to wish on a star."

"Sounds interesting." He yawned. "Tell me more."

"Some of the dream made sense, and some of it didn't. But there was this thing in the dream called the 'Father's Star'. And he told me to make a wish but I don't remember what it was. So I was wondering if you could try and look it up."

"You're asking me to search for information about something that came to you in a dream, at-" he squinted at his clock radio "-a quarter past midnight?" He frowned. "Jeremy, tiny little children all over the world learn about making a wish on the first star they see at night. It's nothing novel."

"Yeah. I know it sounds crazy. It's just that this all seemed so realistic. And I've never heard about a 'Father's Star' before."

He yawned again. "No, I guess it doesn't sound 'crazy'. Just give me a sec to log off." He tapped his fingers on the keyboard. "OK." He straightened his back. "So I'm looking for anything having to do with the 'Father's Star'."

"Yep." Jeremy looked over his shoulders as the search engine shuffled through its trillions of information bits.

Zero results.

"Let me try another search; 'Star of the Father'." The keyboard clicked under his hands. "By the way, how was the party?"

"It was great, Arthur. I'm actually making some friends here."

"You'll have to tell me when I'm not about to collapse into a coma. Oops, no results again. I don't know what to tell you, old buddy." He shook his head.

"What about wishing on a star, Arthur? Could you try that?"

"Sure, hold on." Jeremy watched as the screen lit up with page after page of potential sites. "What does it say about that?"

"Let me see…there are lots of pages here about silly movie songs… but let me check…no…no…no…Ah!" The page loaded and Jeremy saw rows and rows of writing. "This site says that wishing on a star originated with the Greeks and Romans, who believed that their deities existed in the skies and answered the requests of the righteous." Arthur's and Jeremy's faces glowed the same pale blue as the boy craned his neck to read over the man's shoulder. "And when Christianity came along the Church forbade worship of the old gods, so people began referring to looking skyward as *wishing for something* instead of *praying to someone*."

"So what were some of the names of the gods they used to pray to? Were any of them fathers?"

"There are almost too many here to investigate: Hercules, Cassiopeia, Orion, Perseus, Cepheus, Castor and Pollux. The list goes on and on. You'd have to research each one."

"So they were all Greek or Roman names?"

"Like I said. But maybe we could do this some other time. It's late."

"I know, but maybe you could try doing a search on the Father's Star in Greek or Roman?"

"You mean Greek or Latin."

"Yeah."

"Well Greek has its own alphabet, so that won't work. But I think I remember a little bit of Latin from Catholic school: the Father's Star would translate into *Stellae Patriae*, or would it be *Stella Patris* ? Let me try both." He keyed the words into the computer and hit Return. "Not one result, Jeremy. I'm sorry, but I've got to go to bed. Your aunt has a list of demands for me to do tomorrow as long as a toilet paper roll."

"Thanks anyway." He stood and then turned for the door, shoes in-hand. "And I really appreciate your letting me use your uniform tonight. It got me a lot of attention. Good attention, I mean."

"I'm sure what was *in* the uniform was what got the attention, you bum. But you're welcome anyhow. It brought back some good memories seeing it on someone again. I can't bear to wear it, myself."

Jeremy put his hand on the doorknob. "Just one more thing," he hesitated, then turned to face him. "Does Danny ever show up in your dreams?"

"From time to time," he replied quietly. "Why?"

"Does he ever tell you things you didn't know before, I mean, things that might be true?"

"There's really no way to know if what he 'says' to me is true, Jeremy. But usually he seems so real, like he's never left or been gone, and a lot of the times he seems confused, even shocked that I thought he was dead. Then he tells me that he'll never leave me, that he'll always love me. And sometimes I just sob and wail and I can't breathe because he's there again smiling and I can hold him—I mean actually feel him, his shoulders and all—and then I wake up." Jeremy saw that Arthur was seeing some faraway picture, but then he focused back on him. "So what you're really asking me is if any of what your father told you in your dream might be true, that would mean he's still around somewhere and he's communicating with you. Am I right?"

Jeremy nodded, his eyes glistening.

Arthur pushed himself up from the chair and approached him, then wrapped his arms around the boy, drawing their bodies together. "Of course it's true, old buddy," he whispered, his breath warming his ear. "Your dad's out there somewhere, in the same place where Danny is. And sometimes they come to us...to let us know everything's going to be ok."

Jeremy had never been held by a man before and was stunned by the unyielding solidity of Arthur's body, as well as the vulnerability and heat he radiated. And at once he felt some parts of himself getting squished just as others were stretching, as if he were being remolded, after all these years, from the outside in. He wanted to squeeze him back with strength equal to the exhilaration he felt, but was afraid the volume of his yearning would scare away this moment and leave him, once again, half-finished. So he stood impassively, his arms limp at his sides.

Arthur reached up a hand and smoothed the top of Jeremy's head, and Jeremy remembered Jonathan's hand doing the same in his dream, and his father's words echoed in his memory as loud as if they were coming from a bullhorn: *Mr. Blauefee. Talk to him, he'll help you make your dreams come true. Arthur knows all about the magic.*

Haltingly but steadily, Jeremy lifted his arms and squeezed him back while burying his bursting smile in the rock-like shoulder. Then their hands smoothed each other's backs, and they rocked gently from side-to-side like long-lost brothers, or soldiers from a long forgotten war.

CHAPTER 19

"Wake up, ya' bum, I think I found something." Arthur, in his knee-length terry-cloth robe stood over Jeremy's bed clutching twin steaming mugs of coffee.

"Huh?" Through slitted eyes he saw the sky beyond his windows glowed Easter-egg lavender. He figured it wasn't even six yet. "Something about what?"

"About that silly 'Father's Star'." He placed one mug on the nightstand and slurped noisily from the other. "Get dressed and come down to my room. But hurry, I've got to be at the flower mart by seven." He turned and disappeared.

Minutes later Jeremy shuffled into the man's bedroom where he found him hunched over his monitor scanning thin lines of text. "What did you find?" He leaned tightly over him, breathing coffee fumes.

"Sit down please; I hate it when someone reads over my shoulder."

Jeremy sat.

The mouse tick-tucked and the text on the screen rolled up like movie credits. "Just let me paraphrase this, and I can print it out for you later. By the way, it was my conjugation that was wrong last night; I had forgotten that *Pater* is an a-typical masculine noun, and the genitive, or possessive case, translates correctly into *Stella Patrim*. So once I resolved that I was able to sort through about a dozen different search engines, and finally found this reference. And it's a legitimate one, originating from some brainiac at Oxford. It might not mean anything at all, but I thought it would interest you. Ready?"

Jeremy nodded, and yawned in spite of himself.

"It seems the *Stella Patrim*, or 'Father's Star', is an ancient myth, one that is much older than the most recent Greek and Roman version, which we know today as the story of the constellation of the Gemini twins, 'Castor' and 'Pollux'. In the nighttime Spring sky the Gemini constellation looks like two stick figures holding hands, and one is taller than the other. See?"

Jeremy examined the screen. The connect-the-dots figures did, in fact, look that way.

"But they weren't originally twins, in fact the earlier versions of the Greek myth, from about 1050 BC, suggest they were only half-brothers from the same mother. Castor was reportedly born of two mortals, while Pollux was half-mortal and half-god, and his father was Zeus. The young men were great warriors 'known for their devotion to each other', which strongly implies they were lovers. Castor was killed suddenly in battle by a traitor, thus Pollux begged Zeus to let them be joined together for eternity in the heavens. The two were honored by generations of Greek as well as Roman soldiers and even sailors, who sought their protection and guidance during especially fierce battles.

"But here's more: this source goes on to site a recently translated text which suggests that in the 4th century BC Alexander the Great, after losing his beloved Hephaestion in battle, and as he himself lay dying of grief three weeks later, declared that upon his imminent death both he and his deceased lover would rise up and become this same constellation, the twin warriors of the *Dioskouri*, enjoying each others' company forever in the sky. And since then subsequent cultures have added even more to this story.

"So what does it have to do with fathers?"

"I'm getting to that. But one thing you need to understand, Jeremy, is that the example of Alexander the Great demonstrates how the Greeks altered their mythology to suit their changing political climate, as well as their own evolving customs. And then the Romans altered them further after conquering the Greeks."

"Sort of like propaganda?"

"Exactly. So now I'll read you the oldest recorded interpretation, from the time of Eratosthenes at around 2020 BC. You'll see how the earliest Greeks, the Helenes, believed that Pollux and Castor were a father and son who reigned as king and prince. Listen to this:

"King Pollux, the son of Apollo and a mortal queen, was a man in the fullest bloom of life, magnificent in all capacities, his fairness as a ruler and grace as a warrior was second only to Apollo, and his strength and courage, like Mars himself, bellowed with the ferocity of twenty lions on the battlefield. Prince Castor was the younger image of his glorious father, having the transient beauty of one between boyhood and manhood, and whose virtue had not yet known the pleasures of Eros.

"Because their kingdom enjoyed years of felicitous peace and bountiful harvests the troublesome gods (with naught better to do) bickered with the restless mortals over who might entice the pleasures of the King's virile prowess, and who amongst them was most worthy to relieve the boy of his ripe virginity. A great disagreement arose and a prize was agreed upon for the one, mortal or immortal, who could accomplish both.

"Queen Terpsia, the King's wife and Castor's mother, upon learning of the contest, vowed that she would sooner see her husband dead than unfaithful to her. As a result, she plotted with his own best friend and highest general to murder him in his sleep, and in return promised to make the assassin her lover and the kingdom's royal advisor.

"But as the murderous plot unfolded and the King was being slain in his bed, the virtuous Castor ran unarmed to his father's aid and was struck down as well, and woe befell the wretched woman upon seeing the lifeless body of her fallen son beside her husband. She drew the assassin's own sword and sliced her promised lover's head from his body, then threw it and herself from the highest cliff in the land.

"Then Apollo himself, so distraught over the treacherous deaths of the King and Prince caused the sun to descend to Hades while the heavens rained a thousand leagues for one year.

"Jupiter, to comfort the distraught Apollo and to restore the flooded lands to the miserable mortals, lifted Pollux and Castor from Hades into the heavens where they might rejoice in well-deserved immortality for eternity, enjoying each others' company while providing protection from treachery to fathers and their sons everywhere.

"Finally, Jupiter cast the Queen and the dreadful assassin into Hades where they wander for eternity feasting ravenously on the putrefying flesh of the other."

Jeremy's brows knitted. "That's a pretty sad story, I can see why the Greeks thought they needed to change it around," Jeremy said. "But at least it kind of had a happy ending; the queen and the other guy got what they deserved."

"Actually the Greeks loved tragedies, especially the ones where greedy rulers met grisly endings," Arthur added. "But the core myth even today retains the idea that the constellation of Gemini consists of two noble male family members who were greatly devoted to each other, and who died before their times because of betrayal and treachery."

"That's tragic."

"That's nothing. You haven't read Oedipus, have you?"

"No. Why?"

"Never-mind. Anyway, here's the part that I thought you'd find especially interesting, the elements that relate to your dream: for thousands of years whenever a Greek or Roman father sent his son to war, he would look at the stars and pray to Castor and Pollux for his boy's victorious return. And likewise, before a father left for battle he would show his young son this very constellation and teach him the sacred ancient prayer, telling him that wherever he was at night and no matter how far away they were from each other, they would still be close enough together to see these stars. And even if the worse happened and one was killed, like Castor and Pollux they would someday be together again, side-by-side for eternity. Hence the name *Stella Patrim*, the 'Father's Star', that you say your dad told you to wish upon in your dream." He glared suspiciously at the boy. "Are you sure you'd never heard of this before?"

Jeremy shook his head deliberately. "No, Arthur, at least I don't think so."

"Hmm. It's very interesting, if nothing else. I have a celestial map somewhere. We could try to find the constellation on another night when the sky's clearer. I'll print all of this out for you, if you want it."

"Sure I want it."

"Okay. Now I've got to get moving; your aunt is having a brunch reception at her gallery at noon today and needs a truckload of bunt-orange chrysanthemums that are 'not too red and not too yellow'. I'll have the papers for you later."

Jeremy climbed the stairs to his room and fell backwards onto his bed. Had he heard about this tale before? If not, how could he have fabricated it all on his own? Could it be that his father was telling him something from beyond? And if so, what? He'd remembered something about courage and making a wish in his dream, but the story Arthur just read to him was really about praying for protection in battle from the enemy. *And betrayal.*

He had no opinions about the afterlife one way or the other, so there just didn't seem to be any use getting worked-up over heaven or God or Jesus or the devil himself; he figured that like every other breathing creature he'd find out when his time came, and not a moment before.

But then again maybe the Greeks had been on to something.

With a groan he heaved himself up off the bed and made his way across the bedroom to the French doors, then stepped out onto the balcony where he braced himself, elbows locked, against the chilly metal railing. The morning sun ducked behind a splotch of pewter clouds gathered in the east, while frigid winds skated in from the western sea to herd the devilish Santa Anas back to the desert, where they'd conspire until next autumn. His arms erupted into goose bumps so he rubbed his hands together and was about to go inside when he heard a chorus of squawking overhead. He looked skyward and saw that a flock of white gulls dove and banged against one of their own who'd been fortunate enough to have found some leftover morsel. But after only a few moments the battered bird dropped his treasure and flew off, causing a new battle to begin. And Jeremy came to the conclusion that Darwin had been wrong - it wasn't the fittest that survived, but the greediest.

He went inside and shut the doors.

CHAPTER 20

To Jeremy time was like speeding down a two-lane highway; the approaching days crawled toward him like distant cars in the opposing lane—growing imperceptibly from minute specks until they whizzed by in life-sized blurs, then disappeared forever.

And autumn waned. Even before Thanksgiving he noticed how the crowds of beachgoers shrank as the successive Saturdays grew colder, and the usually teeming parking lots along the highway emptied to become chevron-striped rectangles from Venice north to Oxnard. From his balcony he watched the brilliant blue November skies battle, then surrender, to December's gloom. The landscape faded into the likeness of an old photograph: the once supple beach grasses became straw-like, even the clay-colored cliffs paled beige above their assault from the charging waves. And Summer, to Jeremy, seemed a century away.

He'd dragged his desk next to the French doors in order to labor through his never-ending homework pile in view of sea and sky. From his chair he marked the passage of the chilly afternoons by the faint, creeping shadows of the oaks below, and lifted his delighted face at the occasional flock of geese, honking like furious circus clowns, as they headed south. He even relished the air that poured through the doors smelling like fish and pickle juice, so misty it curled his class notes and made his walls shimmer with sweat.

Ballena Beach had become his home.

During study breaks he walked along the beach by himself. And during these moments, while dodging the sliding tides, he soul-searched and he worried.

During the week before Christmas break he'd thumbed nervously through the admission packages his aunt had requested from Stanford, Berkeley and USC. And although he was now doing solid work in all his classes he knew that neither his accumulation of lack-luster grades from Fresno, nor his lukewarm SAT's, would carry him to the kind of school a Tyler was expected to attend.

His only hope was the promise made him by Coach Tunny.

So he trained ferociously five days a week both before and after school, then on Saturdays and Sundays at home, perfecting not only his backstroke, but also his *rock-from-a-slingshot* start. His aunt had built a 50-meter pool for his father, and she was so delighted by Jeremy's commitment to the sport that she kept it heated to regulation temps, an extravagant—in the winter months—78 degrees.

And his body grew more sleekly defined with each passing week, so he shelved his slouching shuffle, once and for all. He wasn't shy in the showers anymore, and he enjoyed doing his stretches poolside with the other studs, in plain view of the students and faculty who slowed as they passed. To class he wore tight T-shirts under open, flapping shirts and even, consciously or not, adopted the universal affectation of every high school jock: *the rolling swagger.* It dawned on him one morning as he toweled himself dry in front of a mirror that with the combination of his swelling musculature and his burgeoning athletic ability he was quickly becoming Coby's equal; the gap separating them was closing. *Fast.*

Then, during the fourth all-city meet of the season Jeremy won first place doing the Backstroke while Coby was awarded top honors in the Breast, and the duo instantly became the team's shooting stars, their trajectories aimed at the Junior Nationals in early Spring. So the pair settled into an uneasy friendship: two golden boys, one adoring the other adored, sharing positions atop their high school's social totem pole.

Meanwhile Jeremy and Reed sprinted through the rapturous days of infatuation, and then ambled into weeks of familiar coziness. At school they were openly regarded as a couple, and they spent every Friday and Saturday evening together watching TV, or cheering for their football team, or catching a movie with Ellie and Coby (who had reconciled the day after Halloween). They spoke every night before bedtime just to say *goodnight*, and occasionally surprised each other with thoughtful gifts and tender, unexpected hugs.

He cared deeply for Reed. He loved spending time with her and being at her side. They laughed together and looked at the world through similar eyes. He figured their relationship had all the qualifications for success provided they could ride-out the gathering storm of college life; she had opted for early decision at Dartmouth and it looked like he would be attending one the schools his aunt had selected in California, as long as everything went according to his plan.

And they talked about having sex. Both were virgins, so each respected the other's caution about moving forward. One night, while kissing and feeling the sensitive zones of the other's body, Reed told him she was ready for more. But Jeremy confessed he was afraid that if they gave in to their desires they wouldn't be able to stop until they *went all the way*, and he didn't want them winding up like his parents, being forced into a marriage and raising an unwanted child. She sensibly agreed. They decided to drop the subject for the present, and when the right time came they would both know and act accordingly.

So Reed kept her desires as well as her nagging dissatisfaction at bay. She tried to stop comparing him to every other boy she had previously held at arm's length who had hungered for her, had craved the taste of her deliciously ripe breasts, or burned hot as a rocket to be *the first*. How passionate they had seemed shouldn't matter, she told herself, after all they were just horny, everyday guys. Jeremy, on the other hand, was worth waiting for. He was intelligent, and sensitive, and gorgeous, and rich.

And a bit distant. To her therapist she compared him with the abused Irish Setter her parents had adopted from a rescue society who spent the first few months regarding her family with indifference. Farrell ignored them until the dinnertime can-opener groaned, appearing only to gobble his food, and then disappearing under some far-off bush in the yard. But her patient love and constant affection had paid off eventually, he was now the picture-perfect dog who retrieved crooked sticks from the crashing waves, slept at the foot of her bed and licked her hand when she had the flu. Would her boyfriend eventually be the same way?

Dr. Cunningham wanted to say that she'd heard of only a few boys who enjoyed licking hands, but many who enjoyed fetching wood, especially with their mouths, but decided the joke would be inappropriate. Instead she suggested that Jeremy was, judging from his past, probably suffering from post traumatic stress disorder stemming from chronic neglect and unexpressed grief. And she suggested that Reed might want to read up on *codependency*, not so much to understand Jeremy, whom she estimated was most likely a textbook example, but to get in touch with her own behavior so she might establish markers and boundaries to protect herself. Finally the doctor suggested that the boy might be homosexual.

Reed dismissed this explanation. She was in love with Jeremy. She thought of him constantly when they were apart—as she knew did Carlo.

He was guiding the Range Rover carefully up the narrow twisting driveway when his aunt's Jaguar flew down around the last curve and almost hit him head-on. They both slammed on their brakes in time to have the noses of their vehicles nearly touch, like unfamiliar dogs sniffing each other at the park.

Taking her hands off the wheel she held her phone up to her ear and waved frantically at him with her other. He held his own hands in the air in the universal 'what do I do?' pantomime. Like an expert valet she threw her car in reverse and gunned the engine, piloting the car, with the phone still at her ear, backward at an alarming speed up the swerving incline toward the flat pad at the top. He followed her at a safe distance.

Once parked she signaled him over. He obeyed, and she noted upon his approach how, like her dear Jonathan, his posture was now military perfect, and his physique was that of an athlete. And she thought *my, but he is gorgeous.* "You're on vacation for a few weeks, yes?" she asked as her window slid down into the door.

"Yes, Aunt Katharine. Today was the last day of school until after New Year's." He took a step closer to her car and she shut off the motor.

"Excellent. The timing couldn't be better." She pulled off her sunglasses. "Have you any specific plans for the next week?"

"Nothing that can't be changed."

"Good. I have a little project for you. Our property at Lake Estrella has been vacant since just after your father's accident. I myself cannot stand the sight of the place, but neither am I willing to sell it although Bill continuously urges me to. I've had a call this morning from the property owners' association telling me the structure is more than beginning to show its neglect, and the neighbors are up in arms. I would like you to drive up there the day after tomorrow and begin assessing the necessary repairs."

Jeremy's face drained. "But I've only had my license for a month, and I've never driven mountain roads before. Aren't you worried that I might, you know, go over the edge too?"

"Nonsense. Lightning seldom strikes in the same spot."

"But wouldn't you rather have Arthur take care of it? He knows a lot more about those things than me."

"Than I, dear boy."

"Than I." He resisted rolling his eyes.

"Arthur has enough to do right here. Whom do you think would cook and shop and fold laundry? *Me?*"

"Don't you mean 'I'?" he asked sharply.

"*Touché!*" She lowered her eyes, suppressing a grin. "Jeremy darling, the chalet needs immediate attention and it's time you took an active part in the family's holdings; many more things of this sort will soon become your responsibility. Besides, this is an opportunity for you to prove your mettle, as you've done so wonderfully with your swimming, and for you to pick up something your father was unable to finish. You know we never even completed furnishing the damned place. And finally, just knowing you're up there may help me to release your father's ghost, once and for all. It's all rather poetic, don't you think?"

"What's poetic about it?"

"Because in so very many ways you're picking up exactly where he left off, only without the disastrous mistakes. It's like we're all getting a second chance now; we can write a happy ending to a formerly tragic tale. So are you up to the challenge?"

"Yes, Aunt Katharine. I'll do my best." His mind raced and an idea dawned. He spoke quickly in order to herd his scattering courage. "But do you think I could take a couple of friends up there with me? I mean, it might be kind of dangerous there by myself."

She narrowed her eyes at him, and then smiled. "Why of course. I should have thought you'd like some company. If you'll give me the names and phone numbers of the young men I'll speak with their parents personally."

He hesitated. "Well, actually, I was hoping to take along Reed and her best friend Ellie and...maybe Ellie's boyfriend Coby."

Silence.

"Jeremy, please don't ask me for such a thing."

He looked down.

"You'll forgive me, dear one, but having barely survived the disaster brought on by too much freedom I am twice as reluctant to *lengthen the lead.*"

"Aunt Katharine." His eyes pleaded. "You know Reed, she's nothing like my mom was and Ellie's her best friend and Coby's mine. It would really make me feel better going there with them. What if something bad happened and I was by myself?"

"So you'll take along the young man...and what about that nice Mexican boy? They both appear to be capable sorts."

Her suggestion was ridiculous. *Coby and Carlo together for an overnighter?* "I think Carlo's already busy, but Coby's only planning on going away with Ellie this weekend to her parents' place in Tahoe—so I'm sure they could change things around if I asked."

"I see." Her cell phone rang suddenly and she snapped it open. "Yes? Hold on a moment please," and then pressing the device to her breast she continued, "Jeremy, if I agree to sending two young ladies with you and this boy to our home, you must promise me something."

"Anything. I promise."

"That sleeping arrangements will follow the age-old rule of propriety: boys and girls in separate rooms."

He cocked an eyebrow. "Aunt Katharine, *I promise.* Separate rooms for boys and girls."

"Very well. I'll have the directions and keys for you tomorrow before I leave on my trip to Alaska; I'll be gone for about two weeks to meet with some *Yup-ik* Eskimo sculptors. I'm sorry this trip will necessitate postponing our Christmas celebration until after the First, but this is the best time for art scouting in Alaska, as the Eskimos have nothing to do but whittle, and no other dealer in their right mind would travel that far north in December, so I get the best 'pick", if you'll forgive the pun. But I promise to make it up to you."

"Please, don't worry about it." He flashed her the smile he'd just recently perfected. "It seems like everyday is Christmas around here."

"Such a charming boy!" She beamed at him. "Which is why I left a present for you to open, which you may at any time. In fact it might come in handy on your trip to the mountain. Now if you'll excuse me I have a particularly demanding former First Lady at my gallery, she's insisting we extend to her a substantial discount on a Sixteenth Century *Chumash* fertility goddess. Can you imagine the nerve? I'll see you at dinnertime."

She sped away and he bounded into the house and ran up the stairs.

Once through the doorway of his room he catapulted across his bed, snatched the phone from its cradle and hit Reed's number on the speed-dial.

"Hey, it's me."

"Baby, I was just missin' you." Her voice was soft as kitten fur.

"Me too. Listen, I have some great news..."

After he filled her in she called Ellie who in turn notified Coby and on Katharine's word the parents relented and the excursion was a done deal.

After his bedtime shower he slipped on some boxers and flopped back onto his bed, staring holes into the ceiling. Going to Lake Estrella with them was a dream about to come true. He pictured taking long walks with Reed on the lakeshore, and sitting together fireside, and watching the sunrise together over the snow-covered mountains.

But he also guessed there would be times when he and Coby would be alone together, and it frightened him. But he could handle it—he always had. After all, this trip would finally allow him time alone with his girlfriend, which would most likely give rise to an event that would smash the doubts about himself once and for all.

He reached up to the lamp on his nightstand and switched it off, sinking the bedroom into the gray velvet of a winter night.

Boys and girls in separate rooms.

He fiddled with the elastic waistband, arched his back, then slipped his boxers off. In three caresses he was hard. A moment later he slipped his feet into his shorts and yanked them back up.

He flipped over onto his belly, and hugged tight his pillow.

He wouldn't betray her anymore.

CHAPTER 21

Coby checked his wristwatch, his arm slung heavily around Ellie's shoulder. "Hey, we've already been gone two hours. How much longer, Tyler?"

Jeremy glanced in the rearview mirror. "My aunt said it takes about an hour to get up to the lake once the freeway ends, which should be soon."

"Are we gonna stop again before we get there?" Ellie asked. "I'm gonna need to pee pretty soon."

"I don't think it's the kind of road with gas stations on it—but I can always pull over someplace."

"Like in Girl Scouts, right Ellie? Remember when we were twelve and you went behind a rock on that long hike in Topanga Canyon?" Reed giggled. "And you got your tennis shoes all muddy and they stank like a cat box for the rest of summer camp."

"I'll hold it." She wrinkled her nose.

A highway sign loomed into view. Fear stabbed his stomach when he saw that it was their turnoff; in a few moments he would be driving along the same perilous road that had claimed his father. He adjusted the angle of his seatback more upright and cracked his window open.

"How long did you say it's been since any of your family's been up here?" Reed asked.

"Almost fifteen years," he replied. He struggled to keep the Rover stable as drafts from a speeding caravan of snowboard-carrying Cherokees and Suburbans flew impatiently past them in the direction of the ski resorts at Big Bear Lake. Jeremy signaled while checking his mirrors and drifting over to the exit lane, then accelerated as he made the wide, easy turn. They were now on their way up Highway 18.

"So what's this place like?" Coby asked.

"Big, I guess. I haven't seen a picture of it, but my aunt said it was one of the nicest houses on the lake when it was new. Someone even wrote an article about it for *Architectural Digest*."

"Won't it be all cold and empty and spooky, considering nobody's been there for such a long time?" Ellie asked. "Which reminds me, what are we going to eat up there, moose fajitas?"

"The property management company turned on the utilities and cleaned the place; and Arthur packed sheets and towels, and those big boxes in the back are our food. I also have my aunt's credit card if there's anything else we need."

"I'm gonna need to puke if that road up there curves as much as it looks like from here," Ellie warned, checking her seatbelt.

"Then why don't we stop and get you something to eat first," Reed suggested cheerfully, "and that way you won't have to stick your finger down your throat after we have lunch at Jeremy's."

"You're just jealous because you wore out your gag reflex in middle school," Ellie countered. "But at least you got all A's to show for it."

The girls cackled and Jeremy caught Coby throwing him a dirty grin through the rearview mirror. He raised an eyebrow and tossed one back.

It was just before noon by the time Jeremy had driven halfway up the steep, twisting road aptly named *Rim of the World Drive*. The serpentine asphalt hugged the rocky mountainside where the path had been blasted out of granite many decades before, leaving scarred and barren inclines on the left side and dizzying cliffs on the right. He clutched the steering wheel tightly: was it this next curve? Or had it been that really sharp one they just passed? Without realizing it his speed had dropped below the posted limit; he checked his mirrors and saw that the impatient whip of SUVs chasing his tail had lengthened.

"Better pull over at this next turn-out, Granny McSlowpoke," Coby said while looking back over his shoulder. Jeremy cranked the wheel to the right and swung off the main road onto a lookout point and stopped.

"Baby you look sick. You OK?" Reed put the back of her hand to his forehead.

"Maybe I'm just carsick. I need some air." He cut the ignition, set the brake and popped his seat belt. The others released themselves, and then four doors *chunked*.

Frigid winds, like a flock of meddlesome ghosts, buffeted the two pairs as they strolled to the edge of an observation platform at the cliff's edge to scan the panorama. From there they saw the valley floor below, deep as an emerald Grand Canyon, woven-over with bottle-green pines and black oaks, slate-gray boulders and patches of snow. Ominous rain clouds overhead obscured the peaks of the mountains, while far to the west, peeking between the foothills, the city of San Bernardino looked rusty under its blanket of smog.

Jeremy realized how the beauty and the danger of this place were intertwined, like life and death, and wondered how he'd feel coming here today with his father instead of his friends. He imagined Jonathan from the photograph, looking older now, walking out toward the bench next to the railing at the edge of the lookout. He turned and called him over, and Jeremy saw himself running to catch up. "I can see now why my dad loved this place," he told Reed. "It really is incredible."

"If you think this is nice you should see *Val d'Isere* this time of year," said Ellie, know-it-all-style.

"Bitch, shut up," said Reed. She reached from behind Jeremy and shoved her hands deep into his coat pockets. "This high altitude makes her even more uppity than usual, if that's possible."

"So what happened back there Tyler? You were driving like a pussy." Coby punched him playfully on the shoulder.

"Yep, guess I was," he replied, not looking his way.

"You big stupid ding-dong," Ellie chided, pulling her boyfriend by the arm. She stood on tiptoe and whispered into his ear.

"Shit, how was I supposed to know?" he asked. Then he turned to Jeremy. "Hey, sorry dude...I didn't know this was the place."

"It's OK. It was a long time ago." He grabbed Reed's hand. "Come on, let's get going. I can't wait to get off this fucking road."

Sometime later the Rover slowed to a halt in front of 15 Shoreline Drive. Coby jumped out, shoved the squeaking gates open then climbed back in. Then they rolled crunching along through the gravel driveway toward the looming structure at the end.

"Oh," Reed exclaimed, clutching Jeremy's hand. "What a *beautiful* house!"

"It's a chalet, you bimbo," Ellie snickered.

"You're both wrong, it's a mansion," Coby corrected.

Whatever it is, it'll be mine soon, thought Jeremy.

Having been designed and built in the highest contemporary mountain style of the Eighties, the structure looked like a hulking, inverted 'V' made from rough-cut cedar that supported walls of forest-reflecting glass. Jeremy figured it was as long as four or so normal houses jammed shoulder-to-shoulder, and was nearly three stories tall at the shingled roof's center peak. From what he could see the backside of the home cradled an inlet of the lake, and its strip of beach was shaded by a grove of redwoods, and punctuated by giant boulders. As Jeremy approached the front door with keys in-hand he discovered that the house was not only surrounded by huge rocks, but in places had been built atop them, as if protecting a nest of eggs.

"That's the weirdest looking house I've ever seen," Coby said.

"My aunt said it's supposed to look like an eagle landing." He fitted the tarnished key into the door's lock and turned it. The door swung open. "She wanted something that would piss off the conservative neighbors after they pooled their money to outbid an African American family who was trying to buy a lakefront property."

"I think it's gorgeous," Reed sighed.

"I think it looks like a cross between Noah's Ark and the Stealth Bomber." Ellie added, checking her reflection in the dusty windows flanking the entry.

Moments later the foursome stood on the jagged flagstone floor of the foyer. "Phew! Smells like a dog house in here," Coby said, dropping his gym bag onto the floor.

Ellie traipsed delicately down the wide stone stairs to the sunken living room, and then dropped her backpack and purse on the huge sectional that faced the water. "My uncle in Telluride always opens every window in his chalet and cranks the heat up to ninety," she said, spinning lazily then flopping on the sofa. "It's the only way to air out a place like this...like draining and refilling a dirty swimming pool."

"Then let's do that," Jeremy said, grabbing Reed by the hand. "We can explore at the same time." He located the thermostat and adjusted it, then the pair zigzagged from room to room throwing open the windows and doors.

They climbed their way to the third floor, which possessed a cavernous master suite with its own fireplace and bath, as well as a dusty library with panoramic views of the sparkling lake.

"Well, here we are," Jeremy whispered, grasping Reed's waist and pulling her body to his.

"Finally," she replied. They kissed, savoring the familiar tastes of each other's mouths, then pulled away finally with a mutual peck, like a period after a sentence.

"That was nice," Reed murmured.

"Sure was. We'd better get back downstairs so we can unload and get settled."

She led him downstairs by the hand, where they found their friends stretched out on the sectional, lip-locked and panting.

"Hey, you freaks," said Reed, hands on hips. "Do you think you could tear yourselves away for a sec to help unload?"

"In a minute," Coby replied. "I gotta wait 'til I can stand up without it breakin' off."

"You pig!" Ellie screeched, pushing him onto the floor and throwing a pillow at him. He grabbed it and held in front of his crotch, then stood up.

"Come on, Tyler," he said. "We'll do the men's work while the girls fix us a snack. I can tell I'm gonna need all my energy for tonight." He leered at his girlfriend and adjusted himself, then threw the pillow back at her, hitting her in the face.

As they neared the car Jeremy felt a hand on his shoulder.

"Hey," he whispered. "I know it's none of my business but, have you and Reed, you know...hooked up all the way yet?"

Should he be truthful? Why not, it was almost a done deal already. "Not all the way, not yet," he replied, lifting a box. "And you're right, it's none of your business."

"Then why'd you just tell me, dick wad?" He grinned. "So then...do the two of you have anything 'special' planned for this trip?"

"Gentlemen never tell," his face reddened. "All I can say is this is the first time we've been away together...so what do you think?"

"I ain't sayin' what I think," he laughed, and Jeremy saw that his blue eyes matched the clear mountain sky above his head. "Just let me know if you need any tips." He threw an arm around his shoulder. "Just think of me as the big brother you never had."

"Oh sure, like I'd ever take your advice on women," Jeremy laughed, shrugging his arm off. "That would be the end of me and Reed, for sure."

"The offer stands. I'm just a guy trying to help his buddy get his needs met."

They hefted the flimsy cardboard boxes then staggered toward the open double doors. Jeremy could see the girls whispering and huddled together on the sofa.

"It's already after two," Jeremy said, heading for the kitchen. "We should get unpacked and find some firewood."

"I saw a big pile on that side of the house." Reed pointed.

He set his box down on the dining table. "It's supposed to get dark and cold really early up here, so we should set up everything before it gets too late."

"OK by me." Coby picked up his gym bag. "So who's sleeping where?"

Jeremy glanced at Reed.

She looked at the ceiling.

It was now or never. "We're taking the master," he told them all.

Jeremy looked at her and she looked back and he saw the delight in her eyes.

CHAPTER 22

S o, like, what are you gonna do first to this big old place?" Coby mumbled, his words thick with the last of their pizza.

"I'll get the important stuff fixed first." Jeremy pushed himself up from the wooden coffee table, around which the four had just finished their delivered dinner, then stooped to collect their dirtied plates. "You know...like the roof and the plumbing. Stuff like that."

"If it was me, the first thing I'd get is a big fuckin' plasma screen to put up where that buffalo head is." Coby gulped some soda, then pointed with his empty glass to the decapitated bovine hanging over the fireplace veneered with white, jig-sawed quartz rocks.

"I think those head things are disgusting," Reed declared, flipping through an ancient *People* magazine. "What kind of coward hunts defenseless animals, anyways?"

"My uncle used to hunt a lot," Jeremy told them. "He shot that one. And he has this big polar bear rug in his office too. But he's really a nice guy."

"Nobody nice hunts," corrected Ellie. "I mean, who would want that thing around? It's like a trophy you won for murder, only with eyes that follow you like it's still alive, accusing you...accusing you...accusing you."

"Kind of like *The Telltale Heart*?" asked Reed excitedly.

Coby lifted his head. "What the hell are you girls talking about?"

"Shhhh, my beauty." She leaned over and pressed her index finger to his lips. "God didn't create you to understand literary references."

He snarled at her and tried to bite her finger. She squealed, then stood up. "Reedie-pie, tomorrow we should explore this place. I'll bet there's lots of funky junk tucked away."

"I *love* looking through other people's closets," Reed agreed. "You never know how many skeletons you'll find, and what labels they'll be wearing." She turned to Jeremy. "Do you think your family left any of their old clothes here?"

"Probably." Jeremy nodded. "Go see what you can find."

"Shall we?" Ellie asked Reed slyly.

"Why, yay-yes!" She exclaimed. Ellie snatched Reed's hand and pulled her to her feet, then the two disappeared chattering up the stairs.

"Those two," Coby began, after the girls were gone. "I love thinking of them jiggling around in their bras and panties right now playing dress-up. And maybe..." he whispered "...even a little *slap and tickle, pass the pickle.*"

"Ellie and Reed aren't like *that*," said Jeremy dismissively.

"Who knows, man. Nothing about them surprises me." He yawned leaning backwards with his hands clasped, biceps popping, behind his head. "Ellie's got a mind of her own and so does Reed, and we're all old enough to make our own decisions about stuff like that, don't you think?"

"Sure, but wouldn't it bother you? I mean you guys are together just like us, and I wouldn't want Reed messing around with someone else."

Coby lifted himself from the floor and sat next to Jeremy in the spot vacated by Reed. "Hey, if it bugged Ellie every time I connected with someone besides her, and vice-versa, we wouldn't be together. Believe me, I'm not a jealous dude. We love each other and nothing can change that...but we're not ready for marriage—at least *I'm* not." He chuckled. "Besides, how would you know if you're with the right person if you limit your choices? It's like, we all need to test drive the kind of car we're gonna to drive for life—like a minivan or a sports car," he laughed, meeting Jeremy's eyes. "Or even a sparkly pink Monte *Carlo*."

"Carlo's a great guy, Coby. You guys give him way too much shit."

"Look," he began. "I don't have any problem with gay guys, some of my best friends are that way."

"Yeah?" Jeremy raised an eyebrow.

"Sure." He lowered his voice. "And just about every dude I know, even some of the total jocks have messed around with guys." He cracked a smile. "And now they know for sure they like chicks better than dicks. It kind of cures 'em." He leaned back onto the couch. "But what bugs me about your little girlfriend Carlo is he thinks how he gets off should be some big ol' political statement...but instead he's made himself into a big ol' bull's-eye." He nodded. "I'd be careful about hanging around with him too much, if I was you." His eyes shrank into dark blue marbles.

"Folks is already talking, Tyler. You should be hanging out with me and my bros—we're real men."

Jeremy startled at the phrase. "Carlo's real too, in his own way."

"Yeah. Reeeaaaal queer."

The girls emerged suddenly at the top of the staircase. Reed stood in a strapless ivory floor-length formal and Ellie posed in a crisp black *Chanel* suit. She had twisted her hair up into a bun and wore a pearl necklace and earrings.

Coby woofed.

"Oh my God, your mom has such great taste!" Reed nearly shrieked as she sashayed down the stairs.

"Actually those are probably my aunts," he answered sourly.

"You guys should see what you can find upstairs. We saw lots of nice men's clothes too!" suggested Reed.

"Too bad we don't know any nice men," Ellie joked as she followed Reed down, suddenly looking thirty.

"Come on, Tyler. We can't have them lookin' prettier than us," Coby said, pushing up from the sofa. The boys leapt up the stairs to the second floor where they began twisting doorknobs and sliding open mirrored doors. After unsuccessfully searching five or so sparsely furnished rooms they eventually made their way into the master suite on the top floor.

Coby flew onto the center of the massive four-poster bed and, mimicking Reed's southern drawl, began gyrating provocatively. "Oh, give it to me, Jer-uh-maay," he moaned, "I need to get laid *real bad!*"

Jeremy jumped on top of Coby and straddled his chest, laughing.

"I'll give it to you, bitch!" he sneered. Coby grabbed him by the shoulders, tossed him over then climbed atop him, exchanging their positions.

"But I like to be on top, Jer-uh-maay!" he squealed mockingly, fluttering his eyelids and pinning the other's shoulders with his knees. His swelling crotch hovered inches from Jeremy's face. Both boys panted through grins.

Their eyes held.

"OK, OK I give. You can be on top, *this time...*" he conceded, laughing, and Coby jumped off him and stumbled to the closet's dressing area.

"Come on bitch, let's see what we can find. Those girls look as hot as

I feel and I don't want Ellie to cool down. Now what's in here?" He slid the mirrored doors open to reveal rows of dusty suits and skiwear. They scanned the rows of clothes and began pulling things out, but found everything wool was moth-pocked, and the skiwear looked ugly and too hot for indoors.

"Must be my uncle's clothes," Jeremy said. "If you find something you like it'll probably fit, you two are about the same size."

"Ain't nobody the same size as me," Coby leered, squeezing his crotch.

"Yeah, well then why isn't your girlfriend smiling?" he laughed.

"And which girlfriend do you mean?" His eyes sparkled. "Hey, Tyler, with your looks and bod you could have as many as you wanted, just like me. Just remember: never get caught with your pants down."

"Now that's really some useful relationship advice, *big bro*," he replied. "Come on, let's keep looking, they're waiting."

"Hey, look at these old bathrobes!" Coby said, shoving his hand between the rows of shirts, pants and jackets.

"Those aren't bathrobes, they're smoking jackets," Jeremy said, remembering that Arthur had corrected him for making the same mistake early in his stay. "That's why they have matching pajama pants. My uncle's got tons of them at home."

"Now these are cool!" He pulled out one of chartreuse and gold paisley silk with black velvet lapels, and held it in front of himself while looking in the mirror. "This is gonna make Ellie hornier than a nun!" Meanwhile Jeremy searched through the selection for one that suited him, and discovered one made of rich scarlet satin, with chocolate brown velvet lapels trimmed with gold braid. The boys quickly peeled off their clothes and found themselves standing side by side in their boxer shorts, surrounded by floor-to-ceiling mirrors.

"Commando, my friend?"

"You mean no underwear?" Jeremy asked.

"Boxers under these pants'll look like diapers; they'll ruin the effect."

"Whatever you say," he answered meekly.

It seemed to happen in slow motion. Coby's shorts slipped down to his ankles and were kicked across the room. Then Jeremy did the same. They stood naked, an arm's length apart, side-by-side. Their chests rose and fell in unison. Jeremy's eyes fell, with no stream of water to hide his line of sight, boldly onto Coby's cock and he thought *if I reached out right now what would he do?*

Coby took the silk pants in his hand, then bent over and slid in one perfectly muscled leg at a time. He pulled them past his knees, then up mid-thigh and stopped, leaving himself exposed provocatively. Jeremy froze, then mimicked his same movements, but lost his courage and pulled the waist home. Coby likewise pulled his pants all the way up and they both tied their drawstrings.

The reverse strip-tease and the rub of the satin against his skin began to arouse him. He turned his back and slipped the robe over his shoulders, then cinched it quickly at the waist.

Coby did the same. They admired themselves in the mirrors. "Jesus, Tyler, we look like old-time movie stars."

He had to agree. The robes were cut in such a way as to compliment a more mature man's sagging physique, so the effect on the young athletes was breathtaking. The satin and silk draped exquisitely around their square shoulders while falling open at their necks down to just above their belly-buttons, framing like artwork the sculptured pectoral and abdominal ridges hewn from their years of grueling swim practice.

"Come on, we better get back downstairs," said Jeremy.

"Just a sec, I thought I saw something else in here..." He bent over into the closet, searching for whatever had caught his eye. Jeremy, safe now to stare, admired the way the flimsy silk stretched over Coby's Olympian buttocks, looking like a statue artfully painted with green and gold paisley. "Here!" he announced at last, straightening himself up and turning to offer Jeremy a pair of black velvet slippers embroidered with gold. Jeremy reached for them but Coby instead folded down onto one knee. "Allow me." Jeremy lifted his right foot into Coby's hand, and the slipper slid perfectly into place. Then he raised his left foot, but this time Coby held his calf muscle and squeezed it gently as he pushed on the delicate shoe. Jeremy's breath stopped. Coby set his foot back down and looked up at him, face at crotch level, smiling.

"Is...there another pair for you?" Jeremy asked, trying mask his quickened breath.

"These are all too small for me; I'll go barefoot. Come on."

They made their way from the bedroom down the stairway to the landing that hovered over the living room, then posed scowling and with their chests puffed out like models in a catalogue, waiting for the girls to take notice.

Ellie was the first to catch sight. "Why Reed, I think we've just been transported to the Playgirl Mansion," she sighed from the sofa, her pumps already discarded, her toes wiggling on the top edge of the coffee table.

Reed's eyes followed the descending figures trying to gage which was the more splendid, but realized quickly that they were equally stunning. As Jeremy made his way across the room to her, she ogled him from head to toe. "If you were running for *Playmate of the Year,*" she murmured, "you would've just won."

He leaned over her and planted his lips briefly, yet wetly, onto hers. "Then we make the perfect pair, don't you think?"

"Like milk and honey," Reed cooed.

"More like silk..." Ellie tugged at Jeremy's robe, then pointed at Reed, "...and horny."

"Bitch don't start with me." Reed wagged her finger.

They spent the next hour in front of the crackling fireplace, languishing in their borrowed finery beneath the bison's angry stare. Jeremy's head lay cradled in Reed's lap, her hand gently stroking the hair off his forehead, while Ellie alternately stomped around or sat, gesticulating constantly as she rattled off elaborate decorating ideas for the grand yet neglected home. And Coby stretched himself flat on the floor closest to the leaping flames, occasionally hurling friendly insults between long bouts of silence.

Around midnight Jeremy noticed that a snowfall began dusting white the tree boughs beyond the windows, and this made him think of Christmas.

And Christmas made him think of his father.

He imagined a younger Aunt Katharine sitting where he lay now, smiling contentedly as Jonathan rolled himself a snowman out on the deck, or leapt up the staircase, or dug into a bowl of *Cheerios* in the kitchen. He saw him diving off their private dock then swimming capably in the rippling summer waters, whooping and hollering, scaring ducks into the sky.

A longing twisted in him to know this man...to feel like his son.

But he had known him once. Somewhere within his brain lived a memory, some neuronal impression that held, like a ghostly tape recorder, his strong young voice. And he made himself try to remember the sound, to conjure up the timbre and music of his voice calling *Jeremy*. But only silence echoed.

His dad was as dead as that buffalo.

"Baby, what're you thinkin' about?" Reed asked.

He pushed his lips into a smile. "Nothing important."

"I'm thinking of a nice warm bed," Coby announced from the floor. "I say we hit it, 'cause I'm beat." He pushed himself up with a grunt, then stood over Ellie and offered his hand to help her up, which she hit playfully with her foot.

"I'll go in when I'm good and ready, I'm not the least bit sleepy yet. Are you, Reed darling?"

"Why, the night is young, I must say," she answered coyly.

Coby glared at Ellie. She batted her eyes.

"Whatever," he said. "See you all in the morning." He turned and ascended the stairs two at a time, then vanished into the blackness at the top.

"Why didn't you go with him?" Reed whispered, her brows furrowed.

"You know he only wants what he can't have, and this way I can make sure he won't be asleep the minute after I climb in." She stared impassively into the fire, her face and clothes flickering tangerine. "This whole stupid thing is just wrong; it felt like a mistake the minute we got back together."

"You are one crazy girl." Reed shook her head.

"But you guys love each other," Jeremy said. "Shouldn't you try and make it work?"

"Who said anything about us loving *each other*?" she laughed. "That's exactly what one of our problems is, *I love him*, but he's incapable of loving anyone but himself. Why else would he break up with me, then bring Brynn, that world-famous crack whore, to my party? I made jokes all night about shoving her off the balcony into the water, but it was really *him* I wanted to throw overboard. And the worst part is that he knows if he makes me jealous I'll go crazy unless he comes back. It's all a game to him."

"But why would he do that, you know, try to get you back, unless he loved you?" Reed asked.

She shook her head. "You don't know how his mind works; it's like his ego hunts for sport. He just has this affect on people. It's like his looks and how charming he can be combine to make this weapon that he throws like…a sexual grenade. And people don't know what's hit them." She sighed. "I've seen him do this since he was fourteen, to girls and teachers and moms and scoutmasters and the geek behind the McDonald's counter. It's whoever he needs something from. And since I know this, I'm always asking myself *what is it he wants from me?* Or am I, like he tells me, the exception?

"And in spite of everything that's wrong about us we fit together somehow, maybe because we both want what we shouldn't have. No one knows me like he does, which is both wonderful and scary as shit." She pulled her knees up tight to her chest. "And most guys are scared of me, they're intimidated. But Coby's not," she whispered. "He's one of the only guys I've ever known who isn't afraid to be completely himself around me…and somehow that helps me be more myself, too."

"You've gotta move on, baby-girl," said Reed. "There's a lotta guys out there that would love to be with you, and would treat you like you deserve to be treated, every single day."

"That's for sure," Jeremy agreed, nodding with conviction.

Silence descended, then a round of yawns volleyed. Ellie swung her legs off the sofa, planted them on the carpet and stood. "It's been about ten minutes; he'll probably be all worked up in there by himself. If I wait any longer he'll be snoring and I'll have to sleep in a wet spot." She smiled, waving. "Goodnight." Then she turned and headed towards the stairs.

"Goodnight Ellie," they answered in unison.

And then they were alone.

"Reed?"

"Um-hmm?"

"Let's go upstairs." He clutched her hand and pulled her gently up from the sofa as the last of the embers glittered, then died.

CHAPTER 23

S tay there, I'll be right back. Could you light the candles?" She tiptoed to the bathroom and closed the door. He untied the elegant braided cord encircling his waist, paused, and then re-knotted it. In the nightstand he found some matches and lit the twin red candles— thick as soda cans—which she'd set out on each of the nightstands, and then switched off the lights. The sputtering candles made the thrusting shadows of the bedposts shiver against the walls.

How was he going to get through this? He had little information to go on and, it seemed, even less instinct. What was he supposed to do first, and then after that? He'd heard that the first time was painful for girls; how could he experience any kind of pleasure when he'd be hurting her? What if he wasn't able to stay hard? How could their relationship continue if he found himself uninterested in her, or even—God forbid— totally turned-off?

"I'll be out in a second," sang her cheerful, muffled voice from behind the door.

Moments later she emerged wearing a crème-colored bra and panties, and a confident smile. "What do you think? Is this appropriate attire for the lady of the manor?" Her coffee-colored skin glowed in the flickering light, and her hair, which she usually pulled back, fell down to her shoulders.

"Probably not, but I'll never tell," he said with a grin. "My God, you look so...incredibly beautiful."

She stepped toward him. "No more than you, baby," she whispered as she clutched the lapels of his robe and slid the garment from his shoulders. It fell in a silken heap on the carpet. "Like I said, we go together like milk and honey."

Their mouths opened to each other. Her hands smoothed his bare chest, then he hugged her close to his body. The warmth of her against his naked torso stirred him. He began to relax.

Her mouth broke away from his. "It feels like I've waited my entire life for tonight."

"Me too. I can't believe this is finally happening." As their tongues rejoined, his hands caressed her breasts and pressed them and kneaded them gently, like tender fruit.

"Here, let me help," she gasped, closing her fingertips onto the center-point between the two generous cups. With a *thick* her bra fell open. His hands slipped the disabled garment from her shoulders, then instinctively searched out her delicate nipples. They hardened under his touch.

"Baby, you're so gentle," she cooed. "You sure you've never done this before?"

A smile split his face. "Beginner's luck." He bent down and suckled her.

"You don't feel like a beginner," she gasped, stroking the hair on his head. "Let's get into bed." She pulled his mouth to hers and licked his lips, pushing him backward together as a unit joined at the mouth, like erotic Siamese twins, until his buttocks bumped hard against one of the bed's posts. Their progress stopped and she looked at him expectantly.

Was it his turn to be the aggressor? Her eyes told him *yes*. So he turned her around, grasped her shoulders and laid her carefully back onto the cushy new comforter Arthur had so thoughtfully sent along. Her arms locked around his neck and she pulled his body up on top of herself.

"Won't my weight hurt you?" he asked.

"Only a little," she murmured, "but I like it. I want to feel your whole body covering mine." She reached between their bodies and, with a trembling hand, pulled the knotted drawstring of his pajama pants loose. "I want to feel all of you, baby. Inside me."

Their eyes held, searching for deep truths.

"I love you Jeremy."

She'd been determined not to be the first to say it on this night of nights, but the restless phrase had fluttered out of her mouth before she could slam its cage shut.

"I love you too, Reed."

She slipped her hands under his waistband to the top of his buttocks then caressed them, delighted by their velvet solidity. His breaths deepened, and he began stiffening between her legs. She felt his unmistakable pressure against her and relaxed; her doubts about him, as well as her therapist's admonitions, were unfounded. She felt it finally safe to surrender herself to the coming pleasure.

They were home free.

Her hands began sliding his pants down past his hips. "I want you Jeremy. I want you so bad."

"I want you too." His lips grazed hers, and then traced a trail down her neck. While leaning on his right arm his left pushed his pajamas off and his hardness brushed her thigh.

She'd better say something.

"Baby, isn't there something you need?" she whispered urgently.

Her question shattered his single-mindedness into sudden jumbled static, but he forced a short mental inventory anyway.

Shit!

"Reed, I'm sorry I…guess I forgot to buy some before we came up. But hold on and I'll run downstairs and get some from Coby." He pulled up his pants and pushed himself off her then stood. "I'm sure he's got some." He picked up his robe from the floor and threw it on, then turned to go. His hand was on the doorknob when her voice froze him.

"You forgot to buy condoms," she said calmly, and he turned to face her.

He saw that she looked puzzled.

"Hey, it's not a big deal it's…just that this whole trip was last minute and I had so much to pull together and I was nervous about driving up here on *that road* and I had way too much on my mind. I'm sorry. I blew it." He needed to see this event through to the end, and nothing was going to stand in his way.

"Mr. 'I-Don't-Want-To-Wind-Up-Like-My-Parents-With-An-Unwanted-Child' *forgot* to buy condoms."

He crossed his arms. "We said that when the time was right we'd both know it, but out of respect for you I didn't want to assume that this trip was going to be *that time*. I thought we'd discuss it more before it actually happened."

"Discuss it more?" she asked, her eyebrows identical arches. "*Discuss it more?* What more could we discuss?" She pulled a corner of the comforter up to cover herself. "You must be the only teenage guy in the world who doesn't have a condom in his wallet at this very moment. Even the ugliest, biggest losers carry condoms, if only to prove that they've actually got a dick."

"Look, Reed, I'm sorry. This is all kinda new to me."

"Oh, I get it. Wanting to make love to your girlfriend is something that's new to you." She tumbled out of bed holding her bra across her chest, then stomped to the bathroom where she retrieved her robe. She tied it on hastily, her breasts jiggling underneath. "Look, Jeremy. In case you haven't noticed, something's wrong here. I've tried to deny it since almost the beginning but there's just too many things that don't add up."

"What do you mean?" he asked defensively. "You've never said anything about this before."

"I mean that you're *just not normal.*" She stepped over to the bed and sat on the edge, arms folded.

"Would you mind telling me exactly what you mean by that?"

"Look, don't get angry, I'm just trying to make sense out of all this." She looked down, rubbing her temples. "What I mean is that you're just not the way guys are usually with me, and I feel like I'm always getting things started when it comes to us being…together." She cinched the tie on her robe and Jeremy mimicked her action. "I'm not trying to brag when I say this or make you jealous, Jeremy, but ever since I can remember boys wanted to be with me, to touch me, and they were really obvious; sometimes it was frustrating just keeping them off me, you know? And then you came along and I didn't have to deal with things like that." She raised her eyes to his. "At first I thought it was because you were raised right. You know, a gentleman…which you are." She half-smiled. "And then as time went on I started getting this feeling about our relationship—that we should be going through stages and we're not. Like when someone has a baby and they compare it with their friends' kids knowing that around a certain age it learns to crawl, and after that it stands then walks then…whatever. And I think even you see that we're not going through the stages like we should."

"What are you saying?" he whispered, his eyes a show of calculated ignorance.

"What I'm saying, Jeremy, is I think we've already got our unwanted child…and it's hopelessly retarded. Our relationship's not working, for whatever reason, and it probably can't." She blew out a heavy sigh and her shoulders collapsed.

"All this because I forgot to buy a condom?"

"Look. Maybe I'm overreacting, and if I am it'll all look different in the morning. I think we both need to sleep on it. But in the meantime I think it'd be better if we didn't stay in here together, not tonight at least."

"Yeah, I think so too," he nodded, deflated. "I'll go downstairs and sleep on the couch, none of the other beds are made up." He snatched a couple blankets from the foot of the bed. "Look Reed, for what it's worth, I'm sorry. You're the last person on this earth I ever wanted to hurt."

"I know, Jeremy. Like I said, maybe things will look different tomorrow." She gave him a sad smile. "Goodnight."

He trudged down the stairway past the second floor, noticing as he passed that Ellie and Coby's door was closed and the light was out. He then continued to the first floor, clutching the handrail for support, feeling exhausted yet jittery, like the nights he used to wait up for his mother to come home.

At once he saw that the living room was ablaze with flickering shadows.

The Fireplace! He'd forgotten to douse it before going to bed!

In five leaps he was down the stairs, prepared to see the worst. But all that met his eyes were some hungry flames licking a giant log, and Coby stretched out on the sofa warming his shirtless body, the lower part of him covered in his green paisley pajamas, his feet piggy-pink from the heat of the fire.

"Hey, Tyler." He raised his eyebrows and his mouth made a crooked smile. "To what do I owe this pleasure?"

"I...couldn't sleep. And I didn't want to wake-up Reed so I figured I'd sleep down here." He stood at the edge of the sofa, his bunched-up blankets hugged to his chest.

"I couldn't sleep either. Have a seat, bro." He motioned to the cushion next to him.

He sat instead at the end.

"So...how'd it go?" Coby asked casually.

"Great," Jeremy growled. "It was *great.*"

"Dude, I'm happy for you." The fire popped like a cap gun. "By the way, did you know that it's a scientific fact that once we guys get off we can't stay awake? It's like *Wham! Bam! Snore.*"

"And?"

"And the reason I bring it up, my friend, is it means that if you're here, wide awake, then something went wrong and you guys didn't do it."

"Again, none of your business."

"Yeah, well don't feel bad." He reached across and gently shook Jeremy's shoulder. "We didn't either. It's like Ellie's been rehearsing her never-ending bitch routine ever since we got back together." He stretched his arms back over his head and clasped his hands behind his neck, then flexed with a grunt. Jeremy saw that his armpits were clean as a statue's, having been recently shaved even though there was no swimming practice until after break was over. "I guess I'll never figure out what that little bitch wants from me." He yawned, flexing his biceps again, then moved his hands down from behind his head to the waistband of his pajamas, digging the tips of his fingers in to the first knuckle.

Jeremy could think of nothing to respond with and his mouth was dry, so he got up from the couch.

"Hey now, where you goin'?"

"Get some water. Want some?"

"Nah." He shook his head. "What I want I ain't gettin', at least not tonight." He grabbed at his crotch and they both laughed.

Jeremy turned and made for the kitchen. His face felt suddenly sunburned.

He stood at the spigot, filling his glass and thinking *here we are, alone.* And just after the naked dressing room episode. How many shameful nights had his brain assembled similar fantasies, and then zapped them down his spinal cord to be realized by his tremulous hands?

Could it be?

No. This was no fantasy. For starters everyone knew that Coby Carson loved to fuck girls, and Jeremy wasn't a girl. And neither was he gay. He was reading too much into this. He needed to relax.

The water running over the glass and down his wrist startled him. He shut off the water and gulped some down. He'd finish the rest with Coby then find a bedroom for himself. He returned to the sofa, glass half-empty, and folded himself carefully down into his spot.

"So-" Coby cleared his throat "-what's up with you two?"

"Things are great with us. *Like I said.*"

"Then why are you guys, like, taking it so slow?" He rubbed one hand through his hair and slipped the other down his pants to the second knuckle.

"We just want to be sure; we don't want to rush into anything we're going to regret," he said. "You know, so we don't have to keep breaking up and getting back together twenty thousand times."

"Oh, I get it. Ha-ha. You're making fun of me and Ellie." Coby smirked momentarily, and then his face became serious. "You know, dude, I think I know the *real* reason you can't sleep at night."

The fire popped suddenly, accentuating Jeremy's lack of response. His heart boomed in his ears.

"Jeremy Tyler," Coby whispered, nodding his lovely head. *"I know your little secret."*

CHAPTER 24

He stared hard into the flames. How could Coby know? He'd been so careful. This shouldn't be happening, especially not now—not after the disastrous encounter upstairs. "I don't know what you're talking..." he began to protest but his words died, strangled in his throat. Oddly, his crotch tingled again with that familiar soda pop feeling.

"Tyler, come on! You've been with Reed for a couple months now and you still haven't done it with her?" He shrugged, laughing easily. "And she's one of the hottest bitches at school, and then you throw away the chance to do it with her even when there're no parents within *miles* and you're sleeping in the same bed? It doesn't take *Sherlock Homo* to figure that one out," he laughed.

"I forgot the condoms, that's all. I forgot the fucking condoms and she freaked out." He was pleased that he sounded convincing. "We just don't want to live with any mistakes, like my parents did."

Coby stood from his end of the sofa, shuffled over then sat gently next to him. "We're buds, right?"

Jeremy tipped his head.

"And whatever I say won't change that, right?"

"Yeah?"

"OK then, because I've been wanting to get something out in the open for a long time and I figured you did too." He was so close now that his breath warmed Jeremy's cheek. "I've seen the way you look at me," he whispered. "Every day we're at school, in the gym showers, by the pool, even in your rearview mirror on the way up here I saw it. It's unmistakable, dude. *Unmistakable.*"

He felt stunned, embarrassed, nakedly transparent. It was as if Coby had smashed open the lockbox in his head and was now flipping through the porno magazines—*starring themselves*—that he kept stashed there.

"You're wrong." He turned and bravely met his stare, but as he did so a current passed between them and he felt more of the stirring between his legs.

"If you want me to say it I will." He smiled then crossed his arms across his naked chest. "Then, you tell me if I'm right or wrong. But either way, I promise I'll help you with this mess you're in with Reed."

"*You'll* help me," Jeremy laughed.

"You need help."

"Fuck you. If you've got something to say then say it. *But I don't need your help.*"

"Ooh. I see you've grown some balls since we first met."

"Just say it, Coby! Say it or shut the fuck up!"

"Fine. You want to like girls but you think you like boys, but you've never been with either one so you're not sure."

Jeremy knew that he was officially cornered but he couldn't surrender; too much was at stake, he'd reject this until the day he died. But why was it that the more he denied what Coby suggested the more sexually aroused he became? With horror, he realized that the flesh between his legs felt now as hard as tree branch. He leaned forward and adjusted his pajamas.

Is this what Ellie had been referring to? "You're an asshole. You think everyone in the world is in love with you."

"Now who said anything about you liking *me* that way," he said, innocently. "But go ahead and tell me I'm wrong." He inched closer, his voice sweet and low. "Tell me you wouldn't like to hold another guy, a hot naked dude in bed with you. And since *you* brought it up, look at me and say you wouldn't dig for us to be in that bed like we were earlier." He traced a finger along the side of Jeremy's thigh then rested his hand on his knee. "Picture it. Just you and me...making each other feel the way only two guys can." Twin orange infernos were reflected in his violet eyes. "Now you go ahead and tell me I'm wrong, my friend, and I'll believe you."

"Yes, you're wrong!" He was shaking, his composure finally shattered. His painful erection now strained against the flimsy silk of his pajamas, tenting the crotch provocatively. He held his body perfectly still, knowing that even the slightest friction from the slippery fabric would cause him to ejaculate.

"Say it, Tyler. Tell someone the truth for once." His eyes dropped to Jeremy's lap and lingered there for more than a moment, then lifted seductively to meet the other's humiliated stare. "I see you've already answered my question."

"I don't know," he answered nervously. He'd never disclosed *that* to anyone before, never imagined he'd be in the position he was now of being coaxed into admitting his most secret desires to the very object of them.

"Look. There's nothing wrong with being gay, as long as you're not all faggy like Carlo; just like it's OK for Ellie to sleep with other guys so long as she's not slutty like Brynn. So why don't you just find out if you like it? If you do, the sooner the better…for you and Reed both."

"I'm tired, I'm…I'm going to bed." He popped up from the sofa, turning and gathering his robe while he did so to conceal his condition.

"What are you afraid of, man? I'll never tell anyone." He too stood, then stepped toward Jeremy and stopped, clenching his abs for effect. "Or is it that you aren't attracted to me?"

He whirled around, his nerves stripped clean. "I'm not afraid of anything Coby. *Not anything*! I'm used to living in hell—I was raised there, in case no one told you. I wouldn't even know what to do if things actually went the way I wanted to instead of them getting fucked up and sideways. If anything in my life went normally for a change I'd probably get hit by a bus the next day or my head would explode." He sucked in a breath. *Say it, say it, say it!* "And yes, of course I'm attracted to you."

As the truth was released the gates holding back his adrenaline opened, and every cell in his body sucked it up then trembled. At once Coby and the fireplace and the entire living room seemed distant, as if he were watching the scene before him unfold from backwards binoculars. Suddenly, he couldn't feel his feet.

Coby's parted lips curved into a dazzling smile. He took two more steps toward Jeremy, his naked torso shiny with perspiration, looking even more than usual like a glistening Greek sculpture adorned with human nipples. The light from the fireplace behind him gave his head a halo of frizzled gold.

"It's good to hear it finally because I'm attracted to you too," he admitted easily. "I've been for a long time."

Jeremy grinned unbelievingly, but then Reed's face flashed before him. He was a breath from betraying her. His smile vanished and he took a step backward.

"Why are you running away from me?" Coby said, innocent as a child. He reached up and laid his hands on his shoulders, his face broadcasting both benevolence and determination, like a televangelist readying a miraculous healing.

The contact broke the spell. "I...I can't do this." He looked down, shaking his head.

"Don't be afraid of who you really are."

Jeremy shook his head. *Easy for you to say.*

"It's your decision, bud. But tell me, why not?"

He sighed. "Because if I do this with anyone, I don't want it to just be a one night thing, you know...where just because you didn't get off with Ellie and I happened to come downstairs we're hooking up."

"Oh, please don't tell me you're looking for some guy to pick out china with," he laughed. He'd never been refused before and was surprised at how it stung. "You're even gayer than I thought."

"Maybe I am and maybe I'm not," he replied, his anxiety sinking as his confidence rose. "All I know is that if I'm going to do this, I'd like us to feel the same way. Like it's not just for once."

Coby saw an in. "So maybe you and I do already...feel the same way."

"Yeah, so then tell me how you feel about me—and be honest."

"I like you a lot. You know that. We're buds...and more. I even told you earlier that I've been attracted to you for a long time."

Jeremy swallowed hard. "I'm talking about something more specific."

"Like what?"

"I mean, how do you *feel* about me? Emotionally, I mean."

"I just told you."

"Well then, I guess we don't feel the same way because..." Should he expose the extent of his obsession? He quickly figured he had nothing to lose. "...I think about you all the time. And I've got feelings for you. Strong ones."

"Really?" his eyebrows raised. "What kind? His face displayed a bashful smile and eyes that sparkled. "Tell me."

"I can't."

"Why not?

"Because I can't. It's *stupid.*"

"You can tell me," he coaxed. "I promise I won't laugh, and I won't ever tell *anyone.*"

Jeremy's eyes searched Coby's and thought he saw truth there. And trustworthiness. "I'm in love with you," he said finally.

"You are?" was what his mouth said when *I knew it* was what he thought. He figured he could easily have him, but he still needed to proceed cautiously. He sat down and stared ahead vacantly while considering the rustic coffee table in front of them, smoothing the top with the palm of his hand. Would it support both their weights?

"Yeah. I guess I am."

"But because you are, you don't think we should connect? Not tonight at least?"

"That's how I feel. It's kind of funny, when you think about it." The truth was out—and the relief was indescribable.

The house creaked and popped as if listening on tiptoe.

"I guess I better find a place to sleep," Jeremy mumbled. He stretched his arms high, leaned from side to side yawning, then picked up his blankets and turned for the staircase.

Coby's brain scrambled then focused. He cleared his throat. "Wait a minute."

"What?"

"Sit down. I got something I want to...I need to tell you too."

Jeremy collapsed back into the dented orange cushion.

"I think about you too sometimes, like the same kinds of stuff you were saying."

"And that would be what, exactly?"

"This is really hard to say..." He cleared his throat again then threw his gaze to the rafters. "Like having it be just you and me sometimes, you know? Before we left I was even thinking about what it could've been like if it'd been just us coming up here without the girls because I really wanted to talk about this with you, and maybe find out what it feels like to be...together. I look at you in the showers too; you're a hot guy. And then tonight up in the bedroom when we were wrestling...I mean, man, I got *hard.*"

"So did I, in case you couldn't tell."

"I could, that's why I didn't push it tonight with Ellie. And sometimes I picture us just hanging out together not caring about anything that girls want you to care about, lying around on our beach when no one's home, drinkin' beers and just messing around with each other when ever we felt horny. No girlfriend bullshit, you know? I mean, sometimes it's like Ellie is such a major bitch and it'd be so much easier if I didn't even have to make her, or any other chick happy. And sometimes dudes just turn me on. Especially when they're like you. I mean, Jeremy, I've never said this to another guy before, and I might never again as long as I live, but I could see myself with you. Together, you know?"

"What exactly does that mean?"

"It means...It means that I think someday—soon—I could see myself being in love with you too." Suddenly shy, Coby glanced away.

"Are you sure?"

"Pretty sure."

"Then let me know when you're *absolutely* sure." He jumped up. "I'm going to bed."

"Wait a fucking minute!" Coby snarled. "How come you get to run off after I just told you what I did? I've never told that to any guy before. Doesn't that mean anything to you?" He pushed himself up from the sofa, his arms locked defiantly across his chest. He made his eyes look hurt.

"It means that you, like everyone else our age, has confusing feelings and fantasies once in a while." He took two steps toward the darkened staircase.

"Doesn't it mean anything else?" he whispered.

"Telling someone 'someday, soon, maybe I could see myself being in love with you too' to get off with them is a long way from actually loving them. I should know, because an hour ago I did kind of the same thing to Reed. Actually I was hoping that if we fucked I'd fall truly, wholly in love with her, but now I'm pretty sure it works the other way around." He scrunched his eyes closed then opened them. "Coby, I told you something I've never said to anyone and meant, that I'm *in love* with you and have been for a long time. But it's not a big deal, man. If you don't feel the same way about me then I'll send you the same way Reed sent me—*away*."

"Don't run away from me Jeremy." This was tougher going than he'd imagined. He took a step forward and his hand shot out, solidly cupping the back of the other's neck. He locked Jeremy's eyes and pulled his head forcefully toward him while drawing their mouths together. Jeremy jerked reflexively back as the dense heat of Coby's torso pressed flat against his chest; he staggered under the crush of his twisting tongue as it wrenched his mouth open and licked his teeth. He resisted valiantly, but the scratch of Coby's stubble on his own lips awakened a sleeping part of him; he felt like a character in a fairy tale whose spell has just worn off.

And time slammed to a stop for him; there were no days like menacing cars on the horizon ballooning as they sped nearer, no past or future or dead father or Reed. Only nostrils blowing noisily and tongues thrusting wildly and hands squeezing muscle and the heat, oh the young heat that ached for release from the exasperating silk. "Jesus!" Jeremy hissed as his mouth pulled away, eyes wide. A bridge of saliva connecting them stretched, then collapsed. "We can't do this! Our girlfriends are asleep and waiting for us!" He tried to take a step back but Coby grabbed him by the arm.

"We've got to."

"But what if they see us?"

"So let's go somewhere else. This is a big place"

"I can't..." His head hung suddenly with the weight of his shame. As much as he hungered for completion of their act he hadn't the guts to carry it off and he knew it. He felt the familiar flames of self-hatred spark then leap skyward once again, fanned by the certainty that he would never be a real man, no matter how many muscles he grew. He was paralyzed now, the invisible strings yanking every part of him in opposite directions.

And then: *"...in order to be a real man you must be three things: courageous, honest, and..."* echoed a familiar voice in his head, his father's voice from that crazy dream. He could hear it! But what came after *and?*

Like a flicker of lightning he remembered "...selfish."

He threw both arms around Coby's neck and pulled his face to his own, then sucked in the slippery warmth of his mouth while inhaling the dizzying musk that emanated from his hot, holy skin. His open hands palmed the young man's chest. He broke his mouth away and bent to lick the jutting underside of the other's hard pectoral ridge, then gently bit his nipple. Coby whistled low, and in a single movement pushed the other's robe off his shoulders. Both young men gleamed shirtless, breathing crazily.

"Jesus, you're a beautiful guy," Coby stated, looking down to admire the twisting muscles of Jeremy's torso, while running the flat of his hand across his smooth hard chest.

"I'm nothing compared to you," Jeremy replied, his own hands tracing lovingly the ridges of Coby's abdomen and the sculpted jut of his hip-bones.

I am touching him. I am finally touching Coby.

With their lips locked once more together their arms and hands explored each other's backs, then shoulders, then descended finally toward their pajamas. Coby slipped a hand inside the back of Jeremy's pants and kneaded his naked buttocks, all the while sensuously thrusting his crotch against the other. Jeremy nearly fainted from pleasure. His shaking hand descended in between their bodies and moved it carefully to where he knew Coby's rigid sex stood underneath the silk. His hand made contact and they both moaned.

"Hey Tyler," he gasped. "Let's get naked."

"We've gotta go somewhere else," he whispered.

"Upstairs I saw some other bedrooms at the end of the hallway."

"Let's go." He grabbed Coby's hand and led him toward the dimly lit staircase that curved into cave-like darkness at the top. They took the stairs two at a time on tiptoe.

Halfway up Coby yanked Jeremy's hand. They stopped and opened their mouths to each other, and their bodies met once again.

"Hey Jeremy," he whispered. "If I tell you I love you will you let me fuck you?" He stuck his tongue into his ear and slid his hand teasingly down the cleft of his backside. "I've got some condoms with me." He dug a shiny packet out of his pajamas and flashed it in his palm.

Jeremy's heart thumped wildly. He opened his mouth to moan an answer but before he could get the words out a third voice cut through the air like a whistling missile.

"If I tell you I love you both can I watch?"

They looked up. Ellie sat comfortably wrapped in an old Ballena Beach High sweatshirt at the top of the staircase with her back propped against the wall, her feet cozy in bumpy woolen socks. "I'm serious guys," she continued, yawning. "I love watching gay porn, except for that rimming stuff. *Yuck.* But I've got a feeling Reed would want to be in on this too...you know how much she *hates* being left out." She sprang up, then turned and began sauntering down the hallway. "Let's go wake her!"

CHAPTER 25

The first crooked banners of fuchsia clouds unfurled themselves above Ballena Beach, as the sand's sleeping carpet of seagulls unfolded their snowy wings and rose to circle, in unison, over the waves. Paying no mind to the screeching swarm, a jogger plodded insistently through the wet sand, his heart heavy with grief, the wood-smoke from a campfire nearby reminding him of their ancient life together, the fireplace they used to make love in front of, and next to that their Christmas tree. He hadn't any interest in having one since; their ornaments had been the one possession he'd left behind for the apartment's next tenants. They belonged there. Were the new occupants enjoying them at this very moment or had they thrown them out? It didn't matter. The happy peep-hole reflections in the crimson glass balls would never be right again.

Merry Fucking Christmas.

And above the beach, Bill had taken the opportunity Katharine's absence afforded him to conduct an all-nighter inside his shadowy office, hunched within the wings of an ebony leather armchair, his features Frankenstein-green from the reflected glow of the triple monitors atop his desk. While she was rubbing noses with the Eskimos he'd been hunkered-down, scrutinizing the cleverly re-configured profit-and-loss statement his accountants had fabricated for the upcoming Board meeting.

They'd reassigned insurance premiums and deflated employees' bonuses, attorney's fees, mortgages, taxes, even office supplies—anything to maximize the quarterly profits so the Board of Directors, which was headed by his dear wife, would be ignorant of the lack-luster profit Helikon's software division had yielded, thanks to his ongoing and prodigious embezzling. He'd run the new figures through numerous times, delighted and amused by the air-tight manner in which his team had been able to dissolve, on paper, millions of dollars of the company's operating costs. He just needed to stall the Board until the latest infusion of cash poured in to settle the year's books, as they were having a record-breaking final quarter.

Millions and more millions for Katharine and Jeremy, he huffed, all thanks to his genius. Nearly a year ago he'd had the brilliant idea to build software based on a suggestion of Arthur's, and six months later his development team had a working version of *CaterToo*, a revolutionary program that contained thousands of nearly foolproof recipes, graded for difficulty from kid-friendly to gourmet. It enabled the user to create a meal for any occasion by combining compatible appetizers, soups, main courses and desserts, as well as appropriate wine suggestions, while customizing the quantity of ingredients for the guest list and any dietary allergies or restrictions.

And as a final stroke of genius he had included a prompt which linked the user's computer with a corporation that owned a dozen differently named supermarket chains across the nation, so hoards of hungry consumers could have their groceries ordered from the local supermarket, either to-go or delivered, even pre-cooked and ready to serve. The market chains had eagerly contracted to buy his software and stock it on their shelves, as well as pay Helikon a per-use fee. Thanksgiving, as well as the imminent Christmas season was exceeding even his own grandiose projections. And as for the coming year, well, outer space was the limit.

He congratulated himself; over the past thirty-odd years he'd done a world of good for the owners of Tyler, inc. He smirked while recalling how pathetic Katharine's life had been before he'd married her.

1973. Her valiant brother had gone down in a helicopter in Vietnam, and then her father, the chain-smoking heart surgeon, fell over dead a month later. She'd inherited the family's rotting Cape Cod that listed atop their quadruple-acre stretch of cliff-side oceanfront, a handful of parking lots downtown and something shy of a million dollars in cash. Hardly a fortune, even back then, but adequate for him to begin working with.

The young grief-stricken Katharine was educated and pretty but unglamorously obese, and terrified of spinster-hood, having passed her twenty-ninth birthday unattached. He was in town from Cambridge interviewing for a position at a marketing firm when mutual friends introduced them. They were married three months later, in spite of his insistent objection to her keeping her last name, and the stingy prenuptial he had reluctantly signed.

And just look at her now, one of the richest women on the West Coast, thanks to him, flying around the world in search of her passion: laughingly simple indigenous wood-carvings. And graceful and thin as a debutante, to boot. Of course it had taken Dr. John's then John Jr.'s and finally Jonathan's death and the accumulated years of grief to whittle her down from a bulging size eighteen to the svelte eight she now maintained, with his assistance of course. For if he noticed her putting on a few pounds he would speculate mournfully as to the heights of success Jonathan might have achieved by now, or how the late scion would love to see his handsome son maturing so nicely and *Presto!* she would eat nothing but a little yogurt for a few days at a stretch.

So what about his mysterious great-nephew? He had arrived home from Lake Estrella three days early, sullen and mute, hibernating in his room or disappearing to wander the beach alone. What had caused his much-ballyhooed trip to truncate so abruptly? Even busybody Arthur had only shrugged his shoulders when questioned.

He should check the boy's e-mail. With a swirl-and-click the screen to his left blinked from numbered ledgers to a scant paragraph of text:

Carlo—
We need to talk as soon as you get back. Something really bad happened at the lake and Reed and I broke up.
I hope at least you're having fun in Mexico.
No matter where I live, Christmas still officially sucks ass.
Jeremy
PS—You were right.

So he wasn't dating that pretty mulatto girl anymore; that mountain house seemed to have an unfortunate jinx on it. But it was probably just as well, considering the racial issue: as his West Virginian mother used to say, '*Half- white's never right, likes to drink, loves to fight.*' And how clever of him to have not disclosed the details of whatever incident occurred at the chalet! He scrolled back, disappointed to find no other messages.

Hmmm. Jeremy couldn't suspect that his e-mail also fed into his own; no one but Bernie, his most trusted technician, knew about that. But whatever had happened he would surely find out sooner or later. No one held secrets from him.

He tapped his fingertips together thoughtfully. Jeremy's graduation was fast approaching, and it was clear that Katharine intended for her nephew to replace him someday at the helm of their enterprises—after finishing college, of course. He had recently overheard their conversations swirling with admission requirements, grade point averages and SAT scores. But when pushed for specifics, it had seemed that Jeremy was being purposefully evasive as to his academic history; in fact the boy couldn't recall whether or not he had taken any Advanced Placement classes, and had even stumbled outright when asked what GPA he'd been earning in Fresno. Instead, he'd swiftly changed the subject by declaring his intention to major in business and finance—and with this announcement Katharine had clapped her hands with glee and rattled off the names of half a dozen business schools she believed to be suitable. The maneuver indicated that Jeremy could think on his feet, while demonstrating once again how easy it was for his trusting wife to be duped.

So he was hiding something. *Good.* But how unfortunate if he couldn't muster the grades for a top-notch education, as they could use a crafty professional in the family, especially one with youthful energy and enthusiasm.

Yes that's what he needed: his very own *apprentice*.

For Bill was getting to the age now when he'd like to have someone help him take charge of a business that had become as schizophrenic as the old two-faced Roman god Janus, all benevolence and good cheer as the front-man for the evil, backwards-scowling twin. Jonathan had been too repulsively honest for the task, but this new one had his mother's inglorious genes. Jeremy's proposed participation in their financial dealings could be either fortunate or not, depending on the molding of his character.

Of this he had an inkling already—he knew the drunken sculptor.

Hypothetical situations sprang to mind. For instance, how would his nephew react if he discovered that mountains of *Helikon's* business software were being quietly shipped around the world on the gray market in order to skim profits away from their stock-holders while undercutting his greedy retailers? For that matter, how would he react if and when he found out the truth about the sparkling yachts their now defunct ship-building company used to produce, and how each hull had been built to conceal a multi-million dollar stash of cocaine and heroine? Would he go straight to the FBI upon discovery that the lion's share of the present-day Tyler fortune hadn't been built from judicious real estate investments and clever stock manipulation, as his trusting wife still believed, but from the South American drug and gun trafficking he'd helped orchestrate in the '70's and '80's?

Or like any cunning businessman would he simply re-negotiate his cut?

So was Jeremy his manipulative mother's calculating schemer, or his foolhardy father's shining star? He should conduct a simple test to find out—some way to tempt his nephew with something he wanted very badly but didn't deserve to have. But now that everything material was within his grasp, what might that be?

Of course! He could hack into the school district's database and verify his suspicions, then bestow his nephew with a sparkling GPA. As a result, Jeremy would be accepted to the college of Katharine's desire while subjecting himself to the moral dilemma of a lifetime: if he actually disclosed that his academic records had been altered he would be the crime's prime suspect and not even the local community colleges would take him, but if he went along with the opportunity provided it could send him on his Ivy-Leagued way, and more importantly, it would prove that he could be bought.

He cracked his knuckles. It might cost him some valuable time to figure out how to accomplish his task cleanly, but by God when school reopened in January his nephew would be staring wide-eyed at the fabled *Lady and the Tiger* dilemma, courtesy of Bill Mortson. And the beauty of his plan was that the boy's moral backbone would guide him to chase either his uncle's brilliant footsteps over one threshold, or his dead father's beyond the other.

He couldn't imagine a more exciting Christmas present.

* * *

"Open the bigger one first, it's from your aunt," he panted. "The small one's from me." Arthur sidled grinning through his doorway carrying two colorfully wrapped boxes. Jeremy figured the man was still breathing heavily from his morning jog by the look of his sand-splattered workout pants and the darkened collar of his sweatshirt, and the flush reddening his cheeks. He saw that his shoes, probably caked with sand, had been discarded elsewhere.

He peered up at him vacantly from behind his computer, where he'd been hunched all morning perusing the glossy, albeit humdrum, websites of various California universities. From his monitor each looked remarkably like a giant hospital with clean-cut youngsters milling about and smiling blandly. "I didn't get you anything," he mumbled apologetically. "Aunt Katharine said we'd celebrate Christmas when she got back. Sorry."

"Hey, don't give it another thought. You're the kid around here, at least for a few more months. Brats are what this holiday is about, anyhow." He winked and placed the packages on the unmade bed. "Like I said, you should open the big one first. It's from your aunt. I think there's a card." He pointed.

The boy made his way from the desk to the side of his bed to sit, then yanked the green envelope from under the ribbon and tore it open.

Jeremy,

Merry Christmas, my dear nephew. I'm so sorry I can't be here to celebrate this special day with you, and I hope you will please accept my apology for having run out at such an unfortunate time. I'll make it up to you when I get back, I promise. Enclosed is a little something I've been saving for years. I've dreamed of the day when I could see it put to good use again.

With much love,
Aunt Katharine

He tore at the Rudolph-the-Red-Nosed-Reindeer wrapping paper, lifted the flimsy cardboard lid from its base then parted the thick white tissue.

A red, vintage letterman's jacket, with white leather arms.

Could it be?

"I took it to the best dry cleaner in town and had them restore it," Arthur told him proudly. "It's in remarkable condition, in spite of its being wool. Your aunt must've kept it buried in mothballs all these years. The cleaner had a hell of a time getting the stink out; said he'd been to urinals that smelled better."

He pulled the hefty garment from the box and held it up. *Ballena Beach High School Orcas* was embroidered on the right side of the chest, while the logo of a swimmer, frozen in mid stroke, was sewn on the left.

"Arthur, I can't believe it."

"Look at the back."

He turned it around. TYLER, in huge white letters, was stitched across the shoulders.

He jumped up and slipped his arms through the sleeves, then pulled the zipper halfway closed. He jogged across the room to the mirror to examine his reflection.

The sleeves met his wrists perfectly, but the shoulders drooped ever-so-slightly.

"That looks so great on you," Arthur laughed admiringly. "I can't wait for your aunt to see you in it."

He nodded. "I'm only going to wear it on special occasions."

"You do whatever you want with it."

"Can I open the other present now?"

"Please."

In three seconds he had stripped off the gaily-wrapped paper.

Inside was a buttery leather baseball mitt, a hardball and a black cap.

He furrowed his brow, half-smiling as he blinked. "Wow. Thanks Arthur, but I don't get it. I mean, I never really learned how to play baseball," he confessed. "I can't even throw a ball."

"I figured as much." He beamed. "I'm gonna teach you, old buddy. On the beach. We can play catch together."

Jeremy was overcome. He dropped his head to hide his welling tears.

"Hey, don't cry," Arthur pulled him up into a gentle hug. "Crying's illegal on Christmas." He smoothed the back of his head with his hand.

"I'm sorry," he sniffled. "I can't help it."

"It's OK." Arthur whispered to him as they rocked together peacefully. "It's OK."

CHAPTER 26

"Ellie caught you and Coby, *together?*" Carlo's eyes were huge, his chin slack. "I sure didn't see this coming. Could you be any more of a *puta scandalosa?*" They sped northbound along Pacific Coast Highway in the Rover toward school for their first day back after Winter Break.

"I know, and now Reed won't even talk to me. She won't even return any of my e-mails." He scanned the road ahead, weaving between the slower moving cars and trucks stopped for the light ahead at Paradise Cove. He jerked the big vehicle into the right-hand-turn lane and floored the accelerator as the signal switched green, cutting off the first rows of waiting cars. Horns blared.

"That's cold, man, real cold," Carlo laughed, his eyes sparkling and cheeks rosy. "So when are you and Coby getting married? Can I be the Maid of Honor?"

"Don't you mean Matron?"

"Very funny."

"I haven't had the guts to call him since I dropped him off at his house after we went home the next morning. In fact, no one talked the whole way home. Total silence, except for the radio. Even Ellie kept her big mouth shut."

"So the frontrunner for the *Mr. Heterosexual American Teen* competition wanted to do you, Jeremy." Carlo shook his head unbelievingly. "I said you could have anyone you wanted."

"I mean, I can't say I hadn't thought about it, you know, but I never thought it would happen, *ever.* Kind of like picturing what it would be like winning the lottery, or something."

"Which you obviously keep winning," he noted sourly.

Jeremy ignored the jab. "I wasn't prepared for it, for him. Otherwise it would've probably turned out really different." He swerved to avoid a car braking for a driveway.

"What do you mean?"

"I mean that if I had ever thought it really might happen, I never would've gotten in so deep with Reed," he said, glancing Carlo's way. "I feel like shit for doing this to her. I mean, we said we loved each ·other and stuff—but I'm still not even sure I'm gay."

"Oh, oh oh oh. Now that's a good one," Carlo chuckled. "You and another guy were making out, just two seconds away from having a banana party and you still don't know if you're gay?"

"What I mean, Carlo, is how can you know for sure when you're still a virgin? I've had a couple close calls but nothing I can whisper about at the next slumber party."

"I see your point. So what does your gay butler say?"

"Arthur said he's glad the whole situation happened with a friend, and that everything will probably work out after some time has passed—which is just what I need to decide what my next step should be. And with who."

"Well the offer still stands, bud," Carlo giggled, momentarily caressing Jeremy's cheek with the back of his hand. "I'm not as *Abercrombie* as Coby, but some people have told me I have *some* attractive physical qualities. In an exotic, South-of-the-Border kind of way."

Jeremy swallowed hard and returned his focus on piloting the Rover as it devoured the rushing pavement underneath. "Carlo, you…have lots of great physical qualities."

"Like what?"

"Do I really have to tell you?"

"If you're going to say again that we can't screw each other then yes. My ego needs pumping up."

"You're great looking and you have a very hot body. How's that?"

"More, please."

"No. I can't think about you that way. I really need and appreciate your friendship more than anything."

"Oh, I get it. The old 'just friends' routine," he laughed, remembering that if Jeremy had so adamantly refused to acknowledge his attraction to men, perhaps he was also in denial about the possibility of their being lovers someday. "I can see us when we're ninety: 'Oh Jeremy Tyler? We're still the best of pals, the greatest of *chums*. Yessiree! We made it our whole gay lives without even blowing each other."

"Where the hell did you get 'chums'?"

"The *Hardy Boys* mysteries. Those were the books that first made me think I was gay, because I loved the way the 'two handsome lads and their chums' were always going on camping trips together, then they'd all be kidnapped and tied to each other by some mysterious older man. I read every book in the series by the end of sixth grade. But don't change the subject," he glared. "So what're you going to do then, stay a virgin forever?"

"Hell no. But if I get involved I want it to be with someone I don't know yet, someone I won't miss too much if I screw everything up." He floored the accelerator to make a yellow light.

"Welcome to the world of anonymous gay sex," Carlo noted as they sped past a man changing a flat tire. "So like, what type of guy do you see yourself with, for instance?"

"Well..." he hesitated "...there's this one guy I see around school that I think is really cute."

"*Cute?*" Carlo mimicked. "Geez, I feel like I'm with my ten year-old *prima*. Puppies are cute, Jeremy. Men are *hot*."

"Okay then. *Hot*. Really, really hot."

"Who is it? Tell me tell me!" He bounced up and down on the black leather seat.

"I think his name is Darius, or something weird like that," he stated, peering at him from the corner of his eye.

"Black hair, boyishly gorgeous face, body of a porn god?"

"Yeah, that's him." Jeremy agreed, not ever having seen any pornography but getting the gist. "And he is so incredibly gorgeous." He loved finally being able to share his secret crushes with another, even if it held the risk of sounding like a queer.

"Well I have to say that for an amateur you have great taste," he stated. "But unfortunately for you *and the rest of us*, Darius is really, really straight."

"But he's one of the only other jocks at school that ever smiles at me and says hi, and we don't even know each other," Jeremy argued. "And I always see him with his arms around other guys and stuff."

"That's just his way. He's from this huge Greek family up the highway; I mean, they probably all sleep in the same bed or something. They own those two gas stations up at the edge of town, before County Line..." his voice trailed off, sadly considering that if this was the type of boy Jeremy was interested in then he really didn't have a chance. "But don't feel stupid," he said, his voice suddenly bright. "Everyone's in love with Darius. And he's totally cool with us queer-boys, even goes to gay bars sometimes."

"Really?" *Queer-boys.* The term ricocheted inside Jeremy's brain.

"Yeah, he's just such a great guy he has friends everywhere."

"And how do you know so much about him?"

"He dates my sister Carmen sometimes, and I know a lot about him because she tells me *everything*. And from her filthy descriptions I can guarantee you that there's no sugar in that boy's tank."

Jeremy slowed finally to stop at the back of the long line of cars waiting to turn into the student parking lot at the school. He craned his neck to look for any cars he rrecognized: Coby's yellow Mustang GT, Reed's silver Audi TT..."*Shit!* Isn't that Ellie's car up ahead, the navy-blue BMW with the white top?" he strained forward against the seatbelt and squinted into the morning sunlight.

Carlo followed the line of sight. The car's brake lights flashed, and then the door swung open.

"Yep, that's her. So what?" he replied absently, his attention re-focused on a gang of strutting jocks in baseball uniforms.

"I *really* don't want to see her, not now at least. Do you think I can back up?" He glanced anxiously at his rearview mirror and saw the line of cars packed tightly up the road behind him.

"Dude, *are you nuts?*" Carlo laughed. "You're gonna *have* to see her sometime. Anyhow, what's she gonna do to you? Announce over the PA that you need volunteers for a term project you're doing on dick size?"

"Oh, you know Ellie's mouth," he said sourly, guiding the vehicle ahead at a crawl. "I just feel so embarrassed by the whole thing and she'll just make me feel worse than I already do."

"So what would she do if she'd been caught with someone's boyfriend?"

"She'd say something like, 'If you were more of a woman he never would gone looking for satisfaction somewhere else'."

"That's perfect!" Carlo giggled. "I *dare* you to tell her that."

"You're not helping," Jeremy glowered, then sighed. "I guess you're right, and I'll just have to face her. I just feel like I've lost three really good friends all at once."

"Well I'm glad, 'cause the whole situation finally left some room for me," he said, beaming. "You were pretty heavy with those three ever since Halloween, and don't think I didn't get bummed when I heard the four of you were going to the mountains together."

"And you wouldn't have minded being a fifth wheel?"

"Maybe, maybe not. I guess we'll never know. Look, the line's moving, and it looks like there's a space two-over from Ellie." Carlo pointed. "Now's your chance."

Jeremy sucked in a breath, stepped on the gas and wheeled the big black vehicle close to her car. She was already leaning against her rear bumper, stuffing textbooks from her trunk into her orange leather backpack. When she glanced up and recognized them a flash of indignity washed over her usually unreadable features. He smiled back apologetically, shut off the engine, grabbed his book bag from the back seat and leaned out of the car.

"Hey Ellie."

She swept her head backwards-to-the-side, making platinum locks fly over one shoulder. "Oh, is today Ballena Beach's gay pride celebration? Too bad I left all of my rainbow crap at home," she remarked, her double-barreled eyes loaded and aimed.

"I always though fag jokes were beneath you, guess I was wrong," Carlo said primly. "See you at break, Jeremy." He waved sweetly, then sauntered across the crowded parking lot toward the red brick Science building, his backpack swung over one shoulder.

"'Fag jokes' is redundant," Ellie shouted.

Carlo continued walking and flipped her off. "So's rich bitch," he yelled without turning around.

Jeremy stood, hands in pockets, while she checked her reflection in the windows of the BMW, minutely fussing at her hair and tank top.

"Ellie, I'm really sorry about...what happened."

"Yeah, well you should be, but not about what you think." She dug in her backpack and withdrew a lipstick, then bent over the sideview mirror on the passenger's door.

Objects are closer than they appear.

"What do you mean?" he asked, studying her as she circled her mouth with the rosy substance.

"I mean that you probably think I'm pissed about Coby, but the truth is I couldn't care less." She puckered her lips and made a tiny kissing noise at her reflection.

"Then what is it?"

"What is it?" She jerked up and spun to face him, squinting nastily. "It's Reed, you retard! You should've been honest with her. She thought you were *The One.*"

"Yeah, I know, I feel horrible about her more than anything. But El, please understand that I wasn't trying to lie to her," he insisted. "And I really hoped she was going to be *The One* too, at least until it started happening with him, with Coby that night. The only person I ever lied to was me, and if I could only get her to talk to me for two seconds I could try to make her understand." He saw once again the devastation on Reed's face from that morning, then blinked hard and re-focused on Ellie and noticed that she looked suddenly calmer, more herself. "And Ellie, please know that I have a really hard time believing you don't care about what happened with me and him."

"Well believe it," she stated.

"How is that?"

"Didn't you hear *anything* I said when we were up at the chalet having our little heart-to-heart?" She addressed him slowly, as if he were the stupidest boy on earth. "See if this rings a bell, Jeremy: 'Coby wants whatever he thinks he can't have' and 'Coby's ego hunts for sport'. Do you remember now?"

He nodded simply.

"Listen. My soon-to-be-ex-boyfriend is a genuine, one hundred percent authentic, beyond-any-doubt, sociopath."

"I guess I don't know what that is."

"Technically it's known as *anti-social personality disorder,* but that sounds too, I don't know, *sterile.*" She reached out and took his hand. "A sociopath is someone who is incapable of feeling any real love or attachment or empathy for others. Like a predatory animal they smell your weaknesses, then use them to get what they want for themselves. And they do this in the most convincing and charming way. Coby hunts for sex the way cats hunt mice; partly out of hunger but mostly for sport. And you fell for it, the whole fucking routine. Ha!"

Jeremy noticed how her eyes sparkled when she spoke of him. "You mean the whole thing was an act just to see if he could get me into bed?"

"It probably wasn't an act as much as it was a game. I'm sure he really did want to get off that night; God knows he wasn't going to with me. He just figured you were a horny virgin closet case, *which you are*, and it just made it that much more fun to have Reed and me upstairs at the same time. Like I said, partly hunger, mostly sport, as in *the Olympics*. But take it as a sort of sick compliment, Jeremy. He only pursues A-list people."

"I'm not A-list," he muttered.

She rolled her eyes and shook her head slowly. "You need to lose that *I'm Nothing Special* routine," she snapped. "It's a real turn-off."

They stood together in silence, while Jeremy wondered if he should ask the question she already knew was coming. "Then how come you stay with him—" he blurted finally "—if you really think he's this sick manipulative guy, this *sociopath?*"

"That's what I have my parents paying my therapist to figure out," she announced, then cocked her head, smiling at last. "Of course I'm a little pissed that you got hot with him while I was upstairs, but I understand. I mean, he's *gorgeous*. Everywhere he goes people gawk, they do double takes. So he works everyone, like I said before when you weren't listening. And don't forget that I saved your ass that night from him, *literally*, so you owe me. And you can start repaying me by making things right with Reed."

"I'll do anything."

"Then write her a letter and I'll give it to her; I'll even talk to her myself. And in the meantime," she touched his cheek "you need to realize you've got some pretty heavy power yourself. Start using it to get what *you* want. And by the way, please come out of the closet. This wishy-washy shit? *Not attractive*. There's the bell, gotta run."

"Ellie?"

"Hmm?"

"Thanks."

"No worries, doll. Write that letter." And she was off.

Leaning against the side of his car, Jeremy sighed. Around him other students scurried and chatted their way to their classes; he figured he should do the same but he just wasn't ready. Not ready to face Coby in swim practice, or Reed in English Lit., not his teachers or anybody else. He simply needed to get his thoughts together. And besides, he had to write his letter to Reed.

He climbed back into his car and started it, backed out, threw it into Drive and roared out of the parking lot. After stopping for the signal at the end of the street he made a right and headed toward the desolate beaches south of Oxnard, speeding north along the road that edged the shimmering Pacific on his left.

Eventually, he came to an inconspicuous sign on the opposite side of the road indicating *El Matador State Beach*, so he double-checked for oncoming traffic and made a quick left, then followed the narrow driveway down to a small dirt lot, and parked. From there he spotted a precipitous pathway that wove its way through the rocks, down to an abandoned stretch of pale sand below.

Perfect.

He grabbed his book bag from the car, chirped the alarm and began picking his way down the steeply creviced decline.

Halfway down he paused to look. The blinding shine of the morning sunlight on the water stabbed his eyes as he scanned the horizon. He saw the paper-white sails of faraway boats to the east, then the flock of gulls that reeled and dipped above the froth tipped waves churning the sea to the west. A chilling gale whipped through his jeans and sweatshirt and throttled his body, blowing his hair about his face. He curled his toes within his dirty white deck shoes and jammed his hands into his front pants pockets, squeezing his eyes shut so hard he saw orange tingles floating amidst dim red.

His memories tumbled like shoes in a dryer: memories of sleepless nights lying on the sofa taunted by images of what would surely become of him, a gutter-branded boy with no past to uphold him and no prospects for the future.

But so much has changed, a voice said. *Things are different now.*

Aunt Katharine's face floated before him, then came gentle Reed, then sophisticated Ellie and dangerous Coby, and next his true friend Carlo—and finally sweet, sweet Arthur. These were the people that orbited like planets around *him*, the nebula that had felt too unworthy to gather-up its gas and dust, a fledgling star too frightened to blaze the darkened heavens with its own holy light.

But not anymore. He stood wind blown, still now as the gaudily painted flying lady on the bow of a Clipper ship, drinking in the blaring song of this moment when he began, at last, to understand the magic of how it feels to be *alive*. He embraced the excitement of owning a life so voluptuous with possibility: the chance for love and acceptance and friendship and reciprocal lust, *all within his grasp!*

He began sweetening inside, as if a chocolate vine were weaving its way through him as it bloomed flowers with candy-corn petals, shooting tendrils of delicious bliss stretching and curling through his taut arms and legs, through his heart and inside his lungs then down his cock and up his backbone along both sides of his neck to the top of his nobly-held sun drenched head. He saw Ellie's eyes swimming before him, her voice echoing old movie-style, *"...you need to realize you've got some pretty heavy power yourself. Start using it to get what you want..."* Jeremy opened his eyes, threw his arms in the air and grinned; just like a grown-up Pinocchio, he was truly alive, at last.

He picked and shuffled his way to the bottom of the trail, until finally his feet disappeared into the powdery beach at the base. His skin soaked in the warmth of the sunny-salty air, and he watched the disintegrating lace of the sea-foam inches from his feet.

Paradise. It was as if he'd never seen it before.

He stooped to examine the running cuneiform of a lone seagull's tracks in the suede-like sand, and then lifted his head to follow a squadron of a dozen sandpipers, in bomber formation, as they skimmed the water's surface before invading the soggy beach. Enraptured, he smiled at how they charged the fizzing tide in unison, scurrying furiously on invisible legs. Ambling then toward the water's edge he bent to examine the thick clusters of lavender-shelled mussels, like petrified grapes, who napped between tides while nestled within the protective folds of the low craggy rocks.

His eyes beheld the curl of the waves before they slapped the shoreline, and beyond them the scattered patches of dirty seaweed that undulated atop the rolling waves as they gathered and built toward the sloping beachhead. On opposing, tilting rocks out in deep water he made out twin shadowy cranes, like soldiers from enemy countries guarding their respective borders, while craggy boulders pushed themselves out of the sand, surrounding him like waking dinosaurs.

Peace.

He decided at last that he was ready, so he plopped down cross-legged and took out his journal and a pen from his bag.

Dear Reed,

The reason I'm writing this is because I'm hoping that you'll please accept my apology for what I did. There is no excuse except that I just really didn't have much of an idea about who I really am until now. I want you to know that you helped me so much and for that I will always be grateful to you and so happy that I have had you as a part of my life.

I've learned only recently what it means to want something for myself, instead of wanting something because someone tells me to. I know this might sound confusing, but if you grew up with my mom you'd know exactly what I'm talking about. I never had the chance to be the kid who was asked, "What do you want for dinner, or what do you want for your birthday." Instead I was happy if there was any food in the apartment or if my mom even remembered my birthday. I always learned that it wasn't OK to want something, because if I did it just meant being disappointed more. So I learned to turn all of that off and ignore my desires.

My life has changed so much in the last four months that I can't believe it. I went from one extreme to another, and some days I have a hard time knowing what to do. It's just like I was living in one TV show for seventeen years and suddenly I'm thrown onto another movie set and I'm expected to handle it all. Don't get me wrong, it's been great, but I'm still adjusting.

That's why I allowed myself to be dishonest with you. I really couldn't be truthful with myself because of everything it would mean. I thought when I moved here that everything in my life that had been wrong would suddenly be right. Sure I knew that I was sometimes attracted to guys, but I figured all that would be left in Fresno. And when I found out you liked me I was so happy that I figured you were the missing piece to the puzzle that would make my life complete. In other words, I believed you could fix the deepest, most messed-up part of me. And I was wrong.

I was wrong about you fixing me, and wrong about that part of me that I thought was so fucked-up and really isn't wrong, it's just different from most people. I'm learning that even if I am gay, which I think I am, then it's going to be OK eventually.

I've never been more embarrassed in my life as I was that horrible night, and I wish I could re-live the whole thing again so I could make it all turn out different. But I can't.

Ellie wanted to go wake you up right away when she saw us, but I begged her not to so the three of us could cool down. After she and Coby went into their room I couldn't sleep at all, I just sat there in the living room waiting for the sun to come up so we could get the trip back home over with. It was the longest night of my life, and believe me I've had some really long ones. And then the next morning I actually thought about killing myself, seeing you cry the way you did after she told you what happened. You looked at me with such hatred, which I totally understand, because I hated myself then too.

I haven't seen or talked with Coby since then and don't want to. Ellie says he was just playing a game with my head and I believe her. So now I feel like the biggest idiot on Earth.

But enough about all of that.

Please know that I do love you, just not in the way we both hoped. I really want you to be a part of my life. I miss you and I wish you would email me. There's so much I want to say to you in person. Please don't shut me out.

Jeremy

He tore the pages out of his journal to give to her later, folded them and shoved them inside his backpack, then raised his arm to frisbee the book into the waves but stopped. Instead he cracked the book open and turned back the pages until he found it, the pessimistic sentence almost not written on that first night in Ballena Beach:

I wish I was a real man.

He smiled, took one final look at the beach, gathered his belongings, and then trudged back up the hill to his car. Glancing at his watch he realized that second period was about to start, but there was no way he could make it back in time. What could he do in the meantime until third period?

The counseling office. He needed to go by and pick up some transcripts anyway, and if he did it this morning they could write an excused absence note for him that he might be able to use tomorrow in his first two classes.

He sprinted up the hill and, moments later, was roaring south down the highway toward school, singing a noisy duet with the blaring radio.

CHAPTER 27

The celery-green walls of the group therapy room glared like an ER under the fluorescent fixtures zuzzing overhead. The lights made Tiffany's shoulder-length, recently dyed auburn hair look ridiculous and she knew it. In fact, after rinsing the purple goop from her hair yesterday the reflection in the medicine cabinet startled her, the wig-like uniformity of color clashed alarmingly with her waxen, jaundiced skin. *But what the fuck.* She slumped in her tissue-thin pink T-shirt and matching sweatpants, bra-less and potato-like in her seat, rolling her eyes as the emaciated heroine addict across the circle of folding chairs recounted, as if for the first time, *as if they had all forgotten already*, how her mother had once humiliated her.

"When I turned ten she made me a birthday party," she began, "with everyone from school, but halfway through she came out with a brandy glass up to the top and she got real drunk and started bangin' on our piana singin' *Dearest Jesus*, but she kept forgettin' the words so she kept havin' to start over again." Athena dabbed at her eyes with a wad of toilet paper. "Then she gave up tryin' to sing and just played the piano and told me I had to sing now, but she kept hittin' the wrong keys and I started cryin' so I couldn't remember the words either, and when the mothers started sneakin' their kids out she yelled *what the fuck's wrong with you people? Ain't y'all Christians? Don't y'all love Jesus?* And then she hollered, "You may not leave! You may not leave!"

Noisily, Athena blew her nose then hiccupped.

"At least you had a mother," said David, the bald-headed sound engineer who'd been abandoned at three and was striving to overcome his two-year long addiction to *Vicadin* that started after a botched hair-transplant operation.

"At least she gave you a birthday party," Tiffany added, picking at a ball of lint on the front of her T-shirt, remembering that she hadn't thrown a party for her own child since he'd turned two. She had figured at three and four he was too young to know he should have one, and by the time five came along he was used to not having one so why should she start now?

"Your dismissal sounds like you were avoiding Athena's raging anger from her crippling trauma, Tiffany. Could it be that you wonder what stories your son will tell others about you and your disease?" asked Dr. Bourfay, the group's therapist.

"I don't have to wonder," she replied sourly, then switching to baby voice, "I didn't realize I sounded so *mean*...I'm sorry Athena."

"No one is saying you sound *mean*, Tiffany. Mean is a wildly judgmental term, and we stay away from that here." Dr. Bourfay always tried to steer his groups into as neutral a territory as possible, being wholly terrified of genuine conflict and anger himself. "Certainly by now you can see the difference between denying someone their feelings and being just plain *comtemptable*," he stated officiously, glaring at her through his black-rimmed spectacles.

"Like I said, *sorry for being so comtemptable*."

Tiffany despised him. She saw him as a self-important aging pretty-boy with a bland personality and questionable training. He usually appeared for their daily three hour Groups dressed in meticulously pressed khakis and a series of pastel button-down oxfords, the collars of which were clipped closed with the same jaunty yellow bow-tie; she guessed this was his attempt at impersonating the WASP-y cognoscenti he lacked the breeding or the intelligence to be. She rolled her eyes as he goaded the participants of the group into focusing on their here-and-now feelings while adding bland advice, and mimicked his platitudes, most of which were laced with overused hyperbolic phrases and—usually mispronounced—polysyllabic words.

As for herself, during the previous three months she had channeled her considerable sober energy into earning herself an early release by adhering to the minutiae of every conceivable rule, and by passively irritating Dr. Bourfay every chance she got. It was unusual for any client to be discharged early, but she had petitioned the Case Review Board each week since her arrival and had finally worn them down by her dedicated composure, unflagging determination, and a signed affidavit stating that if she betrayed her sobriety they would not be held liable. The Board voted 5-4 in her favor, with Dr. Bourfay having cast the deciding ballot.

Finally, it was Tiffany's last day and her final Group at the *Arbor Vitae*

Rehabilitation Centre, just outside Camarillo between LA and Ventura, less than an hour's drive from Ballena Beach. They had already been going for two-and-one-half excruciating hours; if she managed to make it through this last thirty minutes she was done. And she would lick the linoleum clean if it would guarantee her release this afternoon.

Dr. Bourfay cleared his throat.

"Since we are finished with the main part of the Group for today, I would like to devote the last few minutes to saying farewell to Tiffany, who as we know is leaving today to return to the arms of her loving family." He continued scribbling on his clipboard as he addressed the five people circled around. "So, now is the time for us to say any last words to her, and to share any parting thoughts." He turned to face Tiffany, the friendly lilt in his voice contradicting his frigid stare. "Let's go clockwise, starting with you, Priscilla." He nodded to the globe-shaped lesbian methamphetamine-addict to his right.

Tiffany scanned the motley gathering for the last time, her back and shoulders tense with anticipation for her imminent release; her feet tapped, she had to stop herself from sprinting for the door.

"I just wanna' say one day at a time girl," Priscilla told her, raising her caterpillar eyebrows and nodding in earnest as she spoke. "'Cause you know it's gonna be tough out there. Hang in there Tiff, and know you'll always be right here." She accentuated the word *here* by punching herself in the collarbone with her fist.

Tiffany smiled. "Thanks."

Therese, the quietly poised alcoholic suburban grandmother with the tall red bouffant spoke next. "Never forget what you will be throwing away by taking that drink," she warned, her voice a whisper-on-velvet, her cinnamon eyes boring holes. "And every morning and each night you should remind yourself what you'll be putting your son through again if you do."

Tiffany nodded appreciatively at Therese, wondering for the hundredth time how she kept her hair-do in place at *Arbor Vitae* without a resident beautician.

"I have faith in you Tiffany, I know you can do it," bald David stated, his eyes avoiding hers. "You're a strong lady. And I'm...going to miss you."

Miss the occasional fuck in the basement is more like it.

"I ain't gonna miss you one bit, you stanky bitch," Athena huffed, folding her matchstick arms across her sunken chest, her Tootsie-pop head swiveling side-to-side as she spoke. "We all know you gonna be slammin' down *Thundermug* by sundown and wakin' up tomorrow morning with the Devil's hangover at the county morgue."

"I'm hearing a lot of anger there, Athena," Dr. Bourfay said with a sly smile.

Tiffany stood up, grinning ear-to-ear.

"Fuck you all," she stated gaily, making slow and deliberate eye contact with each person except Therese. "I'm outta' here."

She picked-up her jumbo ZipLoc of personal belongings from the front desk, sneering at the sight of the raggedy slippers, sweatpants and bra she'd worn the day of her last binge back in October. She rifled inside the baggie and withdrew from it her California ID and her Casio watch, which had subsequently quit working. These two items she threw into her new sky-blue-with-pink-piping overnight bag, a gift from the *Thousand Oaks Women4Women Foundation*, along with her toothbrush, half a box of tampons and a month's worth of insulin and syringes.

But no cigarettes.

Shit.

"Bye-bye," said the round-faced Filipino attendant behind the counter, waving her short-fingered hand in the air like a cheerful robot.

"Bye-bye," Tiffany mimicked, not bothering to make eye contact.

After the automatic glass doors slid swiftly apart for her, she strode evenly out of the building's sparkling terrazzo-floored lobby into the blinding January California sunshine, then tossed her plastic-wrapped clothing into the concrete trash receptacle standing just outside. The overnight bag she hoisted over her right shoulder, momentarily imagining herself a businesswoman at an international airport waiting for a taxi instead of the car Bill had promised he would send for her.

Imagine: me a business woman.

Glancing skyward she beheld the bristling tan hills that surrounded her in all directions like a giant stadium constructed of mud.

My own little dust bowl.

A smattering of images made a sudden slideshow in her head:

Jonathan making love to her even as she plotted

Jeremy's face at the hospital

Jonathan screaming at her that night at Lake Estrella

The newspaper broadcasting his accident

Bill Mortson.

Her blood surged at the thought of seeing him after all these years and she ground her few remaining molars. Here she was always the one perceived as the villain; everyone, including her own son, blamed her for everything. But that would change soon enough. She wasn't the guilty one.

This was no dust bowl she was gearing up for, this was the *Super Bowl.*

A whoosh caught her ear, and she turned to see the gleaming limousine Mr. Mortson had ordered to take her to the Tyler Compound. She squinted her eyes as the majestic vehicle lumbered to the curb and stopped, looking to see in the reflection of the onyx glass just who from inside the building in back of her was watching her celebrity-style departure. But instead of seeing a gaggle of wide-eyed hospital workers, the reflection that met her was one belonging to a scrawny, haggard faced woman with pulled-back hair and huge pink ears. She realized sadly that she looked about as out of place entering a sparkling limo as a cleaning lady would look walking down the red carpet with a bucket and a plunger at a Hollywood premiere.

She waited impatiently for two, then five, then nearly ten minutes for the driver to get out and open the door for her, not knowing that Bill had given explicit instructions for him not to, under any circumstances, or there'll be hell to pay.

The car idled imperceptibly while she shifted from foot to foot, her arms folded across her drooping breasts. And then with horror she noticed reflected in the glass a number of *Arbor Vitae* employees, first three, then five, then eight and more, some laughing and pointing and all of them looking at the spectacle of her being snubbed by the driver. Finally exasperated, she reached down and grabbed the door handle and pulled, but nothing budged.

Locked.

Muffled laughter stung her ears.

She pounded belligerently on the glass until a velvety *chick* issued from the door. She grasped the handle, threw the door open and slid herself inside the black leather cocoon, then sealed herself inside with the hardest slam she could muster.

"Fucking asshole!" she screeched at the driver who dutifully ignored her, and in spite of her outburst accelerated gently and expertly away from the curb. She settled back in her seat opposite the obscured glass of the chauffeur's partition, glancing first at the brush-littered hills as they sped by ever faster, then at the polished walnut compartment in the forward center console whose unlocked contents gaped tantalizingly at her like a fresh bouquet of roses and hemlock.

She narrowed her eyes at the car-bar between the seats. It proposed just one glittering crystal high-ball glass filled to the rim with ice, a perspiring bottle of *Absolut Mandrin,* and a bulging manila envelope with *Tiffany Tyler* scrawled on it in Bill's unmistakable hand.

Jackpot!

Her hand settled briefly on the vodka bottle just to caress its frosty sweat, noticing at the same time how the contents were up to the neck but the protective plastic seal had been removed.

Courtesy or poisoned?

With a shaking finger she pressed the window switch, and the black glass descended with a hum into the door; at once turbulent air buffeted her scowling features. She grasped the frigid bottle from its cradle then cocked her arm back quarterback style, ready to heave it onto the rushing asphalt.

No. She wouldn't give him the satisfaction of thinking she'd stolen it.

Delicately, she placed the bottle back in its tabernacle-like holder, and then snatched the bulging envelope from its resting-place. She tore away a corner of the flap and dragged a ragged fingernail across the width of it then peeked inside.

Her breath caught.

Suddenly the driver honked and swerved and the huge vehicle listed like a cruise ship riding a Tsunami and the envelope slid off Tiffany's lap and emptied its contents onto the floor and surrounded her feet with faded, crinkled, hundred dollar bills.

She giggled.

Then her eyes spied, amidst the flotsam, a bright yellow post-it-note with three little words scribbled on it:

Remember our agreement.

CHAPTER 28

Upon his arrival home from school he was startled to find Helikon's most notable employee, a squat man known only as Bernie, scrunched into a bloated ball under the desk in his bedroom hammering and screwing away busily. He was the bear-like technician who had installed the original computer equipment the week after Jeremy had arrived from Fresno in October, the day after Uncle Bill had presented his computer to him.

"E-mail should work fine now," the man bellowed over the squeal of his drill. "You got a bad cable, and some Irish-made software we recalled a month ago kept trash-canning your mail."

"Great! Thanks!" he shouted back. For the last month he'd been receiving intermittent warnings from his computer that his 'firewall' was down, whatever that was, and subsequently his friend's communications were being transformed into cyberspace-junk.

"Let's try her out," the man announced, unfolding himself from inside the rosewood kneehole and pulling himself up to collapse onto the black leather desk chair.

His thumb-like index finger pressed a button and the machine whirred to life. The screen flashed and blinked, and within moments his hands were flying swiftly between mouse and keyboard, his eyes never leaving the ever-changing monitor. "Your peripherals are coming up fine, let's just see if your mail program'll launch. Hang on...yeah...here it comes now...*good*."

Jeremy blinked at the screen as the inbox registered seven waiting messages. "How'd you do that?" he asked.

"Years a' practice." He heaved himself up from the chair, and then bent to gather the scattered tools littering the carpet.

"No. I mean, how did you open my e-mail without my password?" He narrowed his eyes, searching the man's face.

"Oh, *that*. Your password must've been stuck in there from the last time it wouldn't launch." He nodded. "Yeah, the last time you used it, it probably crashed right after you punched it in. Am I right?"

Jeremy nodded. "Yeah, I think I remember doing just that." And he did. But the sudden relief on the technician's face told him that maybe there was something else going on; years of living with a pathological liar had earned him a sixth sense keener than any FBI polygraph—except, apparently, where lust was concerned. But why would this man, this most trusted employee of Uncle Bill, be doing something fishy with his computer?

"Just let Mr. Mortson know if you have any trouble again."

"Sure, thanks."

The man turned and vanished.

He eased himself into his desk chair, then stretched his fingers onto the keyboard and opened the first of his belated messages.

There were four from Carlo, trying to answer his request over vacation to contact him as soon as possible, one from Coby and one from Reed. Finally, there was a broadcast message from the Prom Committee regarding an electronic vote on three proposed locations. He trashed it.

First he opened Coby's:

Hey Tyler,
Left my red sweatshirt
At your place in the mountains.
Could you bring it back?

So was this how he was going to play it, that nothing ever happened? And his oddly Haiku-like request for Jeremy to return his sweatshirt clearly indicated that he had no intention of ever going up there with him again, of having it be 'just the two of us' as he had confessed so convincingly that night. So Ellie had been correct—the cat had probably moved on to more challenging mice by now.

He stared zombie-like at the screen, clawed hands hanging over the keys. He should read his other messages and get it over with. He scrolled down to the message from Reed dated a week ago, and then opened it.

Dear Jeremy,
It's so hard sitting here not being able to talk to you or hear

your voice. I was always so afraid we would break up, and now my worst fear has come true. This is really hard for me to say, but I miss you so much.

Alot has happened that I wanted to share with you and I can't.

I want you to know I've been thinking about what happened and I think we need to talk it out, only just not yet 'cause I'm not ready to see you. It just hurts so much.

I'm so confused. But I know that I can't stand your silence.

I need to talk soon. Write back.

Love, Reed

PS I still have your Christmas present

He nearly collapsed with relief. He would respond later, after she got his letter and had time to read it. But he still needed to find out what Carlo's final message had to say, it was dated late today and tagged re:*Frat House*, which Jeremy knew was a dance club and coffee bar that catered to gay boys.

Dear Chum,

Since you still profess to being sexually confused I figured it was about time you saw what you've been missing, being holed up (!) in your castle and all. It just so happens that Carmen and her sometimes boyfriend Darius (!!) and I are going to the Frat House this evening to celebrate her exceptionally high MCAT scores (for Med school, dummy).

Yes, I know it's a school night, but you're only seventeen once, right? By the way, we need you to drive, my dad won't let us take the Tahoe. Says we'll drive his truck to a gay bar over his dead body. Personally I don't see a problem, but Carmen objects for some reason. Let me know ASAP. We're leaving at 8.

Your homosexual chum,

Carlo.

He pushed himself up from his desk, and then ambled out onto to his balcony.

A gay bar. Was he ready for this?

He leaned with arms crossed on top of the wrought iron railing,

211

noticing a strongly-built Latin man in shorts and a hooded sweatshirt jogging easily along the beach below with what looked, strangely, like a coal-black golden retriever. The glorious dog leapt joyfully at his master's side, baiting him to hurl a neon-green tennis ball far out into the water, after which he streaked along the beach and retrieved it sopping wet, then dropped it at his master's feet to have the happy game repeated. The creature was ecstatic, as if each throw were the first.

A dog. He'd never had one. He'd never even allowed himself to think about getting one; the possibility had never crossed his mind. So many things that he considered acquiring now had never even interested him before—like going to college, establishing a career, *having a boyfriend*—it was as if the unspoken law which prevented him from living his own life had finally been repealed.

At once a moldy dampness tickled his nostrils. He turned his head, noticing an Olympus-sized palisade of black hovering over the northwestern sea.

Another winter storm to be sure, but this one far off. Might not even hit Ballena Beach since most made landfall in Santa Barbara, and then petered-out as they drifted south before reaching Ventura.

An unexpected gust of wind whirled around his head as if he'd slipped on a little tornado helmet, and he shivered despite the heavy sweater he wore. He went back inside and tapped a reply to Carlo:

> *Dear Gay Chum,*
> *I'll pick you and your gang up at 8, unless I chicken out.*
> *But I can't stay out past ten because I've got swim practice in the AM, and I can't be late because I cut my first two classes this morning. (I'll explain later.)*
> *Chumly,*
> *Jeremy*

"Jeremy dear, are you there?" Katharine's voice inquired from his intercom. He leapt across the room to answer.

"Yes, Aunt Katharine?" She must have arrived back from Alaska within the last hour. *What was he going to tell her about Lake Estrella?*

"Will you please come down to the living room? Your uncle and

I wish to speak with you about something. Immediately." Her voice sounded unusually stiff, not her more recently relaxed self at all.

His alarm sounded.

Maybe it was only that they'd found out about his skipping class.

No. He had an alibi: his transcripts. But he'd forgotten to look them over.

Later.

"Sure. I'll be right down."

CHAPTER 29

He glanced at his watch while loping down the stairs on his way to the living room. It was nearly 5:30, so he still had a couple of hours to eat, shower and change before picking up his companions for tonight's pilgrimage. So was he ready for this? Probably not. But at least he could rely on Carlo to get him through the evening. And the fact that Darius and Carmen were going also helped calm his fears; he pictured their forming a human wall he could hide behind, if needed.

He spotted Uncle Bill first, looking—if possible—more grim than usual, seated opposite an elegantly-dressed red-headed woman whose back faced him. His aunt stood stiff as a wax museum figure by one of the pair of gold-leafed tables that flanked the elaborate marble fireplace, her hands clasped politely, her bearing as poised as ever. *Shouldn't she look jet-lagged?* He was just weighing the pros and cons of wearing boxers versus briefs under his jeans when the woman turned to him and the recognition sucker-punched him in the stomach.

"Hello Jeremy."

His head swiveled from his aunt to his uncle then back again.

Poker faces all around.

"Hi Mom." He felt his confidence deflate.

"You look good, son," was what she said, but *it's Jonathan from the dead* was what she thought.

"Yeah, *they* take great care of me. I really like it here." His arms and legs kicked back to life, and he, remembering Katharine's instructions to *stand tall, imagining a string*, padded over to the chair next to where his aunt stood.

He sat down and crossed his legs, scissors-style.

"You look good too," he said, taking in the expensive but ill-fitting brass-buttoned navy dress suit she wore with the matching, although visibly undersized, pumps. Where had she gotten such a conservative get-up? Of course, she was wearing his aunt's clothes. It touched him to see that as much as Katharine hated Tiffany she had cared enough about him to try and make her look presentable.

Now that was class.

"I didn't recognize you at first with your hair that color," he said. "It looks pretty," he lied, figuring any attempt at grooming should be complimented.

"Yeah, well it's a whole new me," she replied, meeting his stare. "I even did so well they let me out a little early."

"Three months is a little early?" His eyebrows arched.

She glared back. "Ten weeks, exactly. They wouldn't have let me leave unless they thought I was ready. The doctor said..."

"But you *promised*," Jeremy cut in. "You *promised* you'd be there for the whole six months. So what the fuck happened?"

"Jeremy!" his aunt chided, her eyes sparkling.

"It's OK, I expected this, Katharine," she pulled the hem of her skirt down to cover the top edge of her knees, the picture of propriety. "I need to talk to you about that, Jeremy honey, that's why I'm here."

"You can make excuses all you want, *Mother*," he said, "but there's no way I'm going back with you to Fresno or anywhere else. I've got friends here now, even a girlfriend," he lied, "and I'm on the swim team, just like Dad was. And I'm doing really well in school now; I even picked up a transcript today for my application to USC-" he caught himself; his aunt was standing in the room too and she certainly didn't need to see all of his grades, not right now at least.

"Why don't you share your transcripts with her later, son?" Bill interrupted, not wanting Tiffany's input on the obvious discrepancies he'd orchestrated. "I'm sure your mother believes you."

"Thank you, Bill. Of course I believe him." She nodded. "Let me start by saying that I understand how you must feel toward me."

"You *what?*" he laughed, shaking his head. "You've got no fucking idea how I feel about you!"

"Young man!" Bill barked. "Your manner is completely inappropriate."

Jeremy glared at him beseechingly. *You're supposed to be on my side.* "Look Uncle Bill, Aunt Katharine, this is between my mom and me, and I think we really need some time to work this out on our own. So maybe we should just go outside, where we won't disturb you." He popped up from the chair. "Come on Mother, let's go walk down to the beach."

216

"Whatever you want." She pushed herself up from the sofa and stood wobbling in Katharine's pumps, her feet like loaves of bread spilling over their pans. "Katharine, Bill, will you please excuse us?"

"Of course," she replied.

"Absolutely," said Bill, his button eyes fixed on Tiffany. Then Jeremy saw that hers met the old man's, and then both looked away. "Will we see you back before dinner?"

"Who knows," she replied, heading toward the doors that led outside.

"Oh Tiffany, *dear*," Katharine inquired, "If you're going to walk in the sand would you care for some more comfortable shoes?"

"I'll take 'em off once I get to the stairs."

"Of course."

He led the way confidently down the zigzagging staircase that descended between prickly cactus clusters and gaudy blankets of fuchsia iceplant, to the sand at the base of the cliffs. Trailing behind, his mother fought her way down one riser at a time, her right hand a claw on the handrail, her left dangling an elegant handbag. Finally she reached the base and set the purse on a rock, then kicked stocking-footed through the sand to the nearest boulder. She groaned as she sat.

Her eyes tried to engage his, but he was looking elsewhere; she followed his line of sight to the gargantuan cloud wall, looking like a mountain range of charred cotton advancing from the West.

Storm.

"Jeremy," she shouted over the sudden overlapping thunder of the waves.

He turned to face her, his hands shoved deep in his jeans. "Let me go first—after I tell you what I'm thinking you might not have anything to say."

"I doubt it, but go ahead."

"I...I can't believe you're here, three months early. No warning, no nothing."

"I tried calling you and you just yelled at me, so I figured what's the use in trying again?"

"You were saying horrible things about my uncle, what did you expect?" She only glared dumbly in response, so he continued. "This is the first time in my life someone has actually cared enough about me to take care of me. And now here you are trying to make everything like it was before."

"It'll be good, Jeremy, I promise," she said. "Everything's going to be different. I've got money now, and I've been sober for three whole months. Doesn't that mean anything to you?"

He shook his head. "It's really hard for me to believe you could actually change—so quickly. Maybe if you'd stayed the entire time I might believe you, like if you'd shown up here in March instead of now." He looked down. Why was he wasting time talking to her about this? After all, her sobriety wasn't the real issue here, for once. He should just say it, the real reason he believed she wanted him out of here. "You just can't stand the thought of me being happy."

His words stung. "That's ridiculous."

"You were the same way with Dad. That's why you trapped him. You knew that you could never be the kind of wife that he deserved but you trapped him anyway."

"It's a lot more complicated than that, you know..."

"That's besides the point. You made a mess of three lives and I've finally got the chance now to clean up mine and have a future. Even you can see how much better off I am now, and *you can't stand it.*"

"Of course I can see how much better your life is here, I'm not stupid. But I'm your mother and I want the best for you and we both need each other, even if you can't see that right now. We *need* to be together."

"Why? Because I'm almost old enough to buy cigarettes for you legally? Or is it because I'm almost out of high school, and pretty soon I'll get some crappy minimum-wage job?"

And then it hit him.

The Tyler Trust.

"You just want my trust money!" he yelled. "You selfish monster, you'll never change. I hate you!" His eyes spilled tears and he fought with every shred of dignity he owned not to collapse sobbing into a heap on the sand.

"No no no no no, Jeremy! That's not it I *swear*!" she pleaded, waving her hands. "I don't want your money, believe me! I have thousands of dollars now, of my own. Look!" She snatched her purse off the rock, opened it, and thrust it at him. "And there's more where that came from! Lots!"

"What, are you robbing liquor stores now?" he laughed bitterly. "Where the hell would you get that kind of money except...from Katharine and Bill?"

His heart sank with the realization.

Did they give her the money to take me away?

"Where I got it doesn't matter."

"Of course it does! I'm not stupid either. *Tell me the truth for once!*"

She'd always known this moment would come and here it was: the head-on collision of her past and future. She closed her eyes and felt the sea-wind tussle her hair and swirl about her body as if she were falling up, up, up, into the sky.

She made her way to him. But as she drew closer she saw that he was shaking. Not *cold* shaking but *ready to explode* shaking. And at once she was reminded of a time when, at the zoo, she hurried past the cage of a drooling lion that paced, out of exasperation, back-and-forth while bumping his head against the bars at either end, as if he'd forgotten since the last trip ten seconds ago that they were even there. She'd never seen anything so pathetic, this magnificent creature trapped like a hamster. And she saw now that it was the same for her son: he stood before her aching for release, but bound by the strings her greed and lust and self-hatred and laziness had wound around them both.

She figured this was it, the moment to cut him loose.

She folded her arms. "For starters, I got the money from your uncle."

"How?" he snarled.

"He just gave it to me so that I, so that *we* could get on our feet."

"You can do whatever the fuck you want with it." He turned and began trudging toward the stairway. "I'm not going back!"

"I know you're upset right now, Jeremy, but you can't stay here!" she shouted, laboring through the sand after him. "You just *can't!*"

He stopped and turned. "And why not?"

"Because I know...that Bill killed your father, and I'm afraid he might do something to you next."

"Bullshit." he began pacing nervously back and forth, his feet generating tiny sandstorms.

"Sit down. You need to listen to what I'm saying now, and you've got to swear never to tell anyone about it unless you're in real danger." She rummaged beneath the cash in her purse for her smokes and found none. *Shit.* Why hadn't she remembered to pack her cigarettes? She had plenty now; she'd made the limo driver stop along the way here and had bought herself four cartons.

"I swear. I won't tell." *It was probably a lie she was about to tell, anyway.*

"Something big is gonna happen soon. With him."

"Yeah?"

"Yeah." Reflexively she checked her pockets again for cigarettes, and finding none tucked her hands up into her armpits. "First off, I've always blamed myself for Jonathan's accident, for your father's death."

"Aunt Katharine says the whole thing was your fault."

Her eyes bugged, then narrowed. "Well, in a way I guess it was. Not directly, but I guess I had something to do with it."

"Then she was right?"

"Well, if there's one thing I've learned, honey, it's that nothing is ever black and white. But things affect each other. I mean, you do something wrong and it causes someone else to do something bad and then suddenly there's an out of control situation. First of all, as you know by now I got pregnant so Jonathan would marry me. So I could be a *Tyler.*"

"That's what Aunt Katharine said."

"Yeah, well that's no big secret. Your father lived in a whole world I could never have unless I stole it. So I did, yes I did. My sister'd done the same thing a couple years before, and she went from living in our family's crappy old mobile home in Paradise Cove to a mansion in Montecito. I thought well, if she could do it then so could I. Johnny Tyler was smart, and athletic, and funny, and cultured, and *rich.* And he was good looking, like no other guy I'd ever seen. When I saw him at those swim meets my heart pounded. He was real classy."

"Did you ever love him?"

"Honey, I don't even think I know what love feels like, from a man I mean. Maybe I did, deep down. All I know is I wanted him and his kind of life so bad it hurt. Hurt like I was in jail and there was a park outside with people laying on blankets and eating fried chicken on the grass, and their happiness was out of reach for me. My friends laughed, they said, 'Jonathan Tyler won't ever go out with you because he has servants to take the trash out'. That hurt."

"I know the feeling."

"Anyhow, I bleached my hair and borrowed my sister's clothes and hung out at the swim meets, and pretty soon we were dating. And you know the rest."

"But what about his accident?"

"I was getting to that. After we got married and you were born I thought I'd be happy, but I was miserable. No one treated me any different, in fact they treated me worse, like I was a *total fake*. I couldn't go out because everywhere I went they laughed at me, they even called me *Tiffany Trashler*.

"So I stayed home and watched TV. And I started doing drugs—coke mostly—and lots of it. Johnny tried to treat me good, he was too nice of a guy to treat the mother of his son like the junkie I was. But the drugs started messing with how I acted and I became a total bitch to him. I guess I was trying to punish him, probably because I hated myself, if that makes sense. Then I realized the only way I could get out of the situation was to divorce him, get some alimony and child-support and take you away. But he wouldn't let me.

"So I made his life miserable. I screamed at him and laughed at him and tried to wreck any bit of good feeling he ever had for me. I even stole some of Katharine's jewelry once to buy coke with, mostly because I needed it, but also to make myself look even worse. But he still wouldn't let me go; he wanted to keep you near him. He said he wouldn't divorce me unless I gave you up for good."

"So you held me for ransom."

"I'm not proud of what I did, Jeremy. But let me finish. One night your uncle made me an offer. He said they just finished that big lake house and I could live there with you in the meantime, and he would work on getting it so I could divorce Jonathan and keep you, and he could supply me with anything I needed. But I had to trust him and do everything like he told me."

"Like what, exactly?"

"Like I had to get Johnny up there and Bill had a photographer hide, and I tried to get your father to hit me so we could prove to a judge that he was violent."

"And did he?"

"Sort of. Anyone else would've given me four black eyes." She nodded

221

slowly. "But he…only grabbed me hard. Just then the photographer snapped a picture and I could see in Jonathan's eyes that he was more hurt than anything else. Then he took off out of the driveway going about 90. From what I understand, it was-" her voice caught "-only about fifteen minutes later that he…you know…he went over the side."

Amazed, Jeremy saw tears filling her eyes and two snot slugs peeking from her nostrils. He'd seen her cry too many times before, as a sort of *do this for poor me* manipulation, or a *you don't know how hard all of this is on me* routine. This, however, looked wholly different. Genuine, even. He looked at the wreck she was with her wrong fancy clothes and clown-wig hair, her papery yellow skin and bloated belly. Had he ever seen anyone so sorrowful in his life? "I can see why someone might *think* his death was sort of your fault," he said gently, "but it really sounds like it wasn't. He shouldn't have been going so fast."

"But that's not all, honey. It happened a month before your father turned twenty-one."

"So?"

"After his birthday his part of the Tyler Trust would be his, including the parts of the businesses that Bill controlled."

"And?"

"So Jonathan hated Bill, and Bill hated him back. They fought all the time about the way things were managed, and I even heard Jonathan accuse him of stealing money. Right to his face."

"Embezzlement?"

"And running drugs besides. My old connection here in town slipped up once when I couldn't pay, he told me I should go see Mr. Mortson from now on—that he could get it cheaper and faster. So one night during a fight I threw that in Johnny's face. But he didn't believe me at first."

This was too much even for his mother to fabricate. "But how could Bill have been involved in all that? Wouldn't Katharine have found out?"

"I can't tell you what Katharine knows or doesn't," she replied mysteriously. "All I can tell you is that Bill does all the money stuff. The point is that your father was trying to get some solid information to go to the police, in case he needed to."

"Why wouldn't he have just gone to Katharine first?"

"I think at the time he wasn't sure of her involvement, and even if he found out she was caught up in all of this he'd probably already decided not to blow the whistle—he loved her that much. All I know is that your father was getting close to his birthday and closer to the truth and Bill knew he would lose everything if the FBI found out about the drugs. Then your uncle has me do this whole photographer thing and the next thing I know they're dragging his car back up five thousand feet of mountain because Katharine wants to make sure I hadn't sliced the brake lines."

"It still could have been an accident."

"But he was a really great driver, just like he was a great swimmer. And he had a real level head. Remember what I said about him not hitting me when I was trying to get him to? And he never drank or did drugs, and the weather was clear that night, I remember like it was yesterday."

"So what do you think happened?"

"I think someone pushed him off that road, or he swerved to avoid something. Believe me," she laughed, "I wouldn't put it past Bill to tie up his own mother and set her in the middle of the highway if it meant more money in his wallet."

"But you can't prove it."

"I know. But after Jonathan's accident I went to Bill and said I knew about the drugs and the embezzling and the accident really being a murder. I just bluffed my way through my whole theory and told him I would go to the police unless he paid me off. Which he did."

"He let you blackmail him?"

"In a way. But I didn't have proof and he knew it. He said he just didn't want anyone poking around because *no big corporation was run by the book*, and he also said I had a colorful imagination—that's how he put it. But he did say if I talked to the police then he was sure it would come out about my coke habit, which he couldn't have known about except from Ari, who was my connection. They were communicating, see? And if the court found out about my addiction they would take you away and I wouldn't have anything—no child, no support, maybe even some jail time. He even said the authorities might think I had something to do with the accident, since I was the last one to see him alive."

"You're telling me things I can't believe," he said, shaking his head.

"Maybe I'm wrong, but I doubt it." She wiped her nose on the sleeve of Katharine's suit. "So now do you see? You've got to get away until it's safe. And in the meantime I can talk to him like I want to make another deal with him to keep quiet."

"Why did you let me come here in the first place if you knew all of this?"

"First of all, the real reason why I fought so hard to get out of rehab early, besides hating every second of it, was to make sure you were OK. I couldn't wait until March because that's when you turn eighteen and I might be too late to help you. And second, I didn't have a choice, the State placed you here. Plus, they had me on some heavy meds to get through the DT's, and that shit makes you feel really good." She nodded. "Besides, what was I going to tell your social worker? That the Tylers are drug dealers and probably murderers?"

"Why don't you just tell all this to the police? You're not doing coke anymore, are you?"

"Of course not. That's when I started drinking, to get off the coke. And believe me, I found out real quick that booze is a lot harder to give up than blow. And maybe I'll still go to the police someday soon, but I'm afraid of what'll happen. I mean, I think there's still this whole zero tolerance thing about property owned by drug dealers. They could take everything away from your family. Then we'd all be screwed."

Jeremy checked his watch. "I've gotta get moving soon, to go pick up some friends."

"That's good. It'll give me a chance to talk to him, alone."

"Will you be OK?"

"There's not much he can take from me, Jeremy, except you. And he certainly wouldn't try to kill me, because I'm not important enough to threaten him. I'm not, as they say on TV, a 'credible witness' in court. But I'm happy you're worried about me."

They sighed in unison.

"Mom, there's one more thing I need to tell you..."

She looked up and was stunned by his poise, by his emerging grandeur, as he stood tall against the wind with the setting sun casting a tangerine halo behind his rumpled hair. She saw that her son was a man now, and, like it or not, he'd proved just now to be an independent spirit governed by free will and bursting with hopes and dreams and determination that both awed and amazed her. Like a bone that heals stronger once broken, she figured the years living with her had somehow made him more perfect, even more imposing than his father. She thought of how Mary might have felt beholding the grown Jesus, although she figured she was more the Mary Magdalene-type.

How could she have produced this noble creature with his finely molded features; those amazing brown eyes—the mirrors of Jonathan's—so deeply expressive of the pain he'd endured because of her, yet miraculously devoid of bitterness. Those eyes, they shined with something like…love.

Love, love at last. Exactly what she hadn't known she'd been looking for all along. What all the money in the world would never buy her. How stupid she'd been! She ached suddenly to take back every drink that had stolen moments away from him, as well as every other reckless and self-serving act that dotted the landscape of their collective history like a thousand steaming piles of shit.

"Honey, Jeremy, son. You don't have to tell me right now. We both have important things to do tonight. We can talk about it later." He was probably going to tell her how much he loved that girlfriend he'd mentioned earlier, and was thinking of asking her to marry him. But she was too exhausted for the ensuing conversation, and besides, she needed to get back to the guesthouse for her smokes and a snack. "I think we're already out of time for now. You go on ahead; it'll take me awhile to climb back up."

And he thought he saw in her face that she knew already what he wanted to say, and for the first time in his life he was certain that she accepted him and loved him exactly as he was. His heart nearly exploded with joy as he leaned over and kissed her cheek, and she threw her arms around his neck and pulled him close, warming the wind-blown side of his face with her tears. They held each other for a moment, and then she released her son and watched as he bounded through the sand toward the stairway.

Upon reaching the top Jeremy turned and waved at the diminutive woman below. And as he watched her waving enthusiastically back, he missed seeing the furtive figure that moved from the guesthouse across the flagstone path to the main house.

His stomach growled. He needed to grab a bite and then get moving.

He trotted through the kitchen, where he snatched two slices of cold pizza from the refrigerator. He was nearly to the top of the stairs when the gravel-grind of Bill's voice raised the hairs on the back of his neck.

"Did your mother and you have a nice chat?"

He turned around slowly. "Yeah, Uncle Bill. We worked a lot of things out—between us." He began moving upwards again.

"That's wonderful, Jeremy. Family comes first, as I always say."

"Yep. Me too. Well, see you later." He started upward again.

"Just a moment, son. What was it that you were saying earlier about your grades improving?"

"Oh." Was that what this was all about? "I picked up a transcript today for USC."

"Why don't you bring it down and share it with your aunt and me? She's been bragging for months about your academic prowess, but I don't believe we've ever seen your actual grades." He smiled in his lipless way. "We'll be waiting in the drawing room."

"But I've got to get going. I'm supposed to be somewhere by eight."

"I'm sure it will only take a minute. Your aunt has been waiting for this for months."

"OK." He rolled his eyes. "I'll be back down in a sec."

He jogged down the long hallway to his room. Why did his uncle care so much about his transcripts all of the sudden? He only had a few minutes to spare, so he couldn't even shower or figure out what he would wear or anything.

Fuck!

He stuffed both slices of pizza in his mouth at once while snatching the thickly taped envelope from the top of his desk, then threw open his closet door and pulled his father's jacket off the hanger. He figured it would be the perfect garment for his 'outing' to the Frat House, seeing as it was a letterman's jacket, and it had TYLER spelled out clearly across the shoulders. Besides, Aunt Katharine hadn't seen it on him yet, so maybe it would help diffuse the shock of learning what his actual grades were, along with the realization that he had been stretching the truth to her all along. What a night to deal with this!

He scampered down the stairs, and then padded apprehensively into the elegant parlor where the Christmas tree still shimmered in the corner.

His aunt's face broke into a huge, goofy grin upon seeing him in the jacket. His uncle's face registered cold shock.

"I gotta go soon, but here are my transcripts, Aunt Katharine. Uncle Bill said you guys wanted to see them right away." He held out the package.

Bill snatched it from him and handed it over to his wife.

"Jeremy, how remarkably that jacket fits you!" she noted happily while unsealing the envelope. "I can't tell you what it does for me to see you wearing it."

"Neither can I," his uncle added quietly.

"I love it. Thanks so much for saving it for me."

"As if I could ever have done anything else," she murmured, then unfolded the thick papers. "Now let's see what we have here, dear one, then we'll send you on your way." She carefully scanned the first page, then the second and third, and then went back to the first. "Jeremy, darling! Why didn't you tell me?"

Something was wrong. She looked altogether too happy for a 'C' average.

"Bill, just look at these grades!" she exclaimed, handing the stack over to him.

"I can explain," Jeremy began.

"I'll say," Bill interrupted. "Why with these, you could go to any Ivy League school in the nation! And look at those SAT scores! *The ninety-eighth percentile!*" He stepped toward the young man and clapped him on the back. "We knew you were being modest, but this exceeds even our wildest hopes. Doesn't it, dear?"

"I must agree that it does," she chirped. "But I don't want you to think that we ever doubted your word."

"Of course not," the old man added, sending him a friendly wink. "A Tyler is always to be trusted."

"Can I see that?" Jeremy asked cautiously, hand outstretched.

"Of course. I should think you'd even want to frame it," Bill nearly bellowed, handing it over.

He blinked unbelievingly. Here was a list of all the classes he had taken since middle school, and next to each was an 'A', or an 'A-', even an 'A+'. He scanned up and down the lines for the ones he remembered for sure. His 'D' in Algebra was an 'A'. His 'C-' in American Literature was an 'A'. Even his tenth-grade 'D' in Government was an 'A'.

What the hell was going on?

He looked from his uncle to his aunt and back again. They wore identical, adoring smiles.

But why was Bill tapping his foot?

Of course! He changed my grades.

He couldn't tell how or why, but he had. Maybe he'd paid someone. He thought about what his mother had told him. *Does he want me on the other side of the country for four years, so I'll be out of his way?*

"Aunt Katharine, Uncle Bill. There has to be some mistake," he said. "These are my transcripts, I mean these have my classes listed, but these aren't my grades. Someone..." he had to proceed carefully if the man was a dangerous as his mother claimed "...someone must have made a mistake when they sent my records down from Fresno. They must have gotten them mixed up with someone else's. My actual grades aren't nearly this good."

"Jeremy, darling, are you certain?" She was obviously crestfallen, and it crushed him. "How could that be if these are your classes?"

"I don't know Aunt Katharine, Uncle Bill. All I know is that the last time I checked I had about a straight 'C' average."

"But that's not what you indicated to me earlier," she said, her annoyance evident. "You said, 'I don't know what my exact GPA is, but I would be surprised if I couldn't get into any school you wanted to send me to'. Can you tell us exactly what you meant by that?"

"I figured...I figured I could get in because you're all so wealthy and no school would say no to a Tyler." He had to confess quickly before he changed his mind. "And I thought that by the time I graduated I would've already made a name for myself with my swimming." He dropped his head and stared at his shoes. "I'm sorry I misled you both. I hope you'll be able to forgive me."

She stepped forward and took his hand. "Clearly your uncle and I are disappointed, but let's not worry about it tonight. You and I can go to the school tomorrow to figure out what's happened." She looked at him squarely. "In the meantime we both appreciate you being so honest with us. Most other young men would never have done what you just have." She patted his hand reassuringly, lovingly. "These things always have a way of working themselves out. Just know that we'll do everything we can for you, for your future."

"Yes son," Bill echoed. "We'll each do everything in our power."

Their eyes met, and for the first time Jeremy saw the darkness behind the old man's. How could he have missed it before now? And Bill saw something familiar seething now beneath the boy's penitent expression. Fear, or loathing perhaps. That look—he'd seen that exact expression on Jonathan's face!

That bitch told him everything.

"Thank you both," Jeremy said blandly. "Is it OK if I still go out with my friends tonight?"

"Where are you going?" asked his aunt.

"A coffee house. I'll be back by bedtime."

"I don't have any objections, do you dear?"

"Of course not," Bill shook his head agreeably. "Go have yourself a night to remember with your chums. You deserve it."

CHAPTER 30

*P*lease…don't…start…raining…yet she pleaded silently while climbing the stairs, feeling as if malicious little fairies or gnomes were piling more invisible weights onto her feet with each step she took. She knew she needed to reach shelter quickly, as years of beachside living told her that this storm wouldn't pull any punches. Eventually, she made it to the flagstone pad at the top where she'd left her borrowed pumps just in time to feel the shock of the first drops sprinkle her nose. She scanned the blackened sky and curled her lip in disgust, then pushed her feet into Katharine's shoes in spite of her sand-encrusted stockings.

Two flagstone pathways diverged before her, leading through beds of barren rose bushes and crisply shaped boxwood hedges that formed the massive cruciform, with its central Florentine carved fountain, which crisscrossed the grounds between the cliff and the main house. Everywhere she looked now raindrops littered the flagstone like carelessly dropped pennies. She ducked her head and began the long march to the guesthouse, but after the climb up from the beach her stamina collapsed, so she made for the nearby gazebo instead.

Eighteen years before they'd been married here, on this very spot. Then, after Jeremy had been born and Jonathan had forbidden her smoking in their quarters, she'd lolled, hypnotized by the shimmer of the sun on the sea, for hours each day in one of the wicker lounges with a *Virginia Slim* hanging from her lips like a burning soda straw, sending her cigarette ashes into the breeze and her butts conveniently over the cliff. She saw now that the lounges had vanished and the structure had been all but emptied; only a rusty little wastebasket remained.

How fitting.

She crossed directly to the bannister overlooking the ever-swelling waves, scanning north to south then north again at clouds so ominous they seemed to suck water from the very horizon.

A rolling movement caught her eye. Anchored a hundred yards or so offshore a single-mast schooner, nearly invisible in the thickening nightfall, bobbed naked of sail. She figured the skipper had probably been caught unaware by the storm and had wisely dropped anchor here rather than attempt the additional miles south to Marina Del Rey. His position in the water was judicious—shallow enough for a last minute swim to safety, yet deep enough for the craft to avoid the swollen crest of each shore-bound wave.

So was anyone on board? It didn't look like it. Perhaps they'd already gone ashore in a skiff.

And then she saw a spark. She squinted, making out the ghostly silhouette of a man as he reached up to hang a flickering lantern from the boom. She gathered from the quick way he bent and reached and stepped around the tiny craft that he was young, maybe Jeremy's age or a little older. He kept himself busily occupied for some time, lashing ropes and checking knots, vanishing into the cabin briefly only to reappear moments later on deck to continue his capable work. Suddenly he stopped his work and froze, still as a statue, facing the cliffs.

Does he see me?

She was so used to feeling invisible here.

As if reading her mind he raised one hand and waved.

She leaned against the sturdy wooden railing, its beam pressed hard into her pelvis, her torso thrust forward in the billowing gale. She then raised both arms above her head smoothly, like a high-diver readying a flip, hands skyward.

He copied her exact movements.

Her dampened skin flushed with a wave of goose bumps that tingled from the back of her head down to her knees and up again. Was he only mimicking her gesture? Or was he signaling her because he needed help? She remembered the time when Jonathan had been caught out in a squall on his sailboat off Catalina and someone had saved his life by notifying the Coast Guard. So she decided to call 911 once inside, and then congratulated herself on her newfound resolve to help others.

All at once the clouds opened and the storm broke loose. Icy winds whistled through the oaks and raindrops ricocheted upwards from the ground. Her teeth chattered. She knew she couldn't stay here until the tempest passed; this was sure to be an all-nighter.

Her mission to get help for the young man bolstered her energy, so she waved frantically again before turning to leave, then tottered hunched and panting along the rain-varnished pathways toward the safety and warmth of the guesthouse.

She threw open the door and hit the light switch, swathing the interior in a yellow glare, and then locked herself in. The old place looked almost exactly the same as when she and Jonathan had lived here, only Jeremy's crib had been removed from the second bedroom.

She called 911 and was transferred to a handsome sounding Coast Guard dispatcher, to whom she reported the boat and its approximate location off their peninsula. The phone call only took a minute or two. She was amazed at how easy it was to do a good deed and vowed to do more.

She padded then to the bathroom and shucked Katharine's suit into a soggy pile on the tile floor, shivered as she tied on her bathrobe and started the shower, then tip-toed to the living room to hunt for her cigarettes. She was ravenous, but couldn't put anything in her stomach without first executing her tiresome blood sugar routine. She knew a smoke would take the edge off her hunger, so she located her pack next to the sofa, drew one out then lit-up, and with a single gasp pulled the delicious heat hard into her lungs.

Water should be hot by now.

The scalding stream bounced off her back and shoulders while half-extinguishing the cigarette clenched between her teeth, and as the nicotine revived her body and the heat from the shower chased the cold from her muscles her thoughts turned to the young man on the boat. He reminded her somehow of Jeremy, and seeing him so precariously alone made her afraid for the safety of her son. She tipped her head back and closed her eyes, letting the water course down her face and neck while dousing the cigarette once and for all. She spat the butt between her feet and watched it spin clockwise in narrowing circles until it rested finally in the hair trap.

She twisted off the water with a trembling hand, grabbed a towel and stepped out of the tub enclosure, alarmed by how badly she was shaking. She needed to eat. And to call Bill. She threw on her robe and went to the kitchen.

The heavy crystal vase on the counter was filled with a dozen Easter lilies so crisp and white they looked to be made of construction paper.

She didn't remember seeing them when she'd arrived this afternoon; had someone delivered them while she was at the beach? She snatched the envelope from between the leaves and ripped it open. Inside was a florist's card with a brief, hand-written message:

Congratulations on your new beginning!
Call me on my private number:
386-3725
B

She grabbed the phone and punched in the digits. It rang once.

"Yes?"

"Thanks for the flowers. They're lovely," she droned.

"Please, don't mention it."

"Could you come over so we can talk face to face? It's been such a long time and we have so much catching-up to do." She grabbed her cigarettes and lit another.

"I'm afraid I'm engaged at the moment," he stated politely.

"Then I'll come there."

"That would be lovely," he began, "but I'm afraid it's out of the question. How about tomorrow at noon? If the rain's stopped we might lunch in the gazebo; I see that you still love it there."

So he had seen her this evening. She wondered if he used binoculars to spy like most creeps or had devised some spooky closed-circuit camera system. She shuddered, looking around the room. *Is that smoke alarm really what it seems?* She threw the device an obscene gesture, just in case.

She should put her cards on the table. Now. "Thanks for the money. But you mentioned something about an agreement. What do you want?"

"I'm certain you can recall."

"You know, my memory's a little fuzzy on all that; booze'll do that to ya'. Why don't you remind me why you're paying me to keep my mouth shut."

"I'm sure you'll recall all those silly suspicions you had at one time about your husband's accident, and that nonsense he'd been saying about my involvement in certain illegal activities."

"Oh, *that*. Now I remember." She exhaled a plume of smoke noisily.

"Of course I'll keep quiet. But it's gonna cost you a lot more than what was in that envelope."

"I feel strongly that what you received was quite appropriate under the circumstances. As you know, it takes much more than mere suspicions to put someone away. You've no evidence for what you'd threatened to expose."

"Ari told me about drug trafficking, Bill. And if I wanted to I could have him hauled into court."

"Ari has me to thank for the two most profitable gas stations on the Coast Highway. He'd never say a damaging word against me, in court or otherwise. On the other hand I'm certain he would welcome the opportunity to attest to your character, given the opportunity."

"You can't scare me with that old crap. I haven't done any drugs in sixteen years. Besides, Jeremy's too old, so you can't hold being an unfit mother over my head anymore."

"Yes, well, you've certainly proved yourself in that regard," he chuckled. "And you're right—as a reformed woman, there is little I could say against you in a court of law."

"Thank you. So you're willing to cough up some more money?"

"Perhaps. How much are you thinking?"

What was the most she could think of that would be in the realm of possibility? "Two hundred thousand in cash; small bills," she said, sounding like a black-and-white movie.

"Certainly. But you'll have to take a business check; I'll need to show it as a charitable deduction somehow...something orchestrated to help you and your son get settled." He could tell her anything. It wouldn't matter anyway. "So we have an agreement?"

"Sure."

"Good. But just one more thing: please don't sully poor Ari's name anymore, he has the reputation of being one of the best, most honest car mechanics in the area. Don't you recall? He used to service your husband's Porsche, and he now maintains that beastly Rover your son's driving this evening. *In the rain.*"

Her blood chilled. "Bill, tell me you didn't have him do something to Jeremy's car—he was the one that screwed up Jonathan's Porsche? Wasn't he!"

"Now calm down, Mrs. Tyler. Ari wouldn't do anything of the kind, he doesn't have the stomach for such treachery, at least not since giving up that unseemly side business he conducted of which you were such a steady client. In fact his son Darius was picked up in that very vehicle this evening by Jeremy. I believe they went to visit a bar where they can meet with other homosexuals. Quite a coincidence, don't you agree? Maybe their being perverts has something to do with parental contact with cocaine."

"What do you mean, 'a bar for homosexuals'. My son's not a queer."

Was that what he'd been about to tell me on the beach?

"But Mrs. Tyler, I had understood that observant mothers are always the first to recognize it in their sons. I must say I was shocked myself when I discovered the truth." He clucked his tongue. "Such a travesty, thinking of young Jeremy, a *Tyler* no less, on his knees or bent over the toilet in some public restroom providing sexual favors for strange men. What *would* his father think? Whom, do you suppose, would he blame?"

"Don't you talk about my boy that way, you sick fuck!"

"As you wish, I don't mean to be insensitive. Now where were we with our deal?"

She was shaken. "I want the money tomorrow. Then I'm taking my son away from here."

"Of course the money's no problem. But you'll have a hard time convincing him to leave, I'm afraid. He loves his aunt dearly; I must say she's become the mother he's never had. And she's always been an advocate of that dreadful gay rights movement. Would you be as supportive? *Could you be?*"

She needed time to think. "I'll keep everything I know to myself, as long as you pay me off and promise me you'll leave him alone," she growled. "If you try and hurt him, you'll regret it."

"Now you must believe that your son is very important to me," he soothed. "I have big plans for him, in spite of his unfortunate perversion. And, Mrs. Tyler, I very much resent your insinuation that I would hurt him or any member of this family, especially after all I've done to help you. Please assure me you haven't tried to poison his mind with your vivid imagination. After all, I could have done the same."

"No, I haven't said anything...yet."

"That's for the best. So now that our business is done," he began cheerfully, "I should mention that Katharine wishes me to extend an invitation to you for dinner this evening; I believe Arthur's whipped up some of his famous lamb. I myself am off to the airport for an early meeting up north tomorrow morning, so regrettably I won't be able to join you."

"Gee, tell her thanks but there's no way I'm steppin' foot outside again until this storm passes." She needed time to digest the news he had so cruelly reported. "It's really a tempting offer though." She rolled her eyes.

"Very well. In the meantime is there anything else you need? I'm certain Arthur is willing to bring you whatever you wish." He had to get someone else inside that guesthouse this evening.

She threw open the freezer, delighted by the sight of stacked frozen entrees and self-rising-crust pepperoni pizzas.

"Yeah. I could use some wood. A fire would be nice."

"I'll send him at once. And permit me to say again how much I'm looking forward to seeing you tomorrow. I should be back by lunchtime."

"Sure, whatever. Just don't forget my wood tonight. Or my money tomorrow."

She hung up, then flipped on the stove burner and bent low to ignite her cigarette with the pretty blue flame. She sucked in a heavy drag, then saw through the plume of smoke that her hand was trembling.

She needed to eat something quickly. She grabbed a Coke from the fridge and gulped a few swigs. Then after her blood sugar raised a bit she would take her insulin and eat.

She pressed her fingers heavily into her temples and massaged them, scrunching her eyes shut against the swelling headache.

Shit. Her son was gay. She supposed she shouldn't be surprised that he had some kind of major quirk, considering his upbringing. She hadn't ever talked to him about sex; she'd figured that he'd learn whatever he needed in school—that was the teacher's job, after all. And she guessed that being a queer wasn't the worst thing that could happen to someone; at least he had money now and could do whatever he wanted in life. Not like her. She'd always had to fend for herself. No one had given her anything.

Could he do something about my hair color?

As she dug two of the pizzas out of the freezer a frosty glass bottle buried in the back caught her eye. She reached in and pulled it out: a brand new bottle of *Malibu Rum* with the paper seal intact. She used to drink this crap with Dr. Pepper as a teenager. Could it really have been in here for the last twenty years? Or had Bill shoved it back there behind the pizzas when he dropped off those flowers...

She placed the bottle on the counter, and then peeled the wrappers off the pizzas and threw them in the oven.

There was a gentle rap on the front door. "Who's it?" she hollered while hiding the rum back in the freezer.

"It's Arthur."

She found him shivering under an umbrella, holding the handle of a child's red wagon piled high with firewood covered in plastic. She scanned him from head to toe and back.

"Didn't you use to be that hotshot football player two years ahead of me? The one that joined the Marines right out of high school?" She chuckled, one hand on her hip. "Well look what working here's done to you."

"And weren't you that gorgeous girl who married one of the best looking, richest guys on the West Coast?" Arthur grinned slyly. "So the years have taken their toll on us both. Let me in or I'll dump this load right here."

"Come in. Actually it's nice to see you again, and I don't say that to many people around here." She threw the door open wider.

"Thank you, Mrs. Tyler. And it's good to see that you're looking well. I must say the rumors appear to have been greatly exaggerated." He pulled the tiny wagon over the threshold, spilling two of the smaller logs onto the floor. "Would you like me to build you a fire?"

"That would be great, sure. I've gotta get something in my stomach before I pass out. You didn't bring any leftovers with you, by any chance?" She drew the sash of her bathrobe tighter around her waist and made her way to the kitchen while he opened the fireplace screen and began stacking logs carefully inside.

"No, but I made sure everything was stocked when I heard you were coming."

"Right. Thanks." She leaned against the counter, downing more of her Coke. She was relieved to see that her trembling was starting to diminish, so she could probably take her insulin now. She made her way into the bedroom and retrieved the small black satchel where she kept her blood-sugar paraphernalia. She dropped it on the counter, unzipped it and withdrew the contents, which included a calculator-sized machine and a fresh syringe.

"You have to inject yourself with that stuff now?" Arthur asked as he knelt down, and then struck a match.

"Yeah, but it's not as bad as it looks," she answered, while retrieving two tiny glass bottles from inside the refrigerator door. She held them up to the light and shook the clear liquid inside back and forth. "I just pretend I'm Billie Holiday."

Arthur poked at the growing fire while Tiffany fiddled with her glucose test strips. "Arthur," she asked him, "how is Jeremy, really?"

He looked up and grinned at her. "He's a wonderful young man, and he's got the world going for him. He's grown up so much in the last few months, it's remarkable."

"He's gay, isn't he?" She dragged deeply on the cigarette in her hand, her eyes moony.

He froze for a moment, then zipped up his jacket and inched his way toward the door. "You need to ask him that yourself. Just be prepared to be honest with him about how you feel. He's smart, and if you're hiding something he'll know it."

"I'm not so sure; I've always hidden the fact that he means the world to me," she said, tapping an ash into the kitchen sink. "And I don't think he knows that yet,"

"Well then don't keep it such a big secret anymore," he replied, grasping the doorknob and twisting it. "Those sacrificial lambchops in the oven are probably cooked by now, so I gotta go. Call me if you need anything else. I've got an errand to run but I'll be back later."

"Arthur?"

"Yeah?"

"Thanks for looking out for him."

"Just doing my job," he replied. He gave her a sweet smile and opened the door, then faded into the drenching blackness of the storm, the empty wagon banging noisily behind him.

Tiffany bolted herself in, punched the alarm code into the keypad, and then sat at the barstool to take her blood sugar. She only had to wait a moment after pricking her finger, swabbing it, and inserting the swab into the machine before the LCD beeped and announced its verdict. She looked at the number. *That's way too high.* She checked her pocket chart, then drew the corresponding measure of insulin from the glass vial into the syringe. Then she remembered the freezing bottle of *Malibu* in the freezer and sucked in another couple cc's, just in case.

Delicious wafts from the baking pizzas filled the room as she stuck the needle into her bicep and gently depressed the plunger. After the liquid had emptied she pulled out the hypodermic and dropped it into the trash container under the sink. Then she hopped off the barstool, shuffled to the freezer and withdrew the white frost-covered bottle, the thick rich liquid sloshing promisingly inside. She set it down carefully on the sink and returned to the barstool to finish her cigarette and to think.

Four months of gut-wrenching sobriety in that shit-hole hospital. And if she hadn't been clever it would have been six. Four months of individual therapy and group therapy and check-ups and urine tests and pathetic addicts and condescending staff. All for what? So the employees could justify their jobs to the Board of Directors who would continue receiving their foundation grants and overcharging MediCal under the guise of helping others, while avoiding the real issue, which was, how in fact do you get someone to give up something that feels as good as a few cocktails?

Alcohol. During group therapy they were asked to put into words how it made them feel. After listening to such inadequate answers as "...like I'm flying..." and "...really, really relaxed..." it was her turn. She took awhile to respond, which was okay, as Dr. Bourfay himself employed long, pregnant pauses. "A booze high—" she began "—is like this: think of an orgasm being like a ball of clay." They all looked at her as if she were nuts. "Now take that ball of clay and rub it between your hands until you've got a long snake." She pantomimed this concept. "That snake you're holding..." she held her hands wide, with her fingers pinching something invisible between them "...is four cocktails."

The group nodded enthusiastically.

Dr. Bourfay had only replied *yes, but no drink tastes as good as sobriety feels.* And everyone in the group turned to look at him, and every pair of eyes said the same thing: *you are such a dumbfuck.*

And booze was a snake for her, she couldn't deny it. After all, the doctor indicated that her endocrine system was living in dog years and her roaring case of diabetes was only kept to a hum by twice-daily shots. And she had to admit that abstinence from alcohol was making a difference; after all, was it any coincidence that she was only now developing a relationship with her nearly grown son at the same time that she was regaining bladder control?

But to surrender to a lifetime of complete sobriety?

I'd rather die.

So what about that day at *Arbor Vitae* after she'd earned floor-cleaning detail for pulling off Athena's wig during group, when she overheard some of the doctors debating the pros and cons of something called *Learned Moderation*, a treatment for alcoholism favored in Great Britain and Australia, where incidents of the disease were low, though most of the population drank regularly? She'd eavesdropped around an open doorway, dripping mop in hand, as the pair of doctors argued heatedly about the subject, one saying it was just an excuse for drunks to drink, while the other kept insisting that complete abstinence programs like AA have a high failure rate because they don't advocate a middle ground.

She had gotten goose bumps standing there, for not one of her doctors or substance abuse counselors had ever advocated a middle ground for her, or even suggested that such an approach existed. It had always been *all or nothing*.

She knew that *all* hadn't worked in the past, and neither had *nothing*.

And if she was doomed to a heavy relapse, how could she ever face her son again? She considered that by telling herself she could never drink at all, not *ever ever ever* again, she was, in fact, guaranteeing another failure for herself, and another episode for Jeremy to be disappointed in, even disgusted by, her. And she couldn't let that happen again. Not now that they'd come so far together.

Not now that she had Katharine to compete with—*once again*.

It was certainly worth a try.

She unscrewed the cap and poured two fingers into a glass, raised it to her lips and threw the contents down her throat. Then she poured herself a second shot and after that a third.

The sweet rum seemed to wash through every cell in her body like golden light, spreading Happy from head to toes and out to fingertips.

Hello, old friend.

She shuffled her way over to the entertainment center across from the sofa and began reading the titles of the DVDs that lined the shelves. A few old John Hughes movies, some Laurel and Hardy movies, and two Adam Sandler films.

Who the hell picks these things out?

In the corner she saw the *The Perfect Storm*, and thought that sounded startlingly apropos, so she pushed the plastic disk into the player and switched on the television.

By the time the opening credits rolled her eyes were drooping, so she got up, cracked open another Coke and had another two fingers of *Malibu*.

Nearly an hour later, with the first pizza distending her belly and the second cold atop the coffee table, she found herself numb and unusually heavy-headed, as if she were floating in a hot bath. "Those men are so stupid they deserve to die," she said out loud, watching with crossed eyes as the *Andrea Gail* sailed straight into another overblown Hollywood disaster.

Moments later she drifted into a stuporous sleep.

An hour or so after that, the back door opened and the *disarm* code was punched into the keypad. Then Bill manipulated her own hand to push the plunger of a second syringe of insulin into the same spot on her arm he'd watched her use on his surveillance system. Two minutes later he re-set the alarm and dead-bolted the door from the outside, then walked back to the main house with the miniscule spy cameras he'd just retrieved clicking together like giant marbles in his pocket.

Sometime around ten she slipped from sleep into a coma. Then just after midnight she began seizing violently and hit her head on the coffee table as she fell to the floor.

CHAPTER 31

I don't know where the hell I'm going," Jeremy confessed as the foursome sped along Santa Monica Boulevard through Beverly Hills toward West Hollywood, oblivious to the black Ford pickup, five cars back, that had been tailing them since the Corral Canyon intersection back in Ballena Beach.

"Stay on this street until you see some cute guys holding hands," Carlo answered, checking his hair in the visor's lighted vanity mirror. "Then slam on your brakes."

"Then we must be there already, because here I am surrounded by three of the cutest guys I've ever seen," said Carmen from the back seat, nestled into her boyfriend's arms. "Which reminds me, why aren't you two holding hands?"

"Because only one of us knows we make the perfect couple," Carlo replied, his eyes scanning the menacing clouds through the open sunroof.

"By the way, Jeremy, thanks for coming out with us tonight to help celebrate. I know it was really last minute, but I just found out I passed today."

"Congratulations, Carmen, you're going to be a great doctor. But why are you celebrating at the Frat House?"

"There's a bartender there named Nathan that used to go to Ballena High who's going to USC Medical now. He helped me prep for the exam, and promised when I passed he'd treat me and my friends to a night there, on him."

"He sounds cool, what's he look like?" Jeremy asked as he slowed for a red light at the crisscross of Wilshire and Santa Monica boulevards. Was that a raindrop that just landed on his ear? Another tapped his nose. He pressed a switch and the sunroof motored shut.

"He doesn't look like Darius, so don't get your hopes up," said Carlo.

"What's that supposed to mean?" Darius asked, swatting Carlo's head over the passenger headrest.

"I mean that Jeremy thinks you're the tastiest manwich he's ever seen," Carlo replied, flipping down the visor again to check the damage to his hair. "Next to Coby, that is."

Jeremy shot him a threatening look.

"Jer, are you scamming my boyfriend again?" Carmen asked, sounding bored.

"Carlo, you need to shut that big Mexican mouth of yours or I'll leave you at the next bus stop." He glanced at the rearview mirror where Darius' eyes met his. Jeremy's face felt suddenly hot. Darius grinned playfully and threw an air kiss at him. The light changed and Jeremy hit the gas hard, throwing them all back against their seats. Carmen squealed.

"Shouldn't you turn on the wipers?" Carlo asked as the rain began pelting the windshield and their view was becoming obscured.

"Oh." He flipped a switch and the long blades began sweeping. His thoughts about his mother and Bill, as well as where they were headed tonight, had distracted him.

"Anyhow you better start looking for parking," Carmen suggested. "The Frat House is down here at the end of Robertson, and parking there is impossible. In fact, see if you can find a space down this alley." She pointed forward to the left, directing him to steer down a narrow passageway bordered by dumpsters and chain link fences, abandoned shopping carts and warped garage doors. He saw that about halfway down was an empty spot that he might be able to wedge into.

"Jesus, it is really starting to pour!" Carlo exclaimed, his hand resting on the door handle. "We should've brought an umbrella."

"I didn't even bring a jacket," Darius said quietly.

"Maybe you'll get lucky and they'll have a wet T-shirt contest tonight," suggested Jeremy with a laugh.

"He doesn't need a wet T-shirt to get lucky," Carmen giggled.

"Especially here," agreed Carlo.

"Carmen, could you reach back and hand me my jacket and cap from the back?" Jeremy asked as they began unbuckling seatbelts and opening doors.

"Where'd you get these?" She hefted the red wool jacket and black baseball cap from behind the back seat then handed them to Jeremy, who slipped them on as he stepped down from the vehicle. The rest disembarked, and the next moment the three boys and Carmen were jogging along with their hands shielding their heads.

"My aunt gave the coat to me," he shouted over the *swoosh* of a passing car's tires on the drenched asphalt. "It was my dad's from when he was on the Ballena High swim team. And Arthur gave me the hat."

"I wish studliness ran in our family...the only thing of my dad's that fits me is his old sombrero," laughed Carlo, "which I could use right now."

They ran nearly a block south of Santa Monica nearly to Melrose, past two cafes, a nightclub and a hardware store. Jeremy scanned the area but could find no sign advertising their destination.

A fissure of lightning split the sky overhead. They'd better find where they were headed soon; Carmen's eye makeup was looking gothic and Darius' black T-shirt was plastered to his musculature like a wet suit.

"Over here!" Carlo yelled over an abrupt crash of thunder. He was waving them into a ramshackle wooden portico held up by ivy-entwined Doric columns framing a bright yellow door, the center of which had *Lambda Alpha Pi* painted in sloppy red letters.

"Why doesn't it say *Frat House?*" Jeremy asked as they jumped up the steps to the door.

"They used to have a sign with nice brass letters over there," Carlo shouted over the downpour, pointing to the right side of the building. "But someone kept rearranging them to say *Fart House* so they took it down. By the way, the go-go boys here are called LAP dancers." He threw open the door and, after telling the sullen bouncer they were on the list, the four ducked inside and were swallowed by the faintly lit interior and the rapturous thunder of the dance music.

Jeremy looked around. First he noticed the span of heavy ceiling beams overhead, from which hung two rows of old-fashioned glass dormitory lights dimmed so low they glowed like pumpkins, and to his right he saw a long bar next to doors that opened onto a rained-out patio. On his left a fire flickered inside an ancient wooden mantelpiece, around which were scattered comfortably worn sofas, tables and chairs. And perched and sitting and talking and laughing and leaning and listening and walking around were guys.

Guys like him.

By the fireplace stood a bunch of officey-looking men, by the doors posed a clique that apparently lived at the gym. Most were White, a lot were Hispanic, and more than a few Black or Asian. A handful looked typically gay, like you could tell from space. But some of the others looked like coaches or firemen or regular college dudes.

There was no denying that being here made him nervous, considering the throng of men who turned their heads in appraisal of the foursome like onlookers at a parade; he even noticed three or four great-looking guys falling silent and nudging their buddies to look in their direction. But he couldn't yet meet these admiring eyes, not only because he was embarrassed by the shy smiles he was receiving, but also because the place was so crowded he was afraid he might trip on someone's feet. The other three seemed unfazed, sidling their way through to some specific destination only they were familiar with.

The foursome stopped for a moment, so he seized the opportunity to study the dark green walls and their collection of ancient fraternity photos. He smiled back at the princely, grinning young men wearing their sweatshirts emblazoned with indecipherable Greek insignias, their arms thrown over each other's shoulders in gestures of typical, all-American camaraderie. But here, in this fraternity of a different sort, their toothy smiles and puppy-like affection took on a bent suggestiveness. It struck Jeremy that these ordinary faces amidst this extraordinary crowd seemed to say *some of us were only able to fantasize about what y'all do every day.*

"Hurry up, Jeremy," Carlo urged, grabbing his hand to pull him through the crowd toward the rear of the building. Jeremy tensed reflexively at the contact, but then relaxed when he realized that touching was OK here. In fact Carlo's grip felt comforting, reassuring even. Jeremy squeezed a response and the other boy snapped his head back to toss him a toothy grin, his eyes sparkling.

The thumping dance song that had been playing as they entered melted into a faster, more mysteriously syncopated beat, overlaid with minor chords that swirled and spun, lazily harmonizing with a woman's low, haunting voice. Jeremy strained his ears to catch the lyrics between the rowdy conversations and laughter surrounding him:

When she leaves
Your eyes will cry
Sadness reigns
Your heart will die

"Come meet Nathan!" Carmen yelled to Jeremy over the music, waving him toward a second bar against the wall of the room furthest back. He spotted a striking man in his twenties with pale skin and dark hair leaning his elbows on the counter-top and laughing with Darius. As he approached the man did a double take, hitched their eyes together and smiled.

Cry to God
He'll only point
And laugh at you

"Jeremy this is Nathan; Nathan, Jeremy."
He let go of Carlo, then shook the bartender's hand, which held on just a moment longer than customary.

But don't be scared
Of love or life
Kiss her cheek
This one last night
Then you'll wish you'd had more time
To learn what's true

"I'm glad to finally meet you," he said. "Carlo and Carmen talk about you so much I feel like I know you already."
"Thanks, Nathan. You too." He puffed out his chest, grinning. Then glancing toward Carlo, he noticed how the heat in his eyes had cooled. "Carmen told me how you helped her with her MCATs, and offered to help us celebrate. That's so cool." He examined the evenness of his features, the full lips and gentle smile. *Definitely sexy.*
"It's nothing unless you take me up on the offer. What can I get for you?"
"I just want a Coke, maybe with lemon if you have any," Jeremy answered.

"I want a beer," said Carmen.

"Me too," Carlo added, "But I'll settle for a Coke too, at least tonight."

"I better get a hot Mochaccino," said Darius, "I'm freezing in this wet shirt."

"I've got a dry one in the back, if you want to switch," Nathan offered, pointing. "Go change back there. And Carmen, you better go with him. I don't want him getting molested."

"Jeremy wants to watch," Carlo blurted.

"Here's your Cokes, gentlemen." He slid the two frosty mugs towards them as their companions disappeared through the darkened doorway behind the bar.

"Carlo, what is with you?" Jeremy asked as Nathan attended to his next set of customers.

"I'm having a great time," he replied innocently. "What do you mean?"

"I mean, why are you always bugging me about Darius? You know that I know he's straight and he's with Carmen. Why're you trying to embarrass me?"

"I'm just joking."

"Well quit it."

"Sure. *Sorry*. Anything else I do that pisses you off?"

"Not really. But I'll let you know."

"Can I do that too?"

"Of course."

"Well then maybe I will," he snapped.

"Go ahead."

"Let's sit down. This may take awhile."

"Fine with me." He followed him to a tall table in the corner flanked by a pair of barstools, ignoring the admiring leers of a trio who looked to be of Arthur's generation. He took off his letterman's jacket and hung it on the back of the stool, scrunching the hat deep into the side pocket. They sat together in silence for a few moments before Carlo took a deep breath, then began. "You don't get it, do you?"

"I guess not. I'm not sure what you mean."

"About me, about how I feel about you."

"Go on."

"Jeremy, ever since the first time we studied together I knew I had feelings for you, and I kept wanting to tell you, but I knew you had to get the gay thing out of the way first. So now that it is—out of the way I mean—I feel like I want to tell you, I have to tell you how I feel, and how I've felt all along."

"I think I know where you're headed with this, Carlo. You don't have to continue." He studied his beverage.

"But I want to, I've got to. You still think of me as a fag because that's what you saw me as first. Then you got over that a little and started thinking of me as a friend, but kind of the same way as you probably see Ellie now...a *girl* friend." He shook his head. "But I'm more than that. I want you to see me as a regular guy, Jeremy. A guy that feels a lot for you, that..." he stopped, then looked around to see if anyone else was listening "...that loves you. Very much. Someone who's listened to you and stuck up for you and watched as you discovered yourself, and then listened to you as you went on about who you were hot for. And it hurts me that you don't think of me that way. Because I do. All the time."

"*You do?*"

"What are you, retarded?"

"You don't have to get hostile. All I mean is that you never let me know before now, except for joking about it."

"Would it've made any difference?"

"Maybe, maybe not."

"So...you don't feel the same way about me."

"I don't know how I feel about anybody right now." He sucked his drink through his tiny black straw, feeling suddenly like a sissy. "I mean, over the last few months a lot has changed for me. I'm still adjusting."

"Jeremy, you've got to find your own way, just like I did." He lifted the glass to his mouth and gulped down the contents, then set it down with a *clack*. "You're right, you've had a lot to adjust to, and graduation is just around the corner, then college after that. You're gonna have to get used to jumping from one situation to the next, we all will. But during those times you've got to know who you can count on. And I want you to know that I'm here for you, no matter what."

"Carlo, that's nice of you to say, really it is, but I've known all my life that I don't have anyone I can count on."

"That's *bullshit!* Didn't you hear what I just said?" He thrust himself forward on the tiny table so their faces were inches away. "I said I love you and you didn't say anything back and I still said I'd be here for you. What kind of monster are you that you can't trust me?"

"The kind who was *raised by a monster* who used every one around her to get whatever she wanted. So I guess you're right, I'm a monster too. *The next generation.*"

"No! You think you are but you're not. Can't you see who you really are?"

Jeremy turned his head in time to see Carmen with her boyfriend, in a dry white T-shirt, laughing as they made their way toward their table. But she must have read the situation because she grabbed Darius's arm and switched directions.

"You don't know the half of it," Jeremy began. "I've never even told anyone what my mother put me through, like how she got pregnant with me only so she could trap my rich dad into marrying her, or that my father was probably murdered and she might have had something to do with it, or how I pretty much raised myself without any love or support or money or sometimes even food, and how each day is a struggle now because of the miniscule amount of confidence I have to stumble through life with. The truth is, Carlo, that I don't trust anybody, least of all someone who wants to get into my pants!"

"Is that all you think I want from you, you asshole?" His voice peaked suddenly above the music, and a few faces turned their way. "You've just proved my point; that you've never had anyone in your life that loves you the way I do—and yes, in my mind that might include a friendly screwing or a blow job once in a while. But for your information, I've also spent night after night dreaming about what it would be like for us to just hold each other…to walk on the beach together at sunset and make plans for our future, to have your voice be the last thing I hear at night and the fist thing I hear in the morning. I…I *love* your sadness, your smile, your goofy walk, your shyness, your laugh, even the miniscule confidence you stumble through life with." He sighed deeply, closed his eyes then wiped his nose on the back of his wrist. His eyes fluttered open through sudden tears. "When, Jeremy Tyler, are you going to open up to someone, even if it's not me, and start making up for the life you haven't been living?"

Jeremy stared down at his hands clasped together atop the table, at once comprehending that his fingers might as well be made of wood, for they'd never caressed anyone or been held lovingly, at least that he could remember. And the possibility dawned on him that the young man in front of him might actually see him not as the tangled puppet he'd been, but as the glorious man he most certainly would be. The smack of Carlo's confrontation revived something nearly dead within him, and he knew that this was a soul he might actually trust, and maybe…maybe even allow himself to love.

They sat together in silence for several long, drawn out minutes; the party-like atmosphere spinning around them seeming a stark contrast to the depressive mood at their table.

"Carlo," he began gently, "I think you're right about me. Again."

Their eyes lifted to each other.

"Like your email said?" he muttered.

"Just like my email said." He nodded. "And you've definitely given me lots to think about."

"Like what?"

"Like maybe I'm ready for some of the things you're talking about. To trust someone finally. Maybe to even love someone back."

"Don't get my hopes up," he warned, "because if you're saying this only for tonight I'll make your life miserable."

"I need some time, Carlo, but yeah, I mean it." He gave him a careful smile.

"So where do we go from here?" He asked finally.

"Well…I don't know how to dance, so maybe you could show me, because this song sounds like the kind gay boys like to dance to. And I'm almost officially a gay boy now."

"Come on then. There's a teeny dance floor in the next room."

Carlo grabbed his hand and was leading him toward the thundering music when Darius intercepted them along the way.

"Where're you guys going?" he shouted over the din.

"I'm gonna teach Jeremy to dance!" Carlo yelled.

"Great! I'll call my dad and tell him I'm gonna be later than I thought. Like an hour?"

"OK!" they both yelled, and then disappeared into the squish of gyrating men.

Minutes later he was back, tapping them on the shoulders.

"My cell-phone's dead, it must've gotten wet!" he hollered. "Can I use yours?"

"Sure, but I left it in the glove box! The keys are in my jacket at the table, and wear my stuff so you won't get wet again!" Jeremy returned his concentration to mimicking Carlo's simple, repetitive footsteps

"Thanks! Carmen's gonna stay here, I don't want her getting drenched," he laughed. "And make sure none of the guys pick up on her!" Darius turned, then snatched Jeremy's jacket from the back of the barstool and pulled his cap on, and the boys giggled as they watched the distinct white letters advertising TYLER across his broad shoulders disappear into the crowd as he threaded his way toward the exit.

Carlo nudged him. "He kind of looks like you, with your stuff on."

Jeremy nodded. "Now I know what I look like in a gay bar," he laughed, shoving him playfully.

"So do you think you look like you belong here?"

"I never thought I'd say so, but yeah. I do."

Carlo put his hands on Jeremy's hips. "Then you have to move these. You can't dance unless you're willing to shake your ass!"

With the storm beginning to wane Darius strode easily up Robertson toward the alley where Jeremy had parked. The sidewalks were unusually deserted, no doubt because of the rain; in fact the only other people he saw were a couple of heavy-set men across and down the street who had stopped to check him out as he strutted along.

West Hollywood. He figured that if he were gay he could get laid by a different guy here every day.

As he walked an icy chill stung his cheeks and he longed for summer; it seemed like forever until it would be that time again. Then after summer would come autumn and with it UCLA, which he would attend thanks to his hard-won football scholarship.

He stopped to admire a huge oil painting that had been displayed prominently in an antique store's window—an oversized landscape of amber California hills dotted with orange poppies and olive-green oaks under a turquoise sky. It looked like the countryside outside of Agoura where he'd grown up, before his father had bought the gas station on the Highway and moved the family to the flats of Oxnard. He smiled thinking of the wood-sided house between the rolling hills where he'd played hide-and-go-seek with his brothers and sisters during the endless evenings of July and August. Was the house even still there? He'd recently seen a sign for a new development down the same road where they'd lived. Maybe he could take the car this weekend and find out. That would make a nice Sunday trip for Carmen and him.

Finally he made his way up to the alley then turned into it, trotting now at a faster clip toward the Rover while splashing through the puddles, listening to his steps ricochet between the garage doors facing the narrow roadway.

But his echoed steps sounded too fast.

Something wasn't right.

He stopped and his heart seemed to stop as if it, too, were trying to listen.

Someone's chasing me!

He jerked his head over his shoulder and saw the two men he'd seen only a few minutes before bearing down on him—one wielding a baseball bat and the other some object he couldn't make out.

Bashers!

He sprinted for the safety of the Rover, pressing the key fob in his hand to unlock the doors. The parking lights instantly flashed orange twice and the interior lit up like home. But should he keep running down to the open end of the alley, or hop in the car? What if one of them had a gun—was that what was in the other one's hand? No, he reasoned quickly, they would've used it already. If he could just get himself inside and start the car he might even run them down.

He was only a couple feet from the front of the car when the footsteps stopped. He looked back and saw the two men standing five or so garages back, one of them swinging the bat like he was warming up for a blazing curve-ball while the other stood motionless. Maybe they'd given up the chase because he'd made it to safety. His hand shot out to grab the door handle.

He hadn't a clue that a third was standing in back of him until he heard the whistle of the bat through the air. Jeremy's black cap flew off him and the skin on the back of his head split open, exposing his skull. In an instant he fell unconscious, his knees folding like a rag doll as he slumped face-first onto the oily asphalt.

Snickering nervously, the trio convened around the motionless figure. "Poor little faggot didn't know what hit 'em," the first said.

"I never seen one run that fast before!" the second one laughed.

"Shut up and let's do this quick," said the third. "We gotta make this look good, but remember he doesn't want him killed if we can help it."

"Then let's get to work," said the second. "Who wants the honors?"

"I do," stated the first. "You fuck up the car like we talked about, then tear up the porno mag and leave it all over the place. Oh, and stick some in his pockets."

"I can't even stand to touch this disgusting shit."

"Just do it. Now turn him over so I can get a hit at his pretty face."

The first man stood bat in-hand, his legs planted wide, while the second and third grabbed the edge of the jacket and heaved the boy in one movement over onto his back, his slack-jawed face rolling skyward.

"Jesus! That's Darius!" the third exclaimed.

"What?" the first yelled with bugged eyes as he bent down to verify the other's discovery. "I didn't know he was a queer."

"He's not, you shit-head. This is just one big goddamn mistake!" He bent down and stroked the boy's face. "Jesus Christ, not Darius!"

"What're we gonna do?"

"We're gonna leave him here and finish off the car then get the hell outta here. Maybe someone'll find him and call for help!"

"I'm leaving now!"

"No, let's finish up first."

The first stood look-out while the second sprayed *FAGGOT* in huge, uneven red letters on Jeremy's car while the third, with shaking hands, tore out pages—that he littered around the body on the ground—of naked, lasciviously posed men. Then the three ran off leaving Ari's precious son bleeding and mortally wounded, with raindrops on his cheeks catching the amber glow from the streetlights a half-block away, where Carmen dreamed of their future together while watching her brother and his true love sway together on the dance floor, locked in their first thrilling kiss.

CHAPTER 32

The plane streamed through the blackness along its easterly course. A few of the passengers around him snuffled and snored in the darkened cabin, even that creepy flight attendant was sneaking a nap, he figured, somewhere back in Coach.

If everything went as planned he would land in New York at daybreak, stop by one of their subsidiaries for an impromptu inspection, then board a returning plane and be back in Ballena Beach by late afternoon. And if something went wrong he would take an alternate flight that would drop him in Rio de Janeiro in time for cocktails and lobster at his favorite seaside restaurant. Either way he'd made extensive preparations for just about anything; he was even traveling under his failsafe alias: *Martin Guignol.*

He'd been tucked into the supple leather of his First Class lounger for a few hours now, viewing different areas of the house on his laptop via his network of surveillance webcams. At midnight he'd watched with tentative amusement as images of Katharine and Arthur hurried from the house then careened in the Jaguar down the winding driveway.

Good.

Since aggravated assault charges were infinitely less complicated than a murder investigation he'd decided, early on, to spare the boy's life. And the absence of a police cruiser now at the Tyler Compound indicated that Jeremy hadn't been killed, but incapacitated instead, as ordered. So things looked, so far, to have gone according to plan. The boy was most likely at St. John's; the sprawling hospital had an award winning trauma center. He figured that his great-nephew would, after multiple surgeries and months of futile therapy, probably remain in a quasi-vegetative state for years. He'd be lucky to ever tie his own shoes again.

He'd chuckled knowingly when they hadn't even attempted to rouse Tiffany; even under these dire circumstances they must have figured she would only get in the way. He felt relieved, as the premature discovery of her body might have sent everything spinning beyond even his rigid control.

Everything was right with his world.

His baggy eyes drooped more than usual, then closed.

Like delicious smelling salts, the nutty aroma of steaming coffee jarred him awake. He screwed up his eyes at the sunlight blazing through the porthole window across from him then jumped, startled to discover yet another effeminate flight attendant leaning over his shoulder, grinning vapidly.

"Coffee, Mr. Guignol?" he whispered intimately.

He tipped his head. "Black."

"It will be my pleasure." He filled a delicate cup carefully then bent at the knees to place it on the table next to his armrest. "If I may ask, sir, what movie are you watching? It looks like a good one."

"What?" He'd neglected to switch off his laptop before drifting asleep, and the machine's sleep mode must have awoken when he had been startled awake.

This cannot be happening.

A dozen or so haphazardly parked police cars had swarmed his property, their roof lights swirling red and blue beams everywhere. Boxes and computers were being hauled away from the house by jump-suited agents, and then loaded into open trunks. He witnessed two more unmarked cruisers as they sped up the driveway and stopped, and then their doors flapped open. In disbelief he saw Katharine and Ari climb from the back of the first car, then Arthur and Jeremy from the second. Suddenly the frenetic activity halted, little groups froze in place here and there. The guesthouse door opened and a gurney was pushed slowly out through it, the white sheet stretched from toes to hair. Arthur put his arm around the boy and led him toward it. The paramedic pulled the sheet upwards briefly. Jeremy gave a nod, bent down and kissed her on the forehead, then collapsed onto his knees.

"It's a project I'm working on," Bill replied calmly.

"Are you a producer?" asked the eager attendant.

"Something like that."

"Can I give you my head shot? I'd really appreciate the opportunity to read for you."

How about a shot through your head, instead?

"Do as you wish." Bill smiled. "But I'm afraid I'll be out of the country for some time."

CHAPTER 33

J eremy dear, please sit down."

She watched with concern as he shuffled slack-shouldered from the foyer into the living room toward the Chesterfield, then changed directions and planted himself in the club chair across from the picture window.

He drew his white-socked feet onto the cushion and wrapped his arms around his knees, hugging them to his chest. Eventually, he raised his head and looked out through the glass at the cobalt water beyond the cliffs where he saw, much to his dismay, a dozen or so crisp white sails skimming near and far. Then a breeze skittered through the house and his nostrils curled from the sickening perfume of orange blossoms that wafted through the doors and windows. His mood grew blacker at the witnessing of such natural harmony. Why did everything in this world seem to shine more brilliantly the darker his life became? Or was it just a simple matter of contrasts, like the way raw meat looks bloodier in the market when they put dark green parsley around it?

It grieved Katharine to see him so depressed, so completely deflated. He'd made so much progress since his arrival those few months ago; she'd watched him unfolding, blooming really, a little each day. And now it seemed as though Jeremy hadn't made eye contact with anyone in the house for nearly a week. *Not since that terrible night.* It reminded her so much of when Jonathan had first come to live with her after being orphaned, it was almost too much to bear. She'd seen now that lightning did, in fact, strike twice in the same place.

Especially when the same storm hangs around for decades.

"Is there anything on your mind?" she asked him finally.

"I was wondering if they've caught him yet."

"No dear, they haven't. But they're looking everywhere. Give it time, they will."

"Why can't they find him?"

"Because he's very smart."

"I want to kill him," Jeremy said.

"I'm sure you do."

He lifted an accusing stare to meet her worried gaze. "I'm ready to know everything that happened. From the beginning. And don't leave anything out."

She nodded gently. "I'll tell you, if you must know."

"I need to."

She pulled herself up daintily from the chair and drew in a breath, as if about to deliver a complicated soliloquy. This wasn't going to be easy; she'd been dreading this moment since he walked through the door last October. But he needed, he deserved to know. Even about the parts where she herself had failed them.

"As far as we know this is what happened, based on Darius' father's sworn testimony, information from your mother, and the parts that I can remember myself," she began. "This whole ugly situation can be traced back to when Jonathan could take no more of your mother's cocaine use. He confronted her and gave her an ultimatum, that if she didn't quit he would take you away. That was just before she moved you up to Lake Estrella.

"Instead of giving up her filthy drugs or you, she told Jonathan about my husband having been involved in the drug trade from South America to Los Angeles, and if he tried to gain custody of you she would expose Bill. She thought this would frighten Jonathan into thinking she had the power to destroy our wealth, but she was wrong. Only Bill and I knew that my attorneys had drawn up an ironclad prenuptial before we married. The truth was that if the government found out about his drug trafficking, they would've seized his private bank accounts and things of that order. But they couldn't touch anything of mine, which was, and still is, just about everything you see.

"Your father decided to confront Bill, which was a terrible mistake. He thought he could get him to pressure Tiffany's drug dealer, your friend Darius' father Ari, into stopping her seemingly endless supply of cocaine. He refused, saying Jonathan's marital problems weren't his responsibility. Your father, in turn, told him that when he turned twenty-one in a few months and inherited his controlling interest, he would expose him and throw him out of the family's corporations once and for all. He also threatened to open the books and find out exactly why the numbers weren't adding up, and if anything looked suspect he would see to it that Bill spent the rest of his life in prison.

"Right about that same time, Ari was involved in a bad narcotics deal and lost the money with which he was planning to purchase his only competitor's gas station down on the Highway. He figured that if he had the only gasoline concessions in town, he could have his own little monopoly and could make enough money to get out of the illegal mess he was so deeply in. Bill agreed to buy the land and let him operate the concession, as long as he 'fixed a situation' for him. That was how he put it.

"Your father went to Lake Estrella to plead with Tiffany about not taking you away, and to get additional information with which to incriminate Bill. Unfortunately my husband thwarted his efforts."

"But how?"

"Apparently, Ari had a brother with another service station in Crestline, which is a short drive from Estrella. Bill followed Jonathan from *Tylerwood,* and radioed ahead to let Ari know when to cut him off. Then Ari slowed to a maddening pace and prevented him from passing, and finally Jonathan lost his composure, which wasn't hard to do after what your mother and Bill had done with that photographer, and passed him at breakneck speed. As he went around a blind curve, he was driving too fast to see that Ari's brother had moved a snow plow into the oncoming lane, so he swerved rather than collide with it and went over the cliff in one of the few areas where there was no guardrail. The entire filthy operation was orchestrated by Bill, and coordinated with CB radios."

"So Mom didn't really have anything to do with it?"

"No, dear. Thankfully for you she didn't. But your friend's father did. I hate to put it in such terms, but Darius' father murdered yours." She shook her head sadly. "And now look at the price he's paying."

"How much time will he spend in jail?"

"It's hard to say, because he made a deal with the District Attorney in exchange for testimony against Bill. I'm referring instead to what's happened to his unfortunate son."

"He's been out of the coma now for three days."

"I pray that he continues to improve. I don't care what sins his father's committed; no son should be visited by such cruel retribution."

Jeremy stood and looked through the window at the flotilla of

Cormorants bobbing on the placid sea below. He still had more questions. He clasped his hands behind his back then turned slowly to her. "But what about my mom?"

"Her autopsy results haven't been released yet. But what I can tell you is what we'd expected—she'd been drinking."

"Goddamn her! Couldn't she stop, just for me? Didn't she love me more than her shitty booze?"

"Jeremy, you must calm down, and sit down. And please don't speak of her in such a way. You see, a tape was made of a conversation between your mother and Mr. Mortson that night, and I'll explain how that came to be in a minute. But what you should understand is that he pushed her that night, emotionally that is. *Deliberately.* Your mother had a terrible weakness, and Bill set her up to succumb to it."

"But how?"

"I won't embarrass you with the details of the recording—although some day you may wish to review it yourself. In fact I believe it might be healing, when the time is right. Suffice to say that he made your proclivities known to her, and in the most base, defiling manner possible. And he implied that if your father were alive today he might rightly blame your sexual 'experimentation' on her. It upset her so much that she returned to her old escape."

"But how did he know about me? I never told anyone."

"And for good reason, which we shall discuss at a later time."

"What do you mean by that?" he asked, glaring at her. "What's wrong with now?"

"I mean, young man, that I haven't the stomach just now to discuss the ramifications of your 'situation', and what it means for us all in the long run. Please...just allow me to continue."

He looked around nervously and opened his mouth to speak, then thought better of it and sat down. Was he really ready to do battle with her about this?

"Very well." She cleared her throat, and Jeremy saw the tears building in her eyes. "As I was saying about Mr. Mortson, he knew about your 'situation' because, as we just discovered, every e-mail transmission in this house fed into his computers. He knew what you were writing to your friends and they to you, where you were going, and with whom."

"That explains why he said, 'you deserve to have a night out with your chums' when I was leaving that night. Do you remember?"

"Yes. I recall thinking at the time it was a queer choice of words, even for him."

"He said that because Carlo calls me 'chum' all the time. I should've known something was wrong. Especially after that whole thing with my transcripts."

"We all should have."

Their eyes met. Katharine looked away. "So what about you, Aunt Katharine. How could you not have known about him, about how bad he really was?"

"Over the course of the last few years I did." She managed a wan smile. "Our marriage had begun disintegrating even by our third anniversary. But I hadn't the talent or interest for the family businesses, nor the stomach, so I needed to keep Bill around, at least until I figured out what to do. And I told myself he might even really love me to stick around with no possibility of his sharing ownership in our holdings; of course I knew nothing of his embezzling—about his stealing from me, from us. So I braced myself and threw myself into the gallery, and redecorating this...this *mausoleum*, and other such meaningless distractions.

"But two years ago I began working closely with the FBI to snare him, after an officer at one of the institutions we bank with noticed some irregularities. I made an effort to examine the reports more closely, but I couldn't poke around too much or I might arouse his suspicions—and besides, I wasn't entirely certain of what to look for. As you have witnessed my husband was...is a very crafty man.

"Over Christmas I didn't really go to Alaska, Jeremy, but back to Washington to review with the Bureau the most recent batch of evidence they'd collected. We couldn't communicate out of this house because we rightly suspected that he wire-tapped every conversation. Even your mother and I were in contact via cell phone; we were collaborating during the latter part of her hospitalization."

"You were?"

"Yes. I believe Arthur mentioned something to you about overhearing a conversation she and I were having about restraining orders and attorneys. I felt strongly that he shouldn't have said anything, and this was something that he and I continuously disagreed on. But he told you about our conversation with the hope that you would prompt me to include you in the investigation, but I refused to heed his advice. I felt it would put you in more danger if you knew, and now I see that I was wrong." She narrowed her eyes and nodded. "One should always take a professional's advice."

"What do you mean?"

"Arthur isn't a butler, dear. He's an FBI Agent. He was our bodyguard, yours and mine."

"*What?*"

"They sent him to us after I opened the file. You were protected from Bill even when I was away. And your mother knew about Arthur's role here, which is why she consented to send you to me."

His head felt wobbly inside, but it all made sense. "But what about that night at the Frat House? *Where was he then?*"

"Oh, he was there. He just didn't want you to see him, so you didn't. In fact he was standing by the door when Darius walked out in your father's—in your jacket. Unfortunately it didn't occur to him until some time later that the boy could also be in danger, and by the time he arrived on scene the crime had already been committed. He blames himself terribly for what happened."

"Arthur went to save Darius?"

"Whom do you think found him and called for help? He saved your friend's life."

"But what…what about Arthur's boyfriend, that whole story about his being killed in the September Eleventh attacks?"

"That…well that's unfortunately all true. Every bit of it. The Marines wouldn't have him but the FBI was happy to. After all, since their former chief, Mr. J. Edgar Hoover, was exposed as a homosexual transvestite they had no choice but to revise their employment policies. No one wants the ugly finger of hypocrisy pointing their way, especially when it's attached to your own hand."

"So what's Arthur going to do now?" he asked meekly.

"As long as Bill is a fugitive he'll stay here with us. It seems that he's grown quite attached to you and is in no hurry to leave, so he's requested to stay on. Besides, he says he'll never be able to afford a house with an ocean view, and he's begun dating some local fellow he met recently. A bartender named 'Nathan'.

Jeremy nodded. "But why did Bill want to kill me? I never did anything to him, and I didn't know anything about the embezzling or the drugs and all."

"From what Ari said, the instructions..." she choked down sudden tears, unexpectedly looking her age.

He went to her and wrapped his arms around her and squeezed. "You don't have to tell me."

"No," she sniffled, eye to eye. "You need to know. Bill's instructions to Ari were to 'beat in the kid's brains but not kill him'; to render you a helpless 'vegetable' and to 'make it look like a hate crime', because 'no one would ask questions about some little queer who was too stupid to walk around by himself'. That poor man, Ari, was beside himself, he didn't want to do it but Bill threatened him with exposure and loss of his livelihood. So, reluctantly, he called up an old debt from three drug addicts who owed him money. He's a simple man, you know. And he loves that boy dearly." She pulled a handkerchief out of her sleeve and dabbed at her eyes, then blew her nose with a honk.

"But to answer your question," she continued, "Bill wanted to guarantee that, unlike your father, you'd never be in the position to cast him from the family's table. And he probably would have killed you too except that it would have looked too suspicious, especially after what he was planning to do to your mother."

"So you do think he did something to her?"

"Of course. The coroner theorized that she most likely injected herself, had a few cocktails, then forgot she'd injected herself and repeated the dosage. They'd seen it happen a hundred times before. The only evidence we have of possible foul play is the alarm records show a 'disarm' and 'arm' had occurred late in the evening. But then again, it could've had something to do with a call to 911 Emergency that she herself made."

"And they didn't come out?"

"No my dear, the call was made for the benefit of someone else. A supervisor called the guesthouse the day after she passed away. It was the Coast Guard following up on a rescue call she'd made, reporting a boat she'd seen that appeared to be in grave danger during the storm. They wanted her to know they'd sent a helicopter out immediately, but had found nothing. And no distress call ever came over the radio from anywhere in our vicinity."

"Did they mention if she sounded drunk?"

"I had the same thought, dear one, and so I asked. They played the tape for me over the telephone and I must admit she sounded quite lucid, and very insistent. I am convinced that she saw something out there, although it seemed to have vanished quite mysteriously."

"Aunt Katharine, do you think any of this would have ever happened if my mother and I had stayed in Fresno?"

"It might have still, because Bill must have smelled that his time was running out—I'm not a very good actress, you know. And he has connections everywhere. You may have even been safer here in the long run. But we'll never know for sure."

"Thanks for everything, Aunt Katharine."

"Oh, please don't thank me. It was your mother and Arthur who saved your life. It is they whom you should thank."

"That's exactly what I'm going to go do. But first," it was time for his last question, the *grand finale*, "can you please tell me what you meant about my 'situation' and what it means for 'all of us'?"

Her back stiffened, and she sighed deeply. "My dear, have I ever steered you in the wrong direction?"

"No, Aunt Katharine....no you haven't."

"And I promise not to, *ever*. First let me tell you that I've always been a supporter of equal rights for everyone, and have done more than my fair share of fundraising over the years in support of the gay and lesbian movement: AIDS, adoption and marriage rights, *et cetera*. I have been around many wonderful gay men during the course of my life, so what I am about to tell you comes from personal experience." She paused.

"Yes?"

"You, my dear, are not a homosexual."

Jeremy rolled his eyes. "Aunt Katharine, how would you know?"

A deep sigh escaped her. "Jeremy, I am about to tell you something I've never told another soul. And God forgive me for breaking my promise to your father for doing so now."

"I'm sure he would understand."

"Yes, I believe he would." She nodded thoughtfully. "Yes he would. Jeremy, when your father was about your age he had a friend, a *special friend*, his name was Jamie. They were very close. Too close, in fact."

"*No.*"

"Yes. And you can imagine where I am going with this. I found them once, together. By accident, of course. Jonathan was quite traumatized by my discovery, as of course was I, and he agreed to participate in therapy so he might develop normally, which of course he did—and then some. In fact, he began dating your mother while still seeing the psychiatrist. And you'll be pleased to know that I've contacted Dr. Slessinger—she was the one who helped Jonathan so much—and she is anxious to begin work with you."

"You're not serious," was all he could say.

"Oh, I'm very serious, my dear. Being a homosexual may be fine when you're young and handsome, but you'll pay a dear price later in life. It's...akin to taking out a mortgage you can't afford, with a monstrous balloon payment at the end." The smug look on her face told Jeremy that she was pleased with her little analogy.

Had she used the same one with his father?

"Aunt Katharine," he began, trying not to scream at her, "Did you ever think that maybe the reason my dad got my mom pregnant in the first place was to prove to you that he was finally a 'real man', thanks to you and that doctor? And that this would finally explain why he *threw everything away on this girl who was so beneath him*, as you love to say?"

Her face first registered shock, then regret. "I must admit...I'd never thought of it that way...you may be right. But regardless, that was then and this is now. You have too brilliant a future waiting for you. This... *situation* will ruin everything!"

"What's it going to ruin, Aunt Katharine? The way I see it, your trying to change my father is what ruined everything!"

She narrowed her eyes at him, and the color drained from her face. "Don't you *ever* say that to me again, young man! I gave your father the best of everything, including guidance! And speaking of, have you considered *nothing* that I've taught you over the past months? Have you thought about how this will affect your standing at college? And beyond that, your ability to have children, and to socialize with polite society? And what about earning the respect of our Board of Directors and stockholders and employees? What about diseases, for God's sake, and the fact that there are scores of men out there who *will* take a baseball bat—*or worse*—to your head? Have you not considered *any* of these things? Or has your teenage lust for these twisted boys obliterated your judgment entirely?"

Her words stung him, but he summoned his courage and went to her. "I love you, Aunt Katharine, more than anyone in my life." He took her hand and gave her a kind smile. "But you're going to have to listen to me when I say this, and I want you to think about what I am about to tell you and not say anything until you've really, really thought about it."

"Of course I'll listen. Say what you must."

"I'm not my father, and I'll never live the life you wanted for him."

She snatched her hand away. "And what is that condescending statement supposed to mean?" she snapped. "How *dare* you imply that I haven't thought this through, or that I don't know there's a difference between you two! You must think me some addle-brained old crone!"

It was frightening, seeing her so angry at him. But he needed to get through this, to try and make her understand. If he couldn't, he would not stay here—it was that simple; the rest of his life was at stake. "Aunt Katharine, of course you know that we're not the same person." He shook his head. "But I don't think your heart knows it yet. There's a difference."

He took her hand again and squeezed it but she didn't squeeze back. She just looked at him and Jeremy felt like she was seeing him for the first time. And a hundred arguments began formulating in her head and she opened her mouth to respond but felt the truth in his words and snapped her mouth shut. Her free hand picked nervously at her skirt. She looked away then looked back at him. He was still staring at her. He squeezed her hand again and leaned in and kissed her on the cheek.

And then her mouth moved as if she were talking, but at first no words came, and Jeremy thought *is she having a stroke?* And when at last the words did come they were meek and hoarse, as if underneath her polish and manners and education and propriety her soul was finally, after all these years, finding its voice. "I...I could not survive losing you," she managed at last, and Jeremy saw tears spill down her cheeks. "My grief...you have no idea..." And Jeremy caught her as she began to sob.

And sob she did. He managed to hold her up just long enough to guide her to the sofa, where she collapsed into his arms like a little girl.

"You'll never lose me," he told her gently. "You're my family. You're more to me than my own mother was."

"Everyone leaves me," she whispered. *"Everyone has left me."*

"But I never will." He caressed her arm, and then the side of her face.

She turned to him, and he realized that the mask that she had carved for herself was gone. And in its place he saw her real face, and how it was branded by anguish and loss and betrayal, and the sadness that comes from living for so long without love. "Give me some time, dear one," she whispered at last. "You must do whatever you must." Their eyes held and Jeremy saw the submission in hers, and how she seemed to be telling him that from this point forward, he would be the one in charge.

She was finished.

"Will you please help me to my room?" she said at last. "I need to rest."

He reached out his hands and she took them.

Arthur was folding a basket of laundry downstairs behind the kitchen. His face split into a grin at the sight of the young man shuffling toward him.

"So how ya' doin, old buddy?" he asked cheerfully, lining up the dark socks on the ironing board to see which made pairs.

"I'm OK I guess..."

"Good. Are you hungry? I'll fix you something."

"No, but thanks anyhow. Actually I came to thank you. For saving my life."

Arthur looked away shyly. "So she told you."

"Yep. You sure had me fooled."

"Nothing I did was trying to fool you, I just left out a few details. And don't thank me for doing my job."

"You did more than your job, Arthur. Way more." He gave him a grateful smile. "Listen, I know we only have a few hours before the memorial, so I wanted to hurry and give you this before it starts. Remember how we were supposed to celebrate Christmas when Aunt Katharine got back?" He held out a brightly wrapped box. "Consider this a belated present."

"Jeremy, you shouldn't have got me anything." He took the package and hefted it, appraising its unusual heaviness. "When did you have the time?"

"Oh, I've had this for years," he beamed. "In fact I made it in school when I was seven or eight. Open it."

Arthur removed the snugly tied ribbon carefully, then picked open the tightly taped seams to reveal a battered old shoebox. He lifted off the lid.

Inside was a red clay paperweight that had been molded by a child's careful hands. On it was the inscription: *TO THE BEST DAD IN THE WORLD. HAPPY FATHER'S DAY! LOVE JEREMY T.* Arthur saw that its chipping pie-crust edge still held evidence of Jeremy's tiny fingerprints.

"I love it," Arthur whispered, his eyes brimming. "I love it, and I don't deserve this but I'll accept it anyway and I'll treasure it forever." He turned the object over delicately in his hands like a coveted award. "But I don't understand why you made this; wasn't he already gone by then?"

"All the other kids were making one in class and I was too ashamed not to make one too—I didn't want anyone to know I didn't have a dad. Then for some reason my mom kept it all these years in that old shoebox, the one I keep on the top shelf of my closet. To tell you the truth I'd forgotten all about it until I opened the box finally yesterday."

He placed the object carefully on the dryer then threw his arms tightly around the boy, who returned his gesture with equal might.

"Hey," Jeremy soothed as they held each other. "Didn't you tell me that crying's illegal on Christmas?"

It was a pitifully small group that gathered at the gazebo overlooking the ocean on this dazzling January afternoon. They had offered to fly Mrs. Jackson down for the occasion, but she had declined based on her suspicion of airplanes. Instead she opted to have Tiffany's name recognized at this Sunday's service at her own church; Jeremy, in turn, had promised to drive up and visit during the coming summer. And so it was only Katharine, Arthur, Carmen, Carlo, Ellie, Reed, and finally Jeremy, bravely holding his mother's ashes in what looked like an upscale coffee can. He had refused Katharine's offer to have a minister officiate, remembering how his mother hated church people almost as much as she hated God, or so she said. He suggested instead that he perform the service himself, considering no one knew her as well as he did. Besides, he needed to get some things off his chest. Publicly.

The sun had begun the long descent from its peak, laying down a platinum path that stretched from the shoreline, across the water and out to the edge of the earth. Over the heads of the little group a swarm of seagulls hovered, perhaps remembering the days when Tiffany used to bring out bags of bread from the kitchen to throw at them; not because she cared for the aggressive birds, but rather because they roosted in the rafters of the finely crafted gazebo and peppered Katharine's lovely wicker chairs and Persian rugs with their runny white excrement.

"Jeremy," Reed whispered, touching his elbow lightly. "Are you sure you're up to this?"

"Don't worry about me, but thanks anyway," he replied. "I'm more worried about Carmen. Today is her first day away from the hospital." All the heads within earshot turned to look at her. She waved at them shyly.

Ellie peered over her sunglasses at him. "I'm afraid to ask, but what's the latest on Darius?"

"The doctors say it's too soon to tell how fully he'll recover," he answered, "but aside from the huge bandage around his head he's looking pretty good. I was over there last night and he was feeding himself already. And he's getting *plenty* of attention from the nurses—*all* of them, if you know what I mean."

Heads nodded solemnly.

"They say he might not ever play football again," Carlo told them. "But Carmen says he couldn't care less about that. He just wants to go to UCLA."

"Well, he won't have to worry about not having the football scholarship for tuition," Jeremy stated. "My aunt will make sure that he goes wherever he wants."

"Jeremy dear," Katharine interrupted, immaculate in black *Chanel*. "The gulls are beginning to make their presence known." She pointed to a gray smear on Arthur's lieutenant's jacket that dripped from shoulder to medals. "Might we begin?"

He cleared his throat officiously. "Thank you all for coming," he began "even though only a few of you even knew my mother. But if you know me you know my history, and she's a big part of both.

"My mother was an unusual woman," he continued, his voice resonant and clear. "She had her own ideas about the world, and what part she wanted, or didn't want to play in it. Her biggest fault seemed to be her willingness to always take the easy way out. This she did often, and all kinds of disasters happened because of it.

"But in spite of her faults, what will stay with me for the rest of my life is the conversation we had a week ago on the beach just below us, right down there." He pointed, and everyone turned. "She told me that she came back here to warn me, because she knew that I was in danger. If she hadn't, I might be dead and she would be the one holding this can of ashes." He held the silver object up briefly, then set it on the ledge behind him. Glancing quickly over his shoulder, he noticed a white schooner below in full sail pulling dangerously close to the waves cresting for the beach.

Something about the boat caught his attention, so he squinted directly into the afternoon sun to read the words painted in bold script on the stern. It read:

KAY + RON's FERRY TAIL

On deck he spotted the athletic figures of a young man and woman in swimming attire who waved their arms happily at the group high above the beach. *They must think it's a wedding,* Jeremy figured sourly. He raised his hand to wave back politely, and inadvertently knocked the can off the wooden ledge.

"Shit!" he exclaimed as it tumbled end-over-end down the rugged cliffside toward the rocks below.

The group rushed to the edge in time to witness the lid break loose, and the remains of Tiffany Tyler spin away on a gust of wind.

"Good thing it's offshore today," Arthur noted.

Jeremy hung his head and sobbed.

Carlo put his arm around him. "Wasn't that what you were going to do anyway?" he asked gently.

He nodded.

"She just beat you to it. She got in the last word."

Arthur handed him his handkerchief, and Jeremy blew his nose.

"I guess you're right." He nodded.

"Sweetheart," Aunt Katharine urged, pointing skyward. "The seagulls."

"Anyhow," he continued, trying to gather his poise, "my mother let me know during our talk here, and in no uncertain terms, that she loved me and accepted me for the person...for the man I've become. This is important to me, as it came from a lonely woman who said she didn't know what love felt like.

"I guess not many people knew, including me, that my mother had another side to her, one that was gentle and sentimental. In fact, I didn't really know this myself until I went through the box she kept all taped up. A couple of days after her death I opened it and found some papers, a pearl necklace she'd 'borrowed' from my aunt, a couple of photos of me as a boy, something I'd made at school..." he and Arthur smiled at each other "...this letter she'd written for my dad, but unfortunately never gave to him. Anyway, here's what it said:

"'March 15, 1988. Dear Johnny, I know things have been hard and I've been kind of a bitch lately, but I want you to know that I love you and always will. It's just hard for me to tell you that sometimes 'cause I'm afraid of so many different things. So after our fight yesterday I wrote you this poem'." He stopped reading momentarily and faced Carlo, who looked down at his shoes, then looked up to meet his gaze with open adoration. And then he continued,

"'You came to my rescue
And saw beyond my shit
I hope I'll never be the kind of wife you want to hit.
I look at you and think
What does he see in me?
I'm just a girl that's poor
How can his true love be?
When our days are done
And we're old and gray together
I pray that you'll love me
And our hearts will be light as a feather.
You're too good for me,
We both know that's true
I just hope you can love me
someday like I love you.
Luv, Tiffany'"

Jeremy finished reading the poem and noticed the quiet sobs and snuffles coming from those surrounding him. And surprisingly the loudest were those of his aunt.

"Jeremy, you're wrong about that poem, about not ever having given it to your father," she stated, her voice hoarse with emotion.

"Then why was it still in her little box?"

"He, Jonathan, had it with him the day he died. It was retrieved from the accident site; apparently he always kept it in his wallet. And I begrudgingly handed it to her the day of his funeral." The tears streamed down her face from behind her glasses, streaking her pale face powder. "She saved it, Jeremy. Your mother saved that paper all these years."

CHAPTER 34

Jeremy's eyes fluttered open. He looked around the room. He was dreaming about his dad again. Jonathan had been saying something about *off the block*. Had he called him a chip off the old block? He smiled, happily figuring he was one, in more ways than he could have ever dreamed. Or was it something having to do with the starting block of a pool? *What was it?* He couldn't bring it back. Whatever he'd said had evaporated from his memory. *Poof!*

He threw his leg over the other's, then caressed the hollow of his neck with his lips. His lover growled deep in his chest, like a panther purring, and smiled at him behind closed eyes.

Was this a dream too?

Their lovemaking had been ferocious. It seemed that every opening in Jeremy's body had been taught to speak a new language as each was happily instructed by Carlo's fingers, Carlo's tongue, Carlo's cock, Carlo's love.

His lover stirred, yawned, stretched, opened his eyes and grinned. Then with his hand Carlo wiped a dollop of spit from his mouth and rubbed it onto him, teasing him.

"I can't do it anymore tonight," Jeremy whispered, exhausted. He lay spread-eagled in the huge four-poster, the sheets underneath him clammy with perspiration. "You've drained every bit of me."

"Wanna bet?" Carlo's hand reached between Jeremy's legs, then slid his head down until it rested on his chest. "I can hear your heart beating," he cooed, rubbing the insides of his sleek thighs. "And it's speeding up."

Jeremy caressed the knotted muscles of the young man's shoulders, loving the feel of his hot copper skin in his hands. He looked down and saw that Carlo was ready once again, and the sight of his erection made himself lift and lengthen.

"Ah, now that's a good boy," Carlo murmured. "I told you hardons were contagious." His lips hunted with kisses down Jeremy's torso until his mouth bagged its prize.

Moments later they were catching their breath.

"I've got a favor to ask," Jeremy asked mischievously. "Tonight, or more like tomorrow, I want to wear Coby's red sweatshirt and have you fuck me."

"Nothing would give me greater pleasure," he answered cheerfully. "Except seeing Coby wear it while getting screwed by the entire football team, coaches included."

"We'll have to explore the details of that later."

"Absolutely, otherwise these'll fall off." He grinned. "Hey, the sun's almost down. You said we could go down to the boathouse and see your birthday present."

"Sure, if I can find the keys. Let's go." They stepped into their shorts and sandals, then threw on sweatshirts and sprinted down the stairs, through the living room and out onto the deck which jutted over the ankle-high waves splashing the rocky banks.

"My God, it's gonna be a beautiful night," Carlo said, taking in the dimming lavender sky sprinkled with stars, and the sliver of silver moon piercing the silhouetted tree boughs.

"The spring sky is supposed to be the best for star gazing," Jeremy told him. "And there's one constellation that's supposed to be visible now that it's April. Let's see if I can find it." His head swiveled from side to side as he scanned the heavens. 'There!" He pointed, as if spotting a UFO. "Between those two really tall pine trees in the west. It's just dark enough now to see it."

"What am I looking for?"

"It's the constellation of Gemini, and if you can imagine the stars like connect-the-dots stick figures it looks like two people holding hands. Look, you can see the two heads side by side, the arms, the bodies, the legs, even the feet."

"What's so special about the Gemini twins?" he asked, still not seeing what he was supposed to.

"Thousands of years ago soldiers used to pray to them for protection in battle, and the Romans called them the 'Stella Patrem', or something in Latin that means 'the Father's Star'. The twin constellations were supposed to be a father and son who were killed by an evil general, then Zeus sent them to be together forever in heaven." He craned his neck back and sighed. "But now that both my parents are gone, I like to imagine them as my mom and dad up there looking out for me, especially since we're up here by ourselves and Bill's still out there somewhere and Arthur's at the house looking out for Aunt Katharine."

"Do you really believe in that kind of mystical stuff?"

"After everything that's happened this year I'm starting to."

"Then maybe I can think of something else in the sky as my mom," Carlo pondered. "Like maybe from now on the moon will be 'Luna', the mother who never accepted her gay son and was forced to watch him forever, from the sky, do things like this." Carlo pulled Jeremy close and stuck his tongue down his throat.

Jeremy pushed him away, laughing. "Come on, it's almost dark." He grabbed his hand and led him down along the floating dock to the boathouse. Once there he slid his key into the lock, turned it and swung open the door. A glint of glossy mahogany and polished chrome peeked from the shadows. He hit the light switch on the wall.

"Oh, Jeremy it's beautiful! What kind is it again?"

"It's a 1947 Chris Craft De Luxe Runabout, straight from the restorer's. They brought it, I mean her, up from Newport Beach last week. She's been rebuilt from bow to stern."

"That was so cool of your aunt to get it for your Eighteenth," he sighed, running his hand along the mirror-like varnish. "For mine all I got was a new Bible. Can we take it out tomorrow?"

"What do you think," he laughed, nudging him. "First thing in the morning we'll pack a lunch and take it to the other side of the lake. There are some beautiful, really private coves there we can explore."

"Just like the Hardy Boys?"

"Yeah, but no 'chum' stuff, if you don't mind."

"Can we take turns driving?"

"Isn't that what we were doing all day?" Jeremy whispered, cupping Carlo's buttocks in his hands. Their lips met softly then parted. "Let's go back up. I left the doors open and I don't want the place filled with mosquitoes. Besides, I'm starving."

With Carlo in the lead they trudged their way up the stairs toward the sleek structure, its black glass walls reflecting dimming smears of purple clouds.

He looked up, watching the side-to-side shift of Carlo's rear, the solid concavity of his waist, and the confident rolling of his gymnast's shoulders as he climbed the stairs ahead of him. Now that he knew the magnificence that lay underneath his lover's clothing he couldn't wait to touch him again.

Once inside they flicked on as many lights as they could find, chasing the darkness back into the corners. Then they made their way into the kitchen, where Carlo scooted himself up onto the orange tile countertop.

"You're gonna have to do something about the way this place looks," he suggested while popping open a soda can, a dreamy expression on his face. "Can I help pick out the furniture? I'm thinking *Calvin Klein* does Aspen."

"Don't get your hopes up, my aunt says she has a decorator lined up."

"But it's your house!" he pleaded.

"She says letting a teenager pick out their own furniture is like letting an axe murderer pick his own psychiatrist."

"I wouldn't go that far, but I get the picture." He swung his legs happily. "So what's for dinner?"

"Whatever your stomach wishes," Jeremy replied, throwing open the refrigerator door.

"Pizza. Pizza, Pizza!"

He stuck his head back into the freezer. "We ate the last frozen ones for breakfast, so we'll have to order some for delivery. Can you wait that long?"

"I'm patient, remember?" he murmured. "Look how long I waited for you."

Jeremy smiled distantly. How could he have not seen the treasures that Carlo offered? He inched over and planted a wet kiss on his mouth. "Alright. Enough already. You can tell our grandkids how you were right and I was wrong." He snatched his cell phone from the counter and was connected by Information. After placing the order for two large Supremes he set the phone back down.

"One hour," he reported. "She said because it's Spring Break they're backed-up."

"So what should we do in the meantime?" Carlo cocked an eyebrow.

"I could use a shower, or better yet, how about we fill up that big Jacuzzi tub in the master bathroom?"

Carlo scooted off the counter and made for the stairs without answering.

Their hands slipped lovingly over each other in the steaming suds, exploring gently as well as bravely; revisiting a touch that had elicited a moan earlier in the day, experimenting with ones untried. While locked in a hungry kiss they masturbated each other under frothing water, and reached gratification simultaneously.

Tiny mountains of snow-white bubbles grazed their earlobes. Jeremy pulled Carlo onto his lap, wrapping his arms tightly around him in an underwater hug. The yielding solidity of the young man's body comforted him, as if he were joined finally with a part of himself he'd ached for his entire life.

But was this feeling only the filling of the void left by his father?

No. This was different entirely.

Life, it occurred to him, was like the color-wheel he'd constructed once in grade school, where he'd carefully cut out pie-shaped wedges of yellow and green and red and purple and orange and blue, then pasted them onto a cardboard disk. His pretty young teacher, Mrs. Nairod, had shown him how to poke a hole through the center of the completed wheel and spin it on the body of a plastic pen where, to his amazement, the disk briefly shone white.

His life, he reasoned, had been missing specific color wedges for some time, causing his own wheel to wobble unsteadily and to look a murky brown. Then one by one someone appeared and claimed each of the colors: Aunt Katharine, bright yellow. Arthur, his father's vacant green. Carlo, passionate red. His mother, a reluctant purple. Ellie and Reed, complimentary orange and blue. And Bill, he figured, was just the plain old cardboard backside.

"What are you thinking about?" Carlo whispered.

"Just how glad I am to have you in my life...and that I don't know what I would've done without you...and Arthur."

"Is that all?"

"Isn't that enough?"

"Yep," he whispered. "It's more than enough."

Jeremy squeezed him hard, biting his ear gently then kissing the cord of muscle running down his neck. "I love you, Carlo."

"I love you, Jeremy." He twisted his head backward and they kissed.

The doorbell chimed dimly downstairs.

"Shit!" Jeremy exclaimed.

"Don't worry. I'll go get it." Carlo pushed himself dripping out of the water, dried himself quickly, and then wrapped his green paisley smoking jacket quickly around himself. "Besides, dinner's on me tonight. Come down when you're ready. I'll set everything up."

"Can't wait!" He climbed from the tub watching the water rain from his own naked flanks, and then toweled himself off. After that he grabbed his own scarlet robe from the valet stand and knotted the cord around his waist, then stepped into the bathroom and checked his reflection, noting the pink glow in his hollowed cheeks. He rubbed some styling gel into his palm and messed it through his hair, then stepped back and smiled.

He had to admit it, he looked good.

He heard the front door open, some friendly voices echoing in the foyer, then the door closing shut.

The thought of hot, cheesy pizza made him realize he was starving. He figured that after dinner they could build a fire, and after that they'd finally test the sturdiness of that big old coffee table.

Carlo called up to him. "Jeremy, can you come down here? *Now?*"

Why did he sound stressed-out all of a sudden? Had he forgotten his money? He grabbed his wallet from the top of the nightstand and sauntered along the hallway to the staircase. He saw the old pizza delivery man in a red baseball cap standing very close to Carlo.

The head tilted back and Jeremy swooned.

Bill smiled up at him menacingly. "Don't you think it was considerate of me to buy you little sodomites dinner?" He dropped the two pizza boxes on the floor and revealed the gun pressed into Carlo's ribs. "I had to give the nice delivery boy an extra Twenty for the hat, but I'd say I got the deal of a lifetime."

"I didn't know, Jeremy!" Carlo blurted. "I mean, I knew he was old for a delivery guy..."

Jeremy thought *he's been out of the country for three months. I can tell him anything...*

"Hey Uncle Bill," he offered as he began descending the stairs. "We sure have missed you around the compound."

"Not more than I've missed being there," he snarled. "But now that Katharine's got the dogs chasing me I have nothing to lose, so I figured I'd take away the only thing she cares about, just like she's taken away everything of mine. Now don't come any closer or I'll put a bullet through your little brown girlfriend."

Jeremy stopped his approach, his manner nonchalant. "I'll bet it's been hard on you Uncle Bill, a man like you running from country to country. And all because of a big misunderstanding."

"What the hell are you talking about?" He shoved the barrel harder into Carlo's ribs, making the young man's eyes bug out and his chest heave unsteadily.

What would mom say? What would she do?

"Didn't you hear? Ari finally confessed that he thought I was trying to turn his son queer, and that's why he sent those guys to beat me up. It was just a horrible mistake for Darius that he was wearing my jacket that night and they thought he was me." *Like a rock from a slingshot* he thought, and stepped down two more stairs.

Bill's mind shuffled the facts: *Maybe Ari didn't want to implicate me after all, because he knew that if he did, I would seize the gas stations and expose his drug business.* "But what about your mother?" he narrowed his eyes. "Aren't they blaming me for that too?"

"They only suspected you because you disappeared that night," Jeremy stated. "Then the coroner said it was an accidental insulin overdose. You know, she'd been drinking and probably forgot she'd already injected herself." He looked down and shook his head.

Like a rock from a slingshot.

When he brought his eyes up to meet his uncle's they were brimming with tears. "Why couldn't she have just stopped drinking, Uncle Bill?" he asked. "Why?"

"Because she was a drunken whore, that's why."

Jeremy nodded in agreement and stole a glance at Carlo, and while doing so detected that his expression was slightly less horrified than it had been a minute ago, then saw that the gun's barrel was no longer pushed directly into his side.

"I know she was," Jeremy sniffed. "Sometimes I think she's better off dead."

Like a rock from a slingshot.

"Don't we all," Bill spat. "But my sources tell me that I'm under suspicion of embezzling, from charges levied by my own wife!"

"Now Uncle," Jeremy smiled. He only had three steps now to go to the floor. "Her bank made her file those charges, probably because they were stealing from us and wanted to blame it on you. Everyone knows that no business is run by the book," he nodded, reciting the words his uncle had once used himself. "Aunt Katharine still says how brilliantly you handle the money, and that's how you were able to build her fortune for her, that's exactly what she told me." He stepped down another stair and began to slowly bend his knees, as if he were going to sit down for a comfy chat. "She even said, 'Jeremy, I'm sure the accountants can explain everything. I trust my husband implicitly. I just wish he'd come back home so we could work all of this out'."

"Well she's right about that. If I've told that woman once, I've told her a thousand times that—"

Like a rock from a slingshot Jeremy sprang from the step as he'd done a thousand times from the starting position at the pool's edge. His outstretched arms hit his target full force in the chest. The gun clattered to the stone floor at the same instant that Bill's head hit the jagged quartz of the fireplace and cracked like a watermelon. He slid to the floor convulsing and bubbling foam from his mouth, his legs kicking the floor like a spoiled brat throwing a tantrum.

"Carlo, are you OK?" He snapped his head urgently toward him.

"I guess!" He was shaking. "What do we do, Jeremy? *What do we do?*"

"Go call 911! My phone's in the kitchen. *Hurry!*"

He galloped away.

Was he gone?

Bill's eyes blinked wildly at the ceiling and his mouth twitched in a horrific grimace. His arms flopped like someone falling off a cliff backwards.

"You fucker!" Jeremy screamed, leaning over his writhing body. "You Goddamn murdering son of a bitch!" Bill's eyes were beginning to roll up in his head and he sounded as if he were choking on his tongue. His pants darkened from the spreading urine as it was let forth, and a foul stench clouded the air.

"Look at you, you son of a bitch! I fooled you! You're gonna die and nothing can save you!" He bellowed over him, his spittle landing on the wrinkled, paling face. "Jeremy Tyler fucked you! This little faggot fucked you! Ha ha!" He stood up and did a lewd dance around the prostate body as its spasms crested, then began to wane.

And then he dropped to his knees and got within an inch of Bill's face, their noses nearly touching, his yells turning now to sobs. "I hate you for what you did to my father! I hate you for what you did to my mother! I hate you for what you did to Darius and tried to do to me!" Jeremy saw that trickles of blood dribbled from the old man's ears, making little pools like spilled nail polish on the stone floor.

It won't be long now.

"Die you goddamn murderer," he cried. "Go burn in hell! You deserve it! Die! Die! Die! And never forget that I was the one who killed you!"

The old man farted and gasped, then was still.

"You don't have to hurry," Carlo spoke calmly into the phone. "I think he's already dead."

Jeremy glanced up through his tears at the buffalo head above the mantel and noticed, for the first time, that it seemed to be smiling.

* * *

"Just a sec, he's almost done with his laps." Carlo pressed the compact silver phone into the cushy white towel around his shoulders, waiting for Jeremy to reach the side of the pool and come up for air. "Hey!" he yelled as the wet brown head finally broke the surface, looking around. "Hey!" he called out again.

Jeremy looked up grinning and blinking, then shook the water gloriously from his hair. *"What?"*

Carlo held up the phone. "Your fairy godmother."

Jeremy reached up and Carlo leaned over and handed the phone over. "Hey, old buddy," he said, bobbing in the pool like a buoy.

"Hay is for horses," Arthur's familiar voice corrected. "So what no good are you two bums up to?"

"Just finishing my laps. Then we're going into Honolulu for dinner and to try out this new club we heard about; supposedly the go-go boys don't wear anything under their hula skirts."

"Oh, the scandal of it," he laughed, then continued, *sotto voce*. "Listen, I need to talk to you about something. Serious."

"Oh no."

"It's nothing bad. Do you want to call me back when you're finished?"

"Let's talk now. You know I can't take the suspense."

"OK then. The ghost of Bill is alive and well."

"Is blood running out of the faucets again?"

"Unfortunately it's nothing that simple. Business stuff, some loose ends that need tying up. *Immediately.* "

"Anything I can do from here?"

"Unfortunately you can't. This has to do with some big coffee grower in Brazil who goes by the name of *el Gigante*, he's got some huge real estate development that Bill had started to invest a lot of your family's money in. And your aunt admits that it does look promising on paper and in the photos, but before she throws any more money at it she wants you to go down to see how it's progressing."

"But I don't know anything about real estate development," he protested.

"Apparently she was so impressed by your supervision of the chalet's refurbishing that she believes you may have a future in development, *if the young man should decide to pursue one, of course.*"

They both giggled at his uncanny impersonation of her.

"I thought she was through making decisions for me," he noted absently while ogling Carlo as he leaned over to pick up his magazine and sunglasses from the chaise, his square-cut Speedo stretched enticingly over the perfect curves of his ass. "Are you going too?"

"Of course. I haven't taken a single vacation day since Danny's death, and I've even got some Bureau contacts down there that'll help ensure our safety."

"Why would we need their help?"

"You don't know much about South America, do you?"

"Only that it's kind of poor in most of the places," Jeremy offered.

"And where there's poverty there's always corruption, young man. But we should be gone only a couple of weeks at the most, so we shouldn't get into too much trouble. And after we've finished with what we need to do I'd love to show you around *Brasilia*, we could see all those beautiful utopian government buildings like the *Palacio Planalto* and the *Panteao*—that is, if you'd like to."

"Sure, I guess." He shrugged his shoulders. "But can Carlo come too?"

Arthur sighed. "I guess that might be for the best."

"What's that mean?"

"Never mind. It shouldn't be a problem, so long as the two of you are...discreet; Brazil isn't West Hollywood you know."

"Don't you mean the three of us?" Jeremy snorted.

Arthur laughed. "No, I mean the two of you...because you're the ones who are lovers."

"I'd almost forgotten," he replied dreamily. "When do we have to leave?"

"The sooner the better, but I realize you're thousands of miles away. Can you be back by this weekend?"

"I'll have to talk it over with him. There's stuff we still want to do here—we're going snorkeling tomorrow and then we have windsurfing lessons the day after that. And we haven't even been to one of those cheesy luaus yet."

"I know, I know. But just so you know Jeremy, your aunt says there are immediate decisions that need to be made. And she's waiting for you to make them."

He looked over at beautiful Carlo standing at the pool's edge, then up at the coconut trees with their fronds brushing lazily against the silhouette of their gleaming hotel, and beyond that to the brilliant tropical sky and the savage beauty of the coastline. He vowed to memorize this scene; if there was one thing he'd learned, it was that perfect, peaceful moments are hard to come by. "I guess we can be home by Saturday night."

"Katharine will be pleased. I'll have the paperwork and our travel arrangements set-up by then. Does your boyfriend have a passport?"

"Carlo, do you have a passport?" Jeremy yelled (and two thousand miles away Arthur pulled the phone away from his ear).

Carlo nodded enthusiastically and began trotting over to him.

"Yep, he does. Is there anything else, Arthur?"

The silence on the other end made Jeremy think he'd suddenly lost the signal.

"Arthur?"

"Yeah. Sorry. No, there's nothing else—except that...that I've missed you, Jeremy. More than I thought I would."

Jeremy looked at Carlo, and when Carlo saw the sudden grin on his face and the sparkle in his eyes he noisily kissed the air between them.

Jeremy returned the gesture silently. "Me too," he answered finally. "More than I thought I would, too."

ACKNOWLEDGEMENTS AND AUTHOR'S NOTES

I got the idea to write this tale after attending a book fair with my students. I watched them scrutinize the various books for sale—the girls choosing, for the most part, stories about middle school drama and cute boys, while the boys chose books about cars or haunted houses or creepy-crawlies. Twelve year-old Brian—a sweet kid whom I'd rescued more than once from the cruel taunts from his classmates about his effeminacy—asked me to help him find a book, as there was nothing he could find that he wanted. But after examining the offerings on the shelves I saw what he saw: there was little, if anything, that might spark his interest. Thus an idea began to gather in my mind: *write a gay teen romance novel—something that Brian, or the countless other kids like him out there, might enjoy reading.*

And so I began writing my first book. But then over time *STRINGS ATTACHED* grew into something bigger than what I'd originally intended. For one thing, I found that I couldn't accurately portray the anguish that a gay teenage boy goes through with his sexual self-discovery without including a somewhat graphic self-gratification scene—and that made the story *adults only.* And since I was now writing a story intended for adults, I figured I should make the language more 'grown up' as well. And finally, since I was now writing a full-fledged adult novel, I decided to throw in a couple of other sexy scenes and a smattering of violence to jazz things up.

And then I asked myself: *how will I make my book different from all the other kind-of-sexy-sort-of-scary-coming-of-age novels out there?*

One night at dinner, my partner Jaime and I were discussing the progress on the manuscript (over the years, he's heard every incarnation of each page as I'd read them aloud to him). He was telling me how Jeremy's character, as a neglected teenage boy, didn't seem 'angry' enough, and I tried explaining to him that children of alcoholics often display 'codependent' characteristics, which means that in order to survive they must put the needs of their alcoholic parent before their own. "They react instead of act," I told him as, ironically, I downed the last of my wine. "They're pretty much out of touch with their own needs and desires. It's kind of like they're puppets."

And then it hit me: have Jeremy's story parallel the story of *Pinocchio*, where instead of a puppet wishing on a star to be a *real boy*, this codependent gay teen wishes on a star to become a *real man*.

And then the fun began.

I had to draw the parallels with Pinocchio without knocking the reader over the head with them—except for the title, of course, so I decided to drop hints instead. Pinocchio was written by Carlo Collodi; I used 'Carlo' as a name for one of the central characters, and the *Gallery Collodi* is Katharine's art gallery that features elegantly simple wood carvings. She even makes a Pinocchio reference when explaining the gallery's name to her nephew. Other hints to Jeremy's identity can be found when she instructs the slouching young man on his posture:

"Hasn't anyone told you to walk and stand tall, imagining a string is holding up your head?"

"A string?"

"Yes, a string, such as that which holds-up a marionette. If you accustom yourself to visualizing this you shall, with practice, never slouch."

Katharine is herself Gepetto, the carpenter and clock maker who creates Pinocchio, only she tries, and nearly succeeds, to 'carve' Jeremy into the image of what she likes to think his father was—and might have become had she not given him too much freedom (or *cut his strings*) in the first place.

The story takes place in Ballena Beach; *Ballena* is Spanish for 'whale', and when a whale *beaches* itself it dies—which portends what happens to Bill Mortson, whose last name is an anagram. His name is also a double reference, as it points to the French word 'mort' which means death, combined with '-son', which is a reference to the demise of Jonathan, who was, in essence, Bill's son. His selfishness and wealth make Bill immense and unstoppable, like the ravenous shark who swallows Pinocchio in the Collodi version; and like this shark he nearly succeeds in 'swallowing-up' both the Pinocchio and Gepetto characters.

Another reference to Pinocchio is when Jeremy, after being confronted by Carlo about his inability to love, looks down at his own hands and realizes that "...his fingers might as well be made of wood, for they'd never caressed anyone or been held lovingly..." Even Jeremy himself considers dressing as Pinocchio to attend Ellie's Halloween party, but then decides against it.

Perhaps the most telling and somewhat comical parallel to the Pinocchio story is when Coby confronts Jeremy with his suspicion of the other's homosexuality. "I know your little secret," Coby tells the terrified boy when they are alone together. But of course Jeremy denies this assertion, and in a mimic of the original puppet boy's 'physiological' response to telling a lie, with each denial Jeremy tells, the more sexually aroused he becomes.

Another carry-over from the original story is Arthur Blauefee; 'blaue' and 'fee' are the German words for 'blue' and 'fairy'. And although Arthur is gay, he is no 'fairy' in the derogatory sense of the word, but seems to have almost supernatural abilities with regard to the 'magic' he works on Jeremy, and how he sees to the youngster's needs. He is perhaps the most instrumental influence on the boy, and hence is the one who is best at bringing forth the teen's true self. And he is the quintessential 'fairy godmother', providing him with everything from a costume for the 'ball', to protection from 'the great shark', to the role model of a homosexual male who is the embodiment of a *real man* in the semblance of a loving father. At one point Jeremy says, rather sarcastically, "Thanks, Mom." And Arthur replies under his breath, "I prefer fairy godmother." Finally, when Arthur encourages a despondent Jeremy about how controlling Katharine is, the man tells him, "...your aunt may want you to be just like your father, but he was his own man; he was nobody's puppet."

One of the final clues to Jeremy's identity is the song that's playing when he and his friends go to the Frat House. If the reader sings the lyrics out loud to the melody of a very familiar tune, one gets the message in no uncertain terms. But the lyrics are ominous—they tell what ill fate Tiffany is experiencing at that moment, as well as the grief that's coming Jeremy's way.

And speaking of crickets, where is he? For one thing, Carlo Collodi made that original talking cricket appear in his novel for all of a page or so. And in the original story Pinocchio, having nothing but a wooden noggin for a brain, becomes alarmed by its vociferous behavior and smashes it on the cottage wall—just like that.

So there.

The Pinocchio references provided some solid leads to the reader, I felt, without being overly derivative. But what about 'the star'? How could I incorporate something as 'childish'—or even foolhardy in a modern-day novel—as someone wishing on a star then having that dream come true?

First I had to look at the custom of 'star wishing'. Where did it originate? Why do so many people—albeit mostly children, as instructed by their parents—still do it? I started by looking back at cultures with deities as constellations and the concept of *apotheosis*—man becoming god—and figured that the only difference between a wish and a prayer is whom you believe is listening. And then I looked for a constellation that might have elements of my story and found Gemini and the tale of Castor and Pollux. If you read some various accounts of the myths surrounding them—and there are many—you may be as taken as I was with the overriding commonality of them all: familial male-male love that survives eternity in spite of mortal treachery. And it's also true what I found about myths being changed to suit the climate of their times, so I took some artistic license with the Gemini Boys and tailored it to parallel Jeremy's story as a vehicle for warning the reader as to the impending dangers. But back to *the star*: when Jeremy and Jonathan are on the beach in the dream and the boy can't decide on one wish so he wishes for them all, each does come true: at the end his mother stops drinking forever (she's dead), his parents are together again (we see them on the boat during the memorial service, but more on that later...), and he proves that he is a *real man* after all, as he is able to give and receive love, he pursues his true desires and needs, and he defends himself and the one he loves against a foe intent on inflicting immeasurable harm.

So what about that mysterious schooner? The young man aboard it reminds Tiffany of Jeremy somehow because he's the ghost of Jonathan who, in the fashion of the traditional Irish banshee, has come back to forewarn Tiffany of an impending death in the family (remember, the Tylers are mostly Irish, as noted by Katharine). Tiffany reports the troubled boater to 911, but when they send out an escort to look for the craft, as well as its captain, it appears to have disappeared without a trace.

Then, when the schooner reappears during Tiffany's memorial service, it is now Jonathan *and* Tiffany—as their younger, better selves—onboard, and the message on the stern guides the reader as to the true captain of their ship: *Kay+Ron's Ferry Tail* is a reference to Charon (pronounced /kay-ron/), the ferryman who carries the souls of the dead across the river Styx, as well as a reference to this story being a 'fairy tail' in many senses of the word.

And finally, what's going on between Arthur and Jeremy? Throughout the story, they maintain an almost constant level of love, affection, and positive regard for each other without ever getting *nasty*. A friend who began reading the story told me, "I'll bet Arthur has Jeremy in bed by the end of chapter 5," to which I only smiled. Their relationship is holy to me, and I wanted to show that a mature, virile gay man can mentor a gay youngster without any sort of prurient agenda whatsoever on either's part. They have a perfect father-son relationship, one that mirrors the one I had with my own grandfather—who, by the way, used to call me 'Old Buddy'.

But what about the phone call at the end of the story, when Carlo and Jeremy are in Hawaii? For the first time, Arthur refrains from using his pet name when addressing the young man. And at the end of the conversation Arthur hesitates before telling him, "...I've missed you, Jeremy. More than I thought..." to which Jeremy answers, "Me too... more than I thought, too." And when Carlo sees the sparkle in Jeremy's eyes he assumes that his boyfriend's loving look is meant for him. But is it? Now that the reader sees that Jeremy is a real man we must assume that Arthur sees him that way too, so I thought I might open that door for some added pizzazz/conflict in the *STRINGS ATTACHED* sequel, because you know they really aren't related after all...

Ballena Beach is, of course, Malibu. I've enjoyed many afternoons there with a notebook in my hands, my back against the rocks and my feet buried in the sand. There really is an El Capitan State Beach and even an old, immense Mediterranean Villa on the cliff overlooking the ocean. And Lake Estrella (*estrella* is Spanish for 'star', by the way) is a thinly disguised Lake Arrowhead. I've spent plenty of time over the years on the banks of the lovely lakes up in the San Bernardino Mountains, and did my best to portray the natural beauty of both locales.

The astute reader will find many other—sometimes obscure—

references to puppetry and stars and death and magical realism, as well as foreshadowing, peppered throughout this book, so I will leave that task of discovery to those who enjoy searching for it. Suffice to say that I had such fun writing this story, and hope that you have found yourself entertained while being immersed in these pages.

I want to thank Jaime, my partner of eighteen years, for supporting me and encouraging me and listening to me and offering his invaluable input into this novel. Jaime, you believed in me and for that I cannot thank you enough. You have been the gasoline in my tank and the helium in my balloon. This book is for you, as much as it was written by me. And a big cuddly thanks to my beloved Margaret, whose snuffly snores emanated from beneath my desk on many, many a late night; you are my little Margie Doodle and I will love you through all of eternity. I want to thank Margo for her tireless cheerleading and Arlet and Art for reading the entire manuscript without me asking them to, and Claudine for your support during a very difficult time; thanks to Sita White for almost becoming my agent and for giving me wonderful advice along the way; an oath of gratitude to Ayofemi Folayan for being the first person on this planet who told me I could write, and who promised to hunt me down (in her wheelchair) if I stopped, and to Jason Tanner for the wonderful cover photo of his friend Jeff. And thanks to my parents and sisters for their support, in spite of the fact that I was writing a gay-themed novel that would be published with the family name on its cover.

And finally, I must thank the brilliant author Kathleen McGowan, as well as the divine orchestra that made our meeting, as well as our collaboration, so harmonious. Your input and guidance have helped make my wish come true. I will forever thank my lucky stars that we met.

I hope that someday, Brian, some 'magical' force in the universe encourages you to pick up this novel in a bookstore, and then you'll smile when you finish reading these pages. I know that wherever you are—whether straight or gay—you are, by now, a real man too.

Nick Nolan
January 2006

(P.S. And a big, grateful thanks to the late, great Paul Monette, whose amazing and uncompromising works first inspired me to write. I hope that you and Betty are pleased with this.)

For more information please visit **nick-nolan.com**

293453

Made in the USA